The
PLAYMAKER

by

THOMAS KENEALLY

SIMON AND SCHUSTER

NEW YORK

Copyright © 1987 by
Serpentine Publishing Company Proprietary, Ltd.
All rights reserved
including the right of reproduction
in whole or in part in any form.
Published by Simon and Schuster
A Division of Simon & Schuster, Inc.
Simon & Schuster Building
Rockefeller Center
1230 Avenue of the Americas
New York, NY 10020
SIMON AND SCHUSTER and colophon are
registered trademarks of Simon & Schuster, Inc.
Designed by Edith Fowler

10 9 8 7 6 5 4 3 2 1

Library of Congress Cataloging-in-Publication Data

Keneally, Thomas.
  The playmaker.

  1. Clark, Ralph, d. 1794—Fiction. 2. New South
Wales—History—Fiction. 3. Great Britain. Royal
Marines—History—18th century—Fiction. I. Title.
PR9619.3.K46P53 1987 823 87-13127
ISBN 0-671-49343-4

*To Arabanoo and his brethren,
still dispossessed.*

THE

Recruiting Officer

A

COMEDY

By Mr. GEORGE FARQUHAR

As it was first acted at the

THEATRE ROYAL

in

DRURY LANE

April 8th, 1706.

Performed now to honour the
KING'S BIRTHDAY,
Thursday, June 4th, 1789,

By the CONVICTS of the
PENAL SETTLEMENT,
Sydney Cove.

Dramatis Personae

MEN

CAPTAIN PLUME, *the Recruiting Officer*	Henry Kable
MR. WORTHY, *a Gentleman of Shropshire*	Robert Sideway
JUSTICE BALANCE, *a Country Justice*	Ketch Freeman
CAPTAIN BRAZEN, *a Second Recruiting Officer*	John Wisehammer
SERGEANT KITE, *Plume's Sergeant*	John Arscott
BULLOCK, *a Country Clown* ⎱	Curtis Brand
COSTAR PEARMAIN, *a Recruit* ⎰	
THOMAS APPLETREE, *a Recruit*	John Hudson

WOMEN

SILVIA, *Daughter to Justice Balance, in love with Plume*	Mary Brenham
MELINDA, *a Lady of Fortune*	Nancy Turner
LUCY, *Melinda's Maid*	Duckling
	(Sometimes known as Ann Smith)
ROSE, *a Country Girl*	Mrs. Dabby Bryant

SCENE: *Shrewsbury*

THE PLAY IS MANAGED BY
Lieutenant Ralph Clark, Marines

The Players

HENRY KABLE: Sentenced at Norfolk Lent Assizes, 1783, held at Thetford before Sir James Eyre Knight and Fleetwood Bury, Esquire. For burgling the dwelling house of Abigail Hambling, Widow, taking goods to the value of some eighteen pounds. Sentenced to death. Reprieved on account of extreme youth. Seven years' transportation.
Occupation: labourer.
Age at sentencing: sixteen years.
Present age: twenty-two years.

ROBERT SIDEWAY: Tried by the London Jury before Mr. Recorder at Justice Hall in the Old Bailey at the sessions which began on October 16th, 1782. For stealing property value twenty-eight shillings. Guilty. Transported for seven years.
Then at a special session for the County of Devon held at Exeter Castle on Monday, May 24th, 1783, was found at large still within the realm of Great Britain without any lawful cause. Guilty. Death. Respited on condition of transportation for life.
Occupation: watchcase maker.
Age at second sentencing: twenty-three years.
Present age: twenty-nine years.

KETCH (JAMES) FREEMAN: At the Hereford Lent Assizes on March 4th, 1784, before Sir William Henry Ashurst Knight and Jerome Knapp Esquire, Justices. Sentenced for highway attack on Thomas Baldwin and

taking from him twelve shillings in money. Guilty, to be hanged. Reprieved. Transported seven years.
Occupation: labourer.
Age at sentencing: seventeen years.
Present age: twenty-two years.

JOHN WISEHAMMER: Sentenced Bristol, February 10th, 1785, for stealing snuff from the shop of Messrs. Ricketts and Load.
Transportation, seven years.
Occupation: no trade.
Age at sentencing: twenty years.
Present age: twenty-four years.

JOHN ARSCOTT: At Bodmin Assizes, August 18th, 1783. Sentenced for burglary and breaking and entering the dwelling house of Philip Polkinghorn and then the house of George Thomas. Watches and tobacco stolen. To be transported for seven years.
Occupation: carpenter.
Age at sentencing: twenty years.
Present age: twenty-five years.

CURTIS BRAND: At Maidstone, Kent, on January 6th, 1784. For stealing two game-cocks. Sentenced to seven years.
Occupation: no trade.
Age at sentencing: twenty years.
Present age: twenty-five years.

JOHN HUDSON: First tried at Middlesex before Mr. Justice Willes at Justice Hall in the Old Bailey at the sessions of December 10th, 1783. For burgling and breaking and entering the dwelling house of William Holdsworth, and stealing therein one linen shirt value ten shillings, five silk stockings value five shillings, one pistol value five shillings, and two aprons value two shillings. Transported for seven years.
Occupation: sometimes a chimney sweeper.
Age at sentencing: nine years.
Present age: fourteen years.

MARY BRENHAM: Tried by first Middlesex Jury before Mr. Baron Hotham at Justice Hall in the Old Bailey at the sessions which began

Wednesday, December 8th, 1784. For feloniously stealing stuffed petti-coats, a pair of stays, four and a half yards of cloth, one waistcoat, one cap, one pair of cotton stockings, one pair of nankeen breeches and one cloth cloak, the property of John Kennedy. Value thirty-nine shillings. Transported for seven years.

Occupation: servant.

Age at sentencing: not yet fourteen.

Present age: eighteen years.

NANCY TURNER: At Worcester Lent Assizes on March 5th, 1785. For feloniously stealing a silk cloak, a pair of stays, a muslin handkerchief, a lace handkerchief, an apron, and other stuff, goods of Nancy Collins of the Parish of Holy Cross in Pershore. Total value forty shillings. Sentenced to seven years' transportation.

Occupation: servant.

Age at sentencing: seventeen years.

Present age: twenty-one years.

DUCKLING (SUPPOSED NAME ANN SMITH): Believed sentenced at Old Bailey, October, 1786. For stealing silverware, value forty-five shillings. Sentenced to death. Reprieved to seven years' transportation.

Occupation: none.

Age at sentencing: sixteen years.

Present age: nineteen years.

DABBY (ALIAS MARY) BRYANT: Devon Lent Assizes, held at Exeter on March 20th, 1786, before Sir James Eyre Knight and Sir Beaumont Hotham Knight. For feloniously assaulting Agnes Lakeman Spinster in the King's Way, putting her in corporal fear and danger of her life, and feloniously and violently taking from her person one silk bonnet value twelve pence and other goods value eleven shillings eleven pence, her property. Guilty of highway robbery. To be hanged. Reprieved. Trans-ported seven years.

Occupation: forest dweller.

Age at sentencing: twenty years.

Present age: twenty-three years.

Contents

PART ONE

1. The Reading   25
2. Isle of Turnips   31
3. Players   40
4. Recruiting the Perjurer   51
5. Dreams   56
6. By the Spikes   67
7. A Full Company   72
8. The Morality of Plays   80

PART TWO

9. The Hunt   93
10. Wryneck Day   110

PART THREE

11. Perjury and the Play   129
12. The Autopsy   139
13. Hanging the Marines   145
14. Playing to the Indian   151
15. Enchanting the Indian   171
16. The Play and Poetry   182
17. Judging the Perjurer   188
18. Exorcising Handy Baker   199

PART FOUR

19. Letters
20. Bruises
21. The Redeemed Forest
22. Ca-bahn
23. Curse or Cure
24. The Watching of the Ill
25. Withholding Prussian Blue

PART FIVE

26. Tattoo
27. Celebrating the Part
28. Lag Matrimony
29. San Augustin
30. Performance

EPILOGUE

PART ONE

First Ralph heard again how Harry had—one evening in the settlement's first days—discovered Duckling's absence from her tent across the stream. In those days, soon after the women were landed, Duckling occupied her own little bell of canvas close to Captain Jemmy Campbell's marquee, for whom she worked for a time as a servant. Harry had set the patrols of the convict night watch and then gone to Duckling's tent to see sitting in front of it Dot Handilands, the most ancient of the she-lags, rumoured to be eighty years of age. For then, before huts and locks, felons with little else to do were often employed for a small portion of food or liquor to keep watch over people's possessions.

She admitted, only after threats, that Duckling had gone to see Goose.

Harry crossed the stream in the last blue of the evening and walked up through the women's camp, which was then all tents or insubstantial tumuli of boughs, looking for an innocent glimpse of Duckling among the cooking fires.

Even in those days the apothecary she-lag, Goose, had achieved a superior dwelling. Her mere tent had been extended with a length of canvas to become a spacious marquee. It had therefore both an anteroom and a sanctum.

Calling Duckling's name, he went inside this elegant tent.

There, on a pallet, the big Marine, Private Handy Baker, dressed only in a shirt, was plunging and rearing between Duckling's knees.

Harry launched himself, strangling away, onto Baker's shoulders, but was soon thrown, with all the diverted violence of Private Baker's desire, onto the clay floor. Baker landed on top of him now and, with hands which held the odour of Duckling, began strangling him. A shadow passed over Harry's mind. For the first of the two times he would manage it, Baker took Harry's senses away.

Waking later, Harry found himself seated on a square of canvas, a tumbler of spirits in front of him. As his brain reached painfully for the memory of the latitude and the year—the common bread of time and place without which Harry was not Harry—the knowledge returned to him and he hurried to the corner of Goose's tent to be sick.

Looking up he recognised Goose standing calmly by the flap, some firelight from outside richly burnishing her red hair. He knew now that he was still inside her tent. It was a further segment of it than the one in which he had observed Baker and Duckling. Perhaps there was no end to the canvas Goose had already acquired.

She was the same ample, red-haired woman he had seen in Newgate on the occasion he visited Duckling there. He had rarely bothered to face her since the night of Duckling's commutation of sentence. When he discovered that Duckling and Goose were both in the same detachment of Newgate prisoners marched down to Portsmouth and placed with over a hundred other female convicts aboard the *Lady Penrhyn,* he had devoted himself to having Duckling transferred to the smaller female convict hold of the *Charlotte.* This expedient, he now bitterly understood, had been quite fruitless.

Goose sat on a folding camp stool and grinned at him. She had mad, nut brown eyes. "You should never set yourself to stop Handy Baker once he's in his stride. Handy Baker is a runaway coach and four. Handy can take on three coolers a day."

Cooler was flash talk for girl.

She surmised aloud that Harry, in spite of the bruising he'd had, wasn't planning any vengeance based on the letter of the law.

"All the camps might laugh at you then, Mr. Brewer," she told him. Besides, everyone came over here to the women's camp to see Mother Goose, she said, slapping her stomach. To ask Goose for favours.

CHAPTER 1

The Reading

APRIL 1789

RALPH began hearing for the parts in the play early in April, the day after the hanging of Private Handy Baker and the five other Marines. His purpose was to find eleven or twelve convicts for the chief speaking parts. Much later he could find and begin rehearsing the lesser actors in their movements about a stage which he could only dimly envisage as yet, and among leading players he would somehow have to perfect in the coming two and a little months.

H.E. had given him that span of time in which to bring about the very first presentation of this or any other play ever performed on this new penal planet, which so far as anyone knew had gone from the beginning of time till now absolutely play-less and theatre-less.

On this morning of his first auditions, he was heavy-headed from sitting up late with Harry Brewer the Provost Marshal, and from drinking with him a dangerous quantity of brandy. Then, returned to his hut, he'd paid for it with one of those murderous old dreams he thought Dabby Bryant the witch had cured him of. As long as he drank wisely and modestly, Ralph was safe from them. But in occasional drunkenness they returned, deadly and perfectly discreet little dreams to do with loss, desire, and jealousy.

In this one he met a city and a wife he had been separated from almost precisely two years in time and eight months' travel in space. The city was Plymouth, for which his convict transport had sailed to join the others at Portsmouth. The wife was of course little Betsey Alicia, her heart-shaped face sharp as a knife in the dream's definition. He had been holding two chestnut horses, one on either side of him, by the bridles. He had wanted Alicia to mount one of them and go riding with him, but she had refused. He got angry and abused her, falling back on convict insults in his fury, calling her an ulcer, a torment, threatening even to punch her. He hated to satanic lengths her perfect little shoulders and her neat rose of a mouth.

When she had still refused to mount, he'd let go of the bridle of one of the chestnuts, mounted the other and gone flying through the countryside, he and the horse both speeded along and made one creature by a delicious anger. Rounding a corner, however, he had been stopped by the sight of Alicia sitting under a hedge with a sharp-featured young man in a white suit of clothes. And singing a particular song with him, "The Myrtle of Venus—with Bacchus Entwined."

The day-time Lieutenant Ralph Clark had no doubts about the faithfulness of his wife. But the old question was, did the night-time Ralph, that child of the prophets, of the seers and the holy dreamers, looking straight through the eight moons which divided him from his wife, know something better than the day-time functionary and playmaker might know?

He had had Private Ellis erect the marquee again at the side of his hut, and at ten o'clock on a rainy morning at the beginning of April, a month which here, on this reverse side of the mirror of space, was not spring but instead a temperate autumn, he sat in there at a folding camp table, his green coat slung over his shoulders and two copies of the chosen play in front of him. This was *The Recruiting Officer*. It had been written some eighty years past by a sad young playwright called George Farquhar, who had not lived to see it become a great favourite of the theatre or to know any of the wealth and fame it would generate for those who presented it or acted in it.

In fact Ralph had read the play four times in the past week, and during at least one of these readings began to see how the play could be thought of as dull and contrived. Just the same, in all this vast reach of the universe this was the one play of which two copies existed. There was Lieutenant George Johnston's copy, and Captain Davy Collins's. He himself would have preferred *The Tragedy of Lady Jane Grey*, because he could remember how he had wept when reading it aboard the convict transport *Friendship* during an Atlantic storm. But the cultivated Judge Advocate of this penal commonwealth, Davy Collins, commenting on H.E.'s demand for a play, had said with some justice, "Something lively, eh, Ralph? Confused identities, inheritances, lovers, girls dressed as officers, double meanings! We all know the convict lags won't sit still for death and destiny!"

Four large and robust speaking roles for women, seven or eight grand to minor speaking roles for men. Sitting at a table inside the marquee, he felt ill enough to hope that few prisoners would come to be heard, but he knew many would. For the women prisoners liked to consider themselves actresses, and many of them had followed the trade which, cynics always remarked, was so close to that of the stage—whoredom.

He was not prepared for the first auditioner to be the prisoner Meg Long, the woman-beater. He saw her suddenly at the tent flap, her big flat features gleaming at him wetly through a slick of raindrops. Her hair was slick with rain too, and terrible bald patches from ringworm glistened pinkly. As she came closer, her breath blinded him.

"Morning, Captain chuck!" she said gaily. "I ain't no mere pretty nun. I'm a Covent Garden woman of high class."

She smelled like death. She was quite incontinent. The surgeons quoted her as an argument for the building of an asylum. Occasionally she would jump on one of the younger female prisoners and try to caress her, and the girl would scream into those rapt great hammer-flat features until rescued by other women or constables or Marines. But here now her face was lit from within with the hope of Thespian glory. It was so strangely touching that Ralph, despite her madness and her stench, felt it would be inhuman to send her away at once.

"Meg, you must come in out of the rain," he told her.

She stood in front of his desk, grinning and shaking herself. Water flew from her as from a wet dog. "There are not many parts for women," he said. "I am looking particularly for actresses who can write. They will have to make copies of this play for their own use."

He riffled the pages of *The Recruiting Officer*. He saw the names of Plume and Worthy, who before the play was over would find themselves engaged to heiresses, and the name of Silvia Balance, that lusty, forthright girl who—to fit Davy Collins's requirements for a play—dresses as a young gentleman and attracts the desire of a farm girl called Rose. Who would be Silvia and who the virago Melinda? This dull morning Meg Long seemed not only to incarnate the gulf between his own fortune and that of happy Captain Plume, hero of the play, but also to show him too clearly the gulf between the convict women and the true actresses, the women of authentic theatrical spirit, he was seeking.

"Now you can't write, Meg, can you?" he asked.

Meg Long nodded crazily. "I have penmanship, Captain chuck."

"Where did you get penmanship, Meg?"

"From the abbess of my mob, my canting crew, when I were a kiddie. She teached me penmanship to the hilt."

"Oh sweet Christ!" he murmured. He tore off a small slice of paper—there wasn't much to waste of the stuff—and pushed a pen and ink toward her. "Come here and write me something."

She held the pen deftly and with delicacy, and he was surprised. Then, leaning over the desk, dripping on to it and giving off miasmas that stung his eyes, she began to write, dipping the pen twice. There was some blotting, and when she had finished she waved the sodden paper back and forth, helping it to dry. Then she handed it to him. "Eeeeeeeeeeeeeeeeeeeeeeeeeeeeeeeeee," she had written. He studied the succession of vowels, wondering how to get rid of her. Without warning she had her arms around him, threatening to crack his ribs with her maniac strength. Once, in another hemisphere, she'd beaten the wife of a coffee merchant so livid and swollen that members of the jury had wept when the victim gave evidence. In Meg Long's arms, Lieutenant Clark understood how misused the woman must have been, and why Meg had been given a lifetime's exile—what the convicts called a bellowser—to a distant star.

He had only just collected himself to struggle with her when he saw a black face appear over her shoulder. A harmonious voice, marked by elements of French and Kentish and something irreducibly African, came from the face.

"*Ma mère*, you must let go that gentleman. Yes, *chérie*, in the name of the Fragrant One. Ease them little arms of yours. This gentleman is *foko* to me, is brother, so ease your arms, mammie."

Mad, shitty Meg Long let go of Lieutenant Clark and began to caress the black man's face. His name was John Caesar. He came from Madagascar and invoked the Fragrant One, some sort of Madagascan god, endlessly. He was very dangerous—the strongest and hungriest of all the prisoners.

"I have come here for the play, *maître*," he told Ralph, pushing Meg Long deftly to one side. "There was a black servant in every play I see in Maidstone." He had been someone's servant in Maidstone once. His great member was said to be renowned among the convict women, but not always welcomed by them, since he turned so easily to blows.

Lieutenant Clark thought he had better not entertain Black Caesar's artistic ambitions too much, since he had seen how dangerous it had been to give any space to Meg Long's. "There are no black men at all in this play," said Ralph, his head pulsing. Meg Long's lunatic muscles had squeezed all the blood into his brain. "There are no black servants, Caesar."

"There be always *beaucoup* black servants in every drama I see," Black Caesar insisted, frowning.

"Now do not argue with me," said Ralph. "It is not down to me that there are not black roles in the play; it is down to George Farquhar, who wrote the play eighty years ago, before you were born, and who died of consumption before he was as old as you or me."

Now, in the lessening rain, there was a crowd of convict women, noisy but waiting to be invited in, at the flap of the tent. They displayed that delicacy which, apparently, Madagascans lacked. Ralph saw among the faces that of Liz Barber, who had once, aboard the convict transport *Friendship*, invited Captain Meredith to kiss her arse and called him a thief. Now she wanted, of course, to be first woman of the stage in this penal latitude. In her berserkly enthusiastic face, Ralph could tell what a grief this play, demanded by H.E. and Davy, might be for him.

"I will take your name," Lieutenant Clark told the Madagascan, and did so. "If we find we need a black servant, I shall send to the sawpits for you."

Oh what an axeman he was, the Madagascan! "By the Fragrant One," said Black Caesar, almost gently, "you will need a black servant. *Tout le monde* needs a black servant for their play."

"I shall send to the sawpits," Ralph Clark promised again, trying to keep out of his voice the hope that Caesar would return to his labour.

The Madagascan went, but Meg Long sat for hours by the tent flap, just inside, listening without comment or movement as forty convicts, men and women, offered their halting readings to Ralph, some with nearly as much desperation as Miss Long had earlier shown, as if they sensed like her that their best chance out of hunger and lovelessness and a bad name was to capture the first primitive stage of this new earth.

CHAPTER 2

Isle of Turnips

April 2nd 1789

Concerning the play *The Recruiting Officer:*
For the Information of His Excellency.
General Principles of Procedure—

For the chief male parts, those with less outlandish British accents. West Country people—whom the convicts call Zedlanders, I notice, because of their well-known inability to pronounce S—will serve pretty well for the lower and more comic parts. The play is set in Shrewsbury, but there are not many Salopians among the prisoners, and certainly none with any Thespian ability. For the women, Melinda and Silvia should be capable of polite London accents, but Rose and Lucy can be wilder. Nancy Turner, the Perjurer, would be a perfect Melinda—she is handsome and dark. But perjurers should not be honoured, particularly in parts which have been graced by a line of great actresses, beginning with Mrs. Rogers. I might say it is surprising to find her reading for a play the day after her lover Dukes was hanged, reading without apparent grief. There's a steeliness to the woman, however, which might be the mask of grief.

So far I have settled upon only one actor—Henry Kable has the right levity and intelligence to play Captain Plume. His East Anglian voice is very pleasant, and given that he is a convict overseer he will be able to keep order among the others. Your Excellency might remember too he is a characteristic East Anglian Dane, very fair-haired, but his complexion a quite handsome leathery brown. Your Excellency might also remember that he is married to the convict Holmes and that his history is somewhat more interesting than that of the run of felons. He is still a thief—I remember from the *Friendship* how when he was working the pumps with another lag he managed to cut a way into the forrard stowage and take a quantity of flour. But his present behaviour is such, and his engaging character so marked, that we are not likely to find another quite like him. I shall keep Your Excellency informed concerning the preparations for our play.

> Your obedient servant,
> Ralph Clark,
> Lieutenant, Marines.

AT the noon bell he cleared the auditioning convicts from his tent and Private Ellis brought him his plain lunch of rice pudding and bread. He ate the food without joy, and it sat like a cramp on his belly. The sun appeared, and suddenly the tent was full of those great black flies which infested this littoral. He would have liked to sleep, but he had a duty to his turnips.

A pug-faced man of about fifty years, wearing a crooked three-cornered hat, stuck his head in at the tent flap. "Holy Christ, Ralph," he said. "I swear I saw Baker watching me this morning, when I rose at first light to take a piss."

Private Baker had been hanged with the other Marines just yesterday, and it was normal for Harry Brewer, the Provost Marshal and owner of the rumpled face, to see the phantoms of the hanged.

"Did he speak?" asked Ralph, feeling again the oppressiveness both of yesterday's extreme punishment and of the sickly liquor in his blood.

"Nothing. I spoke, Ralph, though I am not sure he stayed to hear. I told him I was the one in possession of the earth, I was the only one with an active manhood left to ply. He was not the sharpest man of intelligence and it will take some days for it to come to his attention that his cock has fought its last fight."

Ralph wondered how Harry Brewer's image of the dead's behaviour fitted with the Christian doctrine of Heaven and Hell, of
deliverance or damnation at the second of death. There was something heathen, Portuguese, or even Chinese about Harry's belief
that spirits delayed and lingered and had to be spoken to harshly to
make them move on.

Harry Brewer came fully into the tent now. There was a bottle
of port in one hand. "If I come out to your island with you, we
could sit in the shade and watch your old lag do the hoeing and
recuperate ourselves. I want to get away from this Bedlam here.
Every whore calling congratulations to me because Baker's hanged.
Sometimes I wish I was a man of virtue, like you, Ralph."

"You have lost a rival." Clark smiled, lively now that the
prospect of going out to the island had been raised—inspired also
to eloquence by having read all morning the playwright George
Farquhar's well-balanced sentences. "And gained only the small
annoyance of a ghost."

A shudder—the sort of spirituous shudder good bottlemen
seem to suffer as they get older—rattled through Harry's features.

Harry Brewer protested, "But you know I am unhappy to see
any rival vanish that way. The hemp quinsey, as the convicts call
hanging, and the shitten breeches. Christ, I swear I hate it."

"Well, there are no executions in our little comedy here," said
Ralph, patting his two copies of the play.

"*Deo gratias,*" said Harry. He had picked up fragments of
Papist Latin in such places as Rio and Narbonne. He and H.E. had
once spied on harbour fortifications in France, but enjoyed the
occasional High Mass as well.

On the way down to the dinghy, Harry murmured, with that
terrifying nothing-to-lose candour of his, "What I fear is that she
had more ardour for Handy Baker than she does for me." Ralph felt
desire pass through him like nausea.

The *she* Harry spoke about was a nineteen-year-old convict
who was still known by the name she had been given in childhood
by her mob, her canting crew. The name was Duckling. Ralph did
not think Duckling was very clever, but she had wonderful breasts
and good sharp features. Harry Brewer, thirty years older, was possessed by her and it did not make him happy.

"When I put my hand on her," Harry continued with his usual frankness, "her eyes deaden. What would you expect? She has been on sale since she was eight years of age. All I hope is that her eyes deadened when she was with Baker."

Private Ellis was already at the dinghy in his shirtsleeves. He grunted in a way Ralph associated with low intelligence as he rowed them forth across the deep anchorages of the cove. Even from a little distance the town looked what it was—a pitiably half-matured conception of some distant and dispassionate idea. On the east side of the stream they saw H.E., "the Captain" as Harry called him, strolling with the native Arabanoo in H.E.'s vegetable garden. H.E. looked comically bandy, but the native—in white knee breeches and naval jacket—dazzled the eye. Harry Brewer gave a little shrug. No more than a lot of other people had he approved of H.E.'s plan of finding one of the savages of the locality and quickly turning him into a gentleman ambassador back to his own people. But Harry could not say so even though others loudly did. There was a sort of balance operating between H.E. and Harry. H.E. did not condemn Harry for sleeping with a convict, and so Harry did not condemn H.E.'s strange enthusiasms.

"I would like to use Ketch Freeman for the role of Justice Balance," Ralph confessed as, groaning and sniffling and muttering to himself, Private Ellis pulled wildly on his starboard oar to yank them round the point of the cove. "Do you think it's proper to use him?"

"Ketch Freeman came to read lines for you?"

"Yes. He has the right sense of bitter funniness."

"I suppose the poor bastard would have."

"If he is known as an actor, people won't spit in his shadow."

Ketch Freeman was the public hangman.

As they rounded the point and H.E.'s garden, H.E. bending to demonstrate the nature of corn to Arabanoo, Ralph was able to perceive in its entirety this outermost penal station in the universe. By its serving officers a number of whimsical names for it had been invented: Lagtown, Felonville, Cant City, Cullborough, Mobs-bury. Actually H.E. had named it plainly after the distant person of a London political jobber, Tommy Townshend, Home Secretary in the government of Britain, who had in his care all prisons—even this enormously removed, out-of-doors one. Townshend had been ennobled as Viscount Sydney, and so Sydney was the name H.E. chose.

Ralph had always thought that to name things was to end their innocence. Naming children, he believed, was so dangerous that no name was put to his son, Ralphie, until the child was actually being christened. In having Tommy Townshend's name stuck on it, the place had taken on the flavour of British factional politics, and it had lived up to its name by being factional, sectional, violent. Though almost a year's travel lay between this convict moon and the politics of Westminster, the members of the officers mess formed crazy little parties and cliques with all the bitter energy of a true parliament. They wrote partisan letters for and against H.E. to old school friends who happened to work at the Admiralty or the Home Office—mail no ships ever came to collect.

T H E place which had been chosen for this far-off commonwealth and prison, and named Sydney Cove in the spirit of events, faced the sun, which here was always in the north. This reminded you, if you thought about it, that home was always on the other side of the sun—eight moons of navigation away if you were lucky, a year or more if not. The land on either side of the cove was divided down the middle by a fresh-water stream flowing out of a low hinterland among cabbage-tree palms, native cedars, the strange, obdurate eucalyptus trees of a type which (as Ralph was assured by scholars like Davy) occurred nowhere else in all Creation. Ralph had not liked to say, in the face of Davy's botanical excitement, that the rest of the world had been lucky to miss out on these twisted, eccentric plants. But if, as Dick Johson believed, it was the great flood of Noah which had drowned the unlovely eucalypts elsewhere than here, then elsewhere than here was lucky to have missed them.

There was a steely tree too which when struck with the axe either took a gap out of the blade or began to bleed a blood-red sap. It was, Ralph thought, a fair symbol not only of the strangeness of this reach of space but of the criminal soul as well.

This penal town station had the literal appearance of a town because of its peculiar circumstances. There were no walls or compounds—space and distance and time were the walls and the compound. So, like London, Paris, Vienna, and any other settlement marked by the European genius, the town had already developed quarters and suburbs—a fashionable side and a rough side. The stream was the divider. If your eye started on the west arm of the town, for example—the exactly opposite pole to the point where H.E. was presently entertaining a savage in his garden—Lagtown began with the hut of Lieutenant Will Dawes, the astronomer, and his observatory. Dawes lived apparently happily over there, always abstracted. He tried to avoid garrison and court duty, since they interfered with his observations. Because the night sky was so different here and so engrossing, he avoided mess nights with Major Robbie Ross. His coat was already merely a mid pink, as if the militariness was being bleached out of him by the moon.

Near them was Surgeon Johnny White's hospital and its garden. Next you could see the bakehouse which stood close to the beach and on the edge of the women's camp. The women prisoners lived under a high shelf of rock and in a suburb of shacks, the walls being panels of wattle and daub, roofs of thatch cut in a hurry from the grasses which grew along this shore.

When the women had first landed from the prison transports thirteen months before, they had been given only a sheet of canvas to make tents and awnings. They camped under those escarpments of rocks, down which the afternoon and evening thunderstorms of Sydney's strange Februarys ran gushing. In the weeks before the six convict transports and their accompanying storeships vanished again, making for India or China to find cargoes, you would see love-struck sailors coming ashore with carpenters' tools, doing their best to work the hard and contorted timbers which grew here, putting up for those women they had known on the endless voyage little huts and cabins—gifts of love which, like love itself, had small chance of keeping the weather out.

South of the camp of women lay a men's cantonment large because of the great number of male prisoners. Then, farther south again, stood the parade ground and the Marine encampment. Officers, the company of Marines and their listless wives lived here, as did Ralph, who had been able to acquire some sawn planks and shingles for the making of his one-room habitation. In this quarter too could be found the courthouse of the Judge Advocate Davy Collins, constructed by the convict brickmaster, Jimmy Bloodsworth, using red clay he had found a short walk behind the cove. Bloodsworth's bricks were scarce, were treasures. Between Capetown and Valparaiso, between the South Pole and Batavia, Bloodsworth's bricks were the only materials of any substance.

The little stream which divided the city of lags was able to be forded. The water of the spring came down from no snowbound mountains, but from a temperate inland, and it was pleasant to wade across keeping a lookout along the banks for the iguanas of the region, who were large and muscular and full of arrogance.

Once you were across the stream, you were on the better, or eastern, side of things. Ground had been rationally cleared to make some large vegetable gardens. Those convicts who had trades and a good record lived here. So did many public officials. Henry Kable, the convict overseer who Ralph considered might make a good Captain Plume, had the dignity of living here. Will Bryant, the only lag who knew fishing and spouse of that Dabby Bryant who had eased Ralph's dreams, had also lived over here until caught stealing part of the catch. You found, too, on the east side of the stream a number of women convicts who occupied the suburb by right of concubinage: the Jewish prisoner Esther, who lived with Lieutenant George Johnston, H.E.'s aide-de-camp, or the London thief Duckling, who lived with Harry Brewer. But they all knew that like Bryant they might be cast back over the stream for any criminal act, and that their official protectors might not be willing to prevent it.

T w o bays around from Sydney Cove and still deeply within the great blue protection of the harbour lay Ralph's island garden. Once Ralph had worked it on his own, but then convicts began swimming around the shoreline to it to steal carrots or turnips. So the old convict Amstead, a West Country thief of roofing lead, had been put out on the island as a nightwatchman and a day labourer.

As Ralph stepped ashore on the island with Harry Brewer, he heard Amstead's little dog ranting. It was a strange dog from Africa which Lieutenant Maxwell had picked up at the Cape before he had gone mad. When poor Maxwell had begun wandering around the penal colony with his pants off, trying energetically to find any reach of water into which to throw himself, and having to be soothed out of Johnny White's small stock of laudanum, the wise dog had switched its affections to old Amstead.

Amstead farmed a sunny slope on the north side of the little island—he had beans growing there, potatoes, and three orange trees from Brazil. Turnips and carrots grew on the flatter south side. Amstead's little hut and campfire sat between the two. "I be as good as a lord here," the old lag had said exultantly to Ralph one afternoon. Private Ellis brought out Amstead's weekly rations, and he was happy, after four years in a prison hulk in Plymouth and on the packed convict decks of a transport travelling farther than prisoners had ever travelled, to live an eremitic life here, separate from the younger, sharper, more turbulent lags.

Amstead appeared now on a shelf of rock above Harry and Ralph and Private Ellis. "Zur," he called to Ralph and Harry, taking off his convict cap. "I did not see you yesterday, Mr. Clark." Amstead had lately got a little imperious about Ralph's irregular visits to the place.

"I couldn't come," said Ralph. "There was a hanging."

"Ah," said Amstead, shaking his head sagely. Hanging was the sort of thing they got up to in that other world two bays away. "Come then, zur. I have just dug up a turnip I swear to weigh close to three pounds."

On the far slopes of the island, where the best ground was, Amstead had filled a number of straw baskets and jute bags with potatoes and turnips. Ralph and Harry exclaimed at the robust quality of this produce. There was no landing place this side, so Ralph ordered the old convict and Private Ellis to carry the stuff over the ridge to the dinghy.

Freed now of Amstead's tyranny, Lieutenant Clark and Harry Brewer sat in the sun on the edge of the tilled earth and Harry began to smoke his pipe.

"Old Ketch Freeman," murmured Harry, thinking of the hangman who wanted to be an actor. "Is it a part with any laughs in it?"

"Many laughs. Many comic exchanges between Justice Balance and Captain Brazen."

"You ought to ask the Captain whether he wants Ketch to act in a play. I mean to say, Ralph, hangings are a sort of theatre, and maybe the Captain wants Ketch to give his all talents to the business of execution."

And, Ralph decided, if H.E. says yes about Freeman, I'll then ask him for definite approval of Nancy Turner as Melinda.

CHAPTER 3

Players

April 4th, 1789

Concerning the play *The Recruiting Officer:*
For the Information of His Excellency.

Sir,

Among those I have audited for the forthcoming presentation of *The Recruiting Officer* is the public hangman, the convict James Freeman, popularly referred to as Ketch. Since he shows every capacity and willingness to take the role of Justice Balance, a role for which he is suited—though he is so young—by the ageless quality of his features, I have spoken to the Provost Marshal, Mr. Henry Brewer, concerning the propriety of engaging him in such a happy event as the presentation of the play promises to be. Mr. Brewer believes that, subject to your approval, there would be nothing inappropriate in Ketch Freeman's being given the part of Justice Balance. If you in your turn have no objections, then I shall engage Freeman.

Your obedient servant,
Ralph Clark,
Lieutenant, Marines.

R A L P H had also seen some small theatrical gift in Duckling. But he did not mention it to Harry Brewer until the next morning, at the end of the convicts' church muster.

There was no cathedral in this new penal commonwealth. Dick Johnson, the priest, had to preach to the lines of convicts in the open—as was the case that morning—or, during the colder season, in a large marquee or somebody's borrowed hut. H.E. kept delaying the building of a visible church for Dick to occupy. That was because H.E.'s vision of God was very different from Dick's.

For H.E. saw God not as a father, loving or stern, but as a sort of quintessence of British order who didn't need any particular architecture to enable Him, or more likely It, to be invoked. It was murmured by H.E.'s enemies, including Dick, that this was a result of H.E.'s Jewish parentage. "He'll build a synagogue before he builds a church," Dick had once murmured to Ralph, who was one of Dick's most prized parishioners.

Dick called himself a Moravian Methodist and an Eclectic, terms Ralph understood very inexactly. He didn't want to offend Dick, however, by asking for an explanation. The Reverend Johnson and his wife, Mary, had always been very interested in the state of prisons, so it was appropriate that they had been sent to serve in this ultimate one.

Among the tracts Dick and Mary had handed out to the convicts in the transports at Portsmouth, before the journey even began, was *Advice against Swearing,* and Dick seemed a little unhinged by the idea that if he could only convince the convicts to stop profaning the name of God, all else would fall into place. Their clean tongues would spread a Divine reform to all their limbs. The lags had from the first treated this proposition with contempt. When Dick had first visited the hold of the *Lady Penrhyn,* which held over one hundred women prisoners, the girls put him to flight by pulling their skirts up over their heads. "Convincing him of their trade," as the surgeon, Johnny White, said.

H.E. had once offended Dick by telling him to preach on straight moral matters—the main issues of stealing, deceiving, and whoring; the secular virtues of reasonableness, obedience, and industry. He'd also insisted that Dick be not too particular about marrying couples here, whether they were rumoured to have partners in the old world or not. For this was a new state of being. The eight-moon passage to this place had been nearly as absolute a change as death, he argued, and therefore altered morality.

The Reverend Johnson then was a florid young man about Ralph's age. He had been permitted to bring his wife with him all this way. Dick was kindly: he had concerned himself with the terrible brand of smallpox which was afflicting the natives. But even a devout parishioner like Ralph could not help but feel that Mary Johnson, who was capable and pious but more worldly, might have made a better pastor.

For Dick's sermons were dreadful—a mixture of plain moral advice as H.E. had requested, but also warnings to the convicts about falling into the Papist heresy of Pelagianism and Justification by Works. When it came down to it, Dick considered that a whore or a pickpocket could always reform and be redeemed, but a heretic was beyond help. So, even in a criminal community where doctrine and orthodoxy were not common subjects of conversation, he was determined to save the minds of the lags from every nuance of Papist heterodoxy. His sermons, therefore, were capable of making your average sheep thief's eyes cross.

As Harry, leaving the small hillock where God had been praised that morning, told Ralph now, "Jesus, Ralph, what a cracked sermon that man preaches!"

Ralph made some moderate answer. Then he sprang it on Harry. "Duckling has some capacity," he murmured.

"Christ! Who hasn't come forward to claim a part in this bloody play? But she can't read."

"I have had to lower that high standard in favour of those who cannot read but have good memories. I had the lag Mary Brenham rehearse her in some of the lines, and she spoke them back well to me. She didn't tell you she would audition for the play?"

"She didn't. I shall beat her for it." But Harry wouldn't. He was a pitiably indulgent lover. His face was bunched like a fist now, yet it held no vengeance in it at all. "I would not like it to turn her head."

He feared too much success would draw younger men to her.

"It is a lesser role," Ralph reassured him. "Lucy. Melinda's servant. She would be quite overshadowed by the other performers."

Harry chuckled. "So she has some stagecraft, does she? My girl?"

"She is a different person if you let her act."

"I hope she does not have many risqué lines."

"Not really. She wears a mask at one stage and pretends to be her mistress. But all the risqué lines belong to the part of Rose, who is a girl from the countryside. A Salopian shrew."

"I would not like it to go to her head," said Harry again.

"At the end of the play she will hardly be remembered by the audience," said Ralph, arguing—to his own amazement and delight —like a theatrical manager. "Yet she will have a justifiable sense of personal success nonetheless."

Ralph watched Harry weighing the matter, pressing first one eyebrow, then the other, blowing speculative air first into his left cheek, then into his right.

Ralph knew it was fashionable for gentlemen to take an interest in girl whores they had known who might suddenly be on trial for theft. It was counted elegance for a man to go over to Newgate prison to help out some young tart, whether she sat in the remand section waiting to appear before the Middlesex jury, or in the condemned hold waiting to be hanged or reprieved. But there had been none of that mere modishness in Harry's attendance on Duckling which had begun at the Old Bailey one dim autumn afternoon nearly three years ago, and had even earlier causes. Harry had had no choice. He had therefore gone to see Duckling's trial not out of idle kindness but out of a compulsion he could not control.

Duckling's crime had had no distinction. She had stolen some silverware from a client, a young jeweller's clerk who had been to a sale, got drunk, and employed her for an hour's joy. She had, a little later, been making off down Dean Street with the sack of candlesticks and salvers when her client, awakened from his brief post-coital stupor, dressed, descended the stairs of the tenement to which Duckling had taken him, and came running after her.

Harry Brewer was in Dean Street that evening, his last visit to the streets where he had paid out his youth. It was an evening when England seemed to lie under a fug, a cloud of felonies great and minor. A young curate had just confessed that he had married the Prince of Wales secretly and illegally to the Catholic widow Mrs. Fitzherbert for a bribe of five hundred pounds. The Whigs in the House of Commons were claiming that the aging governor general of India, Warren Hastings, had bullied the Nawab of Oudh into handing him jewellery worth a million pounds. The Whigs wanted Hastings impeached, but there would never be an execution for His Excellency Hastings.

Humbler servitors of crime than Hastings sat hip to hip in London's dozen prisons and in many county gaols, all of them much condemned by reformers, by Messrs. Wilberforce and Howard and members of the Eclectic Society. An over-spillage of prisoners was chained up in aged warships whose hulks rode at moorage in every harbour. Once a portion of all these felons would have been shipped off as farm labourers to Virginia and Georgia and the Carolinas. But now Virginia, Georgia, the Carolinas, and nine other unfilial American colonies had violently ended that penal connection.

As the children of that criminal deity, the Tawny Prince, accumulated in the streets and prisons, H.E., who had been farming in Hampshire since the war with the Americans came to an end, was commissioned to bear some of England's lags away to the limits of space and time. Harry had been his secretary at sea, and remained so on land. H.E., that is, was the only officer on the Navy lists in whose company Harry had a standing and something like a rank. So there was no question that Harry would go with H.E., who provided him with the only breathable air in the universe.

First H.E. moved into an office at the Admiralty to plan the enterprise. Harry was placed in a small closet next door, where he kept accounts, wrote letters, and contemplated the gulf before which he and his Captain stood. H.E. himself did not understand quite why he had been selected. He was one of a number of competent officers. He had, before his appointment, shown no particular fervour on the question of prisons and prisoners. But he was captivated by the idea now. Could a new Virginia made of utterly sullied beings be perfected by distance? It was clear to Harry the Captain would spend some years testing that question.

In Dean Street for a farewell, therefore, Harry had seen two young culls, as the felonry of Britain liked to call themselves—both of them members of the same criminal mob as Duckling—emerge from a public house in answer to Duckling's cries, jump on the jeweller's clerk, and rake him with punches. Both of them vanished, however, when two constables appeared. The jeweller's clerk now grabbed Duckling, who had waited too long in the hope of seeing him brained, and pushed her into the arms of the constables.

Not wanting his employer to know he had been foolish enough to bring items of jewellery up into the Parish of St. Giles, the young man—Harry watching—swore to the constables that she and the two culls had held him up with threats right in the road, that he had never seen any of them before. Harry intruded—his profligate youth had given him a sympathy for whores. He reminded the young jeweller that he should swallow his embarrassment and avoid both perjury on his own part and a death sentence for the girl.

The legal point was, as Harry would often in later days explain to Ralph, that if she stole the silverware from the boy while he was still sleeping in the room they had rented, she would be condemned to death only if the goods were valued by the jury at more than forty shillings. And even then she might have a good chance of a reprieve. But if she had attacked him in the open road, with her two companions, then she was technically a highway robber and was all the more likely, by statute, to take the jump.

Harry, with his terror of hanging and his plague of dreams and ghosts, argued with the boy and the constables while Duckling struggled in their arms. But the jeweller's assistant kept stubbornly to his story and at last the constables ordered Harry away.

Harry had attended her trial before the second Middlesex jury, who doubted the jeweller's clerk but still placed the value of the stolen goods at a hanging level. Harry had seen her accept the fatal sentence with a nightmarish composure. It was that—her terrible equability at the prospect of noose and lime pit—which had drawn him in.

He had told Ralph the story of her reprieve every time they had drunk together, whether in Rio, the Atlantic, Capetown, the Indian Ocean, or here in Sydney, this new extreme of space. He was fatally drawn by her strangeness, her incapacity to utter a tender word. He bore, by his own confession, the fear that she might one day say aloud that she might as well have been hanged in front of Newgate Arch—that a mouthful of lime meant about as much to her as a mouthful of air.

He was equally terrified that she might find a younger man. He did not want her to do it by Thespian success in the role of Lucy the servant.

"I have had great problems finding convicts who can act," Ralph pleaded. "Mainly the mad and the stupid and the relentless villains have presented themselves, sniffing an advantage."

Harry reached out his knotty hand and slung it around Ralph's shoulder, hugging him. The Provost Marshal gave off a not unpleasant musk, sweat, an excess of the bottle, a strain of brotherly bemusement.

"I have no rank, and to some I am laughable. Many of your brother officers are very careful not to be too genial to me when they are being watched. You are genial at all times. You are welcome to her, my friend."

Ralph felt a flush of shame. He was himself sometimes careful not to be overwarm with Harry when too many of his brother Marine officers were near. For Harry had been, until an accident had made him Provost Marshal on this distant sidereal shore, the oldest midshipman in the Royal Navy, and the unspoken fear was that he would pass on to others an inability to achieve promotion.

T o prepare the costuming, Ralph got the convict Frances Hart, who had once, aboard the *Friendship*, made him some shirts. She dipped canvas in dye and began cutting layered skirts for the two ladies of the play, a suit of grey burlap for Mr. Worthy, a suit of white for the scenes where Silvia disguised herself as a man.

But who were the two ladies to be? "Don't fret, sir," said Frances Hart, who had once taken possession of morocco leather pumps, knowing them to be stolen. "I can hem it and tuck it to fit the player. But since I must make men's clothes for the figure of Silvia too, I must make a beginning now."

For the dark, erotic malice of the character Melinda—a malice which (Farquhar indicated) would repay Mr. Worthy with high times in the marriage bed when by the end of the play he had won her—no one still had come near Nancy Turner the Perjurer. But aging Captain Jemmy Campbell of the Marines, who was querulous and could cause a lot of dissent during the play's one night, wanted Nancy Turner hanged for her perjury. What a fog of bile he would give off if he saw her queening it on the stage.

Ralph had already chosen his Silvia, however, the true heroine, the girl who would promise herself to Captain Plume at the end of Act Five when Melinda was doing the same service for Mr. Worthy.

His Silvia was Mary Brenham. She was about eighteen years old, Ralph guessed, though she had the presence and the calm of a much older woman. You kept forgetting that she could have been no more than fourteen years when sentenced. She showed a strange mixture of diffidence and honesty, as did Silvia herself. She had a fine unpocked face and brown hair—again, brown was Silvia, and black was Melinda, at least in Ralph's mind and, Ralph was sure, in Farquhar's. Her nose turned up sweetly at the end and the nostrils had a most uncriminal delicacy. All together, she showed the sort of well-formed English features that could make the sentimental reflect on the ruggedness of the basic English stock, even as it manifested itself among felons, and on other more sensual mysteries as well. She was tall too, or at least as tall as Ralph, who was not considered a particularly small man. She could read, and by special dispensation she lived on the eastern side of the cove. She was, as far as Ralph knew, no officer's concubine; her habitation of that eastern shore was entirely a case of merit. Possibly her lack of visible lovers was explained by the interest Reverend Dick and Mary Johnson took in her. She seemed to be—as Ralph himself feared he was as well—one of their special concerns. Though she seemed a little shy, she expanded when you gave her something to read, whether it was Silvia or Melinda. At the auditions she had a small child with her, about twelve or thirteen months, who tottered about the marquee contentedly. The child's name was William, but she called him Small Willy on the rare occasions when, during the audition, she had to call out to him.

"Refresh my memory as to why you are here?" Ralph asked. For there were some crimes which would disqualify you from belonging to Lieutenant Clark's Theatrical Company, even though he doubted Mary Brenham had committed any of them.

"I stole clothing from my employer, sir," she told him. There was no shamed hanging of the head. Convicts were used to answering such questions.

"Who is the child's father?" Ralph had asked her.

"A sailor," she said, looking away now yet still with the accustomed convict frankness. "I was on the *Lady Penrhyn*. The child's father is Bill Crudis, a sailor a long time gone away from here. But a decent fellow."

Ralph wondered for an unfaithful second if his Betsey Alicia could have lived through the eight-month journey on the *Lady Penrhyn* without taking on a protector, someone who would be a source of oranges and chickens in such places as Rio and Capetown.

"You say you stole clothes?" Ralph asked, filled with a genuine curiosity. She was one of those instances where the stated purpose of this penal enterprise had surely not applied. What had brought such a young woman—an unhabitual felon who carried, artificially or naturally, a lack of taint in her face and bearing—to the limit of things, the place meant for ultimate punishment?

She told him she had been sent at the age of thirteen years and eleven months to act as a maid in a house belonging to a Mr. Kennedy in Little Queen's Street. She had put Mrs. Kennedy's baby to bed and had then wandered into the parents' bedroom and discovered there clothes of a richness she had never seen so close before. She took two petticoats, a pair of stays, and four and a half yards of fine cloth from Mrs. Kennedy's wardrobe, and various items of male clothing from Mr. John Kennedy's. She had never stolen —or so she said—anything before or since. She had been sentenced to seven years at the Old Bailey. The length of the sentence meant nothing now, however. She inhabited a shore which was a fair model for eternity. Lord Sydney had chosen it for that quality: the unlikelihood of her or any of the others ever making a return.

Ralph sat her at the desk in the marquee and asked her to copy out and read Act One, Scene Two, the meeting between Silvia and her cousin Melinda. Outside, in the town, the work detachments straggled off to the sawpits and to H.E.'s farm, the fishing boat put off into the great harbour, the she-lags and the Marine wives fed wood into the fires beneath the great boiling coppers down by the shore and threw in their soiled clothing. Behind the hospital Reverend Dick Johnson was burying a forty-year-old she-lag from Manchester who had been destroyed by flux. It seemed that all the cove was engaged in tedium and the remembrance of mortality, except Mary Brenham, who gave herself to the copying of the living words of George Farquhar. It took her most of the morning to complete the task—she was occasionally distracted by her little son. Then Ralph read it with her, himself taking the lines of Melinda and pronouncing them in a monotone, since a few of them embarrassed him by their raciness.

Silvia asserts, for example, that she doesn't care that Captain Plume is not constant in his affections.

"I should not like a man with confined thoughts. It shows a narrowness of soul. Constancy is but a dull sleepy quality at best, they will hardly admit it among the manly virtues; nor do I think it deserves a place with bravery, knowledge, policy, justice, and some other qualities that are proper to that noble sex. In short, Melinda, I think a petticoat is a mighty simple thing, and I am heartily tired of my own sex."

To which Melinda—in this case Ralph—has to reply without blushes, "That is, you are tired of an appendix to our sex, that you can't so handsomely get rid of in petticoats as if you were in breeches. On my conscience, Silvia, hadst thou been a man, thou hadst been the greatest rake in Christendom."

Ralph liked the way Mary Brenham, ravager of the Kennedys' wardrobe, read. She was very careful not to commit herself to too much ardour, but there was a promise of great liveliness at some future date when she and Silvia would be one creature. She listened to the earthier lines of Melinda as if they were readings from Isaiah.

There was no arch smile or lifting of eyebrows. This demonstrated to Ralph not that she was somehow unworldly—no one had ever been in the *Lady Penrhyn*'s convict hold and emerged unworldly, except maybe Dick Johnson—but that she was weighing the part, circling its edges, her eye fixed on its centre.

He commented that she read well, and she told him that in the convict hold of the *Lady Penrhyn* she had read to the she-lags on the bed platforms around her stories from *The Gentleman's Magazine*, bound copies of which had been loaned to her by Lieutenant Johnston, a young officer with a like-sounding name to Reverend Dick's but of very different disposition.

"You used to read to Esther Abrahams?" Ralph found himself asking. He was delighted and disarmed by the image of Mary Brenham, leaning forward over a bound copy of *The Gentleman's Magazine* to catch the light from the charcoal brazier in the aisle between the two convict platforms, and all the other women hushed; Esther Abrahams, the Jewish convict, hushed, her baby daughter, conceived in Newgate gaol, swaddled in a blanket beside her. Lieutenant Johnston, who travelled on the *Lady Penrhyn*, had admitted and celebrated his love for Abrahams early on in the voyage, and one token of it had been this gift of bound magazines to the women's hold.

Ralph was so seduced by this image of Brenham, perhaps already plump with Small Willy, reading aloud deep among the thwarts of the *Lady Penrhyn*, that afterwards he would hardly remember having uttered the words "Do your duties, Brenham, permit you to take the part of Silvia?"

CHAPTER 4

Recruiting the Perjurer

RALPH wrote for his own instruction:

> For the role of Mr. Balance, Ketch Freeman the public hangman, who has H.E.'s approval and is overjoyed, since he believes that as an actor he might not be disdained by the young she-lags, as he is in his role of executioner.
>
> For the role of Captain Plume, the recruiting officer, Henry Kable, the convict overseer.
>
> For the role of Silvia, daughter to Balance, in love with Plume, Mary Brenham, who is as well as a competent player a good copyist.
>
> For the role of Lucy, Melinda's maid . . . the girl Duckling.
>
> For the role of Melinda, a Lady of Fortune . . . Nancy Turner, if we can do so without seeming to condone perjury and bringing down Major Ross and Captain Campbell on our heads.

DAVY Collins, Captain of Marines and Judge Advocate, spent Sundays writing his journal. It was a journal intended for publication, since fantastical voyages such as Davy, Ralph, and all the convicts had undertaken would be considered remarkable in England and even in Europe at large. Ralph had no literary ambitions of his own and was unrancourously certain that Davy's book would be a journal of great quality and popular appeal, since Davy was a natural scholar. That did not mean he had ever been to Oxford or Cambridge; he had entered the Marines at the age of fourteen. But he had a scholar's nose—he was interested in everything to do with this strange reach of the universe. In the wild sweet tea with which Johnny White treated scurvy, in the more extraordinary species of fish Will Bryant found in the harbour, and in the language H.E.'s savage, Arabanoo, spoke: its terms for uncle, turtle, death, and God. Many of the gentlemen had been taken in by the repute the very first visitors, James Cook, his artists, and his scientists, had— some eighteen years before—given the place. Through them it had acquired a name for being a miraculous reach of earth. So that ordinary commissioned oafs like Lieutenant Faddy and Captain Meredith had expected it would pamper and entertain them all the time. But it did not do that. It was not concerned with entertaining people. Its dun forests affronted them, its vivid birds shrieked and were inedible, its beasts mocked the Ark. Its Indians lived by rules further removed than the stars from the normal rules of human-kind. Cook had named the country New South Wales, as if it were an echo of a British corner. But it was no echo. It was a denial of all that. It was the anti-Europe. You needed a subtle mind if you were to find wonders here once a month let alone daily. Davy Collins had such a mind. Where others were bored or appalled, he was diverted frequently and grew excited. His journal therefore multiplied and was now the size of a three-volume life.

As well as working on his history of the new planet and its novel society, for the past thirteen months Davy had administered and been the embodiment of the law in a latitude which had not previously been acquainted with statutes. To help him in this exercise he employed a few inviolable texts: the Letters Patent, Clode's *Armed Forces of the Crown,* and Hayward's *Principles of Civil and Criminal Law.* Davy was no fierce judge but extended to the criminal something more terrible than ferocity—a calm and generous curiosity.

As well as that, he and his young and inquisitive friend, Captain Watkin Tench, were the leaders of a party among the officers who saw this particular new world as picturesque and curious and worthy of future study. Their military pride was not offended, as was Major Robbie Ross's or Captain Jemmy Campbell's, to find itself engaged with convicts in such an odd back-pocket of a barely known world.

"At least in other nations," Robbie Ross had fulminated, "Adam and Eve arrived innocent. Here they arrived with their crimes already written all over their faces." But reasonable Davy had accepted the lags as they came. He, like George Johnston with Esther Abrahams, had made a careful friendship with a convict called Ann Yates, seamstress. Ralph, still determined to be true to his wife, Betsey Alicia, nonetheless saw Davy's association with a lag not as a lapse of morals but as a willingness to take the new felon society on its own terms.

Ralph approached the door of Davy Collins's old shack through the brick steppings of the new one Bloodsworth was building for him. The site was yet another proof that in its little more than a year the town had had three incarnations—one canvas, one bark and wattle, and a third slow transformation to stone and brick, based to an extent on H.E.'s powerful sense that a brick was a statement of civilisation and social order, an appropriate declaration to make to the convict population.

Davy welcomed Ralph and told his Marine servant to make them some tea. Ralph asked for the sake of form after the state of Davy's journal. Davy picked up a page as if to refresh his memory and looked at it through his overhanging silvery curls, which, it was rumoured, had changed colour from gold under the deadly fire of the American colonists—or, more exactly, *rebels*—at Bunker Hill some nine years ago. "At the moment I am writing about the hangings," Davy said. "I state the opinion that the worst of the women are to blame."

"Do you think that could be classified as fresh news, Davy?" said Ralph despite himself, slapping his knee.

The flippant answer annoyed Davy and he shook his head. "Remember what Robbie Ross said once. The breast of every whore will become a food market."

"He said the *quim* of every whore," Ralph amended.

Davy nodded. "The reader will understand what I mean," said Davy. "In a country without, as Robbie is also always saying, top-soil and a mint, food and wine are currency, and flesh is the chief industry." Davy smiled then. "This is pretty serious talk for a Sunday."

A soldier brought in the tea and Davy poured some sugar into it from a small sack he kept in a Delft canister for protection from the ants.

"You remember Nancy Turner, who perjured herself to protect Private Dukes?" asked Ralph then. "She has some ability as an actress."

"She came along to your tent to read for a part?"

"These she-lags," said Ralph, "they keep a fairly short period of mourning."

"Yes. About half an hour, I'd say. Well, Mister Covent Garden, do you want to make use of her?"

"I don't want to seem to approve of her perjury on the one hand. And on the other, I do not want to begin her in the role and then find in two weeks' time that she is arrested and on trial for her perjury. I wouldn't be speaking of the matter with you if there was another woman of equal talent. But I have had the dross of all dross pouring through my tent—Meg Long, Liz Barber, Mrs. Dudgeon. I don't know . . . they see pardons in it, and the love and respect of their fellows. If Garrick and Palmer are able to dine free at Chuddock's Chop House in the Strand just because they've done well in Drury Lane as Captain Plume, then some of the sorriest convicts imaginable believe they too will have fame and a free table. That's the way it goes."

They drank their tea for a while, Davy frowning. At last he said, "It would be improper for me to say Nancy Turner couldn't be used. She will not be arrested, as much as people would like to see it. There is no women's prison here, other than the open-air one in which we all subsist. No men's prison either to speak of, not as prisons are built at home. And, although we all knew she was lying, that is not enough to convict her. By the time your play is performed, also, most of the present argument about Nancy Turner will have been forgotten. What you should remember is that Captain Jemmy Campbell might froth a little if he sees her on the stage. But who can live their lives according to the ebb and flow of Jemmy's ardours? Robbie Ross, however, has immediate say in the matter of your promotion and mine, and you might want to take better care of *his* sensibilities."

Ralph could sense that Robbie would never make his colonelcy and that therefore a man's military career could perhaps survive his disapproval. Above all, though a careful officer, eager to please, Ralph felt in his blood the maddest, purest, and most fragrant triumph. He knew at once that this was why people were theatrical managers, so that they could have this god-like excitement frequently—the excitement of bringing together on the one stage the dark volatility of Nancy Turner and the coy strength of Mary Brenham.

"This play will amaze everyone," he told Davy, who had the grace to laugh in celebration with him.

"Your whole damn cast has definite and unarguable crimes written against their names," said Davy. "It would seem a little crack-brained to cut an actress off the list for something that can't be proven. Is it a large part you intend for her?"

"One of the two larger of the women's roles. But not the better of the two women. Melinda has a spite and wilfulness which prevents the audience from loving her completely as Act Five ends."

"Nancy Turner should not be loved completely," murmured Davy. "I have seen at least three performances of this play and remember Mrs. Jordan acting the role of the other girl, the one who disarms and enchants the entire theatre . . . "

"The role of Silvia," Ralph supplied.

"And who will be Mrs. Jordan in this world, and disarm and enchant all of us, eh, Ralph?"

"The clothes thief Mary Brenham," Ralph told him, wondering himself for an instant why it was necessary to specify Brenham's modest crimes. Yet again he savoured the correctness of that balance between Nancy Turner and Mary Brenham. It was the correctness of all art, of all balances; when the elements demanded each other's existence, the way a recidivist criminal like Turner seemed to demand the existence of a one-time offender and accidental mother like Brenham.

CHAPTER 5

Dreams

FOR the part of Rose, a lively country girl with a number of pointed lines to speak, Ralph wished to have Will Bryant's wife, Dabby. He knew from his brief time in her arms a year before that she had a capacity to utter pointed lines. Added to this, she was able to mimic the thickest Cornish accents. Since the days of the Elizabethan dramatists, theatre managers had been gouging laughs from audiences by exploiting such West Country tones. Yet most of the time she herself spoke more or less exact English, for she had been educated at a point of her girlhood when her father's fortunes were higher than usual. Her father had been what they called in the West Country a "Mariner," a smuggler, and possessed for a time the money needed to live in town, in this case the town of Fowey.

Later, when peace and excise officers had been searching for him, the Broad family (that was Dabby's maiden name) had lived in a shack of wattle and osier in the forest, amid a wild community of forest dwellers, part Gypsy and all devotees of the lord of all thieves, the Tawny Prince. She was therefore a strange balance of town girl and forest savage, of the polite and the unspeakable. She had been given seven years for holding up an unmarried woman on a country road, stripping her of her hat, her clothes, and her jewellery, and leaving her defenceless and naked in a hedge under an early moon. Such were the extremities you went to when your father was no longer a "Mariner."

Ralph had first heard of Dabby Broad-Bryant in terms of certain acts of mercy. When Duckling had been sick in the Atlantic, aboard the *Charlotte,* Harry had crossed from the flagship to offer money to Broad so that she would keep on forcing water between Duckling's lips. For Duckling had the flux, and was also losing her hair in lumps the size of coins. Dabby Broad was to be Duckling's irrigator. When Duckling got better, Harry had praised Dabby Broad to Ralph during a dinner on the *Sirius* one evening in Capetown.

And very early after the women convicts had been landed Ralph himself had an experience of what he thought of as Dabby Bryant's compassion.

This had been in the first weeks. Ralph had been doing duty in charge of the guard at Government House. The Captain, or H.E., was at that time still living, a little comically, in a large gubernatorial canvas and wood structure not far from the place where Harry Brewer and the convict bricklayer Bloodsworth would later build him a more orthodox two-storey residence.

Beyond H.E.'s place a fishing camp had been set up on the shore. There were three huts, a long boat, and nets. The nets attracted Ralph. The crusty, twiny, salt, and fish-gut smell possessed a beguiling familiarity. A different star pattern hung above his head at night and he was still learning to read it. But though the heavens had altered, fishing nets maintained their universal reek.

Whenever Ralph wandered past the fishing camp in the settlement's first high summer, which in that country was February, he would usually see Dabby Bryant sitting in front of her hut jiggling her baby daughter, the one she had called Charlotte after the transport which had brought her so far. She would be chatting either with Susannah, the wife of the convict overseer Kable, or with Duckling, or with some other woman from that select side of the stream. Bryant would call greetings to Ralph as he went past. He would look back surreptitiously to see if she were making the inevitable convict jokes the women made in the wake of any officer's passage. But in Dabby Bryant that sort of frantic malice seemed to be lacking.

Once, when he went by the fishing camp, the child was sitting waist deep in the water, and Mrs. Bryant had her skirts belted up around thighs olive as sin.

The West Country convict Will Bryant, who had married Broad the Sunday after the women came ashore, had mentioned to Surgeon Johnny White and Davy Collins as well that he did not believe he was married in the Cornish sense of the word, that if ever he were to return to Cornwall—in spite of the hope of the Home Secretary to the contrary—his marriage to Dabby Broad would be annulled by that very passage. So that Will Bryant clearly harboured the same suspicion as Ralph himself did—that here you were a different sort of being from the one you had been in that world of rational starlight from which you had now been exiled. But in spite of Will's doubts about the universal value of his marriage, Dabby seemed very much the chatelaine, the confident possessor of the fishing camp.

Because so many of the lags were London criminals, more used to lifting watches than casting nets, Will Bryant was the only fisher of any experience in all that felon civilisation. He had been sentenced for what might be seen as a characteristic vice—bringing Norman brandy, collected from French vessels standing offshore, into the complicated Cornish and Devon coast. In a fight on some isolated beach he had wounded an excise officer. Indeed he had all the dark intentness of a wounder. But he was also muscular, quick-witted, and energetic.

The affair between Dabby and himself had begun aboard the prison hulk *Dunkirk* in Plymouth Harbour. The *Dunkirk* was an old naval vessel moored in place a short row from shore and peopled by the overflow from the city and county gaols. The overflow included Dabby and Will. Prison reformers like the Reverend Dick Johnson denounced the hulks as sinks of lechery, but here was a remarkable marriage which had come out of such a hulk!

Because of the stature of Will, the Bryants were the only convicts with a servant—a servant, that is, offficially permitted by H.E.—a slack-mouthed boy called Joe Paget. They had a gardener too, an older prisoner named Nat Mitchell. So that in this way, in those first days of the new society, Bryant and Broad reminded Ralph a little of Harry Brewer—this version of a new world had given them a standing they could never have enjoyed in the old.

The time her child Charlotte was in the water and her own skirts belted up and her husband out in the harbour in the fishing boat, Ralph had found himself talking to her about lightning. At that stage he was much concerned with lightning. Every afternoon and evening that first February there seemed to be a thunderstorm with the most remarkable and vengeful lightning of its species. Recently he had been dining in Major Robbie Ross's marquee when a thunderbolt had struck a tree fewer than ten paces from the door, bowling the Marine sentry over and frying three Cape sheep and a pig. Ralph hated the lightning, especially when he was alone in his tent and all the canvas turned a violent blue, and one lay naked under a drench of unearthly light. Even in Ralph's frequent dreams there was no lightning so thorough in intent as the lightning of this new penal universe, as it flashed down out of the west, out of an unseen and unguessable hinterland.

Ralph had asked Dabby Bryant about the influence the lightning had on the baby girl.

Dabby Bryant laughed robustly, the olive flesh above her knees jiggling. "She isn't so afraid as I am," said Dabby.

Encouraged by this frank confession, Ralph suddenly said more than he had intended, uttering a sentence from the journal he was writing for Betsey Alicia: "It is the most terrible country for lightning that I have ever seen." It was a small part of the substance of his marriage that he'd let slip away into the hands of this Cornish looter of spinsters. Ralph had an absolute temperament and believed that if you betrayed a little you would ultimately betray everything. The concept of betraying everything excited him more than he dared utter.

Though that fishing camp redolence nagged at his brain, he did not go back there to smell the nets for some days. When he did return, on a Saturday, he was delighted to see the shore deserted. The convict gardener Mitchell worked in the Bryants' garden, planting turnips, as Ralph himself would soon start doing on his island out in the harbour. Gulls argued about the place where Will Bryant usually gutted the fish before taking them to Surgeon Johnny White at the hospital. Ralph was passing the Bryants' shack, the slab bark shutter of its one window propped open, when he was surprised by a flat statement from within the hut. "I am famous for dreams too."

He saw through the window that Dabby Bryant was there, talking to him directly. She could not have seen him coming, so her statement, so exactly timed for his arrival at the window, was somehow based on foreknowledge.

Ralph stopped to face her. He could feel the extremities of his face burning. He had become the most notorious dreamer in the colony, with his night cries and his wailings. Aboard the *Friendship*, across three oceans and through eight whole moons, he had with his dreams attracted complaints from Captain Meredith and gross Lieutenant Faddy. Faddy had once told him those who cry out in their sleep were not fit to command Marines. That was the only time in his life Ralph had ever proposed a duel to anyone.

Now that everyone was on shore, it seemed even the convicts knew about his loud dreams. Perhaps Dabby Bryant had heard him cry out at night in the Quarter Guard tent.

"I heard you when you stayed at Mr. Harry Brewer's tent there. You are heard all the time, poor fellow, wailing away like that."

And not only wailing away, but keeping his journal of dreams so that Betsey Alicia could later interpret them to him.

"It is someone else you've heard," Ralph stupidly claimed.

"Oh," she said, "it's a known thing. Mr. Brewer sees ghosts, and you have your plague of dreams. Everyone knows you dream that your wife and son are dead. They die every night for you, between the lightning and sunrise. So much to bear!"

Ralph felt a flush of anger. "My dreams aren't for picking over, you know."

"Listen here," she told him, extending a brown hand through the window and grabbing his wrist. The familiarity of her touch took him by surprise. "I have dreams like a Pharaoh. When I was fourteen and asleep in Fowey, I was here on this exact shore. I saw

Will Bryant—it's none of it a surprise to me. These days and nights, I have dreams I cannot utter. I know I will be an old woman in Fowey—that is one of the dreams."

"Dreams aren't to be directly interpreted," said Ralph, grateful that the attention had turned from his sleeping self to hers. "You should reconcile yourself never to see Fowey again."

"Oh," she said, "if we have made the longest journey in the history of lagdom, is there any surprise if I could make it back the other way?"

I will go back, he thought, pitying her, and I will remember you and this place only as an anecdote to be related at a northern fire. Yet he certainly loved her olive skin.

She maintained the hold on his wrist. "Listen, darling! You go following your wife into a field, don't you? The field is all ploughed. There's snow on the clods. Yes, the field is all ploughed. And she wears her wedding dress. And from her breast she takes a louse. With her eyes fixed on you, she gives the louse to you. And you don't know what the louse means, darling—death or hate."

Ralph tried to get his wrist back from her now, but to his surprise her hand held it.

"Oh, duck," Dabby said, "what a sad little lord you are!"

He was free all at once. He walked to the door, halted in front of it, and began weeping. She had so neatly presented one of his chief dreams! He entered the hut and Dabby put her arms completely round him, vice-like. There was no child here. The infant Charlotte, a favourite throughout the encampment, must have been with one of the other women. She drew Ralph down onto a low cot which held a feather mattress she and Will had somehow acquired. The bed was so close to the clay floor that snakes and scorpions and giant ants could have struck the sleeper without leaving the earth. But in the circle of Dabby Bryant's arms Ralph did not fear any of these blunt, earthy dangers. Releasing him, she dropped the fairly fashionable scarf from her shoulder, opened the grey penal blouse the Home Secretary had given her. Within the sullen fabric lay two olive and, so Ralph thought of them, feral breasts. Images of Romulus and Remus being suckled by a she-wolf came to his mind.

As Ralph tore at his own military jacket and unbuttoned the sides of his breeches, there was more than the desperation of lust. For he knew it was specifically the seed of his dreams that he was about to pass to her, and that chance must be taken instantly.

Her legs now locked over his shoulders, she too worked at him like someone ministering an urgent mercy. And soon they lay together gasping cruelly, like two people who had somehow mutually rescued themselves from drowning in a canal.

Later he was astounded by the ease and blamelessness of this infidelity. Given the whole story, as he hoped she never would be, Betsey Alicia might nonetheless understand that he had put off an inhuman burden. He no longer dreamed those well-arranged but mystifying dreams which he had suffered in the Atlantic and Indian oceans, whose cries had awakened other officers and, for all he knew, reached even the lags on the convict decks. His dreams now became chaotic, like other people's, and dimly remembered. There was nothing to write down of them. They possessed no story. He woke from them feeling strong and normal.

Without those intricate dreams to set down, the journal he had been keeping now possessed no meaning. Davy Collins's journal was fuller in describing this remarkable penal station and the outlandish mysteries of its animals and plants, and of the Indian inhabitants who had lived here *ab origine,* from the start of time. His own journal had never had any distinction apart from the dreams. The Pharaoh-like burden of dreaming significantly, which he had caught from his wife, Betsey Alicia, had now been lifted from him by Dabby Bryant. And so, when the convicts had been ashore fewer than three weeks, and himself ashore barely a month, he abandoned his journal so rigorously kept aboard the *Friendship.*

Not only did he never approach Dabby again for a repeat of the exorcism, he was not even tempted to. Dabby Bryant had got the balance right. Now it should be left to itself. He saw her sometimes when she was in the company of other convict women from that side of the stream, and heard reports of her from Harry Brewer.

Now, a full year after she had delivered him of the dreams which until then had oppressed his days, he went across the stream to ask her to play Rose.

W H E N Ralph got to the door of the Bryants' shack, the venue of his cure, he was shocked to find the convict Cox there. Cox was Will Bryant's foreman. His face was large and disordered from an excess of imprisonment and now from the cruel reflections of the sunlight off the harbour. Neither Dabby nor the child was there. Ralph felt the Bryant hearth had been violated.

Cox reminded Ralph that Will had been turned out of his house. "Turned out of being chief fisher too. He were flogged and sent across the stream. And now he works for me, that kiddy, that Will."

Ralph *did* remember now having heard that Will had been tried for keeping back some of the catch. He had been sentenced by the Court of Criminal Jurisdiction on a day when Ralph had, thankfully, not been sitting on it.

Crossing the stream again, Ralph found the Bryants in poor Charlie Wilson's hut in the male convicts' encampment. He felt shame at having been ignorant that his Cornish exorcist, Dabby Bryant, had been forced across the stream and into a hut which had gone empty and haunted since Charlie Wilson had fasted himself to death months before. Charlie, working at the shingle-cutting camp, had starved himself, selling off his rations to other lags. He wanted to raise money for a return to that England which had spat him out. What a terrible faith there was in that shingle-cutter as he wasted to a skeleton. For there were no ships in the harbour, and barely a rumour of possible ones.

Charlie's body had been found near the shingle-cutting camp, on its back and already black with putrescence. Poor Harry Brewer had attended the post-mortem examination and had of course promptly enough seen Charlie's ghost, black-faced as at his death, waiting among the alien acacias and tree ferns at dawn.

As Ralph approached the door, he could see Dabby moving about in front of the place. Even in her eclipse she looked un-abashed. And as he knew, no one had greater power to appease and quench a querulous ghost.

Getting nearer, Ralph saw Will Bryant lying face down on a blanket, profoundly asleep, his body half in shade. The infant Charlotte played with her father's hands, tripped over his sizeable upper arms, probed scars on the back of his neck with a small finger.

"That girl Duckling tells me you don't cry out so much, Mr. Lieutenant Clark," Dabby called lightly to him, not careful at all of her husband's presence. He wondered was she punishing him for ignoring her decline from the east side of the penal city to the west. He did not speak until he was close to her.

"I am so sad to see you have had a change of fortune," said Ralph.

"We will go back, darling," she said, smiling frankly.

"I hope that's so." He paused. "Did you know I was making a play? On H.E.'s orders. I would like you to act a woman named Rose in this play. Rose is a country girl, very funny."

"So you want a sawney, a stupid Zedlander?" she asked him, winking.

"Dabby," said Ralph, "you know how you have to be very clever to seem stupid on stage. Take the role of Costar Pearmain, who is a dull country boy, whereas Rose is sharp. Well, let me tell you that the great Garrick himself, in his first season on the stage in London, played Costar Pearmain."

He had taken this item of theatrical history from the copy of the play which Davy Collins owned.

"I know in my blood," he pursued, claiming the same degree of special sight which she possessed, "that you can be damned clever on the stage."

He noticed Will Bryant had stirred and was sitting upright now, holding his daughter by both her wrists and gazing darkly at him.

"Why should I play a country girl?" asked Dabby. "To fetch myself men? I have a man."

"It will give you great enjoyment," Ralph told her. "There is nothing as sweet as making plays."

Ralph heard a piercing female catcall behind him, the sort which had transfixed him so often aboard the *Friendship* whenever he appeared below decks near the women's bulkhead or walked amidships to inspect them in their exercise pens. Turning, he saw the call had come from some of the women he most abominated in any world and under the influence of any system of stars. It was a clutch of *Friendship* women—Liz Barber, Liz Dudgeon, a third Liz,

Liz Huffnell too, whose Marine lover, Private Handy Baker, had only the week before been hanged. Huffnell, passing now with the other two, seemed in no way inconsolable.

"They always envied me," said Dabby. "Now they take joy in Will's punishment."

Will was standing up, yelling at the women. "Get away! Whores and slop buckets!"

Liz Barber yelled, "Taking in extra laundry, Lady Shit?"

They meant Ralph's laundry, of course, and Ralph burned, so easy was it for them to make him burn. And they knew it. There were officers they would not mock so openly—some because of their dignity, others because they were mad and vengeful. Ralph sat uncomfortably somewhere between these two parties of gentlemen.

Dabby took a disk of sandstone in her hand and whirled it against Liz Barber's ankles. There were flurries of abuse. Ralph ordered the women to disperse, threatening to call the Quarter Guard. He was relieved to see that this had some effect. As they turned away, sneering and jibing, Dabby continued to shout insults after them, and Ralph did not bother to stop her. It was as good as rehearsal, it was as close to Rose slanging Bullock as he could have wished. At last the *Friendship* women veered away, up a track among the cedars, toward the Marine cantonment.

"Have you ever been flogged, sir?" Will Bryant asked Ralph then with dark suddenness.

"Of course I haven't."

"Ah!" said Will Bryant, shaking his shoulders in a way which implied he had not yet healed, though of course he had.

"Some people," said Dabby, taking up the running from her more reticent husband, "look on flogging as an awful insult. To show your arse in public and be beaten on it, darling. And then to lose your house on top, and have to work as a hand in a boat."

Will said, "It'd be better for a child on that other side of the stream. There's less riot there."

Ralph understood at once that they were offering him trade. He should write to H.E. and say that Will was repentant, and had suffered enough, and wished to expiate now by the daily competence of running the fishing boat. And in return Dabby would play Rose and speak those lusty lines.

Will was asking without apology for a large favour. And Ralph hoped it was not because Will was aware of the larger kindness his new world bride had extended to a bewildered dreamer the year before.

"I can say with some confidence in any letter I write to H.E.," Ralph asked, "that you intend never to steal fish again?"

Will would not answer. "You can say it," said Dabby.

He had to demand something. "I want you, Mrs. Bryant, to come and meet the other women of the play at noon bell tomorrow."

"I must bring Charlotte with me," said Dabby, "for there are no servants for me now, and no one on this side I would like to leave her with."

Ralph turned to Will himself, who again held Charlotte by the wrists, a tethering the child seemed to delight in.

"Forget the lashes you took," Ralph advised Will. "They are behind you."

"That they are," Will agreed with the intentness of a man who might make a mob, or take an oath as a radical, a United Englishman, and happily bring down monarchies.

CHAPTER 6

By the Spikes

THE greatest enthusiast for the play among the women was Mary Brenham, the young thief with the small son. She copied away all day in Ralph's tent, sometimes smiling to herself as she worked through the more comedic passages.

The greatest enthusiast for the play among the male convicts was not Henry Kable, the convict overseer who would play lively Captain Plume, not Ketch the hangman, who needed a role so he could restate his humanity to the convict population—not Plume or Justice Balance, therefore—but Robert Sideway, a dark-haired and reflective actor who had seen Barry and Palmer and Smith, the acclaimed Mr. Garrick, Miss Litton, Mrs. Sterling, and Mrs. Peg Woffington. Sideway was to play Mr. Worthy—he told Ralph he had seen Mr. Munden play it at Covent Garden in the autumn of 1782. Later in the morning, he would confess that this was the autumn in which he had been found guilty of sundry acts of theft. "Anything," he confided solemnly to Ralph, "which could give me genteel access to the best theatres. And those coffee houses where by spending threepence a day you can meet fine minds, Mr. Clark, fine minds. And when it came to the theatre, Mr. Clark, if I could not have a box, I was in a fever to sit by the spikes."

"By the spikes?"

"The bars they put across the orchestra, to protect the actors from either hate or—and this was ever the case with me—adoration."

"We didn't have spikes in Cheshire when I was a child, or at the theatres in Plymouth," said Ralph. But then, you didn't get the same theatrical passion out in the counties that you did in London.

"I know," said Robert Sideway. "I have been to the Royal in Plymouth also."

Ralph had not known Sideway as an enthusiast of the theatre when he had met him during an inspection of the hold of the *Friendship*. He'd not thought of him *sub specie* an adorer of Peg Woffington the day Sideway insulted drunken Lieutenant Faddy while the *Friendship* had been hurtling east before a bitter westerly on a cold sea. Sideway's insult of Faddy then had been so wild that Ralph, who sometimes would have loved to have put Faddy himself in chains, was moved to put Sideway in them. And even when chained—the ankles alone carried twenty-eight pounds of fetters —Sideway had gone on offering both Faddy and Ralph such London criminal insults, such cant-talk abuse, that the two of them were united in temporary friendship. He'd called them cooler-kissers (sodomites), and catchfarts (sycophants), sirreverences (turds wrapped in paper) and scabbados (syphilitics), satchel-arsed sons of whores (unfashionable dressers), nonesuches (female pudends) and horse-leeches (satyrs), hap-harlot snufflers (fanciers of women's underwear) and fencing culls (receivers of stolen goods). They could go and live at the Cock's Tooth and Head Ache (a mythical hotel) before he would cry *peccavi* (beg their pardon).

But now, in this penal world ashore, he was a different man, urbane, unlikely to descend to low insult for fear that might cast doubt on his capacity to act Mr. Worthy the way Mr. Munden would do it at Covent Garden.

"You say you have been to the Royal in Plymouth?" Ralph asked him. The Royal had been an occasional delight for himself and Betsey Alicia.

"After Torbay," said Sideway, smiling wanly. In Torbay, away to the east of Plymouth, convicts due to be transported to North

America had some years ago rebelled and overrun their ship. It had been a renowned incident and had filled the region for a time with terror, though all of the escaped lags had been in the end fairly peaceably retaken. Sideway hoisted the sleeve of his convict jacket and showed Ralph a scar on his right arm. It was of the kind Ralph had only seen on the bodies of old soldiers.

"A bullet wound?"

"The ship *Mercury*. It was to take us to Nova Scotia, a cold country."

In the case of the mutiny on the *Mercury*, what Sideway was offering as a pretext was the ice of Nova Scotia. He could have more credibly said that he had mutinied on the *Mercury* out of a desire to see a performance of George Farquhar's *The Beaux' Stratagem* in Exeter. "The surgeon shot me when we overran the ship. They found me again on the road from Plymouth to Taunton. Of course, I was making my way to London."

"To the theatres?"

"To the theatres, and the friends. But my life would have been different, I swear, Mr. Clark. For I was not one of the instigators of mutiny on the *Mercury*. I availed myself of it. That was all."

"And did the surgeon shoot you for mere availing, Robert?"

Sideway laughed, gentleman to gentleman. "The surgeon was in terror. He shot wildly, and I was on deck . . . "

Sideway would be a polished Mr. Worthy and a guide to some of the coarser actors. Ralph was pleased though that handsome and practical Henry Kable, the overseer and the new world's Captain Plume, would keep Sideway's wilder theatrical affectations in check.

April 9th, 1789

Your Excellency,

I am happy to report that a number of the better convicts are approaching the task of supplying the entertainment for the celebrations in connection with the coming King's birthday with great zeal. Among the parts hitherto not decided, I have now settled upon Robert Sideway to play Mr. Worthy, a Gentleman of Shropshire. John Wisehammer, the Hereford Jew, will take the role of Captain Brazen, an over-florid recruiting officer in competition with Captain Plume, and a role which suits exactly John Wisehammer's engaging but excessive temperament. For the role of Sergeant Kite I have selected John Arscott, the carpenter, who will also be of great service to me in the construction of scenery, etc., as frugal as our arrangements for scenery and decoration must be. Arscott's demeanour seems to have amended itself since his quarrel with the *Sirius* sailors a year ago.

Since many of these people are engaged on labours of construction and farming, I would be grateful if you instructed the Provost Marshal, the Superintendent of All Works, and the convict overseers that they should, within reason, be given free time away from their places of labour to polish their skills and enhance their chance of delighting the entire civilised population of Sydney Cove.

I would be pleased also if I could be temporarily granted the services of Susannah Trippett, the artificial flower-maker and—as the time for the performance draws near—those of John Nicholls, who before his sentencing was a hairdresser and perfumier.

I will conclude this report by telling you that I have recruited—if H.E. will excuse the pun—Mrs. Bryant, popularly called Dabby for her sharpness and cleverness, to perform the part of Rose, a Country Girl. In this regard, I hope Your Excellency will forgive me if I raise a plea for the situation of Bryant's husband, the government fisherman. I witnessed an instance of the invective and insult to which these two are treated by former fellow prisoners aboard the *Friendship* and other ships. Bryant's eminence as the only adept fisherman in this distant region, and the privileges you so generously extended him, which have now had to be cancelled because of his misdemeanour, have attracted the envy of the sort of convicted felon who could never —in anyone's wildest expectation—hope to enjoy similar kindnesses. Bryant is aware of the shame of his demotion and is palpably embarrassed also by his flogging three months past. Since there is no one else as able as Bryant in the matter of the government fishing boat, I recommend him to H.E.'s clemency for possible return to his old hut on the east side of the cove and to command of the boat.

I hope these theatrical arrangements meet with Your Excellency's assent.

Your obedient servant,
Ralph Clark,
Lieutenant, Marines.

CHAPTER 7

A Full Company

SHITTY Meg Long, the one who had first come to his tent to be admitted to the play, sat in the shade of a native fig and watched the rehearsal go ahead in the shade of another.

"A drummer," Ralph read, "—and we shall arrange for one . . . a convict drummer, I think, rather than a Marine—enters the market place in Shrewsbury beating 'The Grenadier's March' or any other suitable tune. Sergeant Kite also enters."

Ralph, in the fear and exaltation of this first massed reading of the play, felt willing to make his players any promise. His instincts told him that for their own reasons of corps pride they wanted the play all lag, all convict. Not even the Marine trumpeters or drummers were to be invited in. Now that he had made that skittish pledge he felt a tremor of exclusiveness pass through his actors.

"Kite enters," Ralph went on. "That is you, Arscott, and you are followed by Curtis Brand in the part of Costar Pearmain and young John Hudson in the role of Thomas Appletree." Curtis was Harry Brewer's gardener, and John Hudson, a Cockney fourteen years of age and much favoured by motherly convict women. He had been used by older housebreakers to wriggle through broken fanlights and had been sentenced at the age of nine. Brand, a little sullen but an adequate worker, a man in his twenties, had given Ralph a passable reading.

"Nor can we start just at this moment," said Ralph, "since, Sergeant Kite, I believe it would be clever of us perhaps to flatter the gentlemen of the officers' mess by changing all reference to Grenadiers to references to Marines. Therefore, you say, 'Besides, I don't beat up for common soldiers; no, I list only Marines—Marines, gentlemen.' Likewise it might amuse the gentlemen who saw service against the American traitors if you changed all French references to American ones. Thus, 'If any gentlemen soldiers, or others, have a mind to serve Her Majesty'—which of course must now become 'His Majesty'—'and pull down the French King'—the 'French King' now becomes the 'American traitors.' "

After these gestures in the direction of recent history had been completed, John Arscott the carpenter began, reading one of the two printed copies of the play and having already been privately tutored by the theatrical Robert Sideway.

"If any gentleman soldiers, or others, have a mind to serve His Majesty and pull down the American traitors . . . if any apprentices have severe masters, any children have undutiful parents . . . if any servants have too little wages, or any husband too much wife: let them repair to the noble Sergeant Kite at the Sign of the Raven in this good town of Shrewsbury, and they shall receive pleasant relief—"

"*Present* relief," said Ralph Clark, delighting in his first exercise of theatrical management and in this first sight of Kite incarnated in the carpenter.

"—present relief and entertainment. Gentlemen, I don't beat my drums here to ensnare or inveigle any man, for you must know, gentlemen, that I am a man of honour. Besides, I don't beat up for common soldiers—no, I enlist only Grenadiers—"

"Remember, John Arscott, that I have altered that."

"I list only *Marines*, gentlemen. Pray, gentlemen, observe this cap. This is the cap of honour, it dubs a man a gentleman in the drawing of a trigger."

Arscott even offered a cap of air in the direction of Curtis Brand. The tribal magic of the play had begun to circulate among the actors.

Curtis Brand was slower in his response, a more halting reader.

"Is there no harm in it?" he ground out. "Won't the cap enlist me?"

"No, no more than I can."

And clever Arscott went to set the unseen military cap on Curtis Brand's head, a gesture so quick that Curtis reacted despite himself, and flinched as he would have to flinch when it was done on stage.

In the shadow of the native fig, Meg Long was farting with amusement. Curtis Brand read gamely on now, solemn as the rustic he was playing. Industrious, though. By the night of the performance, he would be close enough to Arscott in performance to delight the crowd, especially since there would be wine and spirit rations that day.

"My mind misgives me plaguily," read Curtis. "Let me see it." And as if by the miraculous contagion of talent, he reached out and took the quantity of air from Arscott's hands and held it—even with the right tentativeness—in front of him.

"It smells woundily of sweat and brimstone. Pray, Sergeant, what writing is this upon the face of it?"

"The Crown or the Bed of Honour."

And Arscott wore a divine smirk.

"Pray now, what may be that same Bed of Honour?"

"Oh! a mighty large bed! Bigger by half than the great bed of Ware—ten thousand people may lie in it together, and never feel one another."

"My wife and I would do well to lie in it," read Curtis Brand/Pearmain, "for we don't care for feeling one another."

Meg Long screamed with laughter and beat the earth. So doing, Ralph surmised, she became the first theatregoer of this earth so new they called it by such a name—New South Wales.

Brand and Arscott were aware now, from Meg's snorting, that even this tentative performance could delight. There seemed to be an expansion of their presences before Ralph's eyes—they *leaned into* their parts.

"Look'ee, Sergeant," groaned Brand, "no coaxing, no wheedling, d'ye see. If I have a mind to enlist, why so. If not, why 'tis not so. Therefore take your cap and your brothership back again."

Kable and Sideway, watching, were both engrossed, with smiles on their faces, and as the noon bell rang Mary Brenham emerged from the marquee, holding her son. From the direction of the dividing stream appeared the other women of the play—Nancy Turner the Perjurer, Duckling, who must not have risqué lines, and Dabby Bryant, the benign witch of dreams. They sought shade apart from Meg Long and sat and watched the men. For Arscott was shouting compellingly.

"I must say that never in my life have I seen a man better built. How firm and strong he treads! He steps like a castle! But I scorn to wheedle any man. Come, honest lad, will you take share of a pot!"

Curtis, fearing now perhaps that the newly arrived women would mock him for his halting reading, began to mumble.

"Louder, if you please, Curtis Brand," called Ralph, like an authority. He went over then and spoke privately to Curtis. "It is early days, and we must all make fools of ourselves many times over if we are to cause the crowd to laugh when the time comes."

He nodded to Arscott to carry on.

"Give me your hand then," boomed clever Arscott. "And now, gentlemen, I have no more to say but this—here's a purse of gold, and there is a tub of humming ale at my quarters! It's the King's money and the King's dish."

"Now, John Hudson," said Ralph, "you have to call, 'No, no, no!' "

"No," said John Hudson obediently but dully. "No, no, no!"

"You must do better with your 'no's,' Johnny," Ralph observed.

But Arscott took up the slack.

"Huzza! Huzza to the Queen, and the honour of Shropshire!"

" 'King,' John Arscott," said Ralph. " 'King'! Now you, Curtis, and you, John Hudson, you yell, 'Huzza!' "

"Huzza!" yelled the two lags, so wanly it made the women laugh for the wrong reason.

"And now you enter please, Mr. Kable, from the right of the stage."

Henry Kable entered trembling. Once in Norwich Castle,

when a housebreaker of seventeen, he had been reprieved at the base of the gallows and then—within a minute or so—witnessed the hanging of his own father and his father's accomplice. It struck Ralph for the first day that some of the terror of *that* public performance had now transferred itself to this one. In Kable's mouth Plume's gallantry withered. He muttered that he, Plume, had left London at ten yesterday morning and ridden a hundred twenty miles in thirty hours. "Pretty smart riding, but nothing to the fatigue of recruiting."

Kite, according to the play, implies that Plume has begotten a child on an old friend of his, Molly, at the Castle Inn and tells Plume she has just been brought to bed. "Kite, you must father the child," muttered Plume with an uncertainty of delivery which made the women hoot. Kable looked up, glowering. "Take no notice, Henry," advised Ralph.

Arscott, who was now the darling of the women in the shade, took the attention away from Plume by reciting the women he was already married to—an Irish potato saleswoman, a Whitehall brandy seller, a carrier's daughter at Hull, "Mademoiselle Van Bottom-flat at the Buss, then Jenny Oakum, the ship's carpenter's widow at Portsmouth. But I don't reckon upon her, for she was married at the same time to two lieutenants of Marines, and a man of war's boatswain." It was a famous speech and Kite delivered it famously, far more vividly than the delivery of his fellow players.

"A full company!" said Plume flatly, under cover of the women's frank amusement. "You have named five—come, make 'em half a dozen, Kite. Is the child a boy or a girl?"

"A robust boy."

"Then set the mother down in your list and the boy in mine. Enter him a Marine by the name of Francis Kite, absent upon furlough. I'll allow you a man's pay for his subsistence. And now go comfort the wench in the straw."

T H E N, according to Farquhar's invention, Kite goes to soothe Molly and to set up as fortune teller as a means of deceiving recruits into Captain Plume's company. Kite/Arscott was applauded out of the glade by the women, and now it was time for Robert Sideway to enter, in the persona of Mr. Worthy.

He did it so excessively, Ralph thought. He staggered and pressed the back of his wrist to his forehead. He blinked and clutched his left breast to subdue a quaking heart.

" 'Tis indeed the picture of Worthy, but the life's departed," read Henry Kable. "The man has got the vapours in his ears, I believe. I must expel this melancholy spirit.

"Spleen, thou worst of fiends below,

"Fly, I conjure thee by this magic blow!"

Kable, as the play demanded, slapped Sideway on the shoulder, and Sideway—thinking it was expected of him—tottered like someone shot. Ralph did not dare look in the direction of the women for fear of being ignited to laughter himself. He clapped his hands and moved in closer to Sideway.

"Perhaps, Robert, it might be better to begin in a more modest theatrical way and to build on that. Layer upon layer of gesture and feeling. Rather than to try to accomplish a finished performance on the first day."

"You think I am overdoing it!" Sideway accused thunderously, looking like the old Robert who in the cold southern seas had had to be fettered in the forrard chain hold.

"For the first day, Robert, I think you may be attempting to be Mr. Munden at too early a stage. If you spoke to Mr. Munden, if you *could* reach him and speak with him, I think he might confess that at first reading he himself would not be as full-fledged as you are trying to be. Come now, Robby, I won't stand for any black brows! We're here to make a play and not for vanity. Though some would say that making plays is the greatest vanity of all."

In vengeance at being corrected, Sideway muttered his first line without any inflection.

"Plume! My dear captain, welcome. Safe and sound returned?"

"Do it as you will then, Sideway," called Ralph. "As you will. I should have made you Captain Brazen."

For Robert Sideway, with his ridiculous gestures, was stealing the excesses of behaviour proper to the part of Brazen, which the

Hereford Jew John Wisehammer would play in the overdone way normal to Jewish players. Ralph had spoken to Sideway only to save him from the scorn of his fellow players. But if he would not accept advice, Ralph concluded, then let him be mocked and so educated! "Remember," he called at one stage, "Worthy is a noble person, not an oaf."

"I know, I know," sang Sideway, in an artistic fever, his face glowing and beginning to sweat, since there was no line he recited which did not have an accompanying gesture or even a new orientation of the body. So that he worked as hard as any dancer, glancing only sometimes at the text Henry Kable held in his hands. If Sideway could have convinced everyone he had seen the play so often he knew it by heart, then he would have been delighted.

Henry Kable could see at once the chance of defusing Sideway's theatrical grandeur and of playing to the women, sharing with them the joke of Sideway's overbaked style. Gradually he tailored his acting to that end. For he knew Sideway could disobey an officer and be honoured with a sentence from Davy Collins's court for it. But you couldn't disobey the convicts. They above all had the power of ridicule.

Mr. Worthy is in love when he enters. He is in love with Melinda. Melinda is beyond his reach, since her aunt in Flintshire, Mrs. Richly, has died and left her a nearly unimaginable fortune of twenty thousand pounds.

To which news Plume/Kable responds with military imagery. "Oh, the devil! What a delicate woman was there spoiled! But, by the rules of war now, Worthy, blockade was foolish. After such a convoy of provisions has entered the place, you could have no thought of reducing it by famine. You should have redoubled your attacks, taken the town by storm, or have died upon the breach."

Now, laughter of the right kind from the she-lags in the shade! And more laughter as Plume/Kable continued to give his earthy advice. "The very first thing that I would do should be to lie with her chambermaid, and hire three or four wenches in the neighbourhood to report that I had got them with child. Suppose we lampooned all the pretty women in town, and left her out? Or what if we made a ball and forgot to invite her, with one or two of the ugliest?"

Soon they had reached the point where Plume speaks of his own desire, Silvia. Ralph saw Mary Brenham blink and smile vaguely as if it had only just struck her that Kable was to be her love on stage. Plume says, "The ingratitude, dissimulation, envy, pride, avarice and vanity of her sister females do but set off their contraries in her. In short, were I once a general I would marry her."

Ralph had to call to the carpenter, who had joined his admirers in the shade and had his hand on Nancy Turner's hip.

To end the scene, Kite enters and tells the Recruiting Officer, Captain Plume, that he has visited their old friend Miss Molly and has discovered there a footman in blue livery, Silvia's footman, who has delivered to the unfortunate girl ten guineas from his mistress, a gift intended to be spent on baby clothes. (Kite, of course, being sharp, has at once married Molly and taken his share of the money.)

Voicing his enthusiasm for the girl, Captain Plume leads sad Worthy off the stage. Departing into the shade on the edge of the clearing, Sideway did not stagger, gasp and groan quite so much as he had at his first entry.

"This is wonderful," cried Ralph, his eyes prickling with tears at the energy and craft of his players. He felt the particular surge of gratitude for the pace Arscott and Kable had already worked up. He waited till his blood ceased quaking with delight before calling, "Melinda and Silvia for Scene Two."

Mary Brenham covered her mouth with her hand, looked toward her son profoundly asleep in the shade, and rose.

CHAPTER 8

The Morality of Plays

RALPH was soon depressed, though. He had gone to such lengths to cosset everyone's sensitivity in the matter of having Nancy Turner the Perjurer as Melinda. But reading her lines she showed a shyness she had not exhibited as a lying witness in Davy Collins's courthouse. "Welcome to town, cousin Silvia," she mumbled. The happy and arrogantly artistic state the men's performance had put him in now vanished. H.E. and Davy Collins would forgive him for using Nancy Turner the Perjurer if she were a dazzling Melinda. Those frightful Scots, Major Robbie Ross, H.E.'s deputy in government and commander of the Marine garrison, and his crony Jemmy Campbell, might even be appeased. But they would blame Ralph if Turner were poor, and their blame would be of the furious variety.

But his sweet, composed thief, Mary Brenham, saved the balance of his hopes by expanding before his eyes into Silvia, the way Arscott had expanded into Kite. It was the mystery again. It was the word made flesh. She took fire at the lines: "I need no salt for my stomach, no hartshorn for my head, nor wash for my complexion; I can gallop all the morning after the hunting horn and all the evening after a fiddle. In short, I can do everything with my father, but drink and shoot flying; and I am sure I can do everything my mother could, were I put to the trial."

At "put to the trial," she thrust her right thigh forward mannishly. It was sublime. Gardening could not match this, unless the turnips spoke back to you in the tongues of angels!

Nancy Turner the Perjurer continued to cast him down in her rendering of such pert lines as the one about Silvia being tired of an appendix to her sex that can't be as easily got rid of in petticoats as in breeches. The joke fled into the air, mute and muffled. Even Meg Long, sitting in her own mist under the native fig, could see nothing to beat the ground over.

"You are meant to be a tease, Nancy," Ralph told her. "You are—as Mr. Worthy says—a jilt. You must have levity and malice!" He nearly added, "You had enough damned levity and malice in the courtroom!"

As Melinda maligns Plume's character, Silvia storms out of her cousin's house. Yet even for a first reading, the argument between Turner and Brenham came off dully, Nancy Turner's mutterings and stumblings dragging Mary Brenham down. When Brenham vacated the clearing and Duckling entered representing Lucy, Melinda's maid, the end of the act died, as it were, in their throats.

Ralph took her aside again. "You must be quarrelsome, Nancy, quarrelsome! You have seen women quarrel? Weren't there quarrels in the hold of the *Lady Penrhyn*? I want you, Nancy, to believe in your enmity for your cousin Silvia, and to put some fist into it!"

To his surprise Turner began to weep. In the heat of her grief, freckles became evident on her dark, luscious face. "You'll work it up, there's time yet," he soothed her. "You will be a fine Melinda." Duckling stood by like a true maid, frowning, and as he put his hand on Turner's shoulder, an act which from a distance would look quite intimate, the Reverend Dick Johnson walked into the rehearsal.

R A L P H invited the Reverend Dick into his hut. It was one the clergyman was familiar with, since he had sometimes held Communion services there. "I seek always a house whose bed has not been sullied by convict concubinage," florid, earnest Dick had once confided to Ralph. This standard disqualified many of the officers —George Johnston on account of Esther Abrahams, Surgeon Johnny White because of the young Southwark barrow woman he sometimes invited into his bed, and even Judge Advocate Davy Collins with his weakness for a milliner, that handsome Yorkshire woman named Ann Yates, condemned to death at York Summer Assizes for breaking and entering and now regularly reprieved in Davy's arms. The unstained cot Dick Johnson sought was therefore a rare item of furniture in the convict town. Those officers who did not have a mistress were too scientific and self-assured for Dick's raw evangelism—the astronomer Will Dawes, for instance, and elegant Watkin Tench, and even H.E. himself, who was rumoured to be an atheist.

In Ralph's small hut there was little but a table, a full display case for butterflies to take home one day to Betsey, a desk, two chairs run up by the carpenter of the *Friendship,* which had returned a year past to the known world, and that celibate bunk which made the place a suitable site of worship. There were also two sea chests, in one of which lay folded the Communion cloth from the first Communion taken in this quarter of the universe—the service having been held in Ralph's marquee in the first days. Ralph's mind was teased by such things—the first Communion, and now the first play. Ralph called for his servant, Private Ellis, a sullen man of about forty years who suffered from a permanent cold, and ordered him to make tea—not too strong. Ralph had a mere seven pounds of the stuff left—he had sent an order to Capetown for more with Captain Johnny Hunter of the *Sirius,* but Johnny and the *Sirius* had yet to be seen again, and it was feared the sea had consumed them.

Ralph noticed Dick Johnson had his chin tucked down against his clerical bib and seemed embarrassed. He had broad and generous features, and his lips were wide and sensual, and all of that was at variance with his evangelical fury, which Ralph could sense simmering away in him as Private Ellis boiled up the water for the tea.

Ralph asked him about the health of Mrs. Johnson and of the native girl, Booron, a child of perhaps ten or eleven whom Dick and Mary had just taken into their home. A horrifying form of smallpox had erupted among the *ab origine* Indians of the place—a mystifying plague, since no one in the city of lags, in Sydney Cove itself or at the outstation called Rosehill, had been stricken with the illness. Bodies of natives, swollen and thickly covered with pustules, were found unburied in various bays around the harbour, sitting propped against sandstone ledges or lying in caves. It was known that the strange unearthly beings of this region favoured some sort of burial, but the bursting out of these terrible rashes and tumours must have sent the healthy ones fleeing farther into the forests, leaving their stricken relatives to putrify in the open air. Watkin Tench, who always inquired into such things, said that the abandonment of the bodies of the wretched victims meant that the natives had never seen the disease before. But Johnny White and Davy Collins argued against that, since they had discovered through taking H.E.'s native Arabanoo to the hospital, where four stricken Indians had been placed, that the natives had a name for it. *Gal-gal-la.*

H.E. had enquired at one time whether glass flasks containing variolous matter which Surgeon Johnny White had brought with him for some scientific purpose, could have somehow spread the malignancy among the natives. But Johnny mocked the idea.

At the height of summer then, Johnny had gathered a party of convicts and Marines who had been marked by the disease in their earlier lives. He ordered them to carry to the hospital four Indians discovered stricken in an abandoned encampment. At the hospital the two grown male natives died, but the two children were nursed through. Johnny White wished to adopt the boy, whose name was Nanbaree but whom the surgeon had already christened Andrew Snape Hammond Douglas White. The less assertive Johnsons had adopted the girl, and surprisingly saw no urgency to lay the weight of a Christian name upon her. So she was still Booron.

The mention of this new and fascinating member of his family did not, however, cause any generous rising of Dick's chin this afternoon. Reverend Johnson was for some reason in torment, and Ralph guessed what it was. It was the use of Nancy Turner as Melinda.

P R I V A T E Ellis left at last, perhaps to see *his* convict paramour, Liz Cole, another of those shoplifting London milliners. Liz Cole was already married to a quarrelsome lag called Marshall, whom she had jilted for Ellis. Once or twice, Ralph had warned him of the danger of this sort of affair, and Ellis had nodded away for the sake of politeness. What Ralph couldn't understand was how any-one would leave anyone for Ellis's sake. It was one of those mys-teries of passion.

With Ellis gone from the hut, Ralph turned to the priest. "Please. You must feel unconstrained, Dick, speaking with me. I beg you."

Dick hid his full upper lip behind his full lower one and stared miserably at Ralph. At last he unclenched his mouth and spoke. "I must ask you to use any pretext to abandon this play which you are managing. I ask you to do this both in my capacity as a friend and as Christ's priest in the vastest and most decadent parish in all Creation. I know certain people like to see me as a Methodist lunatic and an enemy of decent joy. You know I am not that, Ralph, and I beg you to go on believing I am not. My motives for asking you are based on the most serious considerations of both private and social morality."

And he closed his eyes, put his hand to his brow, and began to explain himself.

"Mrs. Johnson," he said, "has the convict Mary Brenham in a few times weekly to wash and iron. Brenham brought with her when she came to us yesterday a written copy of Act One of the play you propose to present. Mary—Mrs. Johnson—began turning the pages idly, and was astounded to find enshrined in the lines some of the principles of behaviour which have brought the pris-oners to their present unhappy condition and led to their being located at the end of the earth like this."

"Dick, it is a *comedy*," Ralph pleaded, astounded. He was as good a member of the Established Church as anyone, and he could not understand why Mary Johnson had not been consumed with enthusiasm for Farquhar's work. That she had been in any way appalled looked to him like a wilful misreading.

"In an ordered society"—Dick sighed—"one might be able to

consider it a comedy, though I have to say there are some lines at which civilised people should not laugh. Here, however, in this society, where violations of property and person are the standard of behaviour, the play cannot be considered as anything but a dangerous incitement." Dick made an appeasing motion with his left hand. "I hate talking like this to a friend, Ralph. I sound like a sermon."

And indeed the uneven white of an embarrassed friend was showing through Dick's tanned face.

"This girl Mary Brenham," he continued. "She has a child by some sailor. She begot it while she was coming here aboard the *Lady Penrhyn*."

"So I believe," said Ralph.

"She tells me this. You remember that the *Lady Penrhyn* was the only ship in all the fleet which carried a convict shipment entirely of females. Aboard the *Lady Penrhyn* then, you had to align yourself with a sailor. If you did not—if you were not known to be the property of one of the seamen—then you stood the chance of being violated by the entire pack of sailors. So Brenham aligned herself with the sailor Crudis, one of the few who were better than beasts. But even so he forced her favours from her."

"Perhaps she did not give them entirely without wishing to," argued Ralph, moved by an obscure fraternal defensiveness for Crudis.

"Brenham was raised decently—you can tell from the way she carries herself. Consider that there is nowhere aboard a convict ship, neither in the hold nor in the sailors' quarters, where bodily commerce could be carried out in the sort of privacy you and I, and for that matter Mary Brenham, would consider essential for the purpose. It was different for the officers, since they had cabins of their own, and indeed in some cases made use of them!

"Let me assure you, therefore, that Mary Brenham's sensibilities were outraged by the voyage and yet, even here, they still exist. So there is Brenham at one pole of our convict community, and she is encouraged—positively urged—by the arts of comedy to abandon her delicacies. And at the other pole we have the Perjurer Nancy Turner and others of that kind. Lacking in any moral sense, they will now see in *The Recruiting Officer* all their amorality exalted and laughed at by the members of this penal civilisation. This was always the peril of the theatre! The events even of Act One, which I have read and made a copy of, will serve as an exemplum for events which will no doubt occur later in the evening of the performance. No, no, Ralph, let me specify. First we begin with Sergeant Kite, who enumerates five women he is already married to simultaneously. Then we have Captain Plume asking whether Melinda is as great a whore as she is a jilt, and when Worthy denies it, Plume exclaiming, ' 'Tis ten thousand pities.' Next, Plume's advice on how Worthy should go about assuring Melinda's affections. 'The very first thing that I should do, should be to lie with her chambermaid, and hire three or four wenches in the neighbourhood to report that I had got them with child.' "

"But," Ralph pleaded, "the play makes it clear that Captain Plume is in fact a virtuous man, and that all his racy talk *is* merely talk."

The Reverend Dick thrust his head back now, looking at the ceiling. Ralph could see nothing but his chin. "Ralph, Ralph, talk is *everything* in a play. What does he say of Silvia—that she would have the wedding before consummation, and he was for consummation before the wedding, and so as far as he was concerned she could go and lose her maidenhead her own way!

"And it all continues in the second scene," Dick went on, sitting upright now and hunting among his notes. "There you have Melinda, who will—as I say—be the Perjurer Turner, talking to Silvia, who will be that better type of convict, Mary Brenham. Oh, yes. Here. 'You are tired of an appendix to our sex that you can't so handsomely get rid of in petticoats as if you were in breeches.' That, I tell you, Ralph, is an inflammatory sentence to utter before the combined felonry of this place."

Dick let his notes fall to the floor. He blinked at Ralph. "Is there further need to quote, my friend?"

Ralph felt calmly enraged. In his new zeal for theatrical management he felt an almost brotherly urge to defend the words of George Farquhar, who—ill and poor—had written *The Recruiting Officer* and *The Beaux' Stratagem*, the latter from his deathbed, dying on the evening of its third performance. Oh what a lusciousness there was in George Farquhar's words, and what a valour in the way Farquhar's own tragedy was excluded from the scenes, so that the play had all the body and lustiness of a tall masculine presence in fierce health. And Dick, in his Eclectic Society sternness, could not see, sense, or appreciate that valour. He was worried merely that Liz Barber might have a belly laugh and that this might in turn vitiate the moral universe.

"If you are convinced this play is a scandal," Ralph asked with deliberate emphasis, "why do you not appeal to H.E., who authorised it?"

Reverend Dick Johnson stamped a foot and rose, clenching his fists.

"You know why, Ralph. He's cross-grained when it comes to me. He will not order a church to be built for me. If I show any concern for the personal redemption of a convict, he advises me to preach on moral subjects and leave redemption. If I show any concern over the play, he will become convinced it is above all the work best designed to be the comedy first seen in this place. No. *You* must quash the play using any excuse—lack of actors, or even by voicing the same concern as I have voiced to you: that the words will have a poisonous influence."

"But I do not *believe* it, Dick."

"You do not believe in the impropriety of what I have read?"

"It is there only to get a laugh."

"And that fact justifies it?"

Dick no longer spoke as a friendly counsellor but with the sort of dissenting rectitude Ralph found most irksome. That was the trouble with evangelicals. They were always increasing the demand on your behaviour. *You do not have a convict mistress? Good. Now renounce the theatre forever! Expunge the comedy! Geld the tragedy for the sake of the convict population!*

"Am I not an honest Protestant?" Ralph asked in exasperation.

"That is not an achieved and permanent state. It is a state you possess only by grace of your Saviour, Jesus Christ. You do not stay there by your own merit but by favour of the blood of Christ.

Officers in this garrison speak of being a Protestant as if it were something political, like deciding to be a Tory. I did not expect to hear this nonsense from you, Ralph. You have been an honest Protestant, yes. Though there is the text which instructs us to call no man honest, let us say *you* are honest. But even so, you are mistaken in this matter."

A dangerous impulse to theological debate entered Ralph. He welcomed it heartily.

"Are you dictating to my conscience, the way a Pope would?" He knew that a mention of the Whore of Babylon would half rout Dick.

"My God, I am *not!*" roared Dick. "I argue what is self-evident to any properly informed Christian conscience."

"The very woman whose virtue you wish to protect—Mary Brenham herself—is brought to life by this play. Brought to life! I do not exaggerate. It is the only urbane thing which has happened to her since she stole as a servant and was caught and sentenced. The highest civil authority in this place has not only permitted the thing but encouraged it. I will *not* pretend I am squeamish about it and opposed to doing it. For I too have a difficulty with H.E. and cannot pretend that I am as well-liked by him as are the more obviously cultivated officers like Davy Collins and Watkin. If I felt a real moral concern, then I would go to him. But I do *not*. I disagree with you absolutely, Dick. I will not abandon the play!"

"Then it means you cannot expect to enjoy Communion in your own household in the future."

"Do not bully me with the sacraments of Christ, Dick. I have not taken a whore yet. Be kind enough to wait until I do."

"I have to tell you that this matter is important enough to Mrs. Johnson and myself as to preclude any further intimacy with you, Lieutenant Clark. In a felon colony which is entirely against us we have always counted you an ally. It is with grief that I realise we no longer can."

And indeed poor silly Dick was suffering so much he had torn his cravat and clerical collar away from his throat.

"Then," said Ralph, with a heady feeling of heresy, "I must choose to be theatrical."

"God save you, my brother." The Reverend Dick Johnson said it like a curse, and his lips contended with each other for a few more seconds before he rose and left.

T H O U G H Dick Johnson might be a somewhat extreme, Wesley-leaning priest of the Established Church, as darkness fell Ralph began to grow wary about his condemnation. The truth was that in his deepest being Ralph believed in the same God Dick Johnson did—and this was a God of Lightnings. In all the universe, this penal harbour was the home of lightnings, the sounding box, the focussing glass. Extravagant coruscations continued all summer and half the autumn.

To the primitive Ralph Clark, then, who quavered at this sound and light, the withdrawal of the blessing of the one representative of the Established Church in millions of square miles of space seemed by darkness a powerful invitation to the God of Thunders to send a bolt. Ralph was pleased, therefore, that the summer was ending as the playmaking began and Dick's excommunication was uttered. The season of lightnings was all but over now.

He did not in any case think of Dick Johnson's anathemas once he was in the clearing with his players. This morning the starting players were the young hangman Ketch Freeman, the convict overseer Henry Kable, the mutineer Sideway as the exquisitely exercised Mr. Worthy, and Mary Brenham as Silvia.

The executioner, Ketch Freeman, had one of those withered young faces. Hook-nosed and ancient, it seemed to be waiting for the rest of Ketch's body to catch up to it in age. John Nicholls the perfumier, who had once too often and far away stolen powder and pomade, had appeared briefly at the marquee just to show what could be done to age an actor's face. He marked some lines either side of Ketch's nose and covered his features with a grey-blue powdery wash which instantly made them plausibly the visage of an aging squire and Justice of the Peace. When Ralph saw this, he knew such alchemy was worth the risk of lightning and pulpit condemnation. Behind the deathly wash, Ketch, too, was radiant. For he knew the world forgives actors anything.

Plume says, "Pray, Mr. Balance, how does your fair daughter?"

And Balance replies, "Ah, Captain! What is my daughter to a Marshal of France? Whereupon a nobler subject. I want to have a particular description of the Battle of Höchstädt."

Ralph, according to his policy, altered "Marshal of France" to "rebel general," and "Battle of Höchstädt" to "Battle of Bunker Hill," and the scene was ready to be played. Ketch as Justice Balance performed it with his chin in the air and his eyes nearly closed —it is how perhaps the politer people of that great city looked on him in his days as a footpad and mugger. He also kept both his lips stiff, his lower lip barely parted from the upper.

"No no," called Ralph, "you are showing him like a Londoner. He is *not* a Londoner, Ketch. He is an honest, bluff, straight-talking fellow." Oh, thought Ralph, what a pleasure it is to argue character. "What does Balance say to Plume about Silvia? When he accuses Plume of wanting to debauch Silvia and Plume denies she is at any risk, Balance says, 'Look'ee, Captain, once I was young, and once an officer as you are, and I guess at your thoughts now by what mine were then, and I remember very well I would have given one of my legs to have deluded the daughter of an old plain country gentleman . . .' You see, Ketch. He's *that* sort of fellow. He declares war on all cant. Now a man like that uses his lips when he talks. So you, Ketch, you can use your lips too."

Ketch gave up the stiff lips during that morning only a little at a time. For having been for so long the centre of all groans, he now wanted to be the centre of all laughs. Ralph saw him stealing looks at Meg Long, who sat under her usual tree. Even Meg was not laughing much. Perhaps she was becoming jaded, as theatre-goers do. When large Black Caesar stopped in the clearing, a dangerous-looking adze over his shoulder, to see if Lieutenant Clark needed him yet for the mob scenes, Ketch kept looking to him, too, for applause and laughter. But Black Caesar did not give him any.

PART TWO

CHAPTER 9

The Hunt

FEBRUARY 1788

RALPH'S friendship with Harry Brewer, the oldest midshipman in the Royal Navy, had been enlarged by Harry's habit of treating him as his confessor. Harry had sent in Ralph's direction such a reckless tide of confessions Ralph had no choice but to avoid the man altogether or to become his brother. Since Harry was such a competent storyteller and unabashed by the lifetime he had devoted to folly, Ralph could not imagine giving up the friendship. He did not know when he might need a confessor himself.

The warmth between Ralph and Harry Brewer, notable enough while the convict transports were on their endless voyage, was augmented during a hunting expedition the two men set out on during the first month of the history of the penal city. Everything was novel then. People still had the sense that, even on a small excursion, wonders might be found.

It was in that continuing season of lightning, the one in which Dabby Bryant later rescued Ralph from the onus of perfect dreaming, that Ralph took Harry's invitation to go shooting with him. One of Ralph's back teeth had been throbbing, but the Irish surgeon, Considen, the planet's foremost tooth man, had put a wad of cloth dipped in some brown narcotic into the socket that was paining Ralph to allow him specifically to go into the woods.

Ralph met Harry on the eastern side of the stream, which was less precipitous than the hills to the west, and headed into the forest, each of them accompanied by a man whose task was to carry the firearm until it was required. Harry's piece was carried by the Jamaican lag Jack Williams, and Ralph's by his servant, Private Ellis.

At first Ralph thought he would be disappointed in his hope that Harry Brewer would entertain him. The Provost Marshal had slept badly. He said it was the Dutch spirits he'd bought in Cape-town. Those Dutchmen had unloaded all their rubbish on the bottlemen of the fleet, who, on their way to a star without distiller-ies, were not too squeamish about what liquors they took with them.

As everyone knew then, there were other reasons for Harry to worry. He was an old man in insecure harness with a young girl. It was an ancient joke he was fulfilling, and often he knew it bitterly.

So at first Harry did not talk much. A further stillness, like the barely concealed intolerance of some enormous force, an alien omnipresence, closed over them as soon as they moved among the trees. The vast eucalyptus trees affronted the normal rules of botany by shedding all the time, and now released leaves onto their shoul-ders with a dry murmur. You could see where cabbage trees had already been lopped to make huts and thatching. Apart from these signs of human intrusion, none of it was like forests Ralph knew. It gave off a kind of ancient stubbornness.

Yet the foreignness seemed to tantalise Harry and revive him. The otherness of New South Wales. Which was not "new" and certainly not Wales. Whatever it was, it had nothing at all to do with the old Druidic kingdom. The gods were different here.

They talked about the thunderstorms. As it had been between Ralph and Bryant, lightning was a standard conversation opener at that time of the year. Harry told a comic yarn of how he had to keep getting up in the night to loosen the guy ropes. Ralph had an image of what Duckling might look like by the blue flare of light-ning and wondered if a punitive God, misjudging Harry's folly, thinking he was really *enjoying* the company of the girl instead of being tortured by it, might with one bolt fuse Harry and his pullet.

The second most common conversational gambit was the

French. The voyagers James Cook and Sir Joseph Banks had made
Botany Bay, that shallow anchorage some seven miles south of
where Ralph and Harry now walked, so famous with their mistaken
praise that two French ships had appeared there within days of
H.E. and his entire penal circus. They were scientific ships, and
their crews had been attacked and wounded by savages on islands
far out in the Pacific. Their demeanour was polite and devoid of
political intent. They had buried on the low foreshore an abbé
supposedly famed in France as a naturalist. They were slowly refitting their ships down there and preparing to go out again into
the latitudes of cannibals. They would make leisurely and exhaus-
tive enquiries in a multitude of islands, paying strenuous attention
to the barbarous night skies, as well as to the foliage on the shores
and the depth of lagoons. It would be years before they were released from their monk-like investigations.

A painful etiquette ran between the French men of science
seven miles south and the British in the penal settlement. One
afternoon, a scientific Papist priest walked up from Botany to Sydney to see the astronomer Dawes, and during his visit had been
very taken with the butterfly case Ralph was keeping for Betsey
Alicia. The butterflies were beautiful here and the moths as big as
finches. Ralph had often enough described to Harry how he had
resisted the abbé's outrageous offer to buy some of the collection.

F o r the first hour of their hunting they saw very little to shoot
at. Some good-sized white cockatoos with fine yellow sprays of
feathers at their crest took their eye, but already the rumour was
that they were gristle through and through. The red-breasted lori-
keets were so lovely, said Harry, it was as well that they would be
safe from such a bad marksman as himself.

They tired quickly in the humid day, and barely had their
marching legs back after their time aboard ship. They came gratefully down into a clearing where it was cool. Here the trees had
bark resembling paper. Harry and Ralph sat in the shade of one,
Private Ellis and the Jamaican Jack Williams fifty paces away under
another. Harry took out a flask of brandy and handed it to Ralph.

Ralph merely wet his lips. It was the stuff Harry had been maligning an hour earlier, and in any case liquor easily befuddled him. Harry took a long draft, though, and placed his head back against the tree, and sighed as if getting ready for sleep.

"I might love this place, my friend," he said, "if it were not for lags. Though if it were not for lags, there would be no place at all. The puzzle, you see."

"You talk as if you had come home," said Ralph, massaging his dully painful jaw.

"I have, Ralphy, I have."

He took some more brandy. "Look at that black boy," he suggested. "The islands he comes from! He'll never go home. I'll never go home." He pinched the moist sandy earth beneath him. "I am transported too. So this is the loam that will get Harry."

Ralph laughed at him. The laugh admitted a needling blast of air to his tooth. "So you have found your homeland, old Harry. But it don't seem to have made you very happy."

Harry said, "Do you know, Ralph, that though Provost Marshal, I am hangable material? Of course you do. Every man I have ever met and liked has guessed I am hangable material. H.E. knows it. I am so pleased he never sets down what he knows about me. He pretends not to know that Duckling is my lag-wife, but he *knows*. And he knows I am hangable. And you are such an honest little bugger, Ralph, such an upright little lover, who hasn't touched one of those she-lags yet, but you know, too, that I am under the eye of God and the Sun, material as hangable as any."

He really drank now—a quarter of the bottle vanished.

Ralph could gauge that he was now about to receive the life history of Harry Brewer, and that, like most intemperate lives, it would be dressed up as a cautionary tale.

The two besetting questions of that life were Duckling and the latent duty he carried as Provost Marshal to hang people.

Harry began with Duckling.

"D u c k l i n g was sentenced four o'clock in the afternoon, very dull October. The courtroom nearly dark. Baron Ayre and the second Middlesex jury. She'd taken too much *stuff* from a man called Fannock—solid silver stuff, a damned candelabra, the stupid little bitch. The jury valued it down as far as they could, but it was still too much. I went to take her three shillings in Newgate; there's a taproom close by the condemned hold. You can drink there, debtors have their visitors in, and they drink and chat with the condemned. Sport, eh, Ralphy? I took her three shillings two days before she was to take the drop and they thought I wanted to hire her—there are men who do that too, the night before the hangings. That is one of my nightmares. A girl who in a day will be hanged and be thrown into a lime pit, willing to do a jig with me because I've got three shillings."

He groaned. The brandy—as he liked to say—was burning his pipes.

"I am not like Davy Collins or Watkin, that clever bastard. I am one of the *others*. There is only a hair between me and the lags. I *am* one of them, and they can sniff it out in me. And you, Ralphy, you find it there, too. How I became an ancient oaf of forty-seven years, carrying shillings to a fifteen-year-old moll, is—to a decent fellow like you, Ralph—probably not lacking in interest."

With a blinding candour, Harry began to tell the full story of his youth and why he went to sea just before he reached the age of forty, and shamed himself for nearly ten years, carrying a boy's rank, living a life to which only the Captain gave any content.

When Harry was young, he worked for a London firm of architects and builders named Cuxbridge and Breton. He was likeable, he said, as if that quality had now been leeched out of him, and he was an excellent draftsman, and he was wild. To go out with money in your pocket and not knowing in what pub and with what girl you would end the evening—that was all life's richness to Harry. So Harry paid away his youth and his life to Soho girls, in that dangerous parish of St. Giles—to girls with fever in their cheeks. He had a system of overstating the price on bids for building contracts, and if Cuxbridge and Breton received the contract, of pocketing the difference between the real and the stated price of bricks and window frames. His favourite reading, as it was for many young Londoners, was *The Newgate Calendar*, a journal which gave a digest of the activities of all the more notable and recently arraigned criminals. And his vigour was unlimited, he told Ralph. He could have two or three girls a night. He confessed he would sometimes incant, while drinking, a sort of rhyme. "My name is Harry Brewer, I'm in every public ledger, and Heaven is my desired end."

In the cant language of St. Giles, they called whores public ledgers.

And in his folly, Harry said, he saw Seven Dials, Soho, the parish of St. Giles, not as an accurate mirror of his own inner disorder but simply as another kingdom, its own commonwealth, separate from the rest of England, which he could visit for a mere outlay of cash. For it was, said Harry, barely a borough of Britain, that reach of St. Giles. Home ground of St. Giles's Greek or cant, the criminal language, bristling with words he had not previously known. The young Harry would walk among the strange tongue, would approach Seven Dials up Drury Lane, and in the theatre they'd be performing *The Provok'd Wife* or *The Beaux' Stratagem.* There were always hundreds of peddlars in front of the place, selling watercress, lavender, apples, and sheets of ballads and doggerel by the foot. And coaches creaked up and sedan chairs arrived, and expensive men and women held their breath as they pressed through the crowd and made for the theatre door. For everyone knew that every hawker was a criminal waiting for a chance. Among them, nut-brown and knowing Irish girls, who smoked clay pipes so short in the stem Harry couldn't understand how they did not blister their noses.

Ralph could see, as Harry talked, that this wilder region of London—if it was a region of London and not its own governance—was still potent in Harry's imagination. During a year or so's service in London, he himself had never found the place so engrossing as Harry had, but then he had not had access to the cashbox of Cuxbridge and Breton.

Meanwhile, said Harry, Cuxbridge and Breton had got quite old and were dependent on him, as he was on them. They thought his way of life and pallor after liquor represented a human enough moral fallibility which might one day mar his career. They did not understand *they* were paying for all his excess.

So Harry worked for them twelve, no, *fourteen* years, years of total rakishness, éxcept that he *was* a good draftsman and good at bookkeeping, and the old men certainly had no sense they were missing money.

Then one sodden midnight he found himself in an infamous public house in Monmouth Street, the Bear and Dog, in the company of a girl called Flora. Both of them were drunk and in the company of three or four stylish young gentlemen-thieves. To his bemusement, Harry heard himself boasting to the young men about his years of embezzlement at Cuxbridge and Breton. There was a smile on his face as he bragged away, and a freezing terror in his guts. He wanted them to know that, like them, he was a serious practitioner. He thought he'd cheated Cuxbridge and Breton merely to pay for his mad life, but now he knew he had developed a criminal pride. He knew at once that he was now not a visitor and a dabbler, but rather a member, a limb of the criminal commonwealth. He woke up next morning with the knowledge that he had laid himself open to the most dangerous people in London.

One of the stylish young thieves came to his rooms one night and ordered him to present himself back at the Bear and Dog the following Friday. Harry should realise, said the young man, that there were benefits in joining a canting crew, a criminal mob, and swearing allegiance to a Dimber Damber, a chieftain of the crooked way, who could look after you if you were arrested and send you comforts in gaol.

So he had put himself in the hands of a canting crew, a gang, a mob, colourful social oddities when you read of them in the *Calendar* or made quick, polite, drinking visits to their public houses, but fierce in their grasp. Harry knew that if he did not come to the Bear and Dog and take the oath to the Dimber Damber, Cuxbridge and Breton would be alerted to his fourteen years of what the canting crews called tickling the peter.

So he went back to Monmouth Street on a Friday night, to enlist in the mesh of allegiances centred on the Dimber Damber of the canting crew of the Bear and Dog.

The Dimber Damber was a small man who wore an earring in his left ear and laughed like a hound harrying a rabbit. His wife stood two inches taller and wore an old-fashioned wig to hide baldness brought on by ringworm. Such were the king and queen to whom Harry was to take the first oath of his lifetime. Everything that passed through the Bear and Dog, the Dimber Damber took a tax from—from jewel theft, from the income of the whores of the so-called pushing academies, from the haul of pickpockets and tricksters. In the Bear and Dog, Harry told Ralph, there was always a child of eight or nine sprinting through the place, running with loot in his shirt, going to ground, and a permanent traffic of pals and other pickpockets' associates. Little ratty runners with a good turn of pace would appear from nowhere and disappear into holes in the floor. And from all their speed, the Dimber Damber and his unhealthy wife took a percentage.

The stylish young thief who had come to his rooms recommended him heartily, like a brother, to the Dimber Damber. Harry was, said the young thief, definitely on the cross, a practitioner of the crooked way. He had tickled the peter of a West End company. As Harry listened to the young thief, he felt a terrible pride overtake him, and feeling the Dimber Damber's eyes upon him, he felt like saying, Here I am, as fit a candidate for hanging, for twisting, for the hemp disease, the gallows quinsey, as you're likely ever to see.

The Dimber Damber, with all the reasonableness of a lawyer, hit on the sum of ten shillings a week as Harry's offering to what he called the "Fund." Harry now had a new employer, and he knew he could not support or, strangely, could not give loyalty to more than one. In that hour in the Bear and Dog, he felt a terrible filial love for poor old Breton and doddery Cuxbridge.

It was all a ridiculous scene, said Harry. He spoke his oath at midnight, standing on sawdust, surrounded by the solemn and wavering crew of felons, who took the affair with all the seriousness appropriate to the installation of an Anglican bishop. And a sort of criminal lunacy overcame Harry. He found himself strangely touched and affected by the oath, and was so drunk by then that he promised himself he would, on waking the following morning, somehow give up being a surreptitious villain and a sneak and become an honest professional.

In the glade of paperbark trees at the end of the universe,

Harry repeated to Ralph the oath he had taken at the Bear and Dog on a Friday night in '73.

"I do swear to be a true brother, and that I will in all things obey the commands of the great Tawny Prince and keep his counsel and not divulge the secrets of my brethren. I will not teach anyone to speak the cant language, nor will I disclose any of our mysteries to them. I will take my Prince's part against all that shall oppose him, or any of us, according to the utmost of my ability. Nor will I suffer him or anyone belonging to us to be abused by any strange villains whether abrams, rufflers, hookers, pailliards, swaddlers, Irish toyles, swigmen, whipjacks, jarkmen, bawdy baskets, dommerars, clapper dodgeons, patricos or kertles. I will defend him, or them, as much as I can, against all other outliers whatever. I will not conceal aught I win out of libkins or from the ruffmans, but will preserve it for the use of the canting crew. Lastly I will cleave to my moll wap stiffly, and will bring her duds, marjery praters, gobblers, grunting cheats or tibs of the buttery or anything else I can come at, as winnings for her weppings."

What Harry had been swearing to was to protect the Dimber Damber from any strange confidence tricksters, pretending to be madmen to put even the cunning off their guard; from pilferers and jewellery thieves; from professional beggars; from those who robbed with violence; from Irish tinkers notorious throughout the counties of England; from thieves who travelled the country pretending to buy old shoes and clothes, or selling brooms or mops; from those who got money out of people by pretending to be shipwrecked sailors; from forgers; from sellers of pornographic songs and books who might be unwilling to pay a cut; from those who pretended their tongues had been cut out by the Turks and so extorted charity; from fake ministers of religion; from thieves of cloth.

Harry had further sworn that if he took to male prostitution he would pay over whatever he earned either inside the walls of a house or from rolling in the open. Lastly, he would make love to his girl, Flora, or whomsoever, on a regular basis and would give her gifts of clothing, hens, turkey cocks, pigs, or geese, or anything else he could lay his hand to, as plunder in return for any pleasure she gave.

"Poor damn Flora," said Harry. "I knew her for a month and then lost her for life. I wonder what winnings she has for her weppings these days."

"I KEPT paying that damn Dimber Damber for four years," Harry confessed.

Then all at once old Breton had a stroke and it stoked up that part of his brain which dealt in suspicion. He had a man in to look at Harry's bookkeeping. That was when Harry, at the age of thirty-nine years, joined the Navy, straight into the crew of the *Ariadne*, a twenty-four gunner under the command of a post-captain named Arthur Phillip, who would later become H.E.

It was in those years though, between taking the oath to the Dimber Damber and his joining the *Ariadne*, that the dreams of hanging had become entrenched. One day he had confronted the beast and attended a morning execution in front of the Newgate gatehouse. There was one criminal in particular in whom he was interested. A Henry Berthand had feloniously impersonated one Mark Groves, the proprietor of one hundred pounds' worth of three-percent annuities, and had transferred the same as if he were their real owner. Harry attended because he was aware that Berthand was, in terms of money stolen, less of a criminal than he himself had managed to be.

Harry's dreams had become more intense after seeing Berthand turned off.

For in the four minutes it took between the drop and the final beat of Berthand's heart, said Harry, the poor fellow became a public fool. He danced, he urinated, his body went to every effort to prove its humanity. And the more his body beat the air and showed off its last humble tricks, the better the terrible crowd liked it. There was a man, too, called Charlie Woollet, hanged that day for stealing a watch. "Have you noticed that in every batch of condemned you find watch thieves? Stealing time seems a heavy crime with the judges. As a friend of mine once said, Those who steal time get removed from it. But Charlie Woollet, he didn't measure up to Harry Brewer. Not as a thief. Not as hangable matter.

"It is clear now that there will be a hanging," murmured Harry to Ralph after a somnolent pause. "The idea of it does not worry anyone. Dear God, Duckling . . . Duckling in Newgate, with a day and a half to live, was calm. Twisting is part of the landscape to these people. It honours the Tawny Prince. It's the highest honour."

"Who is the Tawny Prince?" asked Ralph, though he felt he might have glimpsed him in his dreams.

"The Tawny Prince . . . he's the god of the cross. When I say cross, I don't mean the cross of Jesus. He's the god of Disorder, and is heavily worshipped by lagkind, Ralph, for twenty mad years by Harry Brewer himself. The Tawny Prince sponsors all twisting —it's the Tawny Prince's Mass, his evensong. His folk down in the men's and women's camp are getting ready for it without knowing they are, for they are his unwitting servants in this matter. And as for the others, Davy Collins, the Captain, even you . . . you know it must happen and you take it equably. I am the only one who cannot. I dream of it every night without fail and I have such loathing, Ralph, that it is beyond my power to put the rope on another being's neck. My constables are full of the same dread, and I cannot depend on them to do it either. Ambition has me in a corner, Ralph, the way the bitch always has us. Right, Harry, says ambition, do you wish to be Provost Marshal? Then you must be a sedate hanger. You say you cannot turn people off? Then you cannot be Provost Marshal. But you cannot live without wages and rank and the esteem of men like Ralph Clark? Then you must use the rope!"

Ralph had to admit there were stages in Harry Brewer's confession when he wondered how much of the Provost Marshal's recital was still accountable to criminal pride. Yet at this point in the tale, you could not doubt Harry's anguish.

Beneath their tree Private Ellis and Jack Williams had dropped off to sleep, lying together innocently in the paperbark shade.

"Even the Captain knows the state I am in," murmured Harry.

Harry explained how H.E. had called him to the four-room government house built of lathes and canvas, and H.E. had been sitting on a chair in the bedroom and had asked Harry to feel his heart, which had seemed thin and febrile and as if it might beat itself out at any second, depriving Sydney Cove, the new world, of the organ on which it depended for sanity and hope. Then H.E. told Harry that when he appointed him Provost Marshal, it was in the belief the post would not be too onerous. There had never been a world like this one, said H.E., where to be a person under sentence was the normal thing and to be a free man abnormal. H.E. had fancied that this very fact would make the convicts act in terms of reasonable self-interest, as a few were already doing, but not enough. H.E. had expected that landing on this shore would alter the convicts, make their condition apparent to them. As well as the demands of the strangeness of the country, they had something to look forward to at the end of their sentences, more than expulsion into the mere streets. They had the prospect of becoming landholders, of having the labour to their land provided for them out of future shipments of felons.

These novel conditions, H.E. had thought, could mean there would have to be little further discipline apart from that offered by their isolation eight moons out in the earth's space. But this was already promising to be a withered hope.

So, H.E. had asked Harry, still clamping Harry's hand up against the rib cage where the heart uncertainly beat, could Harry stop a heart if it were necessary?

Harry had been a little aggrieved and had let H.E. know it. But H.E. was not deluded. Could Harry do it without too much torment? All the normal business of society, free and bond, had been carried out on the shore in the first three weeks. There had been weddings, and the christenings of bastards begotten by seamen, Marines, and convicts during the voyage. The Reverend Dick Johnson had preached on the grass from the 116th Psalm. "What shall I render unto the Lord, for all His benefits toward me?" And now it was likely that *other* ceremony would occur. It was in fact H.E. who had raised that picture in Harry's mind of an execution waiting to happen.

"If I were dismissed," harry confessed to Ralph, "or replaced for being slow, there is nowhere I could go. I am already at the end of things."

And suddenly, careless of being seen by Ellis and Williams, he began to weep in a way that made the crooked pegs of his remaining teeth jut forth until they dominated Ralph's view. Ralph checked on the Marine and the lag, and saw that the Jamaican had stirred, taken one lustrous-eyed look at Harry, and then, with the wisdom that said you should never catch an official at a disadvantage, clamped his eyes shut again.

It was a case of Harry's confessions and the intimacy they had forced on Ralph now being compounded by a series of astounding events. Feeling that Harry had to be quickly distracted from his morbid expectancy of a coming hanging, Ralph pointed off to the south. "Look," he said. "That's the Prince of them all." Harry blinked, and Williams and Private Ellis woke up.

"Prince?" asked Harry. Perhaps he was still thinking of the Tawny one.

"It was a giant of a kangaroo," lied Ralph. He stalked off south into the woods, waving at the others to follow him. He came close to swallowing his tongue when he saw, in an open area at the top of the ridge ahead of him, exactly the giant beast he had predicted, taller than a man. It surveyed him. Behind him, he heard Harry mutter a prayer and stop, panting, transfixed by the kangaroo's placid gaze.

Anyone who brought back game earned a temporary renown in Sydney. Ralph took his gun from Private Ellis's hands and aimed. He could hear Harry going through the same motions, disconsolately, discomposed by the animal's serene eye. As Ralph aimed, Ellis reached over the weapon, striking the flints together to light the fuse. The hunting gun exploded with an awesome concussion, worse than Ralph had expected. He noticed Ellis sitting on the ground, nursing smashed fingers and cursing. Ellis, by pouring too big a powder charge around the pan, had caused a flash and blown away a part of the breech of the gun. Wrapping up Ellis's hand in a handkerchief, Ralph was aware that his own face had been lightly burned and his brows perhaps comically singed. The kangaroo had of course vanished. Ellis cursed as if the gods and not his own inexpert hand were to blame.

The accident had absolutely restored Harry. He fed brandy to Ellis, helped him upright, and told the Jamaican to carry both guns. Ralph, wanting to keep Harry in a good frame of mind, chatted away about the animal they had just encountered. "Davy Collins tells me," said Ralph, "that they carry their young in a pouch, and give them the tit there. And the penis of the male lies between its buttocks and its balls."

Harry clapped Ellis's shoulder. "Do you think our earthly lot, Ralph, would be easier or harder if we enjoyed a similar arrangement?"

Ralph laughed along with the joke. His mind toyed a second, and no more than a second, with Harry's surmise. For as if to replace the gigantic kangaroo in this garden of wonders, four natives appeared among the cabbage trees ahead. They did not seem to block the path even though each of the two men carried a number of spears between them, as well as the dish-like implements which they used to launch their spears, and hardwood clubs. This was the closest both Ralph and Harry had been to any of the inhabitants, and Ralph watched them with more curiosity than fear. He wanted to be able to report every detail of the meeting to Davy Collins, for Davy at that stage wrote up reports of such encounters in his journal.

The party consisted of an older man, a younger man, a woman, and a boy of perhaps fifteen. The hair of the two grown men was divided into matted strands and the teeth of animals were stuck onto the strands with a mustard coloured resin. The older man had a white bone through the cartilage of the nose. Both the male adults carried ornamental scars across their chests and their upper arms, and so did the woman—the upper line of her breasts, which Ralph thought were good breasts, were delineated with a raised scar. She would look beautiful if she were not coated in the soot and fish oil they rubbed into themselves to keep the mosquitoes off.

"You've been watching the camp," Harry suggested to them. "And no doubt your brothers and sisters are watching the French down there behind us. And the difference is, my friends, that the French are visitors and will shuffle off to the cannibal isles. Whereas Mr. Harry Brewer will cling to this shore for good. What's that you have in your hand, my honey?"

Ralph himself noticed for the first time that the woman held in her left hand a shovel. It was held lightly. Four fingers. As in the case of all the native women, the first two joints of the small finger had been removed—Davy Collins had already noticed this custom, but could not suggest why it was practised. It seemed to Ralph there was a dangerous innocence in the way the woman kept the shovel in her maimed hand. He remembered there was only one intact hunting gun left to them now.

But the natives did not seem to have any guilt about the shovel. The woman did not try to hide her plunder. She had picked up a tool some lazy felon had thrown away. That was all.

Ralph felt a duty to deal with the whole business in panto-mime. "Shovel—it's ours," Ralph said. Harry laughed and Ralph could not blame him. The older man and the woman replied at once, and there was no knowing if their reply was germane to the shovel. By an instinct Ralph reached forward and took the thing out of the girl's slack hand. She had been distracted by the sight of Jack Williams, who through stealing some gin in Deptford at the age of fifteen had four years later merited this encounter.

"Jack," Harry announced pedagogically, comic himself now he was attempting to make sense to the natives. He pointed to the young lag. "Jack."

The four natives glowed and began to laugh and talk at once, to circle the party and point at aspects of their dress and demean-our, and then to inspect the wound in Private Ellis's hand. "Get to buggery," Ellis invited them, fearing their exhalations might in-fect the wound.

But their main interest was in the Jamaican. Harry turned to the boy and relieved him of the two guns he was carrying.

"Go on, Jack," said Harry. "Go up and talk to the lady and the gentlemen."

"Jack," Ralph kept saying, as the West Indian stepped closer to the natives.

Private Ellis stood by with the forlorn patience of the soldier, holding his hand upwards in its sopping bandage to relieve the pain.

"Jack," the natives began dutifully to yell. They were engrossed in the young gin thief. They inspected his mouth, and Jack obliged them by smiling. The older of the two men reached out and pulled open the front of Jack's canvas shirt. Seeing the flesh and nipples of Jack's chest he bleated with delight. The other man moved forward and together with his elder felt Jack's chest all over and gently tested the nipples, as if to see whether they gave milk. When they did not, the men turned and spoke to the woman and she came and joined them in front of the convict. Everyone laughed, even Jack himself, his eyes glittering as she explored his chest and pushed his shirt up at the back and felt the satiny flesh. Then the elder of the men, finished with Jack's upper body, began to feel the crotch of his canvas trousers. Ralph had an impulse to come to the young West Indian's rescue. But Harry cried, "They wish to know if you're a man, Jack. Drop those trousers and inform them."

The boy undid the navy belt from around his waist and let his trousers drop. He held his scrotum from beneath for better display. He was excellently endowed. Harry yelled—Ralph thought it was risky of him, both in terms of dignity and because it might give Jack ideas—"Oh Aunt Martha! Don't go near my sweetheart with that thing, Jack."

The sight of Jack's manhood brought some yelps of praise from the two older natives and from the young woman. The elder of the men turned his rump briefly toward Jack and danced it about in a way which would lead Ralph to report to Davy Collins that sodomy must be known among the natives.

Harry and Ralph began to fear that Jack and the woman would want to copulate now and alter the balance of what had been till then an educative encounter. Harry averted this outcome by telling Jack to give the older man his shirt—it would be replaced out of stores. He himself gave a spare brass button to the younger man, and Ralph felt bound to give the woman a handkerchief. She placed it on her head and set her face at an angle, so much like a European woman trying on a hat that even Private Ellis laughed painfully.

As the natives went off, conversing together in their bird-like language and looking back all the time at Jack and laughing,

Ralph's toothache revived. The surgeon's wad of narcotic had fallen out.

"Perhaps we should have showed more anger over the shovel," said Ralph, biting the air off to stop it penetrating the hole in his mouth.

But the meeting with the savages had been only a momentary amusement to Harry. He had returned now to his own consistent pain, just as Ralph's tooth had.

Harry said, "You will stand by me, friend?"

"When, Harry?"

"On gallows day," said Harry. "Or as they call it, wryneck."

"Wait till it happens," said Ralph, laughing. But they both knew Harry had so compelled Ralph with his frank confessions that he would have to provide intimate rather than mere friendly succor.

"I will support you, Harry," Ralph promised.

CHAPTER 10

Wryneck Day

As Harry had feared, the new penal society in the South Seas worked its way toward its first hanging through a number of petty meannesses, lesser tragedies, and hapless tries at escape.

In that first February, for example, the convict transports still sat in the deep anchorages of Sydney Cove. One day the black cook of the *Prince of Wales*, pulling himself ashore by means of the ship's hawser rope, which was fastened to nearby rocks, was—for a joke—shaken off it by two of the boys aboard the ship and he drowned in the deep opaquely blue anchorage perhaps twenty paces from the beach.

While those who could swim splashed about looking for his body, two of the she-lags were ordered—for some minor thieving —to twenty-five lashes at the tail of the cart, a punishment super-vised by a reluctant Mr. Provost Marshal Brewer and enacted by his convict constables. It was not that Harry questioned that such sentences were statements of public order. He was no radical. It was because he did believe in retribution that his dreams *were* so coloured with punishment.

Because of his gentle spirit, he had ordered the lighter flay for the women. The rumour went around this town at the world's end that he'd instructed the constables to give a high proportion of "sweetheart blows"—blows, that is, which Harry's convict constables deliberately delivered with less than full force. Seven sweethearts out of each ten, it was rumoured Harry had ordered. People thought this quaint, and the women themselves, two of the worst London criminals from the *Friendship,* would later, healing around their campfires, mock him for it.

In those days, too, some were fleeing H.E.'s rational kingdom. A general muster of all the convicts on a Saturday in late February showed that nine men and one woman had gone beyond the boundaries of the camp and were missing.

The French were still down in Botany, refitting their two ships and waiting for their naturalist, the Abbé le Receveur, to die of the terrible wound in his side a Samoan native had given him two months before. You could be sure that every one of the ten escapees had been down to Botany to beg the Compte de La Pérouse and his officers, in the name of French mercy, to take them aboard.

In fact, the Frenchman had recently sent two officers north to Sydney Cove, a seven-mile walk overland through the unearthly forests, still—in those days before the smallpox plague—full of playful and flitting Indians, to assure H.E. that he had dismissed all convicts who came out of the woods pleading with his men. He had, said the Compte, no desire to intrude in the internal justice of Britain. Ralph thought the phrase in one sense funny. The convicts were as *external* to the kingdom of the Georges as you could get!

Omens continued to multiply. In Sydney, it was considered a cautionary sight when on a thunderous afternoon a white arm floated by the women's camp on the tide. Better, the arm signified to the women, to wait around the new township for the familiar rites of the Church of England and of the criminal law than to run away into the forest or expect the aid of Indians or of French scientists.

The rite of punishment, then, towards which the settlement was collecting itself, and the forces of both order and darkness so clearly tending, began with the night arrest of William Murphy, a Yorkshire Irishman and highway robber found singing an indistinct Gaelic song while flat-out drunk outside his tent. Murphy's condition was the first evidence to arise from a crime which had been reported that afternoon by the commissary. Eighteen bottles of wine, part of the hospital stores, had been stolen.

Robbie Ross, who took a particular interest in the stores, undertook the questioning of Murphy. Ralph had been at that time the officer of the day. He had been sleeping in his uniform every night, and very poorly, since Dabby Bryant had not yet delivered him from his terrible dreams. So a number of times a night he still might encounter Betsey Alicia in her coffin, or bearing a louse on her forehead, or a cockroach on the hem of her dress. Thus sapped by his dreams, he went to Robbie's tent for Murphy's questioning.

Major Robbie had his quirks. The interrogation went ahead in the redolence of attar of roses which Robbie scattered around his bed and clothing, and that of his nine-year-old son, John, to ward off fevers. Harry Brewer, as Provost Marshal, was there too in Robbie's oversweet ambience. Harry got no pleasure from the fragrance of Robbie's tent. You could tell from his face that he knew he now stood in the presence of the first capital crime of the new world.

Murphy seemed parched and remorseful, but kept on denying any wrongdoing. He claimed he had traded a shirt for the wine—he couldn't remember who had made the trade. Major Ross circled him with a savage intent worse than blows. In Robbie's apparent hatred of this Irishman, this idiot thief, you could see all his grievance against the country, against Cook and Banks for having recommended this place in the first instance, against Tommy Townshend the Home Secretary for taking them seriously. But all that ferocity was, for the moment, transferred to this young sallow Irishman.

"You will hang," yelled Robbie, his voice somehow reverberating even in a canvas tent. There was an awful Caledonian length to Robbie's vowels. "You will be the first Christian twisted in this awful place. And when it is given over, as it will be, and when we all leave, as we will, you will rot unknown in a grave visited—from now to the first fart of doom—by no one but savages! And you a Papist! A Papist! Aren't you, laddie? Answer me! Answer!"

"I have to confess, good Major," said Murphy, hopefully courageous, as if Robbie was offering Catholic martyrdom rather than mere hanging for a criminal offence, "I have to admit that I am indeed of the Holy Catholic and Apostolic Church."

"Some bastard in a hedge in Ireland," screamed Robbie at Ralph and Harry, "trained him to say that if ever he was challenged by a filthy Presbyterian such as myself."

Robbie placed a knuckle under the young Papist's jaw and raised the boy's face. "And you curious people believe—isn't it so? —in the remission of sins in a yon small Hell called Purg-a-tory. From which you can be delivered only by the prayers of the just. Isn't that so?"

Murphy was panting. All at once he no longer liked this doctrinal discussion. Ralph was pretty sure that though Murphy might indeed die for his faith, he was less likely to die for his accomplices.

"Who will pray for the remission of *your* sins," raged Robbie, "you Papist bastard? Those natives covered in fish oil? Who will come here after we are gone? Not even the Portuguese, who share the same heresies as you, you pickpocketing bastard, you Irish ped-dlar. Not even them."

But Murphy surprised Ralph by refusing to name anyone else. Robbie pushed his face aside and yelled for the corporal at the door. "Take him away. Mr. Brewer will hang him tomorrow morning."

This assurance made Harry Brewer—rather than Murphy— panic. It was this specific boy Harry did not wish to hang. He would for the moment rather deal with the idea of the as yet unnamed ones who were Murphy's accomplices.

Under the thunder and lightning that afternoon, in the gro-tesquely named "prison tent" near the men's camp, Murphy at last told Harry—not Robbie Ross—the names of four accomplices. They had stolen not only wine, but butter, pork, and split peas. Robbie, told of the confession, was delighted that among those named by Murphy and now arrested by Ralph's Quarter Guard was an infamous young lag named Tom Barrett.

T H I S Tom Barrett was only a youth, but the fliest of all fly boys. He had been condemned to death and reprieved twice already—

first when, barely more than a child, he stole jewellery and clothing from a London spinster. He had, like Sideway, then been found wandering the West Country in the weeks after the convict mutiny aboard the transport *Mercury* in Torbay. He was tried with Robert Sideway and others at Exeter for the crime of return from transportation. There, for a second time in his scarcely sixteen years, he had again been sentenced to death. When the sentence was commuted, Tom went to the hold of the hulk *Dunkirk* in Plymouth Harbour and at last sailed on the *Charlotte*.

Even so, up to the point of his transportation, Tom Barrett's criminal career had shown little style to distinguish it from that of a hundred others aboard the *Charlotte* and the *Friendship*. Where he got his criminal flashiness and repute was from an incident on board the *Charlotte* while the convict fleet was tied up in Rio harbour.

Canoes carrying Portuguese traders and black oarsmen made journeys out to the ships to barter, and the convicts who had money of their own, deposited with the ship's master or a crew member for safekeeping, were allowed to buy food and delicacies. This was considered by old-fashioned officers like Robbie Ross a dangerous and faddish innovation of H.E.'s. But Surgeon Johnny White approved the merchandise the traders had for sale—oranges, plantains, cantaloupes, limes, and fancy breads.

The trade went on, aboard each of the convict transports, in the standard barricaded exercise yard aft of the main mast. The barricades stood three feet high and were topped with spikes. Behind them the convicts could stretch in the sunlight and have a sight of the green slopes of the city of Rio, the Sugarloaf, and the palace square.

One of the Portuguese merchants approached a Marine officer and complained to him about a quarter dollar a convict had paid him for bread. It was counterfeit. You could tell by scraping it with a knife that it had a large proportion of pewter in it.

The quarter dollar was traced back to Tom Barrett. A search of his bedspace in the hold showed he owned a bag full of them, manufactured of chunks of pewter, Marine belt buckles and buttons, and the occasional gold coin thrown into the brew. The coins were competently minted, using a metal mould Tom had acquired before leaving England.

Everyone—officers and convicts on other ships—had been astonished that Tom had been able to build in the convict holds the fires necessary to forge metal coins. It did not really take anyone long to conclude that he had got both the freedom to build a fire and the ingredients for his coins by pimping between the Marines and the thirty or so women convicts in the forrard section of the *Charlotte*. In the convict view, by forging aboard ship, Tom had done honour to his canting crew and to the gods of criminality. He wore with easy carlessness the style of a man likely to hang young.

The time for *that*—it seemed—had arrived. In the Sydney Cove version of a new earth, where the new earth looked inhospitable to European grain and the London criminals proved inept at farming, the only certain supply of food could come from what was in the storehouse. No one knew if England, having shipped them to the dark, unredeemed side of things, would remember to send them the staples of life, or if these were sent, whether the ships that carried them could come safely to them. For it was understood even by the brutal convict mind that few sailors could manage to bring a flotilla the distance H.E. and his Scottish navigator, Captain Johnny Hunter, had brought them.

Under these conditions, H.E. had to define the stealing of food on any large scale as equivalent to murder, and to make it a capital offence. Harry understood this: that now Barrett—still less than twenty—was facing his third and inescapable death sentence.

This was, of course, a much worse come-uppance for Harry Brewer than it was for Tom Barrett.

On the day of Tom's trial in Sydney Cove, rain squalls pummelled the town. The water of the cove turned black under a low cloud of the same colour. It began to rain with such intent that it could have eroded Chartres, whose cathedral Ralph had once visited during his service with the Dutch army, and left all the precious units of glass lying around on the clay like so many cups and saucers. It could thoroughly erase a city of canvas and wattle and daub. Those who had had the industry to put up a roof of packed clay found it dissolving above their heads now or dropping at their wet feet in lumps.

Trials took place in those days, the settlement's first February, in the drooping trial marquee of the Court of Criminal Jurisdiction. For the trial of Barrett and his three accomplices, Ralph and six other officers sat on the bench under the presidency of Judge Advocate Davy Collins. The defendants—apart from the renowned Tom Barrett himself—were a young London ivory carver called Lovell; John Ryan, a silk weaver of Irish origins, displaced by the new mills and machines and reduced to criminality and now—unless he was lucky—to a capital punishment; and a cadaverous Cockney named James Freeman.

Murphy's King's Evidence this flood-ridden afternoon was that he and Tom Barrett, with Lovell and Freeman and Ryan, had made a number of raids on the supply tent. They had taken what presented from flour casks and pork barrels and the stacked supplies of hospital wine and brandy. They had used this plenty for their own consumption and to buy the favours of women. At this point in the trial, Ralph heard Robbie Ross's Scottish friend Captain Jemmy Campbell groan in the manner of a man whose pet thesis about the society in which he lives has now been proven.

Arrangements in the trial tent were like those in the distant courts which had, in the first instance, exiled these people. Murphy stood behind the accused and could see only the backs of their heads. But these must have seemed to him as eloquent as any frontal features. For at one stage he screamed, "Forgive me, boys! You know the way these here assizes hound a man!"

"I imagined how the gallows would bloom," Harry Brewer told Ralph later. "Four men. Such an exercise would not in London attract a journalist from *The Evening Post*. Here, it's such a terrible proportion of the human population to hang in one afternoon. More than one half of one per centum of the lags of New South Wales."

A little before one o'clock the court brought sentence of death on three of the men before them. There was no choice, Davy Collins instructed them, in the matter of the stealing of such large measures of food—that was a capital offence by H.E.'s executive edict. Ryan the silk weaver, who was shown only to have thieved wine, was condemned merely to a flogging. The sentences were, said Davy Collins, to be administered that very afternoon. Thereby the law's dispatch was to be signified. Harry would confess later to Ralph that he believed it seemed heinous of Davy Collins to demand a hanging in such heavy rain.

R A L P H, though a little awed by the processes of the court he was part of, was not distressed. He knew the face of justice, military and civil. He had seen, through nearly averted eyes, both the Dutch and the Marines hang deserters, rapists, and thieves.

Harry was by contrast overwhelmed by the sentence. Later he would detail to Ralph all his movements and conversations of that afternoon.

For example, crossing the spring by the bridge of planks and barrels, Harry met the Reverend Dick Johnson, transmuted by the severe, thunderous light to a blackbird figure, a gallows phantom. And in a hurry, rushing across to the detention tent to bring redemption to the three. Harry's bowels leapt at the sight of him. Could it be as late as this already?

"There are hours to go yet, Dick," called Harry Brewer hopefully. But Dick answered with mad fervour. "It is not much time when you consider the history of these men. Tom Barrett might be less than twenty years, but Satan has worked in him epochs of malevolence."

Harry would describe how in that second he yearned for one of those agnostic gentlemen of the cloth, who wouldn't take on Satan brow to brow in this way, who would consider it bad manners and a vulgar excess to seem to do so.

H.E. had spoken briefly and reassuringly to Harry. He went so far as to say no one could be sure of the extent to which that afternoon's event would prevent future criminality. But it would demonstrate that society had arrived here and was asserting its order. Harry argued that—in number terms—to hang three in a swipe was equivalent to hanging two thousand Londoners. H.E. waved his hand, saying the court had not taken the trouble to consider percentiles and that therefore neither could he.

So the conference ended with a solemn shaking of hands and

the idea lying between them that when Lovell and Freeman and mad Tom Barrett were hanged and, like potsherds or statues, were socketed away in the earth with the marks of civilised execution around their necks, the place would be confirmed as a European town, the bread of the British law having been so conspicuously broken there. The concept did not seem, however, to comfort feverish H.E. to any great extent. In genial Harry Brewer, it increased a barely concealed agitation.

Ralph had command of the Quarter Guard section at the prison tent when one of Harry's convict constables turned up with a jug of rum, drawn by the storekeeper, for the three condemned men. Harry Brewer trundled behind him in a sodden cloak, carrying three pewter pannikins. The rum was poured into these, and Harry instructed the constable to take them in to the condemned men, who sat on the bare ground, shackled at the wrists and ankles.

The constable seemed as squeamish as Harry. He was a convicted swindler called Bill Parr, and some nicety of feeling prevented him from entering the tent. He confessed it was some quarrel he and young Barrett had had over a woman.

"And so?"

"He'll look at me now, and he'll say, I reckon the argument's settled, Bill Parr."

"And that would be too painful, would it, Bill?" Harry asked desperately. "Too bloody painful?"

The rain was watering the jug of liquor as they stood there. Harry grabbed the pitcher, stood, and entered the tent. Ralph went with him. Lovell the ivory turner took with a sort of fraternal gratitude the measure of spirits Harry poured for him. So also, with a little speech, the skeletal young Freeman. But as Harry poured the rest into Barrett's pannikin, the boy raised his chin and began to laugh. He could see right into the frantic charity behind this issue of rum from Harry's hands, and he despised it. He said nothing, but the laughter got so loud and niggling Harry ended by tipping the pannikin of spirits over the boy's head.

"Drink that in, Barrett, and go to hell," he roared, stamping out of the tent. The boy called after him through the canvas. "Kiss my arse, Mr. Brewer! Into the bargain, kiss your whore's grimy arse for me."

Ralph followed Harry from the tent. They got in under one of the great native fig trees for protection from the rain. The Provost Marshal turned to him with tears in his eyes. Whether they derived from provocation or grief or doubt, Ralph couldn't have said. "It shows you, Ralph," said Harry, "that though they can speak in riddles, they speak clear enough English when it suits them."

Some time during that afternoon, Harry consulted Duckling, for she was his encyclopaedia on the felon mind. Although he had committed frauds in his youth, unlike most London criminals he did not have that sense of being born and consecrated to crime. At a reach as distant as this place, the image of the Dimber Damber, the claims of the canting crew, and all other forms of criminal allegiance were meant to loosen and shrivel in the sun. Harry knew to his grief that this had not happened. And so he went to Duckling for a clarifying word, one which could carry him through the day. His bemusement lay in this. Though he didn't want Tom whimpering—would be absolutely unmanned by it—the idea of Tom taking it with that unspeakable London calm scared him more.

Duckling, thinking she was giving him comfort, fed his worst fear. She thought he wanted to be informed that Barrett and the other two were ready for the drop, schooled to it from childhood. She said she wouldn't have squawked if she'd been turned off that time at Newgate. She wouldn't have cried *peccavi* at any stage.

And—as Harry understood what she was saying—in London's criminal code you got points for that. A show of repentance, even an acknowledgement of Christ, was forgivable either as a piece of last-moment irony, a theatrical trick, or even as a reasonable caution in view of the strongly touted idea of a life after death. But the heroes who spat in the priest's eye were the most remembered. And those who pleaded for mercy disgraced the brotherhood and the great Tawny Prince, that ancient Gypsy god who was honoured at the heart of the act of crime.

"If I'd been twisted there, I'd have kept *that* oath," Duckling assured him.

THERE was a particular native fig tree between the men's and women's camp which Robbie Ross had chosen for the event. As if he suspected Harry Brewer's primitive horror of capital punishment, he himself arranged for the placing of three ladders under the most obvious and strongest bow, as into the dripping glade came that part of the garrison which was on duty and most of the convict population. Will Bryant and his fishing crew, far out in the harbour behind a veil of rain squall, were excused. Pardoned from attending too were the eight men working today, waist deep in water, in a clay pit recently found on a hill to the south whose contents were thought to be potentially suitable for brickmaking. In a city of canvas, the very possibility of bricks carried with it privileges and exemptions.

When the three walked down from the guard tent, wrists shackled behind them, their column fringed by Harry Brewer's convict constables armed with lengths of wood and by the Quarter Guard bearing firearms, Ralph noticed that Dick Johnson walked beside Freeman, the solemn young thief, and that on both their faces was an expression of ineffability. It could only mean that Dick believed he had saved the snake-thin boy in the last hour of life; Freeman, who since babyhood had worked with burglars, slithering into households through broken panes and fanlights not large enough to admit heftier thieves.

Ralph remembered from the *Friendship* how Freeman liked to get pious now and then, and found it exciting, a kind of performance. There was a day off Capetown, in a storm when he had said the prayers over a dead baby, the child of one of the women prisoners. He had been as orotund as any Anglican canon. Therefore, it appealed to his sense of occasion to show a little solemn penitence this afternoon.

The procession arrived at the tree and each of the condemned was pushed to the bottom of a ladder. Harry read the sentence of the court aloud. Ralph could sense—knowing so much about him —that Harry felt intimidated by the ranks of men and women in front of him. As if they were one spiritual mass, as if each of these three villains did not have mute enemies among the convict lines, whose hearts would be chirruping with pleasure to see their enemies from gaol or hulk or convict transport about to be obliterated.

As Harry read on in unexceptional tones, treading the thin

margin between his own criminal youth and his present civic eminence, a soldier from the canvas Government House guard came
sloshing and puffing along the shallow valley by the stream. Rain
continued to fall on the court's sentence which lay in Harry's
hands, blurring syllables and bearing vowels away. It seemed Harry
might get to the end of the judgement only seconds before the
paper in his hands turned to pulp.

The soldier handed a paper to Major Ross. It was from H.E.
Robbie read it aloud. It said that Harry Lovell and James Freeman
were to have a respite of twenty-four hours. Freeman sat on the
wet ground when he heard. Such was the effort of keeping the code
of the Tawny Prince! And then finding you would need to do it
again in a day's time.

Harry approached Ralph, incredulous anger in his face.
"Twenty-four hours? *Twenty-four hours.*" But Ralph, who was
calmer about these things, guessed that the Captain, H.E., intended to give Freeman and Lovell their lives, not simply twenty-
four hours but the whole complicated future. Except that he did
not want to say so straight out.

The event was rendered more solemn rather than less by the
fact that Tom Barrett was now on his own, standing at the base of
his ladder. The ivory turner and Freeman, blinking, confused,
panting, no exceptional champions of the Tawny Prince, had been
marched back at once to the prison tent.

As Ralph witnessed it, Tom Barrett asked Harry if before being
turned off he could speak to Robert Sideway, for they had been on
the *Mercury* together, had been at large together in the West
Country. The idea of Tom's speaking to Sideway was, remarkably,
considered by Robbie Ross to be a fair request.

Then Barrett asked to speak to the she-lag and infamous madame known throughout the penal planet as Goose. "And to
Goose," he said, "who's my lifelight."

Robbie considered Goose the most abandoned woman in the
place. As if she might contaminate Tom at this late stage, he
refused to let her near Tom's scaffold. When Tom heard the refusal,
he closed his eyes a second and took on a pallor which raised Dick
Johnson's hopes for his repentance. But as he opened them, he

laughed and shook his head, then raised his chin and thrust it forward.

No one had to tell him to hurry his messages with Sideway, who began to weep, saying nothing, but now and then nodded. Sideway—you could guess—absorbed messages to women Barrett had known, messages also perhaps to Barrett's parents, messages to Goose, messages to the criminal community at large.

A number of journals, including the one Ralph then kept, recounted that the convict constable Parr refused to set the rope around the boy's neck. In the end Harry was forced to mount the ladder and adjust the rope himself, doing it deftly for fear the boy would say something to him, plead, or—worst of the lot—grant forgiveness.

Luckily forgiveness wasn't the style of the Tawny Prince. In the smallest way, but so that it could be seen from the lines of convicts, Barrett rolled his eyes and, as Harry finished adjusting the rope and pulling on the noose, winked. This is all a show, said the wink, and I mean to give all parties what they severally expect.

Harry climbed down and nodded to the Major. Poor Harry looked diminished and humiliated by the boy's complicated courage.

Asked by the Major for last words, Tom said the sentence was just and he had earned it by his wicked life. He called on the crowd to learn something from his unhappy fate. He was ready now to face a just God.

Most of the gentlemen of the cove concluded from this little speech that the feel of the noose around his neck had brought him to real sense for the first time in his cunning life. Only Harry fully understood—and would later convey his certainty to Ralph—that it was the prescribed lag performance Tom was fulfilling.

As the city of convicts waited for the drop, there were tears in the Reverend Richard Johnson's honest eyes. By all the rules of Dick's evangelism, Barrett was already with God. So Dick was certain his Deity was established in this convict city for good. All local gods who might have been watching from the dun forests were now vanquished.

But he was unaware of that other divinity who had traveled

with the convict fleet. In making Dick Johnson ridiculously gratified, Tom Barrett was paying vivid honour to the Tawny Prince,
here at a native fig tree in a new world, by means of his own
whimsical blood sacrifice. You had to be an initiate to understand
what Tom Barrett's act meant, and Harry was an initiate. To understand that tonight in the convict camps those with liquor would
drink to Tom's consummate hanging.

The convict constable Bill Parr's reluctance extended also to
pulling the ladder out from under the boy. Harry Brewer grew
desperate now and began to yell at him, and Major Ross told Parr
in his compelling Scots that his earlier reluctance had been noted,
and that if he persisted in further reluctance the Marines would be
ordered to shoot him dead. So Bill Parr, averting his eyes, kicked
the ladder sideways. There was an instant silence in which the
tautness of the rope could be heard even in the rain. Then all the
prisoners began to yell, to cheer either in irony or in concern,
advising Tom on weathering the next minute. The rain increased
as Barrett swung, and the thin and piteous stench of his death came
wetly to Ralph.

T H E next afternoon, when the twenty-four-hour respite of execution was over, the rain still fell, and Harry, flushed with brandy
and mad-eyed, followed Lovell and Freeman back to the tree.

Such had been Harry's ravings during the evening before, so
unhinged had he been by the ceremonial hanging, that Ralph had
considered writing to H.E. about it, but forebore for fear of the
results such a letter might bring for Harry's barely begun career.

Davy Collins himself turned up in the clearing this humid
afternoon, attended by a convict woman carrying a tray of lime
juice and tumblers to take the edge off the officials' thirst. He
carried in his hand a document which he kept folded and approached Harry, who stood in the clearing by the execution tree in
the company of Ralph and Captain Meredith, Ralph's genial but
inebriate company commander. Together they watched Lovell and
Freeman proceeding down the hill with their retinue.

All the officials in the execution parade seemed to have a

fever—Ralph, suffering diarrhoea and terrified it was the flux; Dick Johnson stooped with stomach cramps; and Harry close to madness and looking for Barrett's apparition everywhere.

Poor damn Bill Parr, swindler, specialist in selling non-existent shipments to shopkeepers, and now the kicker out of ladders, had, Ralph saw, placed the halters round the necks of Lovell and Freeman while the condemned were still in the prison tent, so they already wore them as they entered the clearing.

"Look at that," said Davy. "An understandable sensitivity on Parr's part, but for Christ's sake we have to get beyond these queasy little stratagems."

He turned to Harry. "We have to get you an executioner, Mr. Brewer," said Davy. "It is improper for you to have to quarrel about these things with your convict constables. But whomsoever we choose, it can't be one of the black men. The other prisoners would not tolerate it."

Just the same, the Jamaican lags—or even the Madagascan Caesar—seemed suited to the work by their air of calmness and their bulk.

Having for the past two days drunk too much and rested too little, Harry got petulent. "You intend I should take my hangman from among those condemned by the court?"

Davy Collins lowered his voice, "In view of the code operating among the criminals, this was the only lever which could be used to enlist an executionist. This is not like an open society, Harry, where a hangman can be recruited or advertised for."

"Lovell? Or Freeman?" asked Harry, unbelieving.

There was no hope either of them would ever resemble an august instrument of the law. Duckling told a story of Freeman—it was hearsay—that he and a pal had held up a gentleman in the streets of Hereford and taken away his wallet, but when the victim saw Freeman and the other boy part, he followed the thin boy, caught him, beat him up, and delivered him to the peace officers of the city. How could the condemned be awed by a boy who'd been served up by his own victim?

As the procession neared the tree, the dozen or so Jamaicans and Africans among the crowd of lags maintained a strange chant, singing almost under their breaths but in sublime harmony. Oh that black antiphon cramped Ralph's stomach cruelly! He noticed the way the condemned boys began to gaze about, taking in the ranks of witnesses. The event all at once took on the stench of long habit, as if the ceremony of hanging had already become ancient and fixed here.

Freeman and Lovell, looking very young and pardonable in the thunderous light, now stood on their ladders. Their halters had already been tied to the branch by the constables, when Davy walked to the tree, the folded document still in his hand. Opening it, he began to read aloud from it. Lovell was to be reprieved and sent into exile on the exposed rock out in the harbour. He was to dwell there in caves and his supplies would be thrown to him weekly from a longboat. The next time the *Supply*, the little storeship which shuttled eight hundred miles between this harbour and the outstation on Norfolk Island, set out, the ivory turner would be on it. The document declared that he was never to return from there.

He would not be alone, however, on that small lump of sandstone in the harbour. The Jamaican Jack Williams, who had recently gone hunting with Harry and Ralph, had just in the past few days been sent out to the same place for a lesser disciplinary matter. Black Jack was a man of ferocious hungers and would devour a week's rations at one meal. What a life it would be for young Lovell out there on the rock when Black Jack grew frantic with hunger or passion.

When Davy Collins read that Freeman was also pardoned but on condition he consented to be the common executioner, there was some laughter among the convicts. His Excellency, Davy read on, had been sensitive to sundry petitions he'd received on behalf of the condemned from groups of convicts. But these, said Davy, were the last he would receive.

Collins stepped to the bottom of Freeman's ladder and looked up at the angular boy with the noose around his neck. He asked would he consent to the work he had been offered? When Freeman did not hear there was more laughter. A stammer of indecipherable words came at last from his lips, and Dick Johnson murmured, "The gift of tongues!" but not with considerable certainty. Then the boy's head began to loll. Collins told Bill Parr to help him down the ladder.

Major Robbie Ross intercepted Davy straightaway. "What does that soft-hearted and -headed womanly man mean by all this?" he thundered. He meant H.E.

Davy Collins's defence of H.E. was as brisk as his dislike of the Major. "Why, encouragement of virtue, Major," he answered softly.

"I will nae have my officers wasting hours passing sentences of death which are then transmuted into comedy. *Executionists!* We are to have executionists! I tell you I could appoint one from among my sergeants!"

"There are clear philosophic advantages," said Davy, "in a place where three out of four people are sentenced criminals, to involving the criminals themselves in the mechanics of justice."

"So this earth is not foul enough!" roared Robbie, kicking dust. He hated the soil of this place. He felt it was an insult to reasonable agricultural intent. "But you have to further cover it with a light coat of pretty-boy philosophy!"

The amused convicts were being marched away. New South Wales's executioner, soon to be named Ketch after the famous English hangman Jack Ketch, stood bereft by the fig tree under which the two empty ladders remained. A partly restored Harry Brewer limped up to him and—in Ralph's hearing—gave him instructions. "You're not to mess things, Freeman, and you're not to waver. You are to study the principal parts of the neck—speak to Surgeon White without delay. And you are to learn your knots from Sergeant Scott!"

Harry had got back the voice of command, or at least thought he had. In the attenuated features of Freeman, in which the witnessing felons had seen little but comedy, Harry saw the visible mercy of H.E.

PART THREE

CHAPTER 11

Perjury and the Play

In Act Two of George Farquhar's *The Recruiting Officer* the Sydney Cove executionist, Ketch Freeman, found speeches to his taste. Here, for example, Justice Balance discovers that his son Owen is dying in London.

"But the decree is just," Ketch Freeman intoned, "I was pleased for the death of my father, because he left me an estate, and now I'm punished with the loss of an heir to inherit mine."

Freeman—perhaps, Ralph thought, trained in matters of balance and gravity through his public post—had a surprisingly refined sense of the equilibrium of Justice Balance's sentences.

He had by now been hangman for more than one lonely year. On the rainy eve of his first task—the hanging of a young man named John Bennett, a food thief like Barrett condemned in the first May, Ketch had tried to escape the town and had fallen into a flooded sawpit in the dark. Ralph had been at Harry's recently constructed hut when the night patrol brought Ketch in. Harry had harangued the wet boy desperately, grabbing him by the sodden front of his jacket. Ralph remembered how Ketch, like a crane flown in from a storm, had raised his face to Harry, the long line of his nose glistening with water. He had pleaded that the women would have nothing to do with him.

"We're stuck in this, Ketch, you and I," Harry had screamed, "and you won't go to China on me, you meat-mongering bastard!" (Indeed, some of the convicts believed China lay behind the mountains forty miles out.) "You'll stay with me, you little prigger. I'll have you scragged and gutted otherwise, by H.E. himself, and you can look for sweet sockets in Hades, you great streak of oyster. Listen to me! You'll not move from your purpose, you little squeaker. You'll show me some spunk, you sodomite!"

On the strength of Harry's desperate threats, Ketch Freeman hanged Bennett the next day, and all officials were satisfied with the executionist's deftness. Nor had there been since, on the dozen times he had performed his public function, any inhuman horrors. Unless you counted the day two men, hanging together, had while strangling embraced each other in mid-air, causing Dabby Bryant to scream "Oh, pity!" and the Africans and Irish to keen.

It was because Ketch remained so lonely that he could now bring to his reading of Justice Balance the tenor and wistfulness of a much older man.

R A L P H nonetheless found some aspects of Balance's character and emotions, as portrayed by Farquhar, distressing. In Act Two, Scene Two, he discovers that his son has in fact died. He finds it out from Mr. Worthy (the theatrical Robert Sideway), who has just received a letter from London. To Ralph—to the private Ralph behind the cut-down scarlet military coat, to the Ralph who stood privately behind the all-knowing master of the play—Balance's reaction to his son's death was such as to trouble any man's sleep. "My advices says he's dead, sir," says Worthy. To which Balance replies, "He's happy, and I am satisfied. The strokes of heaven I can bear, but injuries from men, Mr. Worthy, are not so easily supported." And later he declines an invitation to drink at Horton's hotel with Worthy. "I must allow a day or two to the death of my son; the decorum of mourning is what we owe the world, because they pay it to us. Afterwards, I'm yours over a bottle, or how you will."

It was the strokes of Heaven which Ralph could least bear. He knew he could never accept the death of his son, Ralphie, with the philosophic levity of a Justice Balance. Yet he listened to Ketch

Freeman declaim the words and talked to him about the speed at which they should be said, the energy, the attack.

Mary Brenham, clothes thief and now Silvia, moved around the executionist Freeman with an instinctive spirit. She needed no prompting. She strode across the stage like the masculine girl she was supposed to be. To Ralph it was already believable that Kable/Captain Plume should desire Brenham/Silvia.

I n Act Two, besides losing a son, Justice Balance receives a poison pen letter from Melinda which says that Captain Plume has dishonourable designs upon Silvia. These designs, Justice Balance concludes, must have been compounded by the fact that Silvia is now his heiress. Despite Worthy's assurances that Plume is an honourable fellow, Balance sends his daughter into the countryside to hide her from Captain Plume. "Twelve hundred pounds a year would ruin him—quite turn his brain! A captain of foot worth twelve hundred pounds a year! 'Tis a prodigy in nature."

Just as the Established Church in the form of Dick Johnson had interrupted the readings of Act One, the Scotsman Captain Jemmy Campbell turned up in the midst of Act Two. He didn't arrive a step at a time like Dick Johnson or wait for a suitable moment to interrupt. He stormed in between Ketch Freeman and Sideway. Neither did he wait for the end of a speech. "Where is that perjuring woman?" he demanded.

Ralph asked him did he mean Nancy Turner.

"During the trial of Marines," Jemmy contended, "she perjured herself to save her lover, Private Dukes. So at the close of trial she was bound over in custody for her patent violation of the oath. I now find that on the limping pretext that we have no women's cells she has been permitted to wander free and become a darling in a play."

Ralph was pleased to say, "We are at the present reading Act Two. Melinda does not appear in Act Two."

"*Melinda?*"

"Nancy Turner," said Ralph. "She is not here, Captain Campbell."

Jemmy's complexion was speckled with grievance. In earlier

times he had been a more genial man. He would make set speeches in the mess and they were so eloquent people would ask him to repeat them. Like his speech on the reasons one could not find a mistress among the native women. "But yon black lassies," he would thunder, "are a pure antidote to all desire. It's the snot, lads, and the ancient fish oil they put on ten years back. The flies themselves are overwhelmed with distaste. And what a fly won't lay lips to, neither will Jemmy Campbell."

Jemmy was Robbie Ross's main partisan, and the aloes in Robbie had now soured Jemmy, too.

"It's yon wee judge in a red coat," he raged at Ralph. He meant Davy Collins. "And here he is letting the Perjurer wander free and be a damned Mrs. Jordan. I have just discovered this, Ralph, and my breath is taken away. And when I ask why she is not in a prison, that yon aged Midshipman Brewer says, 'She is, she is here!' The casuistry, Ralph, will not be forgiven!"

He glowered at Ralph's actors for a few seconds. Ketch Freeman coughed. Robert Sideway took up a theatrical stance, one ankle hooked behind the other. Perhaps he thought Captain Campbell was there purely to look the actors over and judge their competence. With his right hand he made curlicues as if signing his name on an invisible page.

In younger days Jemmy had stood firm in a lane by the Charles River in Massachusetts while the Yankee general Prescott and his marksmen felled more than half the Marine detachment. But it turned out that Jemmy had been spared for worse things—low rank (though not as low as Harry Brewer's), and this convict kingdom which had the feeling of an invention of the mad Dean Swift of Dublin.

"And now, laddie, I discover you yourself have enlisted the Perjurer for your damned masque."

"But I have the approval of H.E. and of Davy Collins," said Ralph. "And of Harry Brewer of course." It was not that Ralph was afraid of Jemmy's power, which was small even by the standards of a penal star. It was that he did not want to waste an afternoon arguing with the Scot.

"Do you think *they* give a tin cuss about the proprieties, Ralph?" Jemmy raged. "They are employing that wee perjuring slut to defeat me in the argument about the officers and the Court of Criminal Jurisdiction. I've now refused to serve on that court any further, since my fellow officers and myself voted for the Perjurer to be gaoled and tried, and our vote was ignored. You see, any tool yon H.E. and the Judge Advocate and that dog-faced Provost Marshal can lay their hands on, they pick up with hoots of exaltation and belabour Robbie and me!"

Ralph remarked he did not think there was any grand design to make Jemmy look foolish.

"It is time there was solidity of purpose in our mess," remarked Jemmy. "Some loyalty to Robbie Ross. Who after all holds the key to all our promotions. He would want to see you at his quarters this afternoon, when the evening bell rings. If you have the time, Ralph, to tutor perjurers in their lines, I believe you might have time also to speak with your commander."

"You want to see her hanged?" Ralph challenged him.

"There are other actresses, aren't there, Ralph?"

Jemmy Campbell considered the actors for a second. "Yon scrawny hangman," he asked like his old self, his eyes having receded a little back into a normal position under his brow. "Is he here to stretch the lines?" He laughed, prodding Ralph fraternally in the kidneys. Then he strode away like a man who believes he has made an ally. That is my future, Ralph told himself. If I don't make major's rank before I am fifty I'll be as cracked as that.

"Let us start again please, players," called Ralph, swallowing down his dread of the afternoon's meeting. "As Justice Balance reads the malicious letter from Melinda."

As the reading went on, he noticed Mary Brenham, who was not for the moment engaged in the scene, sitting in a square of autumn light. Her small docile son had his hand inside her convict jacket, on her left breast. She looked confused for some reason. Perhaps it was the mysterious increase in homilies she was hearing as she did the ironing in the Johnson household. Ralph was tempted to offer her employment at his own place. But he could not have a she-lag at his hearth. He did not know where that edict came from, from within his conforming self or from without. He knew, however, that for the time being it was inviolable.

Freeman as Balance now read the letter from Melinda in the

most orotund manner, sure to amuse the Marines and the lags, if seeming to the more cultivated taste—Watkin or Davy perhaps— a little overdone. And Worthy/Sideway entered with an effete grandeur which, taken together with the sight of Mary, restored Ralph's soul a little.

What a wonder he would be on the night! With a profound bow, his head very nearly as low as the hangman's knees, he uttered his entry line. "I'm sorry, sir, to be the messenger of ill news."

When Ralph got to Major Ross's residence that afternoon he found the meeting of officers had been ordered not by Robbie Ross but by H.E. John Ross, Robbie's young son, who when Captain Shea died had been promoted—at Robbie's own command—to the temporary rank of a second lieutenant, was not invited, being only nine. He sat in a tree behind the house. He was an officer for the sake of the records and for pay purposes. But in questions of the relationship between the soldiery and the Court of Criminal Jurisdiction, he was what he certainly appeared to Ralph to be. A child.

Robbie Ross sat at the table inside, in the usual attar reek. His face, like his friend Jemmy's, had that mottling which derives from profoundly sustained grievances.

Ralph remembered a conflict which had begun in the penal town's early days, when a court martial made up of five young officers—Ralph was not one of them—had offered a private accused of brawling the option of being flogged or asking in front of the garrison on parade the pardon of the Marine he had assaulted. Robbie had told the court—it was headed by Watkin—that they had to impose *one* sentence, not a choice. When the court martial convened again and decided its original sentence had to stand, Robbie placed them under arrest. This meant they could perform no duties and must remain in their tents.

Both sides appealed to H.E., who made the reasonable point that he could not spare the suspended officers, nor could he give Robbie his wish of trying them before a General Court Martial, which would require *thirteen* officers. Davy Collins, said H.E., could keep the records of the dispute and if ever numbers of officers increased, the General Court Martial could be held. In the meantime, though, guards should be taken from in front of the tents of the court martial officers.

For the sake of conciliation, H.E. invited Robbie to tea. The viceregal residence was still at that stage the canvas affair designed by Smiths of St. George's Field. H.E. also invited Robbie's son. Harry Brewer was there when Robbie turned up alone and bristling. "It is a deliberately devised division at the heart of our society," said Robbie. "To which a bairn should not be required to give witness."

Harry saw in H.E. then the signs he had learned to read as profound anger—a repeated swallowing, a whiteness on either side of H.E.'s Semitic nose, and a pinkness on the neck. He had been accused of trying to use a child as a lever, and any chance he could ever choke down his reserve, take Robbie by the elbow, call him Robert, and tempt him to reason had vanished for good. The tinned biscuits H.E. had brought with him from Piccadilly and had ordered opened by servant Dodds so that young Johnny Ross could choose among them sat untouched. They were the bread which the two of them refused to break.

H.E. had pressed on Robbie, but in the coolest, most distant way, the idea of submitting the entire matter to swift arbitration of the body of officers. Robbie replied that he would not stand for arbitration by the young cronies of those five miscreants, those students of the bottle and close enquirers into the private parts of she-lags!

"I take this," he roared, "as another large instance, among so many, of your intent to geld me of my authority with my own battalion."

That, in the lag city's first March, marked the end of all human conversation between H.E. and Robbie, though an oblique one proceeded, and was proceeding still, a year or more later in Robbie's new-built residence of brick and shingles, when the question was Turner the Perjurer. And whether Ralph should lose his Melinda.

Robbie placed a bottle of brandy on the table for his officers, and each man produced his cup. They poured and drank reflectively as Robbie reminded them briefly of Jemmy Campbell's astonishment that the Perjurer was at liberty. Ralph noticed again that, though Robbie was tenuously stuck at the very periphery of the universe, he played the politician and flourished documents and letters as if he were striving at the very heart of things. He read through Jemmy's letters to Davy Collins on the subject, and then he read Davy's reply. Through this Jemmy could be heard snorting and heaving a fierce sigh now and then—like an accent to this or that sentence of Davy's. Davy had suggested that if Jemmy wanted to prosecute the girl before the Court of Criminal Jurisdiction, he was welcome to. Robbie and Jemmy chose typically to be outraged at this idea. It was not their function as individual officers to enforce the eternal edict against perjury. It was the court's, and the court was refusing.

When the court continued in its refusal to prosecute Turner the Perjurer, Jemmy Campbell had written to Davy and told him he would never serve on the court again. H.E. had been *oppressive* —Robbie used the word twice—in trying to force Jemmy back to serve on a court which wilfully overlooked its own required duty and which heard what its members said, and then let their judgements be ignored, their good time consumed, their reasonable expectations violated.

"And I'll tell you what Jemmy said to yon quizzical man whose power here is vaster than that of a Russian tsar, and who knows and relishes that power. Jemmy declared to him that all you honest lads were taken by surprise when the Letters Patent were read that day when the she-lags were landed and you discovered you were to serve this crackpot court. That we didn't know till we had landed on this awesome soil seemed to come as a wee surprise to the man. Oh, he says, your officers all feel offended by their lack of foreknowledge? They take a lot of opportunities to tell me so, I inform him. Then, he says, I want you to put it to them. First whether they look upon sitting at the criminal court as a military duty, or as an unexpected extra duty in compliance with the Letters Patent. And second, whether they had any knowledge of having to serve on the court before their landing."

Robbie inhaled significantly. "Now you see Jemmy's position. He has made a stand for all of us, a stand properly based on our liberties, our sensibility, and our proper self-respect. I look to you to align yourself with his stand. I look to you not to leave him stranded but to refuse to sit any further on the same bench as that pretty scribbler." (He meant, as everyone knew, Davy Collins.)

Ralph was pleased to see Watkin hold up a languid hand. "So it is a wider question than just the matter of the girl?"

"The girl is a minor section of the entire proposition, Captain Tench. But if we stand fast and all refuse to sit, that judicial posturer will be forced to prosecute the girl, as he should have in any case."

"Oh, I understand," said Watkin, blinking. "You want on one hand to demolish the court because we did not know of it before we landed. And on the other to have it hang Nancy Turner."

Robbie's eyes, the whites flecked with hard little lumps of granite colour, the work of his irreconcilable spleen, ignored this and passed over his officers, fixing for a time on Ralph. Ralph looked ahead and worked his chin into his uniform collar. Let him ask the question, Ralph prayed, of those of private wealth and of such talent as cannot be ignored.

Happily, and in spite of the earlier remarks, Robbie had asked Watkin Tench first, knowing that if he had Watkin he had the rest. Tench was the son of the proprietor of a boarding school in Chester. Once he had been a prisoner of the Americans for three months when his ship was driven ashore in Maryland, but Ralph was grateful to the Americans that they had released him. For this present legalistic emergency at the limit of space, in that adjustment of the Americas known as New South Wales, could not have been imagined without him, without his decisiveness, exactness, his correctness of language. He had the wondrous courage, too, to stand up to a mad commander.

"Major Ross," he began, "previous to my arrival in this country I had no knowledge of the Act of Parliament which would require me to sit on the Court of Criminal Jurisdiction. But then His Excellency kindly proffered me a copy of the act and I read it."

This outshone everyone, because no one else among them had read it, no one else had been so careful—not even those like Jemmy who had taken up disgruntlement as a profession.

"From the moment I read it," Watkin persisted, "I looked

upon it as my duty to sit on criminal courts whenever ordered, and I still look upon it as such."

"Do you realise, my little scribe, Watkin," screamed Robbie, "that such an opinion will lead to the liberation of the Perjurer?"

"That is Davy Collins's concern," said Watkin, closing his eyes. "He is judge and prosecutor. I—thank God—am not."

Robbie made a subtle but terrible noise, involving both the nose and the throat. He feared he had lost, so all the more vigorously did he challenge George Johnston, the young officer who enjoyed an attachment not only to a she-lag, but to Esther Abrahams, who was a Jewess as well. He hoped George would be somehow shamed by his attachment to his convict concubine to come in on Jemmy's side. But Watkin had saved them all, and George stuck with Watkin. The astronomer Lieutenant Dawes also kept faith with Watkin and Davy Collins, since they were not only men of science, but as well men not governed by animus. And by the time Robbie asked Ralph, it was safe for Ralph to fall in with the others and to give his true opinion, one at which Robbie grimaced.

"Return then, gentlemen," Robbie declaimed at the end of the voting, "to your whores and your plays. But you might remember that your promotion lies in my hands."

The officers left Robbie's house like dismissed schoolchildren, yet glowing with their purpose to discommode the schoolteacher. They would happily oppose H.E. on many grounds, his demands on them to be garrison, court, guards. If only Robbie himself was not so odious.

CHAPTER 12

The Autopsy

NOVEMBER 1788

THROUGHOUT the first year of the settlement's existence, Provost Marshal Harry Brewer was often presented with matters to do with his rival Private Handy Baker. So also—either through duty or through friendship—was Ralph Clark.

In the first November, as an example, a private named Bullmore was beaten to death in a squabble over one of the she-lags. Captain Shea would normally have been the officer to go to the hospital to attend the autopsy, but he was ill with the consumption which would later finish him, and Ralph was sent instead.

November was teaching the lagtown how sweet a spring evening could be here. Stars excited the vision. A southerly breeze idly rinsed Lieutenant Clark in sweet, astringent air. Surgeon Johnny White, the tooth-puller Considen, and Harry Brewer the Provost Marshal were all waiting for Ralph in a small room at the hospital. Lanterns were hoisted on all four walls. Thomas Bullmore's naked body, cruelly bruised about the head and ribs, lay on a solid cedar table. The table had a deftly tilted surface, and a drain hole drilled through one corner. Beneath the hole stood a bucket. By these signs, and by the leather aprons Johnny White and Dennis Considen were wearing, Ralph would have known if he did not already that the surgeons were about to inquire into Bullmore's remains.

Charming Surgeon White was an exacting physician, fine featured, black haired, an exceptional water colourist. He was especially good at rendering the native birds. He travelled avidly and always made friends ashore. At the time the convict fleet had been in Rio, he'd gone into town, won over a local surgeon, and—in front of a crowd of Brazilian physicians—given a highly applauded demonstration of Allinson's new method of amputation on the crushed leg of a Portuguese private soldier.

Ralph remembered too that during that Rio stay, when he himself had been afflicted with homesickness and dreams and the loss of Betsey Alicia—when he had only a dull interest in the quirkiness of Latin life ashore, and a poor tolerance of the ceremonial excesses that accompanied the bearing of the Papist Eucharist from the cathedral to the houses of the influential sick—Johnny White had landed for days at a time. He had struck up an acquaintance with some of the beautiful young novices at the Convento de Sao Juda. He would stand at the convent grille and trade his English for their Portuguese by the hour. They were beautiful girls of distinguished families. Soon they would make a decision either to become nuns or to go into what was known as the world and marry. But it had not been the marrying ones who fascinated Johnny White. For by the time they finally made their choice he would be beyond the reach of any European woman other than the women in the convict hold. But the idea that some of these sublime girls might become the brides of Christ seemed to fill him with a dolorous but enjoyable longing.

Johnny White was therefore one of Ralph's complete men, the way Davy Collins was complete. It was a shock to see him in a leather apron, holding the implements of butchery and standing so calmly over Bullmore's body.

"Private Baker did this, Ralph," said the little Irish surgeon Considen. "You know? Handy Baker?"

"Handy Baker and some associates," murmured Harry Brewer for the sake of justice.

Harry, as Ralph knew from Harry's many recitals of the incident, had been beaten once by Private Baker. There had been a time when he came home to find Duckling missing, vanished across the stream to the hut of Goose, Duckling's longtime abbess or madame, who had summoned her as of right.

Crossing the stream to Goose's hut, Harry had found Handy Baker with Duckling. Interrupted in full flow, the hulking soldier had beaten and bruised Harry fairly comprehensively.

When Harry revived, Baker had already fled, but Goose the abbess sat a while with Harry and reasoned with him. She had after all known Duckling since Duckling was nine years old. Duckling and her mother had rented some sort of cellar in St. Giles from the abbess and her late husband, who together had conducted a pharmacy at ground level near the Red Fox in Greek Street. Nursing Harry with brandy, she had reminded him that if he came down heavy on Private Handy Baker, everyone would laugh at him.

Goose had offered Harry some sort of arrangement, something to do with secure tenure of the girl, and Harry implied but never specified that they had come to some sort of grudging contract. Harry had threatened the woman, yet it was to her, and not to the Provost Marshal, that an ancient and obscure power seemed to attach.

Ralph himself knew Goose. She was red haired, plump, genial, and about twenty-eight years of age. But she had a royal agelessness. He had a memory of having been to see her once himself. She had provided him for an hour with a tent and a girl. His memory of the contact both with the girl and the abbess was blurred by the liquor he'd drunk that evening and by subsequent shame. He remembered though that in his guilt and nervousness he had talked too much and specifically about the most sacred matters, including Betsey Alicia.

P R I V A T E Baker had now killed Private Bullmore, or so it seemed, and that might give joy to most rival lovers. Except Harry, who saw ghosts and had his nightmares about hanging.

So, standing by the autopsy table, as that consummate surgeon Johnny White was about to let Bullmore's quenched blood, Harry showed no joy at all. Wanly he and Ralph listened to the two surgeons taking calm bets on what it was that had finished Bullmore. Johnny suggested bleeding in the abdominal cavity as well as under the skull. Considen put his money outright on subdural bleeding.

Johnny White said, "I intend to open the cranium, and although that will not be too horrific, I would understand if you wished to wait outside."

Yet both Ralph and Harry stayed—Ralph out of a sort of military pride, Harry perhaps from a desire to see Handy Baker's malice made visible beneath Bullmore's skull. Both laymen looked elsewhere while White moved Thomas Bullmore's square shaven head, and with a scalpel cut a wide circle in the scalp. With an oblique vision, Ralph saw Dennis Considen pass his superior a bone saw. As the rasping began, Johnny White grew expansive about what had befallen Thomas Bullmore.

It was a characteristic west-side-of-town story. Bullmore had wanted to sleep with Mary Phillips, a Somerset house breaker whose regular man, Private McDonald, was away up harbour at the outstation called Rosehill. When Bullmore got to Mary Phillips's shack, though, he found he'd been beaten there by Handy Baker, who had met her earlier in the evening at the public cookhouse and who was already in her bed. Bullmore had raged around the hut, beating at the timbers, kicking the corner posts and the door, screaming that no cock would have his hen that night.

At last Baker had come out fully dressed to fight him.

There were other Marines in the women's camp that night, some sitting on doorsteps. They agreed formally to second the two fighters. In this first fight, early in the evening, some damage had been done to Bullmore's face, especially when he fell and knocked his jaw against the lintel of Mary Phillips's next-door neighbour's house.

Bullmore had nonetheless come back sometime between four and five o'clock in the morning to disturb Baker and Phillips. This time Baker had apparently waged the fight unmercifully, and other young Marines—Nancy Turner's lover Private Dukes and two of Baker's standard followers, Privates Askey and Haines—had appeared. Seeing Bullmore's blood they turned on the stunned and stumbling young Marine as on a pariah. After that, Bullmore had staggered up the hill, presented himself to Dennis Considen, and after much frenetic anxiety characteristic of a victim of concussion, fallen into a faint and died.

It was believed, said Johnny, that at the height of the savagery Baker had tried to restrain Askey and Haines from crushing in Bullmore's rib cage with their boots.

"His arguments for peace might well help him in court," murmured Johnny White, laying the saw aside. Having cut a clean inverted dish of bone off the top of Bullmore's cranium, he removed that shield to expose what he called the *dura mater*, which he now began to probe with scissors. Harry and Ralph moved their eyes to Bullmore's head, which assistant surgeon Considen, having put his arms under poor Bullmore's shoulders, had lifted toward the light. A glimpse was enough for them to fulfil their duty.

Johnny began devising a report to Harry, in the hope that he himself would not be asked to waste his time in court. "You can say, Harry, that there is a quantity of extravasated blood under the skull and between the *dura* and *pia mater* on the occiput or hinder part of the head. This was caused by blows or a heavy fall and was on its own enough to kill the boy." He shrugged. "So my friend the Irish tooth-puller here was right."

While Johnny White and Considen went on to examine Bullmore's viscera, Harry and Ralph, their duty dispatched, went outside. Harry lit a yellowed clay pipe and sucked on it with a pained expression. Down the hill, in the civil prison, Baker, Haines, Dukes, and Askey slept in twenty-eight-pound ankle chains and under a gallows shadow. The idea, of course, gave Harry no joy.

Again what took his attention was the great puzzle of criminal fearlessness. "When I go down to the lock-up," said Harry, "Baker wants to speak to me. He complains that Haines has shat himself in the corner. Maybe you should choose friends with better habits, I reply. And then he says, You tell Ketch Freeman to leave the knot loose so I'll dance plenty. You'd do that for me, wouldn't you, you old scandal? The bastard asked me if I thought there wasn't a Marine or a convict who would give up the chance of a turn in love lane with Duckling? He asked me, in front of his friends, did I think I was the only general of her lowlands?"

Ralph wondered yet again at the completeness of Harry Brewer's confessions. There was no vanity at all, no hedging of cruel fact. There could not be a doubt that this derived precisely from his having been for ten years the oldest midshipman in the Royal Navy, sharing the rank with sweet-faced twelve-year-olds, and saved only from the indignity of the midshipmen's mess by his friendship and collaboration with the Captain. So that there was no humiliation inherent in the penal city which Harry could not countenance and report to a true friend.

"See, Ralph, he—like all the other bastards—has this indecent lack of fear, which I cannot understand. If the wrongdoer does not fear the punishment, where's the sense of any of it?"

HARRY did not want his troubles with Baker settled by the Court of Criminal Jurisdiction. They were not. Six days later Davy's court found the Marines guilty not of murder but of manslaughter. Davy Collins and the others could not be sure it was Baker, or any other specific soldier, who inflicted on Bullmore that one fatal wound to the brain. Each of the participants in Bullmore's destruction was sentenced to two hundred lashes. Though this was a moderate-to-severe penalty, it would not in any large way impede Private Baker as a lover or a bruiser. Yet the survival of his tormentor seemed to fill Harry with elation.

CHAPTER 13

Hanging the Marines

MARCH AND APRIL 1789

"I THINK a comedy," H.E. had said, appointing Ralph manager and playmaster and leaning forward on his bandy legs, which the lags found comedic indeed. "But I do not want jokes about Jews, Mr. Clark." H.E. then continued in that manner both penetrating and abstract, his eyes at once piercing and myopic. "They are the chosen race, and jokes at their expense come too cheaply to be of value."

H.E., said Harry Brewer, had a German Jewish father from Frankfurt, a Bread Street language teacher and dance instructor. The man had been H.E.'s mother's second husband, but she had taught her son to pretend to be the offspring of her first, who was an officer in the Royal Navy, so that the boy could get into the Greenwich Naval School. Ralph could not tell whether H.E., in raising that proviso about Jews, was acknowledging his own Semitic connections or taking a rational British posture.

The question of Nancy Turner and her notorious perjury arose from criminal events, which occurred at the same time H.E. first approached Ralph with the idea of a play. Early on a morning in the last week of March, the two commissaries came to open the storehouse at dawn and found the shaft of a key stuck in the padlock. They gouged this section of key out of the lock and put it in the hands of Harry Brewer. He fancied he could feel the heat of perfidy in it. It was clear to Harry at once, as it had been to the commissaries, that a consortium of thieves had forged a key, the shaft of which now lay in Harry's hand, and with it were raiding the storehouse in a far more adroit way than that characterised by the thefts of Tom Barrett and his supporters a year past. It was likely, too, that this new crew of thieves were Marines, since even if you had a key you could still not enter the store without being seen by the sentry.

There was one convict locksmith in the settlement. He was a man called Frazer, a greater favourite of H.E.'s and Watkin Tench's. They would recount at the dinner table how Frazer once had made a set of delicate tools for a crew of counterfeiters every one of whom had been hanged. Watkin once described him as a thief in fifty different shapes—a trickster, a forger, a pickpocket, a tumbler and magician at country fairs, taking in the rustics. Frazer released in people that love of the amiable rogue which is common to all men.

He identified the key at once. He had altered it for Joseph Hunt the Marine, who had borrowed it from the widow of a Marine who had recently died of a fast, unnameable fever. Private Hunt told Frazer he had lost the key to his own chest, and he needed Frazer to do a little work on the widow's key to adjust it for his needs.

The commissaries were, by the time half a key was found in the storehouse lock, nearly bereft of pork, and butter would last, they said, only another two months. On top of that the beef was of a very poor and sinewy quality. It was apparent to everyone that victuallers and chandlers of the Thames, Portsmouth, and Plymouth, now sitting in the known world in front of their fires with brandy and nuts, had unloaded all their worst merchandise on H.E.'s grotesque circus, certain no complaints would get back to them from such a deep reach of space. But whatever its quality, the beef, too, was essential as air to the continued life of the convict dominion, and no one could predict when or if new stores, aged a further year by shipment from the known world, would ever supplement it.

The chance of famine was therefore a common subject among

Marines and lags both, though it was not often raised among those engrossed in the making of the play. There were known to be two degrees of hunger in Sydney Cove. The more extreme degree was starvation, generally found among the old and defenceless felons or those who had gambled food away. It brought in the end its own heinous tranquillity. The second and more common variety was an absence of quality and novelty in what one ate, and this was very dangerous to the balance of the mind.

In the convict city, this latter degree of hunger was growing universal—the officers themselves were beginning to run dry of any delicacies they had brought with them. Convicts had swum out even as far as Ralph's little turnip garden in the harbour to steal a handful of vegetables. People had that irritability about food, about the punctilio of sharing, which Ralph had seen before, but only in hard times aboard ship and on garrison duty in Holland. The longer it continues, this species of hunger, the more flighty do people become.

So when Private Joseph Hunt faced his interrogators, who included Robbie and three short-tempered sergeants, it did not take long for him to confess everything—his accomplices, his methods, the quantities they had raided.

Hunt named first Luke Haines and Richard Askey, two soldiers who had helped beat Bullmore to death. Robbie suspected that Hunt was naming first the two he liked least, in the hope that would satisfy.

He locked him up without an evening meal and took him out next morning. Now Hunt confessed there were seven in the group. They had sworn each other in, a blood oath, and borrowed three keys from people, having them altered to fit the locks on the three doors of the storehouse. Members of the group came from all five Marine companies, so that at least one would be on duty at regular times. And when he was, the others could arrive, let themselves in, relock the door from the inside, fill burlap bags with supplies of flour and pork, and steal brandy and wine, while outside the Quarter Guard marched past and the sentry told them all was secure.

The key had broken because Hunt himself had decided to do a little plundering without any of his associates; he had put the key in the door and was about to turn it when he heard the Quarter Guard patrol coming up the road. In his panic he found he could manage to lock the thing but that the key would not come out. He worked at it frantically and then broke it off at the shaft. At least the sergeant of the Quarter Guard had discovered the door locked and all well, and in the dark would not have seen the shaft caught in the mechanism.

Among the others Hunt now named was Handy Baker, the same soldier who had taken part in Private Bullmore's slaughter and who had once taken Duckling away from Harry Brewer.

The Marines Harry Brewer took under arrest also included the soldier generally considered to have been Nancy Turner's lover, Richard Dukes, who was then serving at the Rosehill outstation and had to be brought down harbour by boat to face trial.

As Harry later told Ralph Clark, the six prisoners talked together in a comradely way in the civilian gaol, now an adequate structure of slab timber. Dukes claimed innocence but was overcome with hilarity when the others told him not to bother with it. He behaved, said Harry, like a man on whom a joke had been played. Generally you could say of all six that there was a terrible equanimity about them—that calm in the face of sentence. They all said Hunt had been the prime mover, but were more amused than aggrieved that he had informed on them. Luke Haines had the idea of escaping execution by handing in a string of names of those who had received the stolen goods—Nancy Turner was of course on that list, as was Private Baker's convict wife, Liz Huffnell. But Robbie promised him nothing for the information and when Luke Haines was put in the cell with his friends again, they teased him about his stratagem. "It's a trick that can be played only the onst, Luke," called Private Baker.

At the trial Private Dukes, patently lying, said he had taken nothing from the stores, that he had sometimes turned his gaze away when on sentry duty, but that was understandable in view of what Haines and Baker and Askey had done to Private Bullmore. Besides, it was only in the past three weeks, he said, that he had known of the business the others were in and done this occasional turning away. He named people who, he said, were part of the thieving partnership at Rosehill—two privates and a young convict named Smith.

Dukes's expedient also seemed to fill his fellow prisoners with amusement. By Luke Haines's testimony, Dukes had paid his girl, Nancy Turner, in goods. "Winnings for her weppings," as the lags and many of the private Marines said.

Davy Collins nonetheless brought the two privates and the convict named by Dukes down the river, and Robbie treated them to an intense questioning, offering first one of the privates a complete pardon if he would confess, and then the other. They all, however, stood up to their interrogation with apparent innocence. At last Davy Collins dismissed them and sent them back upriver.

It was Nancy Turner's appearance before the court which would remind Ralph, a few weeks later, of her suitability as Melinda. She was twenty years old, had a kind of fatal darkness to her, a luscious girl with the sort of mannered reserve servants sometimes pick up from their masters. She denied under oath that she had ever received any goods from Private Dukes. She was reminded of the solemnity of her oath, asked the question again, and again denied it. Dukes called to her at once, an indistinct cry which everyone took to be helpless gratitude. She could not be shaken. Davy told Harry Brewer the Provost Marshal to keep her separate from other witnesses so they would not be infected by her perjury.

John Arscott, the carpenter who would soon be playing Sergeant Kite, was instructed to erect a scaffold between the two storehouses. When the six condemned mounted this new structure and met the nascent Justice Balance, Ketch Freeman, a number of Marines were seen to be weeping and hiding their faces in their hands. Ralph and other officers, themselves overcome, permitted this display of grief. Harry stood through it but later said to Ralph, "This is a most accursed business, and I cannot attend to it any further."

Some of the wives and lovers of the condemned called advice and endearments before and after the drop, and wept. Nancy Turner, still held separately from the others and standing by Harry Brewer—a circumstance which might have led Jemmy Campbell to believe she was under permanent arrest—kept her reserve and closed her eyes as her lover was thrown off the platform. Perhaps she would later be comforted by the observations of others that, whereas his condemned comrades had brief though terrible struggles, and Handy Baker bit through his own tongue, Private Dukes seemed to lose his senses at the very instant of the drop.

CHAPTER 14

Playing to the Indian

THE play, Ralph concluded after a few weeks of readings, though crowded with characters, was in fact a simple matter at heart:

• Two gentlemen, friends, desire two country cousins—fortunately each a different cousin, so that their friendship is enlarged by their longing.

• Both girls, Melinda and Silvia, inherit a terrible degree of wealth which puts them beyond the two friends.

• Through the loud stubbornness of one lover, Captain Plume, and the painful melancholy of the other, Mr. Worthy, the women are won over. But this doesn't happen until Melinda has persecuted poor Worthy by pretending to prefer the ridiculous Captain Brazen, or until Silvia has disguised herself as a young man and enlisted herself in Plume's regiment.

All the other characters, Ralph saw as he considered the play, were for high colour.

It was, he concluded, at the beginning of Act Three that the chances for love seemed leanest. Mr. Worthy, expressing the bitter equation which has overtaken his own life and that of his friend Plume, brought to Ralph a painful but languorous sense of his own hollow desire, which was part for the impossibly distant Betsey Alicia and part nameless, even though the name Mary Brenham did present itself in one corner of that yearning.

"I cannot forbear," says Worthy at the start of the act, "admiring the equality of our two fortunes. We loved two ladies, they met us halfway, and just as we were upon the point of leaping into their arms, fortune drops into their laps, pride possesses their hearts, a maggot fills their heads, madness takes 'em by the tails. They snort, kick up their heels, and away they run."

And of Silvia, who has vanished from town, Plume says in Kable's Norfolk accent, "The generous good-natured Silvia in her smock I admire, but the haughty, scornful Silvia with her fortune I despise."

Ralph had been waiting for this act to see how Dabby Bryant would play the country girl, Rose, described by the playwright as possessing particular beauty. When she first enters she is accompanied by a large oaf of a brother—his name Bullock. Ralph had made his Bullock Harry Brewer's gardener, Curtis Brand, who did double duty as Costar Pearmain, a bumpkin recruit. Brand was a convicted poacher who knew the rustic manner well and, not being quite a bumpkin himself, could convey it.

Rose enters selling imaginary chickens. Soon Dabby and Curtis and Kable as earthy Captain Plume were well advanced into Farquhar's double-meaning jokes, which Dabby delivered with a succulently slack mouth and a slight breathiness. Most of this passage of the play, Ralph reflected, the Reverend Johnson would no doubt indict.

Plume (feeling Rose's chickens): Let me see. Young and tender, you say?

Rose: As ever you tasted in your life, sir.

Plume: Come, I must examine your basket to the bottom, my dear.

Rose: Nay, for that matter, put in your hand. Feel, sir! I warrant my ware as good as any in the market.

Through all this, Melinda/Turner the Perjurer, the threats of Jemmy Campbell and Robbie Ross building behind her like an unregarded cloud, sat in the shade of a native fig, waiting for her first appearance since Act One. She paid attention as the bizarre Captain Brazen, acted by the Jew Wisehammer, arrived on stage with Ketch Freeman as Justice Balance. Mary Brenham had already mentioned to Ralph that John Wisehammer was in his English past a theatregoer like Sideway. But unlike the excessive Sideway, Wisehammer knew exactly how to handle a grotesque line with the proper pitch and emphasis, and so Nancy Turner studied him with calm intent as he spoke.

Brazen (to Justice Balance): My dear, I'm your servant, and so forth. Your name, my dear?

Balance: Very laconic, sir!

Brazen: Laconic! A very good name, truly. I have known several of the Laconics abroad. Poor Jack Laconic! He was killed at the Battle of Yorktown. I remember he had a blue ribband in his hat that very day, and after he fell we found a piece of neat's tongue in his pocket.

Balance: Pray, sir, did the Americans attack us, or we them at Yorktown?

Brazen: The Americans attack us! Oons, sir, are you a rebel?

Balance: Why that question?

Brazen: Because none but a rebel could think that the Americans durst attack us! No, sir, we attacked them on the Charles. I have reason to remember the time, for I had two and twenty horses killed under me that day.

It was remarkable to Ralph that Wisehammer, like Dabby, somehow had a gift for the exact theatrical emphasis to place on a line. He believed that if he had had to find his players from among the officers and the better wives of the Marines they would have brought to Farquhar none of the instinctive touch which seemed to be there in Arscott and Wisehammer and merciful Dabby Bryant.

I N the midst of that scene of farce and complication, Harry Brewer turned up with Bill Parr his constable on the edge of the glade. That he had Parr with him was a sign he was not there as a private man, and a number of the players grew nervous and forgot their lines. Ralph held up his hand and went and spoke with Harry.

"How is my girl, Ralph?" Harry murmured.

"She has the manner, Harry. And no risqué lines."

"There is the line about Flanders lace, Ralph, how soldiers bring it back as presents for women."

"You've read the play, Harry. But that is mainly Melinda's line. 'Flanders lace is as constant a present from officers to their women as something else is from their women to them.' That is Melinda's whimsy."

"Fair enough. I cannot lock the girl away from all earthy meanings, not when she was a whore at nine years. But tell me the truth. She's good?"

"She is excellent," said Ralph, overstating it a little and understanding all at once that he was bargaining for Nancy Turner and wanted his Melinda safe from arrest.

And certain now that the preamble was over, Harry called Turner out of the press of players.

"The order is that you consider yourself under arrest," said Harry. "You should not take to the wilderness. Stay here with Lieutenant Clark and learn your lines. For the case against you can't be proven, Turner. A better thing to stay here and learn Melinda than go out there and become a shadow for nothing. So should I chain you up, Nancy? Or will you stick with the playmaker here?"

"I will stay, Mr. Brewer," said Nancy Turner.

"For God's sake, Nancy, don't be found outside your hut after curfew. At least not at ground level. If as some say you are a witch and a necromancer, by all means avail yourself of the upper air."

As Harry laughed and nudged her upper arm, she smiled and looked away.

Harry sent her back to the rest of the company. "Jemmy Campbell says he has a witness," Harry murmured to Ralph. "It's a worse business than I told her."

"Witness?"

"Someone who saw her take the goods from Private Dukes."

"If it's the truth, I won't have a Melinda."

"The court has not hanged a woman yet."

"But even if she is commuted to life imprisonment," said Ralph, "they will not let her act."

"You must be philosophic, Ralph," said Harry, patting his arm as he had earlier patted Turner's. Ralph wanted to say, You should be philosophic when you see the ghosts of the hanged!

"Isn't there another Melinda somewhere here?" asked Harry.

But Ralph knew now, from his new avocation as a play manager, that artistic necessities operated in the theatre—that was the charm of the thing. All art proceeded by reducing contingencies and accidents to the essential, and to the part of Melinda, Turner the Perjurer was essential beyond all question and quibble of the law.

"I must hope she is not hanged then," Ralph whispered. And he felt oddly, in keeping secrets from Turner, that he was betraying the theatrical and artistic necessity he felt in his blood: by not permitting her to choose whether she would flee into the forest and die quietly there, or await her accuser in the settlement.

T H A T same afternoon of Nancy Turner's arrest, H.E. himself appeared on the edge of the clearing. Ralph was by now used to the continual appearance of officials. H.E. had with him the native hostage, Arabanoo, who wore the uniform of a petty officer in the Royal Navy. Ralph wondered did the native remember Ralph's part as a Marine officer in the painful capture—but Arabanoo never gave any sign of memory or resentment.

Everyone said the native was captivated by H.E.—some said unkinder things still. Arabanoo looked from the players to H.E. and back again, as if to verify that their excessive theatrical emotions were approved of by the man he called father—*Be-an-na*. (Davy Collins had made the point to Ralph once that the nouns of the natives had an emotional conjugation. For when in pain, Arabanoo would call on H.E. by the variation *Be-a-ri!*) And "*Be-an-na?*" he called, faced with Ralph's players.

Ralph had always found Arabanoo an affecting figure. He was a man of perhaps twenty-two or -three years, lean, with a beautiful anthracitic blue to his native blackness. His eyes were a different and penetrating blue and seemed to Ralph to convey polite bafflement. Somewhere in the forests were his relatives, who, as Ralph had once remarked to H.E., might well be dependent on him for their provender. But H.E. had claimed to need the native more, so that he could be cultivated and then sent back to his people as an ambassador. Not that H.E. had yet dispatched him to talk to the natives either on this side of the harbour or on the other, the side from which he had been captured.

There were jokes in the officers' mess about H.E. training Arabanoo for as long as an Oxford undergraduate, and there were the normal insinuations which had prevailed in the matter of H.E.'s friendship with Harry Brewer—stories of how long ago H.E.'s wife had left him, and why she may have done it; the intimations of sodomy.

Ralph knew the imputations were unjust. It was apparent H.E. took his task of communing somehow, soul to soul, with these strange beings too seriously to take easy gratification with a robust young native, even if that had been his taste, a matter never proven by anyone. Perhaps the business of living inside a petty officer's uniform in the city of lags would not have confused Arabanoo as much if H.E.'s appetite for keeping him at his side had expressed itself in some obvious carnal manner. Ralph thought you could tell, by the Indian native's puzzlement, that it had not.

After a particularly flamboyant exchange between Worthy/Sideway and Brazen/Wisehammer, Arabanoo raised both hands in the air, vibrated them and let loose a congratulatory vibrato wail, his tongue trembling between his lips like a bird's.

Given that the native so clearly liked the preparations of the play, H.E. began to visit the playmaking with him every afternoon. Arabanoo was somehow aware these were not the convicts in their normal persons, but in their transformed persons. And given that ritual was not unknown among the Indians themselves, Arabanoo seemed to take some comfort from the rehearsals. It was possible, thought Ralph, that he considered the reading of the lines and the rehearsal of actions to have religious meaning, and Ralph was beginning to wonder himself if it were so.

A R A B A N O O was captured on the lag city's first New Year's Eve in the middle of the previous summer. Or as H.E. looked on it, he was rescued, taken out of his *ab origine* timelessness and introduced to breeches and naval jacket and the Gregorian calendar. 1789, which according to the astronomer Lieutenant Dawes promised— through its combination of cabalistic numbers—to be an exceptional year, would be a lake Arabanoo must enter and swim in, just as Ralph and H.E. and Dawes himself did. He would have to interpret this new and unfamiliar framework of days to his brothers and sisters, the *ab origine* inhabitants.

H.E. had become convinced that a native must be captured and trained as a mediator, since no one saw the Cadigal people any more, the tribe who shared the south side of the harbour with the new penal society. The smallpox epidemic had not yet manifested itself, but there were other reasons the tribe avoided the town— the stealing of Cadigal nets and weapons by the convicts, and the passing of venereal sores to the Cadigal women. There were incidents which H.E. chose to take as a warning of coming battle.

A week before Christmas a number of the lags who worked at the brick kilns came running into town, out of breath and mad in the eye, claiming two thousand natives had appeared from the south that morning and stood facing them with painted faces and bodies. Some of these faces which presented themselves at the kilns were entirely an unearthly white, or were striped with white and ochre in the most frightening way. All were armed with spears whose points of bone, stone, and stingray tails were a poignant reminder to any European that his blood was not absolutely supreme.

The natives had dispersed only when the convicts pointed their spades and shovels at them in the manner of the Marines' muskets. The entire confrontation had proceeded in awesome silence.

Davy Collins had already, of course, made up tables of population for the Cadigal, and he was sure they did not have two thousand warriors. Even so, both he and H.E. agreed on the need to find a man to stand in the middle between the Cadigal and the penal society.

The finest minds in the penal settlement wanted a native seized and groomed: H.E., Davy, Watkin. When it came to finding officers for the enterprise, however, Jemmy Campbell nominated George Johnston and the astronomer Will Dawes. It was believed that reclusive young Dawes was beginning to consider himself a civilian, and that to make him participate in a more or less military expedition would recall his mind to his true position. Dawes, however, who was making the map of these skies and had the authority of *that* behind him, went to H.E. He pleaded not only that he was too busy at the observatory but that he could not in conscience and honour take part in any punitive or man-trapping excursions into the forests. And because of his frankness, and H.E.'s prejudice in favour of science, he was excused.

Ralph was chosen in his place.

The duty made him unhappy. But he needed promotion then —Captain Shea had not yet gone under to his consumptive disease and Ralph was still second lieutenant, anxious for the further seven shillings a week which elevation to a full lieutenancy would bring him. At that time, the last day of 1788, the play had not yet been proposed, and so he could not claim that special judicial, scientific, or other duties had a prior call on his time.

T H E expedition to capture a native required two longboats. One of them was commanded by the officer from the *Supply,* the penal storeship which ran back and forth between the outer settlement of Norfolk Island and Sydney Cove. On its runs, the *Supply* traversed spaces and seas where it knew it would never see another craft. Its officer, Lieutenant Ball, had found in the midst of the ocean, halfway between the principal convict station of Sydney Cove and the minor one, a pinnacle of rock, a blade of stone high as a pyramid emerging from the ocean. To encounter it and to name it was as sweet as the construction of some great monument —as good as an act of creation. It was no surprise that after such experiences in mid-ocean, Lieutenant Ball would be willing to lead an expedition, given that its purpose was to vivify and transform— perhaps with a new name—one of these beings *ab origine.*

The second boat in the excursion was commanded by George Johnston, with Ralph as his second lieutenant. George was a well-made young Scot, popular with his brother officers both because of his joviality and his willingness to conspire. He was no scholar and he drank too much. The rumour was that he was much hectored by his lag mistress, Esther Abrahams, but his temper was too volatile for anyone to mention that to his face.

It was a hot but not unpleasant day out on the massive reaches of the harbour. As they passed Ralph's island, old Amstead hoeing away at the potato beds and taking no notice of any other business, Ralph spoke to Johnston, who sat beside him in the bows, armed with a sword and a pistol.

"Do you think a native will really be changed? Just by bringing him to town."

"First," said George, patting the scabbard of his sword, "we'll have Christ's own time finding one. Their childlike trust ain't childlike trust any more, Ralphy."

"The convicts haven't been changed by being brought all that space. So how can we alter a native by bringing him back across the harbour."

"I wouldn't say the lags hadn't been changed, Ralph," Johnston murmured. Perhaps he was thinking of Esther, who gave him his nightly remission.

"Ralph Clark," said Ralph, "is still Ralph Clark. Fortunate not in any cleverness but in his marriage to a divine wife. People are the people they are."

"You *do* mean to give me proper help in this exercise, do you, Ralph? You *would* shoot a black bastard to save Georgie's life, wouldn't you?" George buffeted him jokingly on the shoulder.

"I would even shoot one to save myself."

"To save a second lieutenant, Ralph. I wonder would Robbie consider that a proper expenditure of a ball?"

But after they had laughed, Ralph said, "Each native has those of his family who depend on him for their food."

"I'm sure they'll find someone to take up the slack for the one we catch."

They had rounded the harbour's middle cape and traversed the swell surging in through the headlands which gave to the open sea. Lieutenant Ball called back to them, drawing their attention to the crowds of natives visible on the sheltered beach on the north side, the beach H.E. had called Manly as a gesture of esteem for the Indians on that side of the water. High up on a rock ledge above the sand two men with clubs in their hands were dragging large iguanas out of their lairs and killing them—not with clubs, but by a deft movement of one hand—which stopped the meat from being bruised. Ralph saw a muscular savage hold up an iguana triumphantly, as if to the applause of people on the beach below, or even of the ghosts in the longboats. For that—said Davy Collins, who had begun his study of the native tongue by trading names of visible things with the Indians, and had then been able to move on to more subtle questions with them—was what the Cadigal and their Gayimai relatives on the north shore thought the convicts, Marines and sailors were. *Bow-wan.* Or *mahn* or *tu-ru-ga*, as Ralph remembered being called by an old native in Botany Bay. *Tu-ru-ga.* A fallen star.

As the longboats worked themselves in stern first to kiss the beach, Ralph thought the native act of primal boasting poignant, given the intentions of all those fallen stars drawing near. From the bows of Lieutenant Johnston's boat, he saw the iguana hunters descending from their rock ledge, old men appearing from the fringe of acacias, women running with strange tentativeness from among the boulders where they had been harvesting shellfish.

As arranged, Ralph and the Marines stayed by the boats, while Ball and Johnston and the sailors walked up the beach to the crowd. Ralph was as always astonished by the strange deportment of these creatures, the way they looked so frankly and curiously into the visitors' eyes. There was no doubt these beings who had lived here from before the Flood, who knew nothing of Zion or the Ark of the Covenant or the Redemption of Christ, who had been protected by eight moons from news of the wheel and the plough, were baffled by their new neighbours, were still looking for a definition of them. They seemed to find meaning in the most accidental aspects: they would seek out a sailor, for example, who was missing a tooth, and the old men would put their fingers in the gap —often to the distaste of the sailor who would nonetheless be under orders from his superiors to stand still. It was Davy Collins's belief that the native Indians were trying to find explanations to the arrival of the lags and Marines in terms of spirit, rebirth, fable, rather than in terms which had to do with the hard-headed plans of the Admiralty or Home Office.

Ralph noticed that it was specifically the youngest and strongest men who hesitated most among the ferns and acacias at the edge of the beach. It seemed they might think their young strength and virtue was what the visitors had come searching for, and of course—Ralph knew—it was exactly so. The women, however, came close, talked incessantly, flourished their hands in front of their enormous eyes; every woman identically marked by the loss of all but the stub of the little finger of her left hand. What did that mean? Ralph had always wanted to know. Why was it essential to the physics of their world that no woman carry a full left hand?

Her own face and shoulders glittering with fish oil, one of the women ran her hand down the sweat on Sergeant Scott's face. The sergeant's moisture astounded her and she began cawing with delight, raising her hand to show her sisters. Some old men began to sing, and through the press two young ones appeared. They were a little taller than the European average, and sinewy, exactly the types of men who had caused H.E. to affix that name—Manly. For since the Creation they had lived on rock oysters, robust kangaroo, sweet-fleshed iguana, and whiting.

The two young men who had now advanced did so silently, as if all the mad singing and wailing had evoked them, had somehow elected them. One smiled as he got nearer. The other stayed sombre. Five steps from Lieutenant Ball, the sombre one was intercepted by a round, gleaming, shrewish native woman who began to argue with him. This amused the sailors from the *Supply*. They were used to the shrewishness of the women's camp and saw manifested in this woman the antiquity and universality of the hell-hag. The young husband argued with her for a while, using moderate tones, while at an increasing pitch she pointed to a large pouch of grass around the other young man's neck, and on the strength of it seemed to be accusing her husband of turning up—in the presence of the fallen stars—improperly dressed.

But he argued her down; he had an authoritative presence.

Clearly, in his innocence, he believed he did not need an amulet to face Lieutenants Ball and Johnston.

Though his muscular friend was animated and laughed a lot, it was this man—the man who had silenced his strident wife—who began playing the word game with Lieutenant Ball. Exchange of words had become the protocol for meetings between the two societies.

"Nose," said Lieutenant Ball, while one of the women ran her hand wonderingly down his blue naval jacket. As he said the word, he pointed to the centre of his face.

"No-gro," sang the authoritative young native and touched his own nose.

Lieutenant Johnston, surrounded by women staring fixedly at his red coat, parted his lips and pointed into the black cavity between. "Mouth," he said.

"Ca-ga," sang the young native, and his companion and all the women and children chortled in chorus, while still the old men sang chants of their own devising and aged purpose.

"Teeth."

"Da-ra."

"Lips."

"Wil-ing."

"Ear."

"Go-ray."

The game increased in speed, and Ralph, standing with his Marines by the stern of Johnston's longboat, small harbour waves sucking at the heels of his boots, had the strong impression the natives were seeking a word of their own which fitted one from the other tongue, and when that word was found, the whole mystery could become clear. With that one coincident word, Ralph was certain the natives believed, the fallen stars, the ghosts, could then unravel their way back to their own place. With this understanding of the native's energy in seeking a word which fitted, Ralph felt, like a loss of breath, an unbalancing grief at his loss of Betsey Alicia, felt weighing on his head the fabulous distance which lay between him and that small divine woman who now ran incoherently through his sleeping hours.

And so the game continued for a while.

"Hand."

"*Tam-mir-ra.*"

"Arm."

"*Ta-rang.*"

"Thumb."

"*Wy-o-man-no,*" sang the young man. His voice was liquid and lyrical.

Lieutenant Johnston pointed to the man's bitter-mouthed wife. "Woman."

All the women laughed now the argument was moving closer to them. Some thrust their hips out and felt their upper thighs, others covered their faces under the impact of such hilarity.

"*Din-al-le-ong.*"

The second young man, the one with the pouch around his neck, jostled his companion. He too seemed now anxious to find the coinciding word and began to look into the eyes of Lieutenants Ball and Johnston with the avidity which had earlier marked the women.

"Belly."

"*Bar-ong.*"

"Leg." Lieutenant Johnston slapped his white breeches. They were kept laundered for him by his little shoplifter.

"*Da-ra.*"

The two Indian men were now standing one-legged, their right legs bent, and the sole of their right feet lodged against their left knees while each patted his upper leg. Lieutenant Ball of the *Supply* gave his signal. Five sailors grabbed the first young man, the one who had been so wisely warned by his wife. Three had him by the upper body, and there was one to each of his legs. The native with the pouch at his neck opened his mouth to roar at this treachery, but the visitors were all over him, too, and a fist was shoved in his mouth as a sort of gag. The women began to scream and advance and Ralph brought his Marines a little way up the beach to block them. The plump young wife took to beating the shoulders of a sailor with a pointed tuber-digging stick, and a magnificent young man emerged from the fringe of trees behind the beach throwing stones, a doomed loving scream rising from him.

The first young man, the spouse of the wise plump wife, was

thrown into Lieutenant Ball's boat, which immediately pulled away from shore. Ralph and his Marines held the line while behind them Johnston's crew tried to load the other native. This one, however, fought valiantly. Dragging one of the sailors with him into deeper water, he commenced to drown him. Ralph, stealing one glance over his shoulder, caught sight of the sailor floating limp while the savage swam vigorously away.

Without particular fear, Ralph now saw spears and firebrands arching toward his line of Marines. All the beach and the entire hillside seemed to Ralph to give off a cloud of missiles. He heard grunts as his men were hit by stones or digging sticks, but he himself was not struck. The spears, even those Ralph hated— pronged with the tailbone of the stingray—seemed to clatter about their ankles, deprived of impetus.

"Fire!" advised George Johnston from Ralph's rear, and without waiting for Ralph's order the Marines let off a thunderous but poorly managed volley which caused no visible harm to the Indians.

"Ralph," George called again more urgently. "We're giving the other one up!"

Ralph tumbled his frightened Marines back into the longboat, while still in the shallows taking one blow across the shoulders from the digging stick of a woman as he launched himself aboard. The sailors pulled away vigorously, the half-drowned sailor lying gasping in the bottom of the boat. The coxswain of the *Supply* threw a burning branch, which landed on the thwart beside Ralph, overboard and into the harbour. Ralph could hear the captured native in the other longboat wailing and keening, and then in deeper water saw him tethered with rope to the thwarts and raising manacled hands.

"This has been damned wrong, George," called Ralph, his shoulder still stinging, and saw two panting Marines nudge each other.

"Black bastard tried to drown poor Johnny," murmured the coxswain.

From the beach now receding rose a wail of loss which some in the longboat found amusing.

T H E arrival of the native in Sydney Cove was something of a raw comedy. A crowd from the women's camp saw the native roped to the thwarts of Lieutenant Ball's craft and came rushing to witness his landing. When he was untied and dragged ashore, in the humid afternoon which did not seem to mark the turning of the year, but to subsist in the meat of some great, unlabelled lump of time, one of the she-lags, a former passenger on the *Friendship*, made a speech in mock praise of the native's manhood, saying it did her good to see at last a man properly endowed after the small company she had been keeping.

Harry Brewer, who was observing the landing himself, untypically cursed her and accused her of having had two men on Christmas Eve. "I would have thought you saw enough combined length then, Amelia," he roared.

The native, pulled along now by the rope around his waist, seemed terrified of the women, perhaps not knowing they were the same species of being as the Indian wife on the northside of the harbour from whom he had been separated. At their core, Ralph wished he could tell the native, under the layers of convict cloth, lies that same bounty of the womb.

H.E. and Harry had taken some pains to choose a companion for this captured Adam. They had decided on a young convict called Bill Bradbury, who had first been sentenced for stealing in London seven years past—he had been merely fifteen then. He was selected for this post because he did not have any of the feverish anger which marked the other lags. Walk behind them and it was as if you saw it splashing from them, hissing in the sand. Bill Bradbury was about to be attached to Arabanoo on permanent terms. An iron wristlet would be locked onto the native's wrist, and from it would run a length of rope which Bill Bradbury held. If a man had to be led with a rope, said H.E., it was better it should be by the wrist rather than by the waist. He hoped the native would thereby become aware that he was not a slave or a captive, but merely an enforced guest waiting to discover the extent of his host's hospitality.

Harry squeezed the man's upper arm as Bill Bradbury took the dangling rope and, under a guard of Marines, began walking the

Indian toward His Excellency's house, which at this stage of history, the turning of the first year, was still that early bizarre construction of canvas and lathes. Bill Bradbury suffered with a good will the taunts of his fellow lags, the viperous anarchic humour of the women. "Walking your terrier, Bill?" they shouted.

But Bill's manner was a comfort to Ralph, who, though his shoulders still smarted from the digging stick, had a sense of a violation having taken place.

"You'll be right as ninepence, Charlie," Harry kept assuring the captive. But from the native's mouth came a constant, low noise which the crowd drowned, a noise something between a single moan and the multitudinous buzzing of wasps.

A hut had been built especially for him; it stood in the garden a little beyond H.E.'s residence. The crowd of convicts dispersed nearing this place, as they saw that His Excellency was working in the open at a portable table set under the scattered shade of a eucalyptus tree. H.E. stood up, laying a glass paperweight down on the page he had been writing. He was then, as ever, engaged in preparing letters and dispatches to London—official reports, informative personal accounts for his Hampshire neighbour, Sir George Rose, who was secretary of the Admiralty. He knew that across the stream Robbie Ross and Jemmy Campbell were writing to everyone they could claim acquaintance with—every official they had ever met at a dinner party, the theatre, a gathering at the Admiralty. They did this with a visible energy. Animus drove their elbows. They sweated ink. Whereas H.E., putting down his paperweight on another page of closely reasoned report, had all the leisure of a man who knows he is remaking an earth—or more than that, creating a new one. It was only a partisan who had no time to rise from his desk and greet a grand symbolic event such as the entry of the Indian into the city of lags. H.E., being no partisan, rose.

For the arrival of the native was in fact a vast event to H.E. As Davy and Watkin, Ralph and Harry would soon discover, he had just received from the *Supply* a report from Lieutenant King, the Commandant on Norfolk Island, a place where—according to the earliest voyagers, wrong-headed Cook and Banks—flax was supposed to grow. As well as that, a native pine there was said to reach astonishing heights. So behind H.E.'s dispatch of young King with a handful of Marines and lags to the small and far-off island was the chance that the flax bushes there and the pines might be of such quality as to unseat the Baltic as the traditional source for those essentials to the movement of humankind across the seas.

Lieutenant King had taken with him a flax weaver who had now proclaimed the flax bushes to be of very poor fibre. The great pines, lopped down, proved to be riddled with knots.

So the promise Cook had given had been aborted and nature had refused to supply an antipodean balance to the Baltic. To compensate, Lieutenants Ball, Johnston, and Clark had found a native, and great things could be done there, in the unknown constellations of the Indian soul. H.E. walked towards the native with his arms thrust out, wearing his strange smile.

He began ineptly by starting the naming game, and George Johnston had to explain why the Indian, the man *ab origine*, might not be so pleased to play the game which had entrapped him that morning.

"Phillip," said the Captain, H.E., slapping his own chest, bony and fever-white through his opened shirt. "Manly," he said, pointing to the new man, choosing to name him.

Arabanoo made a speech and Ralph wondered if it was in protest at the name. He raised his arm, the one with the wristlet, and grasped the elbow with his other hand, as if he were asking for an ascent to the heavens, an escape. It was then—perhaps for the first time—he noticed the bracelet around his wrist and the rope Bill Bradbury lightly held. He seemed at first delighted with the ring of iron. *"Ben-gad-ee!"* he called, which, said Davy Collins, was the tribal word for ornament. Then of course he saw how Bill Bradbury was attached to him and looked back to H.E. and began to rage, as if H.E.'s temperate voice had deceived him. He tried to tear the manacle off with the thumb of his left hand. As he tore and raged he fell to his knees. In front of the Marines and remaining lags, the Captain dropped too.

This kneeling of H.E.'s was not an organised and careful bending of the knee, of the type appropriate to a middle-aged viceroy with a damp fever in his side. It was an urgent, abandoned, excessive genuflexion. H.E. put his arms around the native's shoulders and began to soothe him. The native wept against H.E.'s shoulder and then began to handle the fabric of his shirt and to feel H.E.'s body beneath it. This led him to a desperate sort of embrace.

"*Be-anna,*" he said, apparently to his own surprise. *Father.*

By New Year's Day, it was apparent the native had a name he wished to assert over any which might be laid on him by H.E. The name was Arabanoo. He had kept Bill Bradbury awake all night, mourning away the last hours of one year and greeting the first of the new with tears. He had uttered incantations, but offered Bill no rancour or abuse.

At the dawn of the New Year he was bathed in a half barrel full of hot water. The fish oil came loose from him and turned the water to stew. Then Harry Brewer and Bill Bradbury dressed him in his naval jacket.

The man, by the frankness of his feelings, elicited great affection from Bill, as from H.E. He seemed to accept now that he was bound to H.E.—the feeling of the ribs beneath the cloth of H.E.'s shirt had had such power. But if while Bill was walking him in the garden he got a glimpse across the blue dazzle of harbour to the north side, on one of those mornings when the humidity had not come up and the harbour water seemed as sharply worked and solid as terrazzo, he would begin to weep. And worst was in the evenings, when he would see, under that rock ledge where the iguanas were captured, the sharp speck of a campfire. "*Gwee-un,*" he would tell Bill Bradbury. "*Gwee-un.*" According again to the relentless Davy, in the subtle tongue of the *ab origine* Indians, the word indicated not merely a flame but a circle of kinship bound by fire.

Ralph, though he himself had no chance of seeing around the bends of space to Betsey Alicia's hearth in Plymouth, nonetheless found the Indian's exclamation poignant.

O N the night of the New Year H.E. gave a dinner, and those officers who had time for H.E.—Davy Collins, Surgeon Johnny

White, Watkin Tench, and Will Dawes the astronomer—came. So also did those who had middling, only a little, or no tolerance for the viceroy. Seated at the more junior end of the table, Ralph would be left later with a memory of reiterating many times— having had a glass and a half of brandy and being bad with li- quor—that he took no pride in the triumph of the Indian's capture. The native himself—clothed as a British naval petty officer now—seemed reconciled to this, his first formal dinner. The iron cuff had been taken from his wrist. He ate at a pace. At first he used his fingers, but Watkin showed him what to do with his fork, and he took to it with a delicate but energetic style.

That day Will Bryant had got among a school of bream, a fish of delicate and sweet flesh. There were pounds of bream at the table. One of H.E.'s pigs had been killed as well, and its roasted features were a temporary diversion from the hunger which was growing in the town.

Watkin was enchanted by the man and, typical to his nature, kept count of what Arabanoo ate—near to five pounds of fish and three of pork. Robbie Ross, however, did not see the man's appetite as an engrossing phenomenon. Sitting at H.E.'s right side, he asked a question which proved to Davy and Watkin his relentless talent for taking from any situation the least of lessons. "Do you think, perhaps, Your Excellency, we might wish to exchange him for a black laddie of less pronounced appetite."

H.E. said that if a little pork made the boy at home, that was to everyone's benefit. Robbie replied, "Then I'm right glad the other one slipped away. Twae of yon savage would have eaten the antipodes out."

The Marine band played away in the other room, and the native, sitting on a sea chest by the window, swayed with it, as if he were willing to obey the rites of the spirits, the fallen stars. He had also taken a liking to brandy—which he called "The King" since he had heard that toast proposed earlier in the evening the first time that brandy was drunk. As the young Irish surgeon Dennis Considen began to sing "Young Desire's Plan" in a honeyed tenor, the native subsided onto Watkin's shoulder. Watkin and Davy

Collins withdrew from the sea chest, to enable the *ab origine* Adam
to be spread out.

"At last," said H.E., with a fond smile, "he knows there is
nothing to fear."

CHAPTER 15

Enchanting the Indian

THE native—whom H.E. had begun by calling by the pet name Manly but now called Arabanoo—did very little work as an ambassador to the Cadigal people on the settlement side of the harbour. He became more and more a richly favoured courtier, and while H.E. and Davy and Watkin took delight in his manners, his forthrightness, his courtliness towards the convict women, many officers —including George Johnston, who had captured him—saw him merely as an indulged favourite.

It had grown apparent he was not made to carry messages between the penal governance and the Cadigal. Some weeks after Arabanoo's capture and his enchantment by H.E., a group of sixteen lags had without authorisation wandered south, seven miles overland, to the shores of Botany Bay. There they were attacked by the Cadigal. One of the convicts, defending himself with his shovel, was caught on the back of the head by a native club and fell dead with a shattered skull. Seven others were wounded by thrown clubs and spears. This extraordinary belligerence from the natives panicked the party of lags. They began to flee among the low, salt-smelling paperbarks. Never had such a strong party of Europeans been set upon so vigorously. Apart from the victim.

Some lags paused by their wounded friends to break the shafts of the spears off—the wounded might walk or even run if this were done. But a good half dozen of the group abandoned everyone and came sprinting down on the town screaming that the forest was full of the dead. Calming a little, they said they had been attacked while picking the native sweet pea—an enterprise which H.E. and Surgeon Johnny White considered a corporal work of mercy in view of the shrub's potency in the treatment of scurvy.

A company of Marines was sent into the woods to retrieve the dead. It was not Ralph's company, and Ralph was pleased. He knew the felons were lying about their purpose in travelling to Botany Bay, that they were thieves of women and fishing nets and spears.

The rescuing detachment lurched forth from town unevenly, torn between disgust for the convicts' lying and cowardice and, on the other side, a vengeful unity with the white flesh which had now been violated by savage weapons of stone and bone. Private Marines in their shirtsleeves, sitting in front of the unmarried barracks, understood as well as Ralph that the sixteen felons had been down to Botany for no decent purpose, and called after the departing company, "Tell they lags that a man shouldn't carry stolen goods in his back. The hand is better! The hand!"

It happened that all the wounded were rescued—the Cadigal had given up chasing them. Johnny White and young Balmain and Considen cut the barbs out of their arms and legs and buttocks, using an astringent to prevent rotting of the wounds. The weapons had had subtle points, difficult to extract without wide and excruciating slicing. Some of the wounded—twitching with the pain which Johnny certainly did not intend but which created a confessional impulse—admitted the true reasons they had gone south. This was reported to H.E., who agreed with Judge Advocate Davy Collins that the Cadigal had been provoked and had answered the provocation like reasonable people.

Seven of the party were condemned to floggings—seven separate flogging triangles were in fact placed in front of the provision store for that purpose. At two in the afternoon, H.E. brought Arabanoo over from the east side of the cove with the idea that he would witness the lashing of these men. Then, travelling along with an armed column, he would carry the news of the apt punishment back to the Cadigal themselves. He would tell the Cadigal in their own tongue that H.E. did not propose vengeance but that he expected freedom of legitimate passage.

Fourteen floggers—seven right handed, seven left handed—were appointed. They carried in their hands the standard cats—rope teased out into nine separate, wire-hard heads. These were simply items of civilisation which, everyone in the lagtown understood one way or another, could no more have been left behind in the known world than could the shovels and adzes. So it was all accustomed commerce and as tedious as any military or judicial duty. It was a balance of flush and sweetheart blows; soft and hard.

It seemed Arabanoo lacked any sense of the boredom of flogging or the balance of soft and full-on. After Davy had played the word game a while, so that Arabanoo could understand that these men were about to be chastised for wrongs against the Cadigal, Arabanoo's *ab origine* cousins, the fourteen floggers took to work. For perhaps ten strokes the native watched astounded. Then he began to whimper. The whimper augmented to a roar of disgust. He covered his eyes, taking his hands away only to ascertain that the blows were still landing. As indeed they were—the incisive crack of the exactly timed blow, the leather dullness of the sweetheart. Before forty blows had been landed he was on his knees wailing. There was too much noise to broach the language game with him again, to try to make the rightness of the whole business apparent. In the end Bill Bradbury, his convict keeper, led the appalled Indian away, H.E. pensively following.

This was the first time it came to H.E. and the others that perhaps the task they had proposed for Arabanoo was too large. H.E. and Davy, and Ralph himself, were both gratified and shamed at the horror Arabanoo had shown for what must have been to him a mysterious and novel infliction. But they were as bereft of an ambassador now as they had been before Arabanoo was captured.

It was within a mere week or two of Arabanoo's failure to absorb the social meaning of the flogging that authorised parties, travelling south and east of Sydney Cove, began to discover the first signs of a savage form of smallpox—nowhere to be seen among the lags or soldiers—in the abandoned corpses of Cadigal people. Natives could not be found except those who were dying or dead.

These carried such marks as their fellow Indians had never seen, not since the beginning of time. *Ab origine.*

So that even if now Arabanoo was willing to be a competent envoy, there was no one left for him to speak to.

H. E. BEGAN now to bring him nearly every day to the glade to see the playmaking. This suited the native better than witnessing appropriate punishment. Ralph, observing him, was sure he took delight in the jokes—he could tell when they were well acted even though he could not know what they meant. He would walk towards the women with a most endearing smile and a bent head and sometimes, gently, he would feel their lower arms in a peculiar way, childlike, but less insistent than a child. On the days Dabby Bryant was playing the country wench, Rose, Arabanoo seemed particularly amused and delighted, particularly disarming and fondly touching. So much so that the suspicion came to Ralph as a shock that Dabby Bryant had somehow delivered Arabanoo of evil nights, and thus it seemed to Ralph for the first time the enchantment the lagtown held for Arabanoo might not be totally the knock-kneed grandeur of H.E.

This idea teased Ralph. It was known that male lags seduced the native women when they encountered them. But that Dabby Bryant should fall upon Arabanoo seemed to him a prodigy. Some would of course find it indecent, some would say, "The she-lags are as lickerish as that." But Mrs. Bryant's lavishness didn't seem to Ralph to have much to do with the accustomed ideas of propriety, with recklessness on one hand or tidy desire on the other. It was possible she had succoured both Arabanoo and Bill Bradbury on the same floor. England, Cornwall, and Before the Flood twined as one.

Ralph had a sort of power both as officer and playmaker to ask her if it were so. But as her happy client he did not know how to go about it. So—like Arabanoo—he listened to Rose's robust lines, which were Dabby's robust lines as well. He enjoyed a sense of the strange innocence of Mrs. Bryant calling to the strange innocence of Farquhar's Rose, and the echo coming back again from Rose to

Dabby, creating in Ralph as in the Indian a generous affection and a lust without urgency.

But though this desire was evoked by that good thief Mrs. Bryant, Ralph was surprised to find it did not carry her face. Increasingly, as Silvia achieved all the vigour of a girl playing a boy and enjoying it, his excitement, theatrical and sensual at the same time, called up what he now thought of as the generous features of Mary Brenham.

For in watching Brenham man-and-boy it around the clearing, Ralph began to see a certain size to what she had done in London when she was a thirteen-year-old. She had decked herself with male and female clothing—the clothing of Mr. and Mrs. Kennedy, the people whose child she had been taking care of. The Kennedy wear had not been of astonishing value, but she had taken more than was to be advised by either greed or slyness. There was therefore, he concluded, a streak of excess in Mary Brenham, that excellent convict and single offender, that paragon mother of a tranquil boy-child.

So a chord of excitement ran between Ralph and Bryant and Brenham and Arabanoo during the rehearsals which the native attended, and Ralph was sure he knew not only that Bryant had been so kind to the *ab origine* man, but could also make a guess as to when.

STRANGELY it did not seem as if Dabby Bryant could do much for her large and sullen husband, Will.

Harry Brewer, Ralph knew, had spent some time trying to appease Will over his flogging. Harry felt he owed the lag this, since Dabby had nursed Duckling through the flux aboard the *Charlotte*. Harry had determined by questioning that by the time Will had been flogged for stealing fish from the government catch, he had served nearly five years of a seven-year sentence. Among the documentation which the Home Office had failed to give H.E. before the ships left the Motherbank had been the official court records. There was no absolute way of proving Will's date of sentencing for trying to throttle an exciseman. Harry would comfort him and say the papers would arrive in the end and verify the sentence—that it was merely a matter of time passing and of distances being covered, that there were clerks in the Home Office keeping the score and also, one hoped, being flagellated for their tardiness.

But it seemed that Will shared with Ralph and Robbie Ross and others the feeling he had passed through a mirror, a fiery and transforming one. "It buggers up," said Will, "the numbers on the page." Therefore, times stated at the Devon Assizes did not mean anything here—the meaning of time and term and condemnation had been transmuted, syllable by syllable, during the voyage. Harry argued with Will that his punishment could in no light be looked upon as cruel or exceptional. The same day Will had suffered at the triangle, a convict named John Ruglass, who had stabbed his lover, a very ripe but very drunken London girl, had stood through three hundred fifty lashes, a number which dwarfed Will's. But Will lacked the mind for numeration. The blows which landed on him were absolute blows and not arithmetic. And his mania was indeed strong if Dabby Bryant could not, through her nightly ministrations, deliver him of it.

Will therefore went on answering Harry in the spirit of his perceptions. "It was all too cruel and all too usual, Mr. Brewer. And as for untoward, that savage of your captain's, that heathen catamite, he eats for breakfast more fish than I tried to sell off through my fence, Joe Paget."

So despite Harry's advice and Dabby's consolations, Will could not be appeased. Speaking to Bryant, said Harry, had advanced his understanding of the Americans—the nameless American fisherman behind the screw gun in a smack off Hampton Roads who had once fired a shot at the *Ariadne*, a mysterious shot since it could not hope to do harm and was as evanescent as a political opinion. *That* man's stiff back and sense of self-ownership were what Harry saw again in Will Bryant.

Ralph was uncertain why Will could not be reconciled by his own wife. But he was now very sure that she had with ease delivered Arabanoo of his torment, and he could also speculate with accuracy when she had given the Indian the cure.

It was the last time the storeship *Supply* had sailed off to Norfolk Island. A number of people had gone aboard her for the trip down harbour—Davy Collins, Ralph, H.E., Arabanoo, his guardian, Bill Bradbury. Arabanoo had shown no reluctance to get into the cutter at the landing on the east side of the stream, but as the party drew near to where the *Supply* sat moored he began to speak in a high, musical, alarmed voice. Davy Collins started to question him in the Cadigal tongue. "He says *island, island,*" explained Davy. "He's alarmed that the *Supply* is another country." Or worse, thought Ralph. If he thinks we are fallen stars, he believes we are taking him to the sky.

The *Supply* was a tubby little two-master, no longer than a cricket pitch, as narrow in the girth as Ralph's abominably cramped parlour in the married quarters at Plymouth. It was hard to imagine how anyone could consider it a strange and dangerous continent unto itself. His Excellency and Ralph and Davy had begun at once to utter soft reassurances to the native. *"Pirrip, Pirrip,"* Arabanoo chirped in reply. It was his version of H.E.'s surname, Phillip. He had no doubts that the complexly smiling H.E. could save him from strange passages.

"We are just going down harbour," H.E. kept saying. "A small tour to the Heads. Manly. the land of *pat-a-garam*, kangaroo."

When the cutter nudged along against the side of the *Supply*, the Indian climbed the steps, tremulous, urged along at the elbow by Pirrip. Ralph was aware as he himself reached the deck that the Captain and everyone else artificially stiffened their legs, as if feeling for the first time every nudge of the tidal water against the timbers of the *Supply*, the way it ran like an animal tremor up through the deck and into the soles of the feet. They moved with this comic heaviness—Ralph among them—to demonstrate to the native the nature of the *Supply*, and how it could be walked upon.

Arabanoo seemed to be comforted and adopted a picnic attitude. He asked if he could have "The King." H.E. thought it might be good for the native—in his distraught state—to be given a little brandy.

It was a crowded deck on which Arabanoo drank his tumbler of spirit. The *Supply* had taken on board that day twenty-seven convicts whom H.E. was hiving off to Lieutenant King at Norfolk Island. The volcanic earth of the place and the rich seas would feed them better than the more niggardly soil around the grand harbour here. There was a three-year-old orphan as well—Edward Parkinson—in the care of one of the older females. He was the only fragment left of a ruinous love affair aboard the *Friendship*, one which Ralph had been affected and oppressed by but which later he thought would make a quite suitable romance story for *The Gentleman's Magazine*. Jane Parkinson, a Manchester milliner who had stolen calico from her employer, had been ill of flux aboard the *Friendship*, and was tenderly attended to by the second mate, a likeable young Scot called Patrick Vallance. Ralph and Vallance had got on well, because Ralph had an aunt, Mrs. Hawkings, in Midlothian, in the same village of Musselburgh from which Vallance's family came.

In Capetown H.E. had shifted the women out of the *Friendship* to make room for livestock in the forward hold. Vallance had missed Jane Parkinson bitterly enough to get drunk. It was a day when a strange yellow haze hung over Table Bay, and in the haze Jane Parkinson's lover had staggered off to the heads to urinate, had fallen over the side, and sunk at once as if with the weight of loss. Though three seamen jumped in and dived for him, in that sulphurous mist you could not see an arm's length.

A day later, the baby Edward Parkinson's mother, Jane, Vallance's mistress, was wracked by an irreversible dysentery. Some of the older lags on the *Lady Penrhyn* looked after the child. Five days out of the Cape, she died of exhaustion and wastage just as the fiercest band of winds began to strike the fleet and sweep them on through that mirror of Will Bryant's. The surgeon on the *Lady Penrhyn* later told Ralph that when she was lowered over the side, three whales appeared, giving some bulk to the mute, skeletal presence she had maintained on the *Friendship* and the *Lady Penrhyn*.

Now they were taking her son to the outstation. In all geography there was nothing more ultimate. H.E. had instructed Lieutenant King that five acres of the island were to be farmed in the boy's name from the time of his arrival there.

A similar five acres were to be farmed for the girl child on board, Mary Fowles, whose mother, Anne, had been the one stabbed the month before by her lover. Mary Fowles was five years old, and able to stand on the spardeck with no more restraint than the hand of one of the women convicts. Mary had been taken from her mother by order of Davy Collins. Anne Fowles was a drunkard and could just as easily and erratically be either tender or savage to the child. Fowles's merciful friends had made her drunk the night before her daughter was shipped away in the *Supply*. To those who watched aboard the *Supply*, the Fowles child seemed quite equable about her future, which was to become an outlander of outlanders. She was a small woman under her own management. Whereas Arabanoo was like the baby boy, Parkinson, and did not know what was being planned for him.

The harbour was nearly bisected by a sandstone jut of land which H.E. had permitted to be named—without particular distinction—Middle Cape. This was the home of some natives whom Davy Collins had identified as the Camarai. From them Arabanoo's people on the north of the harbour drew their wives. It was known now that from here Arabanoo had captured his wife—it was all done by ritual abduction, a strange business, thought Ralph, but not so very different from the European mode of marriage.

That plump bitter-mouthed woman, then, who had on the day of Arabanoo's capture tried to prevent him from playing the word game and had hit Ralph's shoulders with her digging stick, that was the wife Arabanoo had raided away from the Camarai. It was understandable that in Arabanoo's geography, therefore, the Camarai headlands, layered in sandstone and covered with the coarse and distinctive foliage of the new earth, shone like remembered combats and desires, and he raised his arm, saluting them, uttering one long and languorous word in the native plainchant.

But then the *Supply* heeled over, as if renouncing those familiar cliffs. The sails were noisily reset above Arabanoo's head and the prow came around to aim itself fair between the harbour's two headlands, which were the pillars of his known world. Now Arabanoo began to struggle with himself. As with an epileptic, you had the impression of a man fighting with hands no one else sees. The effort nonetheless looked to Ralph as if it might split the cords in the native's throat. As H.E. moved towards him, Arabanoo ran to the sky-high weather gunnel and, bruising his leg savagely against it, pitched himself out into the air and thence into the sea. Ralph heard the blow as the deep water of the bay struck him. He swam clumsily, fighting the petty officer's uniform which deadened his strokes. Like a duck he thrust his head towards the profoundest bed of the bay, as if he meant willingly to sit on the bottom and drown. But the naval uniform buoyed him and only his head would go beneath the surface. As he continued to stroke and strain to dive, they swung out the boat to come after him. He wallowed away from Davy Collins's arm extended towards him, but an oar blade—by accident—clouted him behind the ear. Dazed, he was lifted by both armpits from the water and dumped into the belly of the cutter.

They brought him back to the stairs on the port side of the *Supply* and dragged him onto the deck, where H.E., Pirrip, was waiting for him. Ralph helped him sit against the pumpdales and caressed his shoulders. Lieutenant Ball's steward brought him more of "The King." It was clear to Ralph—and surely to Pirrip—that the native now thought he had been absolutely magicked by them. He must, for his sanity's sake, somehow be shown that it was not so, that he was not held by sorcery.

Ralph was therefore surprised to see that although H.E. showed annoyance mildly, he nonetheless showed it. He ignored Arabanoo. When the *Supply* hove to so that H.E. and Davy and Ralph could board the cutter for the return to Sydney, H.E. walked the entire distance of the companionway before extending his hand towards where Arabanoo sat, slumped, a wooden rather than a melancholy expression on his face. Arabanoo became aware of H.E. calling to him. He jumped up, his eyes glittering, his lips parted. He joined his hands together in a sort of candid gratitude. If your soul is absolutely owned by somebody, it is best to be on side with him—that was what Arabanoo was frankly, and by gesture, saying. He rushed down from the helm to the companionway and in ten seconds was seated beside H.E. in the cutter. Davy Collins, climbing in behind him, clapped his shoulder and put a hand on his knee. "We're going home," he told the *ab origine* Indian gently.

Back in Sydney, Arabanoo dined voraciously on two kangaroo rats, both as big as rabbits. He was, Davy Collins said, exquisitely pleased not to have been taken away to the sky. All at once he began to call H.E. *Be-anna*, Father, again. H.E. seemed flattered by the name, simply that. He thought Arabanoo was overwhelmed by honest affection, instead of seeing that the native spoke to him with all the loving, horrified, and ambiguous awe with which Moses spoke to Jehovah. He did not understand how profoundly the native was surrendering himself.

But Dabby Bryant, whose fishing shack was beyond Arabanoo's hut, and who had her ear for unhappy dreamers—she would have understood the native's bewilderment. In a way, she was a native herself, since the Cornish had a tribal disposition.

So it was the night of the day Arabanoo dived from the deck of the *Supply* that Mrs. Bryant had come across from the fishing camp to give the native back some management of his soul. And that, Ralph was sure, was what lay behind the grateful hilarity with which Arabanoo now watched Dabby Bryant play Rose on the afternoons H.E. brought him to rehearsals.

CHAPTER 16

The Play and Poetry

ONE of the scenes which most delighted Arabanoo was the one in Act Four, where Rose bullies her simpleton brother Bullock as Silvia enters dressed in a man's white suit. Mary Brenham had not been in the white suit yet—it was to be a calico thing which Frances Hart had not yet braided and sewn buttons on. But the clothes thief had managed to achieve a sort of white suit strut which—to Arabanoo as to Ralph—went in delicious counterpoint to Rose's country forthrightness.

Since Arabanoo and H.E. both found the sight of women bullying a man so funny, it was apparent to Ralph that throughout the universe one of the comic staples of all societies must be a weak man at the mercy of a sharp woman. Ralph remembered the blow he had taken from the Indian's plump wife on the day of Arabanoo's capture. There had been—according to Harry Brewer—a brisk woman in H.E.'s history too. For H.E. had married a young widow called Margaret when he was twenty-five, and she had left him before he was thirty.

Whenever Harry Brewer spoke to Ralph about the times he had been quartered with H.E., either aboard ship or down on Vernal's Farm in Hampshire, Ralph picked up a slight sulphur stench of eunuch shame—H.E.'s rather than Harry's. For the young widow had brought to the marriage two farms—Vernal's and

Glasshayes—which the young H.E. had run competently. Twenty years after the marriage died and Margaret Phillip went off to London, H.E. was still bound to the conjugal farms, personally running them in peacetime, and during war, in the main cabins of the *Ariadne* and the *Europe*, mailing his directions for harvest and market back to the New Forest from Havana, Rio, Capetown, Goa.

It is one thing to manage a farm while you are a spouse, and another to be still bound to it by obligation after your company at table and bed has been rejected. Harry, loyally, never pointed up the difference in so many words. That H.E. liked farming somehow increased rather than diminished this faint redolence of shame. They were not *his* farms. They were the rump of his marriage. In every attention he gave them he declared himself for what he was —a man without his own fortune, the son of a foreign dancing instructor. A man who had to live, that is, off property that had come to him from his wife's first husband, whose only shame was the excusable one of having died.

T H E nature of the war with the Americans—both the Spaniards and the French having made an alliance with the rebels—had sent H.E. and Harry on an escort journey to India, from which they had returned to find the entire conflict settled by treaty. H.E. had taken his secretary, Mr. Midshipman Brewer, to dinner at Chuddock's. Afterwards they went walking in the polite streets off the Strand and so ran into Mrs. Phillip, with her sister and brother-in-law, about to enter a house in Henrietta Gardens. It seemed to Harry that the brother-in-law was not too pleased to encounter H.E. and tried to hustle the two women he was leading into the house where they were going to dine. The brother-in-law, said Harry, had made a fortune out of pepper, curry, and tea. As he half turned to H.E., the glittering authority of a colleague's splendid house behind him, two black footmen either side of the door, he showed in his face all too sharply his sense of the redundancy of the two men he was trying to avoid meeting.

And they were indeed redundant—the conflict with the Americans and the French had just been settled in Paris; the *Eu-*

rope's men had been paid off. This ship sat at Deptford empty of a crew. In these circumstances a forty-five-year-old captain is a model of superfluity. A forty-five-year-old midshipman is, however, the peak of it.

This meeting was the only time Harry ever had a chance to look at H.E.'s estranged spouse. Mrs. Phillip was slim and slope-shouldered with neat features. Her mouth was small and straight but had in it a large eagerness for experience. Her eyes were round —she was a little bird, said Harry. It seemed to him that there was still an edge of anger in her to do with whatever incident or lack of incident had driven her from the house—though you could just as easily describe it as wry forgiveness.

They discussed very little—the brother-in-law could not understand how the Navy had not been capable of bringing the Americans to heel. What had been lacking throughout, he said, had been a serious intention on the part of the British Government to do so. H.E. asked him with that bright-eyed politeness which would later so annoy Robbie Ross how importers such as he had suffered from the American intransigence. The merchant answered —as if explaining things to a child—that of course Newport News and Savannah and New York and Boston, where he had once sold his East Indian imports free of duty—wonderful markets on a prosperous seaboard—must be a vast loss. The Captain had to remember, continued the brother-in-law, that insurance rates had gone mad and had not come down following the peace treaty.

Taking up his stooped scholarly stance, H.E. had looked out from under his brow and taken on himself the heavy duty of explaining on behalf of the Navy the reasons for American success. Mr. Dennison, the brother-in-law, had to remember, he said, that the Americans had enjoyed the assistance of 2,000 privately armed colonial ships, and that these ships had carried nearly 20,000 guns among them and had been manned by 70,000 Americans—all this in addition to the official colonial Navy, the French, and the Spaniards. The 2,000 private ships were able to act as privateers, and every craft they captured drove up the price of maritime insurance.

Though the rise in the price of insurance had not seemed to Harry to take the gloss off the fabric of the brother-in-law's coat,

Mr. Dennison and his wife still groaned reprovingly as H.E. made his explanations. And all through this, Mrs. Margaret Phillip had kept her eyes on Harry (Harry said) and smiled at him intimately, as if she thought Harry and she had a share in the Captain.

"You see how it was," H.E. explained further to Mr. Dennison. "One in every twenty Americans at sea and behind his screw gun."

Margaret Phillip had then teased him for liking the Americans, and H.E. said they came from the same tradition as we did. To which she said, with that angry lenience Harry had seen in her earlier, "And what tradition is that, Arthur? The German tradition?"

Then she had disappeared into the Nabob's house in Henrietta Gardens, a woman with further friendships to make. Watching her go, Harry was sure she had not heard the last from men burdened with desire.

H. E. HAD a smile Ralph considered watery and remote, and he wore it now as he observed the racy exchanges between Rose and Bullock and Silvia. It raised in Ralph a surmise about what had made Mrs. Phillip angry or impelled enough to leave the farm. It was hard to imagine H.E. sniffing after some other country woman, or being discovered mounting one of the milking girls. H.E., even at twenty-seven, would not have made a credible farmyard satyr.

It was when he saw John Wisehammer waiting under a tree to make his entrance in Act Four, Scene Two, that H.E. again expressed his only dramatic concern. "You do not intend to make a joke of the Hebrew, Lieutenant Clark?" he asked, nodding to Wisehammer.

"That is not why he is present, Your Excellency."

"They are an ancient race," H.E. murmured, as he had when first ordering Ralph to make a play. "And their mysteries should be respected."

H.E. had authorised a modest wine, flour, and fish issue so that the Jewish lags could celebrate their holy days. And it was considered a remarkable ceremony by those Gentile officers invited. Gentile convicts as a race had no knowledge of rite and would have been at a loss to conduct evensong. But the Soho Jewish lags had been exact in their knowledge of ceremonial. This was noted approvingly by Lieutenant George Johnston, who had attended as a guest, being very much the champion of Jews who were among the felons, not because of any Semitic blood on his own part but because of his Jewish paramour, Esther.

COMING to the clearing one afternoon Ralph found Mary Brenham's baby son playing at the flap of the marquee, and inside—at his own deal working desk—Mary Brenham and John Wisehammer in an ecstasy of cooperation, Mary writing quickly, Wisehammer striding around the tent, his hand thrust over to the back of his head where it clutched his black hair, and his feet coming down in emphasis as he tried this rhyme or that. "Applause," Wisehammer was saying, "applause, laws, paws, gnaws, doors, Lieutenant Dawes? Should we mention the gentlemen by name?"

"We humbly beg your kind applause," murmured Mary Brenham, with a creative frown that reminded Ralph of Betsey Alicia and made him sharply aware there was nothing that moved him like a cloud of intellection on a desired face. "And not excluding Lieutenant Dawes," she added, "his telescope between his paws."

Then she laughed, and Wisehammer did, but quickly cleared the joke away with a swipe of the hand and went on rhyming.

"Humbly to excite a smile," said Wisehammer, stamping his foot down to the meter. Mary wrote that down and looked over her shoulder, idly, to the complacent child, over whom Ralph now stood. She put the pen down quickly, as if she had been caught in a crime instead of a poignantly innocent exchange of rhymes.

Ralph himself felt caught out. All he could think to say was, "The future citizens of this lagtown, Mary Brenham, will be peaceful indeed if they all resemble your son."

"We have taken the liberty," said John Wisehammer, in a sort of doing-business manner, "to prepare for your consideration, Mr. Clark, a prologue or an epilogue."

Ralph felt hollow. He longed to be included in their poetasting game. He said he thought an epilogue was a wonderful notion —to show convicts they were capable of literary ideals. He sounded to himself shamefully preachy as he said it, and he felt his blood burning. "Please," he said, "continue." He stepped a little closer and became confidential. "Do not mention Major Ross in your verses. He can be troublesomely political."

"Cross Ross," Mary Brenham ventured, and covered her mouth with her hand, keeping the joke to herself.

Ralph left, feeling that his desire to get a tranquil new world child on Mary Brenham was visible in his face. As he crossed the clearing, he saw Nancy Turner the Perjurer leaning against the trunk of a tree, regarding him with calm irony. Her long mouth was tucked into subtle folds and he feared she might wink like a co-conspirator.

That Sunday it was Easter, and for the first time in seven years Ralph did not attend the Communion service. Beset by Pelagians and rationalists, by the lascivious and double-meaners, and by Papists, Jews, and playmasters, Dick could not find a proper house for the service, so it was held in the open air. H.E. attended and brought Arabanoo, and Ralph heard from Harry Brewer that there was a quarrel between H.E. and Dick over the native's suitability to receive the sacrament. H.E. won it by falling back on the reserves of civil power embodied in him, and so Arabanoo was vouchsafed the bread and wine. "The King," said Arabanoo as Dick passed him the cup.

CHAPTER 17

Judging the Perjurer

RALPH found himself named among the officers to sit on Nancy Turner's trial day when a runner from the Government House guard brought him the list. On receiving it, he went straight to Davy Collins's house on the other side of the stream.

"It could be said that I have a declarable interest," said Ralph, delighted to be able to flourish such a potent legal term.

"Oh yes," said Davy with a smile.

"Since I have worked so hard on her, getting her to a reasonable competence as Melinda, it could be said that I would not like to see her harmed or hanged. If she were acquitted, the convicts might think it was due to my vote, and that plays are greater considerations than the law."

"And aren't they, Ralph?" asked Davy, laughing. But then he grew thoughtful. "For God's sake, I have so many of those bastards refusing to serve. They feel that if they find Turner innocent, Robbie will write to the General of Division and drop shit on their careers."

It was a danger which had certainly occurred to Ralph.

"Please, will you serve? And I shall write a letter to the command in Plymouth, explaining how I gave you no choice."

"I do not want her to hang," said Ralph, thinking of her subtle mouth.

"Remember, Ralph," murmured Davy Collins, with that same blue-eyed intensity which had first deceived the natives into playing the word game, "that you have already aggrieved Major Ross by raising the woman to the status of actress. So you have nothing to lose by serving on the court."

F o R the day of the court, all playmaking had to be cancelled. Leaving his hut about nine that morning, after a poor breakfast of flour cakes seasoned with small fragments of bacon, Ralph heard a voice coming from the marquee. His stomach cramped and his skin prickled, since he thought it must be Mary Brenham and the Jew already at work on their epilogue. Since Brenham was the sort of woman who could be seduced by such a joint literary ambition, he gave in to the mean impulse to part the tent flap. He intended to tell them with a little severity that he had not expected them to be there, since rehearsals were not to happen that day. He would order Mary Brenham instead to do his ironing. He did not want her yet to be exposed to his unlaundered clothing, which carried the ambiguous stains of the long humid summer recently ended. John Wisehammer he would send with a note to Davy Collins. It would say he might not be at the courthouse till a little after ten and that he was sorry. Then of course he could arrive in time, claiming that what he had feared would delay him had not eventuated. For Mary Brenham's sake, he was driving himself to stratagems.

As soon as he was through the flap, he knew he was mistaken in expecting to find Mary and Wisehammer there. Curtis Brand, Harry Brewer's gardener and the player who had been doing Costar Pearmain and Bullock, lay heaving on top of Duckling. Her white thighs were absolutely visible, and it was clear from her barely suppressed hoots of enthusiasm that one of Harry's tenets about her —that she did not know how to enjoy a man—was here disproved.

"Oh Jesus," said Curtis, looking over his shoulder. He was instantly halted, rising to his knees, then rolling sideways off Duckling, dragging his calico breeches up over his red knob. Duckling, however, took her time to see Ralph, though she was better placed in physical terms to do so. She needed an interval to return from the distance which was legible in her eyes. Then she half sat, placing two fingers succulently in her mouth, and only lowering them when she became aware of the visitor. At that she pulled down her skirt to her knees.

By now Curtis was standing. He was expecting heavy treatment—he had been caught not by Harry, but worse still by Harry's friend.

"Does this happen often between the two of you?" Ralph asked quietly. Because to Ralph's eye they had somehow looked like lovers well used to each other.

"Sir," said Curtis, in fair imitation of the moaning and sawney Bullock, "it were a weakness. She asks me, and I don't be no monk, you know that."

"Do you hate Mr. Harry Brewer?" asked Ralph.

"No. Not old Harry."

"And I suppose it's that—the joke of having an older man's woman. A man who takes you out of the sawpits, where the work is fierce, into his garden, where you can make your own time. And then you nub his girl and tell your friends, and everyone laughs at poor knobbly Harry. That's it, you little bastard, isn't it? Take your pounders to Harry Brewer's woman! And if he discovers, he'll be too shamed to punish you."

He turned to Duckling, who was on the ground. He could not understand how Harry was engrossed by this sharp little girl with her joyless way of moving and her blank features. It had to be admitted that sometimes her face took on vivid movement—as when she was being Lucy and earlier, on the few social occasions Ralph had seen her drinking. These observations of her were the basis for his belief she might be an actress. But it was Harry's belief that simulation and acting might be her highest mode of existence.

"Do you want to kill poor dear Harry?" he asked her now, sounding even to himself like a line from a drama.

She reached forward and found one of her canvas shoes, and rose with it in her hand.

"It ain't me that's killing Harry, sir," she said. She was her old blank polite self now. "It's Private Baker's ghost."

"There's the truth, Mr. Clark," Curtis Brand said in a rush.

Ralph had to agree, amid his rage, that if you lived near Harry, you spoke of ghosts in this mundane and accepting way.

"And you see Baker, too?" Ralph asked.

"Maybe a glimpse, two or three times, I'd say," said Curtis Brand. "Remember, my hut is out across the garden. But I hear Harry arguing. Every bloody morning, an hour before the claxon."

"What does Harry say?"

"Sometimes he talks to it like it was a troublesome dog. Sometimes I hear him weeping, though you can't be sure he ain't laughing."

"He keeps his light on all night," Duckling supplied. "And some nights he ain't been sleeping at all, just lushing away."

"All night drinking brandy?"

"All night. Then he waddles out and starts arguing with it."

"And have you seen the phantom?"

"Not so much, except I know it's there."

"And what does it do?"

"It just grins, Mr. Harry Brewer says. It's got dumb insolence." It was a phrase she had picked up in the prisons, both those ashore and those at sea.

Ralph made Curtis Brand leave, sending after him a string of threats. He was to find his relief among the other she-lags, raged Ralph, ordering him to go back to his hut in Harry Brewer's garden. Left behind, Duckling did sway a little on her feet, as if she'd been deprived of sleep too long by Harry's visions and Private Baker's punctual phantasm.

"I will throw you out of the play," said Ralph.

"I like the play, Mr. Clark. Keep me in and I won't touch Curtis Brand."

"You enjoy men?"

"What, sir?"

"You enjoy men?"

"Some."

"But not Harry?"

"I like Harry better than any of them I enjoy. Better than Curtis."

"But not better than Goose."

"I don't always like being tied to that Goose."

"Strikes me you do," murmured Ralph.

"No," she said, looking away. "No."

He made his threats then to her. She was to remember Harry's kindnesses. She was not to go off with any of the men of the cast, especially and above all on the night of the great performance. He reminded her she lived on the far side of the stream and out of all the madness only because of Harry. She would *never* be there on her own merits.

She was already on her way out of the tent, to walk back to that safer side, when she told Ralph the larger news. "Mr. Brewer has this poison. Sometimes he takes it out and puts it beside his brandy bottle, so you wonder is he going to drink it after the next tot. I say to him, don't you drink any of that stuff, Mr. Brewer!"

"How do you know it's poison?"

"It's the same stuff," said Duckling, "my mother used to corpse my father."

D A V Y Collins had been forced to call on the astronomer, Will Dawes, to make up the court. Entering the courthouse, Ralph saw him sitting dolefully on the bench in his faded military jacket. Ralph knew that no one—other than Harry Brewer—abominated the passing of judgement more than William Dawes.

"We don't see you often, Will," Ralph remarked to him.

The astronomer looked at him with wide brown eyes which reminded Ralph of those of a pit pony dragged into the light.

"I regret I have been very busy, Ralph," he claimed. He was always at pains to explain why he avoided the company of his fellow officers in case they grew offended. He lowered his voice. "And you know I hate court work. It you have seen Venus cross the moon's face, what does it matter if Turner told a few lies? All might be liars here, but there . . ."—with a jerk of a thumb he gestured towards the roof of the courthouse and, by implication, to the be-starred reaches above—"there you find no lies!"

The charges had been written out by Davy Collins's secretary and placed before each chair on the bench. Ralph was astounded to read the list of witnesses in this perjury trial of Nancy Turner. There were only two. First was Captain Jemmy Campbell, who would in real terms be acting as prosecutor but refused to be called by such a name, thinking that if he took such a title on himself it would liberate Davy Collins to be no more than another lenient, negligent judge.

The second witness was John Caesar—Black Caesar—who with Meg Long had been Ralph's first auditioner for the play. Caesar's was the evidence with which Jemmy Campbell hoped to catch Nancy Turner. But there could be no less reputable witness than this man.

Reading down the trial list, Ralph saw further that Caesar was to appear later in the day with a Jamaican, accused of stealing food from the locksmith Frazer and from Frances Hart, the dressmaker and costumier, both of whom had built up a small extra margin of supplies, especially in liquor, from trading with customers.

The Scot Lieutenant Davey arrived behind Ralph and at once took his chair beside him on the bench. "A fair load of perjury today, gentlemen," he called. "Black Caesar to give us his canny observations on Turner's perjury, and then merrily perjuring himself when his own time to stand before us comes."

"Please," called Davy Collins, arriving in the back of the court. "Do not discuss the matters before they arise."

For some reason that made Lieutenant Davey laugh.

Ralph was shocked to see the Harry Brewer who now led Bill Parr, his constable, and Nancy Turner, his prisoner, into court. The face looked seamed and dropsical, and the eyes indeed haunted. He must be delivered, Ralph thought. He wished there was a priestlier priest than Dick Johnson available, someone who knew the ceremonies for the expulsion of demons. Wasn't there such a ceremony in the Book of Common Prayer? Hadn't Ralph once, bored at St. Bride's in London, found the Rite of Exorcism hidden away behind the Rite of Burial, teasing the imagination as the sacraments never could?

Harry Brewer sat on a bench at the back of the court as if his energies could not take him any farther. By contrast Jemmy Campbell, gusting in, swept all the way to the front, to the clerk's table, where he stood laying out like the plans of a city all the partisan correspondence between himself and Davy Collins, himself and H.E. Nancy Turner seemed to carry the iron cuffs on her wrists more lightly than Jemmy Campbell his letters and protests and appeals.

Finally Black Caesar was led in, wearing those terrible twenty-eight-pound anklets and holding the connecting chain against his stomach. Turner swiveled once in her seat to consider Black Caesar calmly. From the bench you would have thought it was Harry Brewer who had been listed for trial.

Davy Collins declared the court open, read the charge of perjury against Nancy Turner, and called on Captain Jemmy Campbell to step forward and make his case against her.

"I am not the maker of cases, sir," said Jemmy with a groan. "I am a witness. Will you kindly swear me in?"

He took the oath thunderously and so began.

"I must say first, Mr. Judge Advocate," Jemmy observed, "that it seems a contradiction of interest to have sitting on the bench an officer who has spent the past four weeks teaching the accused how to act certain lines in a poor farce and who must therefore—a reasonable man would say—hope the accusations against her will not be proven."

Davy considered this with his enormous calm. Ralph had no doubt the bullets of the Yankees had been deflected by it on the banks of the Charles River, just as Jemmy had survived that same battle by melting down the flying American lead with his white-hot ecstasy of resentment.

"I am very happy to say," Davy murmured, "that conflicts of interest do not disqualify an officer from sitting on this court. In such a small and fabulously distant jurisdiction, it would be impossible to find officers who did not—in a great variety of the cases we try—have some conflict of interest. All we can do is depend on Mr. Clark's probity as an officer, and since none of my fellow judges has cast any doubt on that, it is hardly a matter for a witness to decide."

Oh how that cool answer roiled in the bowels of Jemmy Campbell! You could hear it being gratefully absorbed with little groans.

Even so, Ralph heard with alarm the size of Jemmy's accusation against Nancy Turner. By the evidence of a number of the Marines who had recently plundered the stores, Nancy had knowingly received from Private Richard Dukes, one of those accused of the theft, a large quantity of provisions being property of this government. These included more than twenty pounds of pork, thirty pints of wine reserved for hospital use, and twelve pounds of flour.

Among those who claimed to have seen Turner receive goods from Private Dukes, said Jemmy, were Privates Luke Haines, Handy Baker, Jones, Brown, and Askey, all of whom were later hanged for their offences.

Dukes had sworn, said Jemmy Campbell, that he had neither been in any large way involved in the plot to steal government supplies, nor had he passed any to Nancy Turner. Turner, under oath, had made the same claim on behalf of her imperilled lover and herself. And it was the opinion of most members of the court that she was perjuring herself, largely for Dukes's sake. The court, of which he—Captain Campbell—had been a member, had very properly demanded that Turner be separated from the other witnesses so as not to vitiate them, and kept in custody while the question of her perjury was further looked into. Days after this decision, he had been shocked to discover that the convict Nancy Turner had not only *not* been detained, but was acting in a play!

Jemmy then read, with a poisonous lack of emphasis, his letters to Davy, Davy's to him, his to H.E., H.E.'s to him. Had oaths undergone a sea change? he asked. Did they have a discounted value in this barbarous place—was that the court's view? Was it the duty of a single officer to prosecute the Perjurer? Or would the court assume its true duty and prosecute the matter itself?

Jemmy then claimed he had, through his own questioning, discovered a witness to Nancy Turner's having with full knowledge received stolen goods, and he hoped the court would now swear in and adequately question this witness. He suggested this should be done before any oath were administered to Turner, since there was a presumptive certainty she would not speak the truth under oath and therefore the oath would once more be violated.

John Caesar was brought forward and took his oath. "By the

Fragrant One, the Fragrant One," he kept on repeating at the end of the standard oath.

"So that we know the value of your oath," said Davy, "could you tell me who is the Fragrant One."

"The Ruler of the Dead, sir. The son of Zanahary. Jesus Christ, sir."

"I suppose that will have to satisfy us," murmured Davy Collins to the other members of the bench. They nodded and looked at their hands. They did not want to lose themselves, this morning, in Caesar's cosmogony.

"Now, John," said Davy. "You say you saw Private Dukes pass goods, knowingly stolen, to Turner."

"That Dicky Dukes, he love Nancy Turner," said Caesar.

She was indeed someone's credible love, thought Ralph, and he felt a gust of dead Dukes's passion sweep across the courthouse, stirring Jemmy Campbell's angry letters.

"So he gave these goods to Turner for her favours?"

"He give more than you need give any mollisher. He love Nancy more 'an breath."

"And where did you see Private Dukes pass all these goods to Nancy Turner?"

"I see him bring this stuff to her at her house in the camp of the *femmes.*"

Jemmy asked when this was.

"It was the evening of the spears. You remember. *Les Indiennes.* When them *malheureuses* go off to Botany and come hoyin' back studded with the spears."

There was some discussion on the bench about the date of the spearing. Early March, said Ralph. In the end, Davy sent Bill Parr over to his residence to fetch his journal. Throughout the delay, Jemmy Campbell sat sideways in his chair, looking at the floor and shaking his head. This finickiness over dates, his manner said, was characteristic of the Judge Advocate and his dangerous attitudes.

The fetched journal showed that the date was March 6. Caesar said that that day love-struck Private Dukes had carried a poke, a canvas bag, which had contained bottles of hospital wine and enough pork to feed two men for a week. He had passed them to

Nancy Turner, who put them in a sea chest Dukes had bought her from a sailor on the *Prince of Wales* before it sailed away. Caesar said the chest was in the same hut as Amelia Levy, a girl who practised whoredom among the Marines and lags, and Caesar had himself been there with Amelia Levy when Nancy brought the stuff in. Dukes had built Nancy a large hut, which allowed her to rent out space, as she had done this time with Levy.

Davy asked John Caesar if he wasn't under a charge himself of having stolen food from the huts of the men who worked at the brick kilns.

John Caesar said it was so, except that every time *Les Indiennes*, the People of the Forest, crept into the encampment and stole things, the lags thought it was him, since he had dark skin too. "They see jest the Negro skin, sir, and what do they say? They say it must be that hungry cull, that Monsieur John Caesar."

Davy remarked that it was not necessary for him to defend himself yet. But had anyone said to him that there could be an advantage to him if he gave evidence against Nancy Turner?

"That Captain Campbell," said John Caesar, "he tell me it will help me if I say the truth about Dukes and Turner."

Jemmy Campbell was on his feet now. He had asked, he said, a number of Nancy Turner's associates if they had witnessed any exchange between her thieving lover and herself. Was this somehow improper? If John Caesar was himself ravenous as a locust, did this somehow cast doubt on what he had seen between Dukes and Turner? Was the Judge Advocate, and those who were still willing to sit on his court, so determined to dismiss evidences which he had through an energy—which should properly have been theirs—uncovered?

A number of the young officers on the bench—Lt. Davey and Faddy, the navigator Ball as well—began to mutter, "Oh God!" and "Christ, what pillocks!" Davy beat the table so everyone would remember his dignity. Ralph did not exclaim at all. He knew that if Nancy Turner were acquitted as a result of a loud and enthusiastic revelation by him he would begin to feature in the correspondence of Robbie Ross and Jemmy Campbell not merely as a fatuous playmaker but as an underminer of the holiness of oaths. So he reached for the pen which lay before him, dipped it in ink, and wrote on the court papers, "The 55th Company, Dukes among them, was at Rosehill on the day of the spearings." He passed his paper to Davy Collins, and after reading it, Davy sent for the orderly book, to find out whether Dukes had been sent down to Sydney by boat that day.

He had not been. He could *not* have been with Turner. Whatever Turner's part as a fence for stolen goods may have been, it was not the part which Jemmy Campbell's only witness, the Madagascan, said it was. By the noon claxon Turner was dismissed by the court.

As she was uncuffed and released to resume the part poor George Farquhar had so long ago prepared for her, Jemmy stood up at his table, made a baton of his correspondence, and brought it down on the wood with a thunderous whack. "This is a fatuous court. It is not worth pissing away one's evidence in front of it. I shall prepare a report for all the British newspapers. I shall make you all famed wee derelictors and traducers. If Jemmy Campbell can do anything to mar your careers, you can consider it from this day hence absolutely done. You have my richest contempt. And I welcome you to charge me with it. I will proclaim in any forum other than this that I spit you out of my mouth and piss on your pitiable procedures. Good day!"

Davy began to call him to order and to remind him of the laws of contempt, but Jemmy ignored him and stumped out to make his apoplectic report to Major Ross.

As it happened, there was nothing inexact about the evidence against John Caesar, who stood trial immediately after Nancy. So many of the brick kilns crew had seen him take their food; so many had seen him work it up into a dumpling and eat it at a sitting. He was sentenced to be sent to the outpost at Norfolk Island for the rest of his life.

The following night he stole the rifle of a Marine and vanished into the wilderness. Perhaps he hoped those he called the People of the Forest would honour the cast of his skin and feed him sumptuously and in perpetuity on kangaroo and iguana.

CHAPTER 18

Exorcising Handy Baker

HIS Melinda now safe from gallows or disabling punishments, Ralph crossed the stream to visit the Reverend Dick Johnson. He found him in his garden, hoeing placidly. His wife, wearing a large straw hat and looking tanned by the sun to an extent not common among the wives of ministers of the Established Church, worked with a pair of shears at a little peach tree. The Johnsons had brought it all the way with them in a tub from Rio and planted out in the small margin of less clayey soil on their side of the settlement. Mrs. Johnson waved the shears at Ralph—perhaps she was not associated with her husband in condemning the play. Perhaps the Reverend Dick—for fear of confessing to his own spouse his lack of power in this remote penal arrangement—had not shared his disquiet over Farquhar's earthiness with her.

The native child Booron, wearing a canvas dress, her features cruelly cavitied by healed smallpox, slept in the shade of an acacia bush.

Ralph had decided his appeals to Dick should be on the basis of friendship rather than official standing. "Dick, I must talk to you," he said. "It is a matter of horrific moment in which you must give me help."

Dick Johnson blinked. He was not used to being summoned in such terms. There were desperate souls in the new earth, but they did not know it, nor cry out in anguish for him. He stuck the blade of his hoe into a lump of clay and walked slowly to the sapling fence where Ralph stood.

"Harry Brewer is beset by a spirit," Ralph confided in him. "His convict girl tells me he has poison and may take it to be delivered of the ghost."

"Is it surprising, Ralph?" Dick Johnson asked. "Has there been since the cities of the plain a place like this?"

"Probably not," Ralph conceded, to get that debate out of the way. "You and I must go and see him this evening, when he is drinking and considering the poison. There is a rite for the expulsion of spirits."

"Do you think I am up to the weight of driving out a spirit?" asked Dick with a surprising grin.

"If you are proof against the seductions of plays, then perhaps you are equally proof against phantoms," said Ralph. "We may have to sit with him through the night. According to his girl, the spirit presents itself at dawn."

"Am I to sit in the house of concubinage?" asked Dick, but with strange resignation.

"It seems you already do," said Ralph. "That we all do. If I come here after supper, we can go to Harry's place together."

Dick didn't seem yet to be sure.

"Harry is not fornicating with her," said Ralph. It was merely a guess. "He has her there only for fear of being alone. Come on, Dick, be an honest friend!"

So after dinner Ralph fetched the Reverend Dick and they walked the few yards to the Provost Marshal's house. It was not yet winter in that country, and Ralph could see faces around a bonfire at the fishing camp and heard one robust laugh from Dabby Bryant. There was a light too inside Arabanoo's shack, which Bill Bradbury still shared. The Quarter Guard crunched past on their way to the convict camps on the other side of the stream. The air of early evening seemed, as always to Ralph, as full of energetic plans, of conspiracies and propositions, of half-stifled cries of hate, surmise, and expectation, as the air of any city. Yet this was only a city in the whimsical sense of the word, and it was no place. It was—as Harry had once said—the unexpected face of the other side of the moon. It was a demonstration of what Ralph believed—that the human spirit, which some thought of as angelic but which in fact might well be a dark and toadish thing, bloated itself to take advantage of available spaces. In Plymouth, Ralph thought, you often had the sense that people were breathing their souls in, tightening the belts of their spirits. Here they breathed out and out. They grabbed the square yardage of the night sky; they expanded beyond reason.

He was shocked at the Harry who answered their knock. In the cooling season, he smelt outrageously of sweat. There was a reek of barely digested brandy too, but that was to be expected. For Harry was a good bottleman. Duckling was indoors by the fire. As Dick and Ralph came in, she nodded for Ralph's benefit to Harry's uneaten dinner of beef dumpling and rice. Harry hooked her around the neck with his arm as she tried to vanish behind a canvas curtain to her bed. "Are you here on behalf of that Deity," Harry asked, "who damns the oldest midshipman in the fucking Royal Navy for lying joylessly beside a ruined child?"

Ralph suspected Dick might be about to say, "Yes."

"Your convict girl told me that Baker's ghost presents itself to you," said Ralph quickly.

"Oh Jesus," said Harry. "I have always seen the bastard. It doesn't matter."

"She says you have poison in mind," Ralph pursued. "Harry, we do not want you to drink poison. We all regard you with too much affection to take your notion calmly."

"Oh, I see," yelled Harry. He called to Duckling. "Do you tell all the players how the old man wants to drink poison?"

"She is frightened for you," said Ralph. "Even your gardener is concerned for you. I am frightened for you, and so is Dick."

It was probably a lie, since Dick was interested in people only in the context of immortal souls vulnerable to heresy. It was only a narrow span in which lovers and believers could breathe as far as Dick was concerned. But he *was* an ordained priest and could *adjure* spirits.

Harry turned to Duckling. "Go to your bed, my baby," he said.

This is his pet lamb, Ralph acknowledged, whom he first met

on a street in Soho and saw reprieved in Newgate. In his capacity as master of the lists for this convict fleet, he included her name. With the result that Curtis Brand could have her in my marquee.

"Then you must both drink with me," said Harry Brewer, getting a bottle and a few cracked cups out of his sea chest. "Oh God, it is good to have friends in the house."

He poured both Dick and Ralph his idea of a modest sup. He poured himself the idea of an immodest one, and then he sat to consider it.

"Where's the poison, Harry?" Ralph asked.

"Oh," said Harry. "It's nearby."

"And when can we expect to see Baker?"

"Oh Jesus! He'll be along. He'll be along."

"While we sit here," said Ralph, "why, Harry, can't you get our your poison so we can see it in the open?"

"Don't talk to me in that wheedling way, Ralph, not if you want to claim friendship."

Duckling's face appeared briefly at the green curtain separating the kitchen section of the house from the bed she shared with Harry Brewer.

"You aren't my favourite girl," Harry snarled at her. Ralph thought that if she had been close enough, Harry might have struck her. "Don't you go telling my thoughts to people, you little moll! Now should I drop dead of stroke, Dick will think it's poison and not bury me in church ground!"

"There is no church ground here," murmured Dick wearily.

Harry refilled his cracked cup from the bottle. "This is poison enough, this Dutch max they unloaded on us in Capetown. Drink it up, Father Dick. It will help your marriage!"

"I'll take it a little slowly, if you don't mind," said Dick Johnson tightly. "And if my unviolated and temperate marriage is to be mocked, Mr. Brewer, I wonder need I stay? After all, I do not mock your connection with that girl."

"You call it bloody concubinage, you turnip. You mock it! You damn it to God!"

"I did not impose the Commandments on humankind, Harry," said Dick.

"No, but you would have enjoyed it, and you would have bred Commandments out of your arse so that there be two hundred fifty of the bastards!"

"Harry!" called Ralph. "We can't have Dick insulted like this. He is here at my invitation. We can go, if you choose, and leave you to those ghosts of yours."

"No doubt you would run to H.E. and tell him I see spirits." Harry touched his cup. "And drink them too. I suppose you would tell H.E. his Provost Marshal is cracked as Black Caesar. I have no income other than from this post, and you two—with your terrible kindness—would do me out of it! That's the sort of friendship Harry Brewer doesn't require. Harry Brewer would rather be tarred and buggered than enjoy that sort of friendship. So go, go through the officer's mess telling how poor Harry talks to the shades, get Jemmy Campbell to write a letter to H.E. How Jemmy and Robbie would love to see me discharged from my post! I tell you, if I have to meet a parliament of ghosts every dawn, I still choose to be Provost Marshal, and only my kind friends can deprive me of it!"

Ralph had to pat Dick's arm and pacify him. Although he was used to being angry with the High Church and the Papists, his anger could also run fairly freely against ordinary people of no apparently heterodox view as well. At the same time, with gestures of the other hand, Ralph began to reassure Harry. The girl Duckling, he said, had spoken of the toxin because of her regard for Harry. He did not mention, of course, that it had dropped from her, like a handkerchief, as she shook off an extreme ardour produced in her by the gardener Curtis Brand. They, Ralph and Dick, would be repeating the news to no one. The Reverend Johnson had come here because the traditional power of a minister of the Established Church included the capacity to command spirits.

"But if you two go talking to other friends in confidence," Harry insisted, "Davy Collins will fall off the bench laughing at me. You must swear, the two of you."

"I do not take oaths lightly," said Dick. "You have my promise, however."

"And mine," said Ralph.

Harry considered them with his tormented eyes and drained his cup. "Well, Dick, have you ever driven out spirits before?"

"It is not a normal exercise for a man of religion," said Dick, half-appeased now.

"Don't you fear to do it?" asked Harry with a spirituous shudder.

"To fear it would be to doubt the power of my Saviour."

Harry began nodding as furiously as a child. "You're probably the right sort of priest to do it," he said, as if to himself.

"Why is that?" asked Dick, suspicious of this declaration of faith.

Harry imitated a West Country drawl. "Ah, thou haz a more certain faith than most fingerposts I've knowed."

"I will not take offence at such an observation," said Dick. "I pray it will always be so. We should prepare ourselves, however, with prayer and not with drinking."

"You deliver me," said Harry, "and I won't have reason to drink. Not in such volume anyhow."

Preparing himself now, Dick called on God to help this our troubled brother and to protect him from the intrusions of the Devil. Ralph was very pleased he did not find it necessary to make an issue about the brandy—he even drank a further cup and a half himself. Within his limits Johnson wasn't a bad fellow, and he would certainly be hell on a ghost.

"I am not a godless person, by the way," Harry then found it necessary to say in a lull in Dick's prayers. "I know you cannot countenance my attachment to the child there." He signalled with his thumb over his shoulder towards the curtain. "But even in my disordered youth, when courting her in Newgate prison, I was not blind, Dick, to the graciousness and the hope which religion lent to our culpable lives. No, I am not joking, Ralph; no smile there please. You have both been generous and friendly to me, and I shall be generous and friendly back. Do you know the chapel inside the gatehouse at Newgate? Oh, I used to go there all the time. I went there after Duckling was condemned too. You climb to the gallery, and you sit looking down on the pews full of warders and leg-ironed lags. It's the sort of place which attracts a particular kind of young man, and I was once that sort of young man, Dick, as I confess freely to you. In the middle of the chancel at the chapel of Newgate is a shoulder-high pen where those under sentence of death sit—the child sat there once, it was awesome to behold her there. For they sit round a table so weighed with chain they are exempt from the normal movements of worship. And in case their condition is not obvious to them a cheap coffin stands, with its lid a little way ajar—it always looked to me as if someone had just escaped from it—right in the middle of their table. It promised certain death, Dick, but also the chance of resurrection. I used to look down on the mob caps of the condemned women when I was young, all of them spaced around that coffin. I wanted to see inside their heads and their apprehensions, but I never did. But how august was divine service in their presence! So I hung over the balustrade with spotty young surgeons from St. Bartholomew's, who were as besotted with criminality as I was and as intrigued by the awful death which hung over all those mob caps. Have you ever taken the last services at Newgate, Dick?"

Dick said he had taken them once when he went there in the company of a certain renowned Mr. Wilberforce.

"Oh, the improver of prisons," murmured Harry dismissively. "Well, you no doubt found it edifying. I can see from your point of view I should have left it at looking down on Duckling from the gallery. But when she was reprieved, it was on condition of trans-portation to Africa for life—they were thinking of Africa then, you see. Thank sweet Christ they never put *that* to law. Then when George Rose—that's the Captain's neighbour in Lyndhurst—got the Captain appointed to control of this circus, I was in our little space at the Admiralty, which H.E. and I shared, when the lists of prisoners for the fleet began to pile up. A list arrived from the Surrey County gaol in Horsemonger Lane, from Marshalsea, a long one from Newgate. Another from Hereford, and even the gaol governors of the city of Oxford hopefully sent in some names. Duckling wasn't on the Newgate list; shitty Meg Long was there, as you'd expect. But Duckling, the redeemable Duckling, did not appear under her most common alias on the list from Newgate. I thought of speaking to the Captain about this, but did not know how to frame it—H.E. is so austere when it comes to women. So in the end, damning the risk, as if I were still a boy stealing petty cash from the merchant I worked for, I crossed out a woman called Dyer and wrote in Duckling's name. Then I went out into the corridor, called a messenger, and ordered him to take the list to the Home Secretary to be signed for approval."

Harry drank lingeringly, his eyes moist with the memory of that exercise of power. Clearly, he considered that that was what had broken the banked-up waters of his stale career and that the tide of modest power had then turned and flowed into his hands.

"You think I am guilty of concubinage," he accused Dick. "I ask you what manner of life she'd be leading now, over in the women's camp, if it were not for me?"

Dick moved in his chair. "Harry, I would be pleased to tell you otherwise. But it does not do to argue according to the good effect of an act which is, by its nature, vitiated."

"Oh, Jesus," said Harry. "A philosopher."

"I would be more comfortable," said Dick, suddenly shivering, "driving spirits from a house that was properly established."

"Jesus, little friend," said Harry, after taking thought. "Put up with me and deliver me as I am."

Harry grew sleepy in the end. He spread two cloaks by the fire for them, and a third for himself. "You will not see Baker before first light," he said, lying down on the cloak closest to Duckling's bed and going wheezily into an untidy slumber. Ralph and Dick found it harder to sleep. Dick lay on his back, Ralph noticed, his arms crossed over his chest, proof against the early arrival of phantoms. It was cold on the floor, on the clay under which Ralph could, with a little recklessness of thought, feel the spirits moving.

He tried to picture Betsey Alicia, but could barely remember her face. He had a guilty sense that she was becoming one woman with Mary Brenham the clothes thief.

A s he waited for sleep, Ralph felt his mind shrink to the size of a coal. But the more it diminished, the more the vigour dropped out of his thoughts, the more that central coal glared and rankled. He could hear Dick Johnson snuffling beside Harry—the just and the unjust united in the same rasping and slovenly breath. He was entertained for a little time by wondering if Duckling would sneak to the gardener's hut, but was distracted from that speculation by waking and wide-eyed terrors for his son, Ralphie. It took so little for children to vanish in married quarters—an afternoon fever could grow and consume them overnight. That was a *known*, from which no Cornish witch could deliver you. Beside it, he felt little terror at the idea of facing Private Baker.

At last he fell into an unhappy sleep.

When he woke, everyone was on his feet—Harry, Dick, Duckling in her nightdress. Ralph had a clear vision of Private Handy Baker with his reckless blue eyes and olive poacher's complexion, standing by the door. In that clarity of first awakening Ralph heard the words spoken, "Not the right key, Harry Brewer."

"Damn you!" Harry was yelling to no one. "Damn you! Damn you!"

The apparition was gone, and Dick seemed not to have seen it anyhow, for he was calling, "Where is the thing, Harry? Where?"

Harry ran to the door and threw it open. "You see him," called Harry pitiably, pointing to a shadow among the eucalypts, which were an impalpable blue in the first light.

Dick tore the *Book of Common Prayer* out of his pocket and found the place. "I adjure you, spirit of Satan, in the name of Jesus Christ our Lord to return to the pit whence you came . . ."

Harry grabbed his own throat and, over a protruding tongue, began to froth. He struggled with his neck to such an extent that Ralph saw a bruise appear there. All the energy was Harry's—there was nothing in the dawn now, Ralph could see that. Then Harry collided with the wall and was pinned there, contending still with himself. Ralph reached for him, but his hand was struck away. With a short but galvanising scream Harry fell to the ground, his legs drew up and back two or three times, and then he lay still with his tongue emerging from his lips like a tranquil serpent from its hole.

"Oh, God!" said Dick. "He has suffered a seizure!"

Ralph called one of the guards from Government House and they went haring off to get Johnny White, the only surgeon who on this bibulous star could be trusted to look upon apoplexy at dawn.

PART FOUR

CHAPTER 19

Letters

IN the days Harry lay unconscious, Ralph had time to reflect on how potent Handy Baker had been, taking Duckling away in the first place, and then somehow continuing that tyranny over Harry's spirit. Harry had lived through a career as a thieving clerk, through the demi-profession of an existence as the world's oldest midshipman. It could not be predicted whether he would live on in this more exalted stature of Provost Marshal of a space vaster than all the Russias. Surgeon Johnny White could not predict when or whether he would wake; and if he did, then certain sections of his face and his body would surely be paralysed.

At the playmaking in the clearing, Nancy Turner, delivered from the threat of death or flogging, was no more or less composed than ever she had been in the part of Melinda. Brenham and Wisehammer, bound together by the conspiracy of their epilogue, continued excellent.

From the clearing one afternoon, during a lapse in the reading, Ralph saw the dreamlike progress of a ship through the heads of the harbour—three masts and sails set for mild south-easter.

"Oh," he said to his players, "look. Quickly!" Children were already beginning to spill from the Marine and the convict camps. Until that second Ralph had without knowing it resigned himself to being the inhabitant of an enormous harbour into which no ships came—to the staleness of that. So, he was sure, had everyone else—locked in time and, as the lags said, doing it.

As the ship drew closer you could tell she was stricken, digging her nose into the sea and tossing it back like a terrier tossing gravel. Her figurehead of the Duke of Berwick was much disfigured but identifiable. It was the *Sirius*.

Last October H.E. had sent her off to Capetown to get flour and medicine. Now she was back, holding what delicacies no one knew. And by her presence in this unknown world, she proved the existence of the known one.

From all points of the convict city boats put out to the *Sirius*. Ralph saw a boat start out from H.E.'s place across the stream. Arabanoo in his tricorn and white breeches could be seen in its bows—H.E.'s standing favourite, as Ralph thought of him.

Ralph instantly suspended the play readings. Large Captain Plume/Henry Kable was anxious to go and celebrate the apparition of the *Sirius* with his wife, Susannah. Ralph went down to the landing to try to find a place in one of the cutters travelling out to the ship. Succeeding, he was on board within a few minutes.

The deck of the *Sirius* had been divided up into cattle and sheep pens, leaving only enough room for the sailors to find their way around the deck to the shrouds. The ship was a floating cattle market in which the stock were disturbed by the jubilance of the crew and the visitors piling aboard. Arabanoo now stood by the base of the main mast, absolutely stunned at the sight of the pens full of restless Cape sheep with the smell of land in their nostrils— the false expectation of sweet grass.

Ralph called to an officer he knew. "How is the Cape?" He was too ashamed to ask, "Is it still there?" But that was the burden of the question.

"They are still breaking people on the wheel there," the officer told him, referring to the punishments the Dutch imposed on their criminals. Ralph felt a tremor pass through him when he heard H.E. murmuring to Johnny Hunter, his old friend and Scots captain of the *Sirius*, "Harry Brewer has suffered a stroke. Johnny White doesn't expect him to live."

The officer Ralph was speaking to showed merely an appropriate but perfunctory grief for Harry. He was a boy of about twenty-four. His name was Daniel Southwell, and under the exigencies of all this distant travel he had already leapt from the rank of midshipman to that of mate. He was the sort of man Watkin and Davy Collins were—a keeper of journals—and in that spirit had plenty of news for Ralph. First, the *Sirius* had gone round the globe—from Capetown, it had returned to New South Wales by the Horn and the Pacific. And it was remarkable, Southwell thought, that it was only on nearing the shores of this last place in the universe that the figurehead had been torn from the cutwater in an almighty gale of wind, and the seas had shocked the timbers.

"And what it shows," said Southwell, "is that this place is surrounded by such turbulence that there is a good argument it was never meant to be approached by the civilised."

In Capetown, Southwell had picked up the political news from newspapers left behind by a whaler. "Your old place of service, Ralph," he said, "the Netherlands. The mob tried to get rid of the King, or as they call him, the Stadtholder, William the Fifth. And the King of Prussia wouldn't stand for having his sister—who as you know is the rather unequally potent spouse of the Dutch king —put to any such threat. So he marched in, and *we* sent a regiment or two. The French wanted to resist us for interfering, but they spent so much on thwarting us with those damned Americans they can't afford it anymore. It is said that France is full of starving mobs. Perhaps we are fortunate to be here with a mob of the Home Secretary's devising."

Ralph remembered the time in The Hague when the horse-faced young queen, Wilhelmina of Prussia, had reviewed his guard of Dutch peasants. A rigorous visage atop a strong little body, itself infused with a most bellicose soul. If her brother the King of Prussia had any such stuff in him, it was no wonder he sent the Prussian army into the Low Countries to acquit the insult she had suffered.

"There's talk that our King went mad, too, at last," confided Southwell, "and not without being provoked by his children, let me say. He thought he was a tree . . . Yes, it's the truth. Yet when people were despairing and bishops were praying for him and all the rest, he got better. In a day, it's said. Robust and capable just one day after his mind was all in a crazy sprawl!"

This, Ralph reminded himself, was the monarch for whose birthday celebrations he and his players were working. It was, Ralph thought in a remote and detached way, better to labour for a sane king than mad Lear.

The next item of news struck Ralph more intimately. The Dutch in the East Indies post of Batavia had told Southwell that the *Friendship*, the ship in which Ralph had lived aft of the slatterns in the forrard hold, above the male lags—the ship which had been his town and his farm and his parish, in which he had swung dreaming his perfect and horrifying dreams of Alicia; whose bilges had grown so sour towards the end of the journey that he had not dared open her cameo for fear it would immediately grow a beard of mould; in which he had a fight with Lieutenant Faddy and argued with drunken Captain Meredith and toasted Alicia's birthday and wept as he read *The Tragedy of Lady Jane Grey;* at the bottom of whose after-companionway the orange trees bought in Rio had withered; on whose penned decks the Cape sheep had died of cold on the long and hectic race through the Southern Ocean; which had carried, jostling in the hold, the separate criminalities of Liz Barber and Liz Dudgeon, which had carried Kable's wife, Susannah, and Kable too, deep into the time of their sentences, time marked and appeased as they fumbled for each other through the bulkhead—*that* ship, the *Friendship*, cancelled of all its reckless human meaning, lay on a bath-warm seabed. Sharks nuzzled the cot where visions of Alicia had held Ralph in tyranny. It was as incredible as knowing that Plymouth or a whole country had fallen into the sea.

Southwell gave the details. The emptied convict transports, the *Friendship*, the *Prince of Wales*, the *Alexander*, had taken five months to reach Batavia in Java. Among all the love-sick sailors, and from Captains Sinclair and Frank Walton, there must have been much carelessness in diet. Because after the *Friendship* and the *Alexander* sailed from Batavia to head north, leaving seventeen of their seamen in graves in that Dutch port, scurvy had become so notable among the crews it was impossible to navigate both vessels against the strong contrary currents and the western monsoon. Off the coast of Borneo, Frank Walton of the *Friendship* had shifted all his men and stores aboard the *Alexander*—there were not enough healthy people to work both ships—and his own ship had been scuttled. Ralph had an image of the froth and rind of his dreams rising from the wreck and floating neglected in that equatorial sea.

The *Alexander,* itself defeated by current and wind, had then made slow way back to Batavia, and when it arrived there hardly a man was left fit enough to work above deck.

"Without H.E. to direct them all," Ralph found himself saying with passion, "the proper procedures don't get themselves followed out on board. Damn that Duncan Sinclair and damn old Frank. They are both indolent buggers at the heart of it and drunk for most of their working day. If we're ever to go back from here to where we came from—and it's something I often wonder about— we need men of some moral bowels to take us."

Yet he knew that when his three years were finished, he might be put on any ship that arrived, without regard to the fibre of its captain.

"I am not surprised, Ralph," said Southwell. "The crews were utterly slackened by too much nubbing with the convict women. But listen, we are carrying mail for you—it was waiting at the Cape."

Ralph had become so accustomed to the conditions of this new existence that when he had seen the *Sirius* he had not even thought of mail. Now the chance of a letter from Betsey Alicia nearly swept his legs from under him. He excused himself from Southwell and went aft to find the *Sirius* surgeon, who had charge of the mails. As he came to the aft companionway he saw Arabanoo stagger along the half deck and lean swaying out over the harbour. H.E. and Johnny Hunter, Captain of *Sirius,* retrieved him and sat him down against the gunn'ls. It looked to Ralph as if Arabanoo had had too much of "the King."

Ralph found the surgeon at last, a musical young man who had brought a piano with him with the convict fleet and had often accompanied that honeyed Irish tenor and tooth-puller Dennis Considen on it. Ralph made a little polite talk with him. The surgeon too had been shaken, as had the structure of the ship, by the recent storm. "It was as absolute, Ralph," he said, "as anything in the Bible or Shakespeare. It was bloody awesome. I have two letters for you, in fact."

Ralph suppressed an impulse to embrace him. If there were only one letter, it could as well be from his business agent in Plymouth, Broderick Hartwell, as from Betsey Alicia. But if there were two, one *had* to be from his wife, as difficult as she found it to place words down on paper, a single letter being the work of a week.

The surgeon fetched the letters, both wrapped in sealskin to protect them from the many onboard seas they had encountered on their long transit. The tenderness and care of those sealskin wrappings prickled Ralph's eyes.

He unwrapped the larger of the two sealskin parcels—he was sure it would be the one from his agent. Inside, the paper was bearded with a blue green mould. The humid seas off West Africa had caused it to grow there, and all the turbulence and freezing of the Southern Ocean had not killed it.

The letter, however, was not from his agent Hartwell but from his best friend, George Kempster, a Marine officer of genuine and independent fortune. He was touched that Kempster should write, but he wondered could it mean that the other, smaller letter was from Broderick Hartwell, and that Betsey Alicia had not yet been able to summon up her chancy literacy. So he opened the second sealskin envelope and found on it her childish handwriting, obscured only in part by the same blue-green mould which had attacked the correspondence from Kempster.

The reality of his wife's existence, which he had come increasingly to doubt since he received the mercies of Mrs. Bryant, fell on him now with such stunning force that he wondered whether he would have to be aligned against the gunn'ls with Arabanoo. "Are you well, Ralph?" he heard Southwell call.

"Yes," called Ralph, from what seemed to him a distance. But he did not hold up by way of explanation his wife's childish calligraphy. He saw that H.E. was helping Arabanoo across the gundeck toward the longboat which would take them ashore. There was something shamefully servile about H.E., as if he were a civil official overlooking the drunkenness of a mayor. Ralph hurried to join them. He wanted to take his letters ashore. It seemed indecent to open them on this crowded deck. He could read them, he thought, on the long walk back from the government pier to his own hut on the west side of the bay.

A coxswain helped drape Arabanoo in the bows. H.E. sat beside the prone native and leaned over the body so closely to inspect Arabanoo's glistening face. His posture was for a second so like that of a lover leaning over a lover that Ralph, settling himself more or less amidships, saw the oarsmen smirk.

"He had only a little brandy," H.E. said to Ralph, as if to excuse the Indian. "I hope it is nothing else."

On the excursions Ralph had shared with H.E. into the wilderness, the pain in H.E.'s side had always flared, impinging on his sleep and appetite. Ralph now saw H.E. favour his right side as once again he leaned over to inspect the native. Arabanoo's eyes opened. There was a snorting noise from him and a spurt of bile and other rank liquid from his mouth. The oarsmen crinkled their noses.

"Something is wrong with the boy," said H.E. to Ralph.

With the sort of awesome humility which had once permitted him to make Harry Brewer his familiar, he began to dab at the puke with a handkerchief. It reminded Ralph of an archbishop washing the feet of poor men on Maundy Thursday, except H.E.'s was not a mere ritual kindness. When he had finished, H.E. held the stained handkerchief still, balled in his right hand. There was no archdeacon he could hand it to.

Arabanoo spoke a plaintive sentence in the native tongue and went to sleep again. H.E. picked up Arabanoo's petty officer's hat from the bottom of the boat and held it a little above the native's face, to protect the wide open features from the sun and the mockery of the sailors. Again there was that strange foreign delicacy of movement and gesture.

"Letters from home, Ralph?" he asked, still keeping Arabanoo's hat suspended in mid-breeze.

Ralph explained—one from his wife and another from his friend Kempster. He was expecting one from his agent as well, but oh the long sea mileages and chancy connections by which correspondence found its way!

H.E. agreed. He said that at Capetown news had been waiting

for Johnny Hunter that the Admiralty had put out tenders for a second convict and supply fleet, but that they had been waiting for the latest dispatches from H.E. before sending them off. "Wagering men could run a sweep on the month and day relief will pitch up here." Next H.E. honoured him with numbers. "From the *Sirius* in any case we have 127,000 pounds weight of flour, Ralph. Dependent on the rate of deaths, it is adequate for four or five months of full rationing. And the ship itself has supplies for twelve months, so *they* are off the stores."

He gestured stiffly with the wadded handkerchief in the direction of the receding *Sirius*.

It was one of the things Robbie Ross found offensive about H.E.—that he gave equal rations to all, to Robbie as to the she-lags, to the shifty St. Giles boys as to the few competent farmers who worked at H.E.'s wheat planting.

Certain luxuries Ralph had placed an order for with Lieutenant Southwell to bring from Capetown would be landed in the next day or so—tea and sugar, smoked ham and preserves. But even with the prospect of restored plenty, Ralph could think only of the letters in their sealskin and tropic mould.

H.E. had sailors carry Arabanoo up to the house in a chair. Ralph congratulated the distracted viceroy over the return of the ship and the rumor of King George's illness and recovery, and went walking past poor Harry Brewer's place and Dick Johnson's toward the stream.

He sat on a ledge of sandstone still on H.E.'s side of town and opened Kempster's letter. He knew now what he expected from it —news of Caroline Kempster's death. For before Bryant had delivered him of his well-built dreams, he had enountered in one of them Mrs. Kempster, a dark-haired girl of about twenty-four years, a woman who resembled Nancy Turner the Perjurer but with a more banked and orderly spirit in her eyes. She and Kempster's mother appeared frequently in the dreams which had beset Ralph during the long passage to New South Wales. She was more pallid in the dreams, a more ceremonious Mrs. George Kempster than ever she had been in the Stonehouse barracks. Ralph had no doubt that as a symbol in his dreams she stood somehow for sickness and mourning, whereas in the real world she stood for laughter, a quick tongue, and great domestic competence. She could breeze through the married quarters, sustaining more tremulous wives, chattering away without malice while left-handedly she attended to this or that fragile wife. Stonehouse Caroline Kempster had good colour and ate well—Mrs. George Kempster Senior sent hams and apples and diced fruits in jars to her son and daughter-in-law. But dream Caroline Kempster was a pole away.

It had been in the last days of the voyage, when the bilges had turned sour and the air in his cabin seemed yellow, that he had dreamed of young Mrs. George Kempster's death. It had been like this. He had fetched her from the door of Mrs. Kempster Senior's house at Yelverton—there had been no quick laughter, no half-comic offer to wipe the snot from Ralph Junior's face. He knew how he had been elected to hand Mrs. Kempster Junior down these graceful stairs, for at the start of the dream he had been engaged in a horse race between himself on a chestnut and Betsey Alicia's brother Matthew on a white horse. It was because he had outridden Matthew that he now had the stature to be here and to have the sombre, dream Mrs. Kempster on his elbow.

When he got to the base of the stairs, a coach drawn by six black horses was waiting. Ralph was aware that when most people dreamed of coaches, they did not take account of whether they were manned or unmanned, whether there were other passengers or not, unless there were faces they recognised which presented themselves. Ralph was so stricken with dreams, however, that he did take account of such things. The driver's seat, as precisely tooled as a driver's seat on the Plymouth Mail, was empty.

He handed Mrs. Kempster into the interior of the coach, very perturbed for her but knowing he could not travel at her side.

That dream of the riderless carriage and six black horses was now some sixteen months past, but he feared the letter he held in his hands would confirm its potency.

After a time devoted to doubt and trembling, he unsealed the message. Part of its bulk was accounted for by an enclosure, which fell to the ground and which Ralph now picked up. It was headed:

Pay Office, Plymouth, December 1st, 1788

It continued:

Sir,

It is with very great concern I acquaint you of the death of
our late valuable friend Mr. Broderick Hartwell on the 18th of
last month. His Executors feel very much for the distress Mrs.
Clark might experience from this unhappy event if they called
in the moneys advanced to said Mrs. Clark by Broderick Hartwell against the guarantees you signed for him before your de-
parture from this country. I fully understand that this is a normal
arrangement for officers who are to serve in remote places, than
which there is no more remoter than the land in which you
presently find yourself. Mr. Hartwell's Executors are therefore
willing to continue to furnish Mrs. Clark with money, waiting
for their reimbursement till the return of the Letter of Attorney
enclosed herein, a letter which we conclude you will readily
execute and send by the first conveyance either to Mr. George
Hartwell, your late agent's brother, care of the Navy Office, or
to myself, we being joint Executors to the deceased.

You are debtor to the late Mr. Hartwell for seventy-six
pounds, eleven and sixpence, and as we continue to supply Mrs.
Clark, we take it for granted no further Bank Drafts of yours
will appear.

I am Sir, your most obedient servant,
Thomas Wolridge

R A L P H felt a wave of that strange sickening impotence which
comes from being not only in debt, but moons removed from the
site where something could be done about it. There was also that
itch of the blood when someone you had cherished and held intimately, Mrs. Betsey Alicia Clark, had to the date of Hartwell's
death somehow exceeded reasonable spending of forty pounds over
two years by some thirty-six pounds eleven and sixpence.

Broderick had been a man about fifty, a reasonable, plump
man who would tend to indulge Betsey Alicia if she made special

appeals. He had had a younger and leaner brother whom Ralph had sometimes spotted moving with a frown through the offices the Hartwell brothers shared in Gibbonfields. Ralph knew he should have taken better notice of this younger brother, since Broderick Hartwell's death had put the Clarks under his management.

Ralph had to bite the webbing between thumb and forefinger to absorb the irony. At this penal reach of the universe there *was* no real entity called money. Money was Liz Barber's thighs. Money was wine, money was spirits. Money was the flour Black Caesar had absconded with. Money was edible, potable, solid. Whereas a sum like seventy-six pounds, eleven shillings and sixpence, seemed a chimera.

> ". . . as we continue to supply Mrs. Clark we take it for granted no further Bank Drafts of yours will appear."

He had given Lieutenant Southwell of the *Sirius* a ten-pound bank draft to make purchases at the Cape. That would have to be added to his debt to the estate of Broderick Hartwell, and no doubt frowning George Hartwell, not understanding the disturbances and the lapses of time under which Ralph Clark laboured, would be aggrieved when this further claim turned up on his desk.

The Power of Attorney allowing Wolridge and Hartwell to collect his pay against the debts had to be signed by two witnesses as well as by himself. He regretted poor Harry's stroke, for Harry would sign it without making judgments about the size of the debt. Knowing of Ralph's modest income, his brother officers could not but raise an eyebrow when witnessing the document. Perhaps he could get Lieutenant Faddy or Captain Meredith to sign it when they were far into their night's liquor. But even under liquor, Faddy had an eye for a figure like that, for a detail out of which jokes and mockeries could be constructed.

(At last, one evening when he dined aboard, he would slip the document first in front of Lieutenant Poulsen and then in front of the surgeon from *Sirius*, and they would both—to his joy—sign it in a cavalier way, without bothering to read it. It seemed that many officers in the place had received legal documents of various kinds from home, and there was a brotherly tradition that you witnessed them without prying into their contents.)

He opened Kempster's letter. News of Hartwell's death had dulled the expectation of Mrs. Kempster's. And certainly Kempster gave in the letter no indication that he was widowed. His main news was also about Hartwell's death.

Stonehouse, December 1st, 1788

Dear Clark,

I hope you received my last letter which I sent to Portsmouth when your strange expedition was there on the eve of throwing itself into the void. I have undertaken to enclose letters for a Mr. Thomas Wolridge, and the purpose of those letters are clear.

Your wife and boy are both well, but by your agent Hartwell's death she is thrown on the mercy of his brother, who takes to Hartwell's affairs and has reduced her allowance to twenty pounds per annum. Do not let that make you uneasy, as hitherto she has contrived to keep out of debt. But what money she will want I will be her banker for, and you must pay me when you come home—this you will keep to yourself as not any person here knows it. To be poor and to appear so is the worst of all evils and therefore I advised her to keep our arrangement to herself.

The dear woman is well and your son, Ralph, recovered from a short but fierce fever. We are taking them with us to Yelverton to spend Christmas—please do not be concerned, they will travel in my mother's covered carriage. All we would need for utter happiness, my dear Ralph, is your delightful company and your funny and serious whimsicality when you have brandy in you.

Mrs. Kempster sends her warmest best wishes. No doubt the ship which bears this will bring fresher news than I can give you here.

However, I should suppose Hartwell's death will be one advantage to you—it will save the nine pounds a year which he paid for insuring your life and then charged to you.

They are forming a second convict fleet and have recruited a new corps for the security of that distant New South Wales. Our old friend Nepean has decided to join it as the eldest captain. I am told you will all be offered Commissions in it— you may all, including our friend Major Robbie, have changed your minds about New South Wales and be now declaring it a decent human habitation. I know not whether it will be advisable for any of you to go into this Corps—you will get an immediate step up in rank, of course, but the question is, will not that be the last promotion you are to look for, unless you can purchase one, which except in the event of Betsey Alicia inheriting her father's estate would seem—forgive me for saying so, dear Ralph—not likely?

Be assured I shall be always willing to serve you and am your sincere friend.

> Lieutenant Quartermaster Kempster,
> Marines, Stonehouse,
> Plymouth

R A L P H was not abashed to find his prophetic dreams of Mrs. Kempster portended nothing. It was not the first time he had dreamed things which should have spelt tragedy but which had not. A dream ran like a fuse toward the final deaths of the players of the dream, but the fuse in Mrs. Kempster's case might run for forty or fifty years, since as everyone knew time was suspended in sleep.

What Ralph took from the letter was therefore not a sense of thwarted vision but a rich sensation of gratitude to Kempster. He would manage Betsey Alicia's business for her. In the most unintruding way, he would have Mrs. Kempster watch Betsey Alicia for extravagance. He wanted to write glowingly to Kempster, but that had to await a ship, and the frustration of not being able to state his thanks was nearly as great as his earlier sense of monetary powerlessness.

Now he opened the letter from Betsey Alicia. As in the case of the Kempster letter, mould had tried but not succeeded in devouring the handwriting. This triumph of good will (together with certain legal documents) over equatorial forces of improbable heat and air moisture struck him again as a savoury and wonderful victory.

Plymouth, December 3, 1788

My dearest Ralph,

How I miss you and what awful dreams I have!

Ralph was pleased in a way that she had not delivered of them, as he had.

> I dreamed we were in Midlothian at your Aunt Hawkings and I saw you looking in at me through a Haberdasher's window, but you did not know who I was. When I chased you to explain, you ran away through the streets.

Betsey Alicia and Ralph always began their letters with dreams, and now it was a habit from which he had been broken, he looked forward to breaking her of it.

> As you know, Mr. Hartwell has died, but though those who manage his business have been very kind, I have been happy to institute certain economies. You will be proud of me, my Ralph. I go to the Union Road markets in the late afternoon when the price of things has fallen and the butchers and grocers are getting anxious. It is quite a game, and Ralphie and I both quite enjoy it so that I do not want you to feel your normal melancholy on the matter.
>
> The same week Mr. Hartwell died Ralphie had a flux, and I was for a few days tormented by the fear that it could not be reversed. Thank God it has been, and he is a boy of spirit again. The Mercers' twelve-year-old boy Philip has gone as a midshipman aboard the ship *Intrepid.* Ralphie has been speaking of nothing else since, which as you know does not too much please me, since I would prefer a life for him other than at sea.
>
> Kempster and Captain Nepean have filled me with news that they are recruiting a new Corps specially for that far off place. Nepean says if you joined that Corps you would go

straight to Captain, Ralph. But I must plead with you that I do not want to live among those awful felons. George Kempster says you would get to Captain but not beyond, and I hope you will take his advice, my love.

We are off to Mrs. Kempster's place at Yelverton for Christmas, and shall have a happy, warm time around that great fireplace Mrs. Kempster keeps in the main hall. Indeed it is as big as our two little rooms here in married quarters. We will all much toast you, and I shall shed my tears.

Missing you, I have been driven to make a verse. I have folded it and put it in this letter.

> Believe me your most loving wife,
> Betsey Alicia

Ralph found the little wedge of poetry, folded four ways. Unwrapping it, he read:

> Written by Mrs. Clark on her husband's birthday.
> May each Returning Year in Pleasure bring
> The glory of his Country and his King.
> May Angels guard his peaceful home with Care,
> Conjugal happiness be always there.
> Forgive oh God the follies of his youth,
> Mould his heart in piety and truth,
> And when Thou callest him to the Realms of Bliss,
> Oh take me too, I am but Thine and his.
> Signed Alicia

R A L P H was disarmed and unstrung by the sweetness of the verse, though his joy was diminished by two aspects of both verse and letter. One was the blanket refusal to join him at this limit of space, this geographic test of devotion. He could imagine perhaps Mrs. Kempster writing to George in the same situation and saying that although she would not *like* to spend all her life in a distant penal nation, she would follow him if that was his choice.

Ralph did not in any case want to remain here, even with a captaincy ensured. But he wished Betsey Alicia had had the wit to make the offer while at the same time conveying she would prefer it was not taken up.

Then, in the verse, the reference to the "follies of his youth." He had at the beginning of their engagement confessed to her a few modest whorings. Yet she liked to cast him sometimes as if he were a rescued hellrake, and so she did even in this verse.

So, in half an hour, reading letters by the stream which divided the convict city in two, Ralph experienced a fast rate of disillusionment with his divine spouse. Mr. Hartwell's executors had begun it by pointing to her mild extravagance. These signs of fallibility in Betsey Alicia surprisingly did not disappoint him. But she had, through her letters and her spending, suddenly lifted from him the burden of frantic adoration. "They change while you're at sea," his friend Oldfield told him once, and it was exactly so. With all that time on their own, said Oldfield, they become more careful of their comforts than most wives have time to be.

He folded the letters and crossed the stream. In his clearing Ketch Freeman the hangman paced alone, reciting lines. "Was ever man so imposed upon! I had a promise, indeed, that she would never dispose of herself without my consent. I have consented with a witness, given her away as my act and deed. No, I shall never parden Plume the villainy, first of robbing me of my daughter, and then the mean opinion he must have of me, to think that I could be so wretchedly imposed upon . . ."

It was wonderful for Ralph to encounter now, in a world diminished by his wife's small frailties, the private and—until he came along—unobserved devotion of Ketch to the play.

He walked towards his hut, wanting to get down on paper his thoughts to Kempster while they were still fresh. Ketch Freeman saw him and came loping in his tracks. Ralph turned to see his comic Adam's apple and bony features drawing close. As Justice Balance his long bones were worth a laugh, though they did not seem quite so amusing when he functioned as an executioner.

"Sir," he said, bowing. It showed Ralph what an excellent means of reform a play is. From a play—and he promised himself to tell Dick Johnson this—a convict learns how politer people carry themselves, which is something he would never learn in church.

"Sir, Mr. Clark, I would like to convey to you my thanks for giving me room in your play. The minds of my fellow criminals are now distracted from my normal exercises, and laugh with me about my gestures as an actor."

"You *talk* like an actor," said Ralph, with a smile.

"If I had known it was possible to be one," said Freeman with grand fervour, "I would never have taken to the highway."

Ralph thanked him. He must have found an uncritical girl to spend time with, someone who did not unman him at the height of yearning by making some joke about his trade.

Where can I find such a woman? Ralph asked himself, going indoors.

CHAPTER 20

Bruises

JOHNNY White's hospital was laid out thus: a ward for male convicts, a ward for females, a military ward, and a small civil ward in which Harry Brewer lay. His bulldoggish features which had always looked ruddy were, in the lee of the stroke and after three days of unchosen sleep, a waxy blue. He smelt of urine and excrement. "What can you do to keep them clean?" asked Johnny White. In that stench the vengeance of Private Baker was clearly conveyed.

Often when Ralph visited, Dick Johnson would be in place by Harry's cot. Dick saw Harry's state as a merciful obliteration. Dick's idea was that while Harry slept, God contended with the Tawny Prince for Harry's spirit. "He will not get out of this without some paralysis," Dick murmured to Ralph. It was what Johnny White had said, too. But Johnny saw whatever wastage Harry would suffer as arising from some cerebral damage, whereas Dick read it as the harm done because of Harry's body being a cockpit for a contest between the Deity and satanic troops.

The day after Ralph read the letters, a chest of tea was landed from the *Sirius* with his name on it, and he took a small caddy of stuff up to the hospital to place beside Harry's cot. It was one of those offerings you make when you are close to a life under threat —you do not know if the gift is given simply in case the sufferer wakes, or whether it is a sort of magical oblation to those forces engaged in the fight for the sufferer's breath and soul. Ralph knew at least that on awakening Harry would welcome tea, and after that would call for brandy and be denied it.

Ralph had placed the small tin of tea on the ground beside Harry's bed and was now checking his friend's features, in which there were certain flutterings of eyelids and tremblings of the cheeks, as if the man himself were trying to wake. His features though, always puggish, seemed now to be tending in one direction, into the lower left corner of his face. It reminded Ralph of the way water seeks the lowest point. This vortex of the flesh, this drag of gravity in one corner of Harry's face, fascinated Ralph, and he stared at the features in a frank way he would not be able to repeat once Harry Brewer awoke.

The room where Johnny White, Dennis Considen, and the others did their occasional surgery, the room which Ralph associated with Dennis's tooth-pulling and the Bullmore autopsy, stood beyond the one where Harry lay. Johnny White kept most of the specifics in there—both the native herbal ones and those he had brought from Europe. He was in fact expecting a further shipment to come ashore from the *Sirius*—diarrhoetics, astringents, digitalis, laudanum, ointments, medicinal wines.

Johnny White one morning hurried through the civil ward, peopled only by undemanding if redolent Harry, on his way to this surgical room. "The native is ill with a fever," said Johnny. "H.E. sent me a note. It says, 'Bring much laudanum.' Can you imagine? These are people, Ralph, who have lived from before the Flood without laudanum, and suddenly they need it in quantity. Or is it really H.E. who needs it for his own sedation?"

W H E N Ralph returned at the end of the afternoon's playmaking, the tea was still in its place, and Harry's uneven features still tended downward in his blue-white mask. As Ralph waited beside Harry, Surgeon White got back from H.E.'s with the story of Arabanoo's fever. Johnny had arrived at H.E.'s new house (the stairwell designed by Harry) to find Arabanoo indeed strongly affected by fever and lying on a sofa in H.E.'s front parlour. And what an Arabanoo Johnny White saw! He had painted himself with orange and white ochres; his limbs were banded with paint. H.E. had admitted him to the parlour fully painted and had let him carry in the weapons he had recently made in idle hours—a flat-faced war club banded in the same colours as the native himself wore, and spears tipped variously with bone and stone. H.E. had permitted the construction of such arms, and Bill Bradbury had not much feared them and had often slept with the native and the weapons at night.

Johnny White found Arabanoo very agitated. H.E. called in Davy Collins to explain all his distress. According to Davy, Arabanoo was aware that his kinsmen, at least those on the south side of the harbour, had been consumed by the smallpox—*gal-gal-la*. Now, stricken with it himself, he had been moved by some sort of guilt for all his fellows who had the same. Davy said, on his basis of some sixteen or seventeen months' knowledge of the native peoples of the place, that there had been some outstanding obligation on Arabanoo to paint himself and take up arms and find the perpetrator of *gal-gal-la*. The native had had no doubt that it was someone among his own people, rather than the European intruders, who had provoked the outrage on the persons of his cousins the Cadigal people and on his own group the Gayimai.

That was why, when returning ill with H.E. from aboard the *Sirius*, he had painted himself in preparation to go in search of the enemy who had laid such a curse. Setting off, he had collapsed among the corn in H.E.'s government garden. Though so ill, he was still trying to rise when Johnny got to H.E.'s house, and any attempt to wipe from his body the paint which signified his purpose, the bands of ochre and white, caused him grief and anxiety. Hence the laudanum, to still Arabanoo, to put a halt to his obligation, to permit a hiatus during which the paint could be washed away.

The fever of Arabanoo, according to what Johnny White told Ralph, resembled that of smallpox, and it seemed likely he might have caught it during the time he attended the two children Booron and Nanbaree when they lay in hospital with the disease. Yet strangely Arabanoo showed no pox at all. There were no sores upon his face or body.

Soon Davy was able to swab the ochre off the Indian's body, for the native's mania had now been dulled with laudanum. Without which, of course, as Johnny said, his race had done from beyond the Fall and the Flood.

D U C K L I N G too would come to Harry's bedside and make lazy motions with her hand across his body, keeping the flies away on the last hot days of autumn. At the playmaking she performed the maid Lucy with the same gusto she had shown in Brand's arms, and it was hard to tell if she feared Harry Brewer's death as an end to her privileges on H.E.'s side of the stream or welcomed it as liberation from Harry's fatherly besottedness with her.

Harry had more than once described how equably she had faced the eve of her own hanging, not even teased by the chance of reprieve, letting herself be rented out from the condemned hold by Goose and the warders for three shillings a toss. And telling Harry when he visited her that she wouldn't cry *peccavi* on the gallows. If she were not too troubled three years past by the question of which side of the lime pit she stood on, it was likely that, despite all Harry's benign care, she did not spend too much time concerned with which side of this penal world she would inhabit.

There was a sort of dull affection, however, in the way she waved her hand above Harry, watching the roof and perhaps remembering her Lucy lines.

R A L P H learned of the attack on Mary Brenham, his Silvia, only when his actors met at the three-o'clock claxon in the clearing by his marquee. He saw John Wisehammer and Dabby Bryant sitting in the coarse grass with a third convict he did not recognise, a woman of ill-assorted features. Nancy Turner the Perjurer, skeletal Ketch Freeman, and Sideway, the histrionic mutineer, stood above the three. The hangman stood back somewhat from the rest of the group, but Sideway crowded in with a pose of stageworthy concern, and Turner—with her usual dark composure—inspected the woman Ralph could not recognise. As Ralph got closer though, he saw with some alarm that the woman was a mute and badly beaten Mary Brenham. The way her bruising and swellings brutally overlay her normally fine-lined face appalled him. An urge to protect her sent him jogging, not like an officer but like a manager, a friend, across the clearing.

"It's that satanic bastard, Black Caesar," Sideway rushed across to tell him.

"Caesar has been retaken?"

"*Retaken*," Dabby Bryant murmured, commenting indulgently on Ralph's innocence.

Mary Brenham raised her contused lips toward Ralph, explaining by this mute evidence why she did not wish to undertake her own explanations.

"Black Caesar did this to you?" asked Ralph.

"All the days he was sitting there," said Mrs. Dabby Bryant, "and we think he likes the play, he'd had the eye for this poor gal, this little duck."

"So he ravished her?" asked Ralph, hollow, looking suddenly at skinny Freeman for some reassurance the Madagascan would be punished but getting none from the boy, who stared away into the woods, like Justice Balance keeping counsel.

Mary Brenham denied rape, shaking her head fiercely once before the pain of the gesture overcame her.

"It'd be her shame," said Mrs. Bryant, to explain the gesture. "It'd be her natural mercy, poor chuck. Any great black cull bruised me that way, I'd call ravishing whether he done it or whether he kept his engine in the mill! I would swear to ravishing to Captain Collins."

"And he," said Wisehammer, his hand hovering in Mary Brenham's direction, "would in his turn appoint a jury of old she-lags to look at you and see if it was true. And I ask you, what if they said it wasn't."

"There wouldn't be any jury of she-lags who'd deny a woman justice for such bruises as poor Mary's!"

"He took flour and beef," John Wisehammer told Ralph, "and beat her while the little boy looked on, screaming. And did anyone come to help, I ask you? No, since they thought it was just a rare fit of the weeps the boy had."

"The things children behold in this place!" said Sideway, already in the role of a horrified Mr. Worthy, a gentle Bristolian squire.

"And escaped again?" said Ralph. He wanted to see Caesar punished for this.

"And escaped again," said Wisehammer. "How would he say it? I'll tell you. That the Fragrant One was on his side."

"What were the Quarter Guard doing?" Ralph asked, his face bristling with scarcely concealed anxiety. "Where was the night watch? Where's Henry Kable to answer me that?"

Wisehammer said reasonably, "How could you stop a man black and strong as Caesar is? Can you spread a net from the brick kilns to the bay on the west side? It can't be done."

"And he carries that private's musket with him," said Dabby Bryant, "and that would make him taller still. There isn't no arguing with a man as big and hungry as that and carrying arms."

"You have been to the surgeon?" Ralph whispered to the girl.

"Time is her only surgeon," said Sideway grandly. "And she has nearly a month to heal before the play is performed."

Ralph saw Wisehammer's hand move discreetly on Mary Brenham's wrist. There was a bruise even there, the size of a large man's thumbprint. There was no question that a woman in her state needed such tender movement of the hand, but Ralph would have liked to have found the authority to order Wisehammer to stop it.

He asked where the child was. Mrs. Dick Johnson was minding it, he was told.

Then he asked her could she walk.

He ordered a rehearsal of Act Four, in which Silvia speaks only in Scene One, though she is much spoken of in the other scenes. This is the act where Sergeant Kite, the carpenter Arscott, who was just now appearing on the slope below the marquee, delayed a little as always by the demands of his trade, dressed as a fortune-teller to deceive country boys into joining the Marines. Plume—the overseer Kable, similarly delayed by work and now rushing toward the clearing in Arscott's wake—hides beneath the fortune-teller's table through all this and impersonates a communicating spirit. He continues to do so as Lucy and Melinda visit Kite, not knowing who he is, and beg to be enlightened on their futures. The players had these scenes paced well by now, and sometimes Ralph would be so beguiled by what they did with them that he would whimper with enjoyment as he circled the actors, sometimes giving this or that eucalypt a little nudge, imparting to the mute wood the secret of his pride as playmaker. Black Caesar, however, had ensured that this afternoon would not be one spent genially nudging gum trees.

"You must come with me if you can walk," he told the girl. "We must see Surgeon White or Considen."

The girl moved her hand stiffly back and forth before her swollen face.

"That's what she fears," explained Dabby Bryant. "That the surgeon will look into her body for signs of the black man."

"No," Ralph said to the girl. "I swear the surgeons will not roughly inspect your body. But your swellings and bruises are too terrible for your small son to see." It was an argument Sideway had given him through the remark about what children witnessed. Sideway, Ralph had decided, was not such a bad fellow. "I swear. If you say the Madagascan did not force himself on you in that manner, then neither will the surgeons force themselves on you. For you are the only witness to the wrong. Apart of course from your son."

She gave in at last, and stood up quaking, helped by Wisehammer and Bryant on either side. Freeman watched his stage daughter rise without extending a hand. Ralph told the players to approach Act Four with good attack. They should not dawdle through it or make their own jokes. Let Farquhar's jokes suffice, he told them. They were to think of how bond and free would both be enchanted and agape with laughter at this scene—for it was the one, which properly acted, would raise all those who saw it to a new level of laughter and wonderment and ensure delighted applause and ample congratulations at the close of the comedy. Henry Kable was to move along any lags who came round to the clearing gaping and making loud comment.

One of the smart lags had said that time was her surgeon, and now Ralph wondered if perhaps they could see that he was forcing her across to the hospital partly out of concern for her violated features, yes, but also to remove her from Wisehammer's touch. In case they had any doubt that he was taking an officerly course in leading her to Johnny White's hospital, he called the buffoon Private Ellis and told him to bring his musket with him. Hence they would look like a small military column as they walked the four hundred paces along the slope to the hospital.

Mary Brenham's pace was a little slow and Private Ellis and Ralph had constantly to stop and wait for her. Ralph considered offering her his arm, but with his fear of mockery thought that would raise certain suppositions in onlookers. Private Ellis at last drifted off ahead, his musket cradled in his arms. He had probably forgotten what he was doing here: he could keep hold of an idea only for limited periods, and though this so often enraged Ralph when it came to matters of cooking or carrying messages, it suited him now. Ralph walked crab-wise, keeping pace with Brenham. He found himself making a speech to her, which, though it might seem to an outsider to be normal and merely friendly, pulsed in his throat like a live animal.

"You have been awfully treated, Mary. I would be pleased to have at my mercy the one who harmed you like this. And I ask you to keep in mind the play, to cling to the play as the thing which will give you your spirit back. I would ask you to do this for me and for your fellow players."

"I shall try it, Mr. Clark," she murmured through stiff lips.

He wanted to embrace her then, in the wake of Private Ellis, but managed to prevent himself.

He was aware of the folly of further admonitions surging up his throat. "Captain Collins's edition of the plays of George Farquhar, the creator of the play we are performing here, Mary, carries a short life of the playwright. He was, as you might have guessed, an officer himself, and like Captain Plume went to Shrewsbury to raise recruits. He would be a man of less than thirty when he died, and that fact can stand as a sign of his rich talent. He wrote *The Recruiting Officer* in great hardship—he never had much income apart from army pay and what he took from performances of his plays. Even so, this was no great amount; no one knew when the play was first performed at Drury Lane more than eighty years past that it would hold its place in the theatre of England over any other play of that year. Within a short time of its first performance, poor Farquhar had to sell his commission in the Grenadiers just to get money to live. He wrote his last play with a loan of twenty pounds from an actor friend, an Irishman. Farquhar was Irish, you know, and seemed to have all the eloquence that went with that nationality. The name of the last play was *The Beaux' Stratagem*—you would have heard of it and possibly seen it before you came to prison." Though he remembered she was less than fourteen years when sentenced! "And so he died on the third night of the performance of *The Beaux' Stratagem.*"

She was listening to him earnestly; her bruises made a sweet amalgam with the tragedy of comedic Farquhar, and Ralph's eyelids itched with tears.

"What I wish to tell you, Miss Brenham, is that of all the roles this great young man wrote, the one to which he was most attached was that of Silvia. He put in his plays a number of characters, brave girls who dressed in men's clothing to achieve their brave ends. But none matched Silvia."

He felt his voice thrumming crazily as he reached the burden of his speech.

"When George Farquhar was a young man first in London, he visited the Mitre Tavern in St. James's Market and heard the owner's niece reading some passages from a play by Beaumont and Fletcher. The girl's name was Anne Oldfield, and Farquhar recommended her energetically to the manager of Drury Lane. Anne Oldfield was the woman he had before his mind when he wrote Silvia, and no one else would do to act that part but her. She was the first Silvia—you can see her name in the list of players at the front of Captain Collins's edition. And as Anne Oldfield was Farquhar's essential Silvia, you are mine, Miss Brenham. No other woman among the female convicts could ever be an adequate Silvia, for it needs a certain quietness of character combined with a strange unboastful liveliness. It needs courage, forthrightness, and a good head. And as I so badly need and admire your acting, so do the other players. We will do anything to restore your soul after this sad bruising. Please, no, you must not weep."

For she had begun to cry, and because of the bruising, she

could touch her face only tentatively to absorb the slick of tears. With the force of her grief the wound on her lower lip reopened and its blood spilled down her chin. It was clear now that she would not be able to talk until one of the surgeons had staunched the flow with styptic or some other painful astringent. This gushing of her wound prevented him now from going on to offer her protection within the shadow of his own household—to provide her with a hut, perhaps, and a guard from his own company. The very success with which he had declared her *his* Silvia in the play had now left unachieved his plan to call her his Silvia more intimately.

Dennis Considen, who considered himself a good repairer of mouths—it was his own term—thought for a time that Mary Brenham's gushing lip would have to be cruelly sewn up. But at last he staunched it with a blood-sodden cloth and let her lie on a cot and begin healing.

"The nose is broken but will mend itself," Considen told Ralph. "I am pleased I did not have to stitch her. As to whether Caesar performed a rape, it's too late even for me to enquire. I could investigate her parts, but it is too late to discover much, and in any case she may have been comforted by a lover since the time of Caesar's attack."

"Not Mary Brenham," said Ralph, his face burning again. "She has a sober reputation and works for the Reverend Dick Johnson."

The Irish surgeon looked at Ralph keenly and then mercifully repressed a smile. "She is seen often with that Jew Wisehammer, isn't it so? And in any case it's wise to presume the convict women are very busy in the commerce of the flesh."

"I don't think Mary Brenham is of the general class of felon," insisted Ralph.

"Perhaps not," said Dennis, now not entirely hiding his smile. "You will be surprised how quickly a young woman mends from injuries such as these. Within three days her face will have returned to normal and she will be able to say her lines."

He placed his hand confidingly on Ralph's wrist. "She is a pretty woman indeed, and I do admit she doesn't have the whorish demeanour of some of them. But she is very taken with the Jew. I would act quickly, Ralph, lest this be his pretext to move her in with him and offer her marriage."

In those seconds of frank and exact appraisal of his fears and desires concerning Mary Brenham, Ralph hated himself for his foolishness, and that little dandy Irish tenor and tooth-puller for his percipience. But he could say nothing, while the Irishman chattered on.

"We all know you are uncommonly fastidious. But it is not yet proven that the Ten Commandments even run here. At this distance the morality of small villages or townships has no meaning. Adultery, that is, is a grievous business if it is done in the street next to the one where you live, with women whose faces your wife knows. But my God, Ralph, there is no chance that anyone's wife will become aware of or appalled by the face of any of these women, who have been removed from the world more firmly than Spanish nuns."

Ralph thought this raciness of attitude was characteristic of the English-Irish, to whom religion was merely a sort of guarantee of their wide property rights in their unhappy nation. He felt impulses both to punch Considen for his presumption and to run from him. In the end he muttered something about how a man must be left alone, without hectoring, to make his own choices. Considen shrugged.

"She should stay at the hospital tonight and tomorrow. Her son can be brought to her if it distresses him to be separated from his mother." Considen smiled very broadly now, this little mocking jockey. "So there is nothing to detain you from your play, Ralph."

Leaving the hospital Ralph swore he would be chaste if it choked him, just to show Surgeon Considen he was not all-knowing. But the memory of Betsey Alicia's extravagance in drawing bills on Broderick Hartwell and her flat refusal to contemplate existence in this new world rose sourly, though not without encouragement from him, in his memory. Since she had in his eyes become something less than the absolute, the essential spouse, perhaps there was room for a lack of absoluteness in him, too.

He would send John Wisehammer to Norfolk or Rosehill, the outer stations of the convict universe, if only he did not do Captain Brazen so well, or have a gift for writing epilogues!

CHAPTER 21

The Redeemed Forest

IT had got cold now. Ralph lay with two blankets, thinking of a third, but knowing his coldness was one which went to the core and could not be offset by an extra layer of naval-weight wool.

On a morning when he felt time could least be spared from the rehearsals he received a note from H.E., asking him to present himself at the viceregal residence at the noon claxon, the hour at which the playmaking was to begin that day.

He sent a message to Henry Kable, asking the convict overseer to supervise the other players in the reading of Act Five. Sideway may perhaps have made a better manager, except that he—as ever —annoyed the other players with his histrionics. And Wisehammer might indeed be the perfect manager, but was disqualified because the stature of temporary playmaster might encourage him in the direction of Mary Brenham.

Having made these arrangements, Ralph put on his heavier jacket and set off for H.E.'s place. As he crossed the bridge of barrels over the stream, he met Dabby Bryant coming in the opposite direction. Her face was set in a spasm which Ralph at first took for laughter but could then see was grief.

"No lines in me today, Lieutenant Clark, boy," she told him. It was obvious she had crossed the stream precisely to seek him out and tell him. "I beg you to let me off *that*. For the sake of what we know."

By *that* she clearly meant all the forced mirth of being Rose.
Ralph touched her wrist. "Is your child ill?"

"Sir," she told him, "the savage is dying. I have it from Harry
Dodd."

Harry Dodd was a servant in H.E.'s house.

"Then you know him well?" Ralph could not prevent himself
asking. "The savage?"

She had no trouble confessing it. In fact she did so at once.
She had heard him crying at night. She had gone to the hut
Bradbury shared with him and had tried to soothe the poor thing
—he was tethered to the corner post inside by the chain attached
to his wrist. At last Bradbury fell asleep on his mattress, and then
so did the native. Her arms, it seemed, were around Arabanoo,
and together they slept like two children in a fable.

"When I woke," she told Ralph, "I discovered the native
sitting up. He was there, cutting shallow little wounds in his chest
with an oyster shell, and he told me by signs to be quiet. He sang
one of those plainsongs he favours, but it kept Bradbury asleep."

It was to this point a normal story which dealt with Dabby
Bryant's usual ministrations. Now, though, it was to become fabulous, a matter of astounding magic which Dabby Bryant relayed in
the same tone she used when arguing ordinary matters—such as
whether or not she should be a player, whether or not Will Bryant
should be boatmaster. Later Ralph would remember with surprise
that he listened in the same manner, as if she were telling him
about a fever or a recipe.

She said that while she watched the native she noticed he
chewed on a tuber, the end of it sticking out of the corner of his
mouth. She did not wake Bradbury—there was no doubt the native's song was deepening his curator's sleep. Arabanoo took the
tuber from his mouth and forced it into hers. She chewed on it.
"My head grew," she told Ralph. "It hung over the place. But it
was there too, small as a beetle, right by him. I saw him fold his
big hand thinly on itself and slide the iron cuff off his wrist. Then
he put down that bloody oyster shell and walked out of the hut."

In the first of the light he led her past the fishing camp, where
of course her husband, restored not only to the decent side of the

stream but to the mastery of the fishing boat again, slept at their daughter's side.

This dream journey she recounted to Ralph seemed very geographic. She said the native had led her eastwards, over a hill covered in native cedars, to certain sharp rock ledges. And so to a crevice where lumps of quartz lay about. Smiling, he had picked up a triangle of quartz, and to her surprise—though not, it seemed, her alarm—cut into his abdomen with it.

This had been a serious opening of the body, unlike the decorative business he'd been engaged with when she first awoke. "He gouged away so hard that all in a hurry I could see his shining guts," she told Ralph, and Ralph nodded, ordinarily astounded. "I'd go yelping at him, telling him not to do that. Yet I know it wasn't a grave wound for him, Lieutenant. For me or Will or Bradbury or any other Babylonian slave it could be a grave wound, and at another time of day or under a different sort of business, it might be a grave wound even for the Indian himself. But I knew that this cutting of his—it was no more to him than peeling off dead skin."

Ralph felt a flush of concern that under certain influences his Dabby Bryant, his Rose, might believe it possible to inflict deep yet —to her confused mind—harmless wounds on her body.

"It was a poison he gave you," Ralph explained, "and it made you see things."

"I understand that, chuck," she told him, piqued. "It was a dream, but—I tell you—a waking and walking one."

So she had, in the manner of dreams, not felt too great an alarm when the savage uncoiled from his intestines a long rope of vine or gut. It ran forth slackly at first, but within a few moments was rising infinitely into the sky, toward the last of the stars. He took her by the waist, she said, and, climbing with her held by the ribs and dangling from him, drew her up that filament—that great green sinew—into a crowded wood. It was like the woods of her childhood, according to her description, the woods occupied outside Fowey by Gypsies and the families of failed mariners.

Yet this was—the way she relayed it—a redeemed forest and an Eden.

"Then we met the Mother and the Son," said Dabby Bryant.

"The Mother and the Son?" Ralph asked her.

"The same ones," she said. "The same ones you meet outside Fowey."

Without being abashed at all, she was telling Ralph the gods of her childhood were Arabanoo's gods. Ralph felt an urge to ask, Who is the Son? Is it this Tawny Prince? But he did not ask it because Dabby Bryant went on about the encounter.

This Son, she said, had drenched the earth with the blood from his tooth, from which everything came, harbour and sea, mullet and oysters, cray and whiting. The clever ropes inside Arabanoo's belly connected him to this wonderful Son.

So Bryant understood—as she told it—that the savage was not a prisoner. "He was able to get out when he chose."

But that Mother, she said, wasn't kind to Arabanoo. She warned him he'd been too easily charmed by H.E. Arabanoo's wife had arranged for him to be cursed because he had looked into the eyes of a pink-faced spirit. "Yet there was a clever man who could take the curse off the savage. She said the man's name was Cabahn."

Hearing the wizard's name, and never having heard it before, Ralph had no doubt he would hear it again. Why, he could not say. It was a reason of the gut. He was connected to that name by a green sinew of thought.

Bryant recounted then how, by means she seemed to take as given, she and Arabanoo had returned from the sky to earth, to the hut and to sleeping Bradbury; and that, folding his hand like a flower once more, the Indian had enslaved himself inside the iron wristlet, while she had gone back to the fishing camp.

"How cruel it now is," said Dabby Bryant, the tears beginning easily again. "the poor black man will perish of smallpox and think it is a curse."

Ralph sat her down, soothed her, and pleaded to the player in her. The player, he hoped, would win over the generous witch. And indeed, perhaps because she knew there was no recourse she could take to help the savage further, she did revive at last. He could see in her face a desire to take on the shrewish country cunning of Rose again. It was as if she had passed on the burden of the savage to Ralph.

Composing herself, nodding—without much belief—at his promises to do what could be done with the Indian, she agreed to go up to the clearing for Act 5. He watched her finish the crossing and stride up to the place where the other players were gathering. He felt a rush of fraternal love for her. She had given him secrets, he was sure, that she could never pass on to Will Bryant.

R A L P H found H.E. sitting at his writing table in the parlour of Government House, at the foot of the only stairwell in all this vast space. This was the stairwell which had so teased the mind of Arabanoo and at the head of which he now lay in fevered stupor, his coma on this side of town running parallel to that of Harry Brewer over on the west side.

By the parlour window sat Davy Collins. He nodded Ralph to a seat by the writing table. Ralph saw that H.E. wore a heavy coat and a fire had been set and was burning. H.E. looked starved. He stuck scrupulously to the rations, with the exception that he had a convict gamekeeper named McIntyre. It was probably a lifetime of griping naval food that had left him pale, and not only lean but crooked. It was known he had suffered extreme privations and dangerous business among the *degradados*, the convicts of Portugal, when as a young man he offered himself to serve with the Portuguese navy along the coast of Brazil. H.E. had confessed to spending time in a Portuguese penal city, Colonia do Sacramento, on the River Plate. There, H.E. had said during the first King's birthday dinner nearly a year past, the Portuguese had placed their convicts beyond the Tordesillas line, drawn by the Pope to divide Portuguese influence in Brazil from Spanish influence along the Plate, the Uruguay, and the Paraguay.

To test that line the Portuguese had founded Colonia do Sacramento far forward of the border, their own convict city. Yet it was not uniquely penal, H.E. had said, not all of it devoted to felonry; some of the land had been taken up by Portuguese orchardists, some by veterans of the Portuguese army. There was a time when Spanish ships in the Plate and Spanish artillery in the hills all about had this city of Colonia blockaded, and at that stage H.E. had been commander of the only Portuguese warship in the place.

The township survived on illegal trading with Spanish farmers, a few fish, and dogs—wild and domestic.

Significantly, when H.E. had spoken of Colonia do Sacramento, the unhappy city, it was not in connection with hard rations and poor food. It was more as a reflection on the ironies of that ancient line of Tordesillas the Pope had drawn out around the earth, from the Amazon to the Moluccas, to separate the claims of the Spanish from those of the Portuguese. The British, out of respect not for the Pope but for their ancient ally Portugal, had drawn the line further out into space still, almost *ad infinitum*. H.E. had remarked at the table on the monarch's birthday a year before that his Letters Patent gave him power over all the country between this convict city to the east and the meridian of 135 degrees to the west, so that the line would not be violated even here, so far out in the earth's undesired spaces.

This unimaginable western meridian of 135, Ralph knew, lay sixteen hundred unvisited miles to the west of where he now sat, looking at the pallid governor and at H.E.'s frequent visitor Davy Collins. The spaces over which His Majesty had empowered H.E. had in any case little meaning when set against the reaches of criminality which still had to be traversed in the souls of the lags. H.E., though by temperament an explorer, a namer, a taker of longitudes and latitudes, here again, as in Colonia do Sacramento, lacked supplies. The fact seemed legible in his skinny frame. The fuel necessary for an inquiry into the millions of square miles which lay untagged in all directions was lacking. The Blue Mountains, forty miles away, beyond which the more ignorant lags believed China lay, were therefore as absolute an end of things as the edge of a flat earth would be. H.E. asked Ralph to sit down now, and Davy Collins asked after the play, and how Nancy Turner the Perjurer was performing? The old woman who worked for H.E. appeared briefly to ask Ralph if he wanted port, which he said he did not. When she left, H.E. began to speak.

"It seems the native is dying," he told Ralph. "But it is very strange, very strange."

"John White says it is smallpox," said Davy. "But the native has no visible pox on the body. There is simply a terrible fever and a sort of poisoning within."

H.E. took up the story again. "In his periods of lucidity he is much distressed, Ralph. It is appropriate—though there are many closed-minded people who might think otherwise—that in his distress he should have the comfort of physicians of his own race. Indeed he cries out for such comfort."

"He calls out," said Davy Collins, "for a *car-rah-dy*—that is what they call their priests. The name of the *car-rah-dy* is Ca-bahn. This Ca-bahn of course lives on the north side of the harbour, in the country from which we took Arabanoo."

H.E. began to cough, took out a handkerchief, and continued his instructions murmuring into it. "I have asked Captain Collins, as a man who understands the importance of our connection to the Indians, to lead a small party to find Ca-bahn, both as a mercy to poor Arabanoo but also because that is perhaps where we should begin in any case to make alliances with the Indians. I mean, so to speak, with . . . something like a prelate or pontiff of the natives. I thought of yourself, Ralph, as an adjutant to Captain Collins in this excursion, since you had never shown yourself infected with that rancorous spirit which we find among many of the officers here."

Davy said, "We will take two sections of men from your company, Ralph, and a small party of convict oarsmen and porters. We will camp tonight on the beach on the north side, and tomorrow go in search of Ca-bahn. It should not be too difficult a matter, and by now the outbreak of smallpox among them should have largely abated." Davy Collins smiled. "You should be back with your playmaking the morning after next. I take it one of your convict players can oversee *The Recruiting Officer* until then."

Both H.E. and the Judge Advocate smiled at him now. He looked away. He heard his own voice emerge thinly in the room. "I must make provision for one of the players, the convict Mary Brenham, who was beaten three nights past by Black Caesar and who has just left the hospital. Though she has been offered to stay in the fishing camp with the Bryants, I do not know if that is a proper locality for her and her son."

He was ashamed of this maligning of Dabby, yet it was preferable to the shame of mentioning Wisehammer as a rival. Ralph was concerned as well by H.E.'s strange opinion of the Jews. If he confessed there was now a chance of Mary Brenham, one of the better she-lags, moving in for protection with Wisehammer, again one of the better lags, H.E. might well approve and tell him there was no need to make further arrangements for the girl. For as Dick Johnson would have complained, H.E. approved of the spirituality of Jews and natives, though not of that of Moravian Methodists.

It occurred to Ralph that Dick Johnson was exactly the man who should be used in this extremity. "I've asked the Reverend Johnson," he lied, "to take her into his household and under his protection. For the present time." For God's sake, not forever, he hoped. "I must now conclude these arrangements."

Davy, who himself had a weakness for a convict girl, looked at him a little ironically but would not humiliate a friend before a viceroy. "We will not be pushing off till three o'clock, Ralph. Is that sufficient time?"

"Yes," confessed Ralph.

"You will of course bring Private Ellis, who will carry your supplies for two days as well as his own."

"Your support does not go unnoticed," H.E. commented.

Yes, Ralph would have liked to have said, but it's Robbie Ross who in the near run has the say on my promotion.

F O R the second time in a few days, Ralph found himself appealing to Dick Johnson in the parson's admirable garden on the east side of the town. Dick's devotion to his two acres reminded Ralph yet again that he had not been out in some time to his garden on the small island to see to Amstead, the convict gardener, or the state of his own turnips. The playmaking, and concern with Harry Brewer and Mary Brenham, had taken up all his recent attention.

Dick listened with sad tolerance as Ralph told his story. The girl had been beaten, she needed gentleness, and, since Black Caesar had threatened him, so perhaps did her placid small boy. One of the lags had a fancy for her and would now use Caesar's attack as a pretext to offer her the protection of his hut. "I do not think it is under these circumstances that Mary Brenham should be forced to choose a companion for life," said Ralph piously.

Poor Dick took one step back, leaned on his shovel, and looked out over the early winter harbour which still dazzled as it did in high summer. When he looked back there was a tear in each eye. "I was not wrong in my original judgement of you, Ralph," he said. "You are indeed a limb of righteousness. I shall insist the girl stay here until the black man is retaken and punished."

As he left the garden Ralph understood how thoroughly he had deceived an old, if small-minded friend. "That is the nature of love," he murmured to himself Harry-like, and went off to pack for the expedition.

CHAPTER 22

Ca-bahn

THEY landed on the very beach from which Arabanoo had been captured on the last day of the previous year. The late afternoon sun was still warm on that strand of fine yellow sand, but the heights of vegetation and sandstone platforms behind the beach, the platforms on which Ralph had once seen a magnificent native stand holding aloft a monstrous iguana, were growing dark already. Davy of course had his own map; given time he would reduce everything to a system. As Private Ellis, the Marines, and the few convicts who had been trusted to travel with them landed rations and arms, pots and blankets, from the two longboats, Davy sat in the long grass on the edge of the trees with Ralph and showed him how they would travel.

Over the hill, said Davy, you came to a spine of land between the harbour and the ocean, and you continued along this—fine lagoons on one side where wild duck might be sighted, and the ocean headlands on the other. Davy hoped they would not have to go too far. Beyond the lagoons lay further hills and ledges and the inland water to the north which H.E. had called Pittwater. Perhaps Arabanoo's relatives, driven along by *gal-gal-la,* had fled that far!

The convicts and Marines assembled now three large bonfires along the beach; there was something about the gathering of wood, the companionable piling of it, which made their voices sound birdlike. A convict cook set up a metal traingle over a smaller fire already burning with a salty crackle. He would suspend the evening pot from that, and everyone's beef for the day would go into it. The sight brought Ralph a saving pulse of elation. It must have had a similar effect on Davy, for now he winked, put the map away, and pulled out a silver flask of brandy and two tiny goblets, the sort of tricky personal accoutrement you would expect a man of his style to possess.

"News of your wife by the *Sirius*, Ralph?" asked Davy, pouring the brandy.

"She spent the Christmas with Kempster. You know Captain Kempster?"

"I do, I do. We were fifteen years of age together in Nova Scotia."

"That is where you met your wife?" asked Ralph, grimacing a little as he took in some of Davy's brandy. He was curious to see how a young man such as Davy would talk about an absent wife while maintaining a lag companion. There might be some instructive mental trick Davy had to pass on.

"My wife grew up in Nova Scotia," said Davy. You would have to assess his smile, Ralph thought, as fond. "She still has the outlandish mode of speech of that region, though when she writes she is far more literary than most of your English-born women. I like her American directness."

High on the beach, where the paperbarks began, Private Ellis was uncoiling Ralph's bedroll. Further along the sand the evening's first three pickets had been placed.

Davy Collins said dreamily, sipping the brandy, "Nova Scotia has such a climate as to encourage embraces."

"Some people seem adequately encouraged to embraces here," Ralph said.

"Oh yes, except our stern master. H.E. seems not to need much love."

Davy poured more brandy still. "My wife attends literary circles," he said, "and publishes novels under false names. She is very accomplished. She is quite beautiful as well, and I must be composed when I think of that—of a young woman of talent living singly in that lizard's nest called London. It's quite possible she would have been enchanted by this country. North Americans have a skill for dealing with the harsh. And certainly if she had been permitted to come with me there would have been no need for me to spend so much time in making a journal and annotating the language of the natives, and all the rest of the particular housework I engage myself with."

"If my wife had come," said Ralph, staring off towards the escarpments where the last light sat, "she may not have been enchanted, but other problems would have been avoided." He was not drunk enough to confess to Davy that the problem which would have been avoided was his wife's prodigality with money.

It seemed Davy thought Ralph was speaking of the temptations of the flesh, and that supposition caused him to smile briefly and privately. "It has sometimes bothered my mind," he told Ralph in a lowered voice, "to consider what the government of Great Britain had in mind when they barred us from bringing our wives. Oh, I know it's a tradition of the service that the wives of officers are considered to be too sensitive in upbringing to stand the stress of campaigning in the field as in foreign places. This is rather a different case I would have thought. Reports from earlier visitors praised the place, however remote it would be, and said it was fruitful and temperate. I wonder, couldn't it have been seen as desirable that the lags should have models of marriage placed before their eyes—your marriage, mine? Oh, I don't mean our marriages are perfect, Ralph, though maybe yours is. But I would guess that most of the time your marriage—like mine—is marked by delicacy, consideration, and a certain ceremony. From observing us close at hand, the convicts might have learned those things which it is harder to learn from observing the marriages of most of the Marines. The Marine marriages teach them no more than what they already know of the institution from their observations in the sinks and stews of Soho and Seven Dials and Stepney and Poplar— screaming, punching, violent rutting, and reckless infidelity. Not that I am a paragon in the matter, Ralph. But our marriages might have shown them there were different ways of proceeding."

The fragrance of the cooking meal, mixed with that of the salt air and the strange bitter eucalyptus smell of the forest, came to Ralph and caused him to smile.

"Why did they not permit our spouses then?" he asked dreamily, without any particular passion at the moment against the Home Secretary or the Admiralty.

"There are only two explanations," said Davy. "First, there is the possibility they were so stupefied by custom they did not even consider our special case."

Ralph laughed. He liked Davy's companionable disrespect. "And what's the other explanation?"

"The other one is more beguiling, Ralph. That they—being men fully aware of the normal male leanings—intended that at this distance of space we *should* take convict wives, and by treating them well and having influence over them, turn them into the future matriarchs of this lag society. Through the exercise of our desire for the comradeship of women and for the usual human solace, we were to make an exemplar of marriage out of a convict concubine—to use Dick Johnson's rather exciting and fleshy term."

Ralph stared at Davy. He was the last man Ralph had suspected would turn into the voice of a rational Satan.

E A R L Y in the day it was dismal journeying—they climbed over rock ledges, sometimes encountering the skeletal remains of an Indian stricken months earlier by the smallpox. It was the only sight of a native they had until well into the morning, and this surprised Ralph and Davy, given that the lagoons were so rich in animal life, that ducks made continual small migrations overhead and that those mounds of genial fur and flesh known as wombats occasionally crossed their track.

They were beginning to climb a spur of hills running north from the last of the marshes when they saw a group of native women fleeing through the trees to their left. More exactly they heard them, for the women ran with shrill pee-wit cries, clutching children to their hips and breasts. This chirping flight distracted the party for a moment from what was ahead of them, but then they saw standing in their path, perhaps twenty paces ahead of them, a tall native, three spears and a throwing stick in his right hand, a war club in his left, and a long, double-pointed bone thrust through the septum of his nose. He did not intend to let them come any further, and he signified it by the bellicose hooting he made in his throat.

"This is what comes of capturing them against their wills," Ralph murmured to Davy. The sight of barbed spears made Ralph angry that H.E. and Davy had with such levity ordered Arabanoo's capture. Davy held his hand up to prevent the Marines from loading their muskets. "Do nothing," he called.

And with that bland, boyish frankness he and Johnny White had displayed on their excursions in Rio, he began to speak the language of the natives.

"Arabanoo *ba-diel!*" said Davy carefully. He was speaking out of the very dictionary of the language he himself had made. His sentences grew in length. The native seemed to ignore him, keeping up the hooting, stamping his front foot, the one which would take the weight, Ralph understood, when the spear was hurled. Davy bravely raised his voice.

"Arabanoo *gal-gal-la!*" claimed Davy.

The native ceased his hooting and frowned. Davy went to step forward, but the native thrust out the knob of his war club to prevent him. *"Diam o car-rah-dy?"* asked Davy calmly. *"Noy-ga Car-rah-dy!"*

He turned to Ralph and translated. "I am telling him Arabanoo is howling for a priest."

"Car-rah-dy," boomed the native.

"Ca-bahn," said Davy. *"Car-rah-dy Ca-bahn! Diam o Ca-bahn?"*

The native began to weep in front of their eyes and made a keening noise like an elongated *e*. "They weep easily for each other," murmured Davy to no one in particular. In an effort to be heard over the keening, he had to shout at the native. He began to ask for the weeping man's name. It was believed that if an Indian gave you *that*, you stood less chance of being impaled.

Davy asked again, and the native ceased his wailing and pointed to Davy less aggressively with the club. "I am Collins," said Davy, with a smile which Ralph thought of as taking some of the sting out of the two-barbed spear, the horrifying acuteness of the shark bone. "I am Coll-ins. And I think you may know me, sir."

The native began to rehearse Davy's name, the way Arabanoo had rehearsed names on the beach on the day of his capture. "Bennilung!" the native offered suddenly as his own name. He pounded his heart to indicate the sincerity of the offering. "Bennilung!"

"*Diam o* Ca-bahn?" asked Davy, his hands spread wide.

At last the native half turned and, with an open hand, pointed north. Tears still sat glinting on the layers of fish oil that caked his face. Davy moved toward him as if they were about to become fellow travellers. But the native turned again full face and, holding the shafts of the spears horizontally across his own chest, pushed Davy back. So they were to follow, but at a distance.

Ralph was astonished the Indian was willing to pay them any service at all. This race was too compliant, Ralph thought. They did not have that crucial talent for malice which had arrived so abundantly here on the convict transports.

The native ran ahead. He led them through further lagoons and across hilltops where the sound and sight of the ocean were immensely and noisily present. He would wait for them at difficult places—rock outcrops or fenny ground. He never let them get much closer than, say, fifty paces before he was gone again, loping among the tall verticals of trees blackened from the fires of the past summer.

He did not permit a stop, and therefore neither did Davy. Ralph could hear the suppressed grumblings of the Marines and convicts behind him.

At last the native led them up to a plateau covered in small, strange olive-green shrubs, all cuffed back and trimmed by the prevailing wind. Here, by words to Davy and by signs, he told them to wait. It was now midafternoon. The Marines and convicts pitched themselves down on boulders round about. The heat of the sun was sweetly cached in the rocks. The men flung themselves gratefully across them and regained their breath. After further words with Davy, the native Bennilung vanished.

"He has gone to fetch Ca-bahn?" Ralph asked.

"More likely to ask for an audience." Davy smiled.

Back in the clearing in Sydney Cove, Ralph knew, they would be mining the comic lode of Acts Four and Five under Henry Kable's direction. Last night, Mary Brenham—with her diminishing bruises—would have slept at Reverend Johnson's place.

The soldiers had lit their clay pipes, and Ralph saw one of them moving companionably from group to group. It was Private Joseph Hunt, a young man of weather-beaten but regular face, who had broken the key in the storehouse lock and by this maladroitness been forced to turn King's Evidence. His six accomplices were buried in a communal grave behind the Marine camp. Private Handy Baker rose from that closeness only to inflict a stroke on Harry. Whereas Hunt meandered on a hill above the sea, the sun on his face. Ralph pointed him out to Davy.

"It don't seem to have marred his friendships," murmured Ralph.

"It never does," said Davy. "The people take a philosophic attitude to those who betray them. As much as they honour those who don't betray others, they are not particularly perturbed by those who do. It's the luck of the catch. On the one hand, the women have avoided Ketch Freeman since he is our hangman. Yet they do not fight shy of Private Hunt. So far from it that in the women's camp the other evening, I saw him sitting and smoking with Turner the Perjurer, can you imagine? Nancy Turner's lover Dukes lies in that grave in the promiscuous embrace of Askey and Baker and the others. While Turner, who perjured herself for him, sits at evening with the one who put him to death more truly."

"Turner?" asked Ralph. For he had thought that if anyone might darkly store up a vengeance it was Nancy. Perhaps she intended, like Judith with Holofernes, to bed down with him and decapitate him as he slept.

Davy seemed very nearly to have dozed off. With his eyes closed, he said, "They are, in their way, as strange to us as are the Indians. Though they speak the same language as us, honour the same monarch, and have recourse to the same common law."

Ralph used the time while waiting for the native to appear

again in imagining how it was possible for Davy therefore to spend his evenings with the prisoner Ann Yates. One evening was no mystery, or two. But how did he occupy lengths of time with her if she were such a different race? Ralph would have liked particularly to have asked him in view of the similarity between Ann Yates and Mary Brenham. Yates was also one of the less outrageous of the she-lags, and like Brenham she had a child, a baby son, the product of an alliance, in the strict sense of the word, the enlistment of an ally, from among the crew of the *Lady Penrhyn*. Ralph considered constructing an honest question on the subject of maintaining a convict at the core of your household. But it took an effort of framing as well as courage. And before Ralph could manage either, the native reappeared. He seemed quite alone. He and Davy had more conversation as the Marines and the few lags began to tap out their pipes.

They followed him now down into a small, steep valley which sat between two fine sandstone headlands. Between them ran a sweet little crescent of beach, a robust surf breaking on it, and on exposed rocks at the northern end many native women and children digging and gouging for shellfish.

As they got lower into the valley, this view was cut off by tall palm trees. "Remarkable!" murmured Davy, the true journalist. "I've not seen such palm trees anywhere else in this region."

But as they emerged into a broader view of the beach, any botanical interest the gully might have evinced was quickly quashed by the sight of some sixty or seventy native males, all wearing patterns of white and red, all as heavily armed as Bennilung. They were grouped in front of a shallow sandstone cave and it was obvious their purpose was to prevent another abduction. As they saw Davy and Ralph and the Marines, they set up the loud hooting Ralph had heard earlier in the day from Bennilung. "Holy Jesus help us!" said a Marine behind Ralph. Expectation that the native had led them into some sort of ambush was like a shameful redolence in the valley, on the edge of the small beach.

Davy was conversing with Bennilung quite coolly, his voice raised only so he could be heard above the noise. "*Diam o Ca-bahn?*" Davy kept asking, and sallying into more complex statements which Ralph hoped would not, through some misinterpretation, bring on a storm of spears.

Davy turned to his Marines only to tell them to do nothing. Ralph was pleased for the primed small arm he himself carried in his sword belt.

Davy discussed Ca-bahn with Bennilung for at least three minutes before—at no signal Ralph could be sure of—the hooting instantly stopped, leaving the *eora* word Davy was shouting comically adrift in the silence. Some of the Marines laughed at this. But Davy went on asking for the wizard.

There was a sort of swarming among the warriors, a coalescing. This melee produced an instant apparition—a small man, not as old as Ralph would have expected, was all at once standing in front of the army. It was as if their massed fervour had somehow manufactured him. He was a startling sight—his face white, his hair spiky, glossed with a luminous blue mud and decorated with the teeth of dogs or kangaroos. Davy showed no doubt that this was Ca-bahn. He took one step and began to make a respectful submission. He explained that Arabanoo was afflicted with *gal-gal-la.* "*Yen-nang-allea o* Arabanoo!" Davy suggested. Let us go to Arabanoo.

The priest with the blue hair made a speech to Davy. Sometimes the inflections rose playfully, sometimes the man's glaring white face took on an ironic but not malicious smile. He spoke for an extraordinary time. The Marines began to shuffle. Two of the convicts sat down. The warriors remained immobile. The wind changed as the priest spoke—white caps appeared out to sea, the horizon grew jagged. The Indians might think the white-faced sorcerer had the wind at his disposal. A cold blast struck the women who had been oyster-gathering on the tidal rocks and sent them shrilling up the beach and into the woods.

Davy looked at Ralph as the priest's speech ground on. It was clear Davy would have liked to have communicated in some way, except that the warriors might be offended by any interruption to their priest's flow.

Suddenly, without any tonal signal to say he might, Ca-bahn stopped talking. When Davy stepped forward again, with the request that Ca-bahn come with him to Arabanoo, all the warriors began hooting once more and—in less than an instant—had spears fitted to their throwing sticks, all pointed at Davy's body. Ralph had a second's horrifying image of the porcupine-like obscenity his friend could so easily become in the next few moments. Davy himself seemed not to be much plagued with such an eventuality. "Do nothing," he told the Marines in a sing-song voice. "He won't come back with us," he murmured unnecessarily to Ralph.

Ca-bahn now took from somewhere on his body what Ralph had first thought was a stone, and hurled it lightly the twenty or so paces between himself and Davy. It landed at Davy's feet. It was a pouch woven of stringy grass. Clearly it was meant to be a salutary amulet for Arabanoo, but when Davy tried to open it and look inside, the hooting reached such a pitch he closed it. Someone— it was done so quickly there was no telling who it was—unleashed one spear, which bit into the sand to Davy's left. "We are intended to go," Davy announced solemnly to Ralph. He gave the order to the Marines, telling them to load their firepieces as they walked crab-wise up the beach.

Soon they were all back among the grove of palms, Ralph walking backwards as if gliding, unaware of his legs or the terrain, for movement in extreme fear was like movement in a dream.

As the Marines climbed out of the little palm grove, Davy had a chance to open the pouch and look at what lay inside. He showed it to Ralph. All Ralph could see was a strange, powdery wad of brown matter.

"I think it is human shit," said Davy. "Though of a considerable age."

CHAPTER 23

Curse or Cure

CARRYING Ca-bahn's charm, they were back at the beach soon after dark. The meal prepared by the few convicts and Marines they had left behind on the beach was eaten quickly. They needed to cross the harbour that night, in case the arrival of Ca-bahn's amulet might help Arabanoo survive the night.

It was cold on the water, but with what clarity did Scorpio in the south-east and the Southern Cross, to which the Cornish witch Dabby Bryant had travelled with Arabanoo, among whose splendours she had met the Mother and the Son, glitter above the harbour entrance. The convicts and the Marines chattered away; they were going home to their women.

The Mother in Dabby Bryant's journey had warned Arabanoo over his congress with the pink spirits. "What if the pouch is some final curse?" Ralph asked Davy.

"The boy is dying anyhow," said Davy, a little airily. "Would they send him a curse? You were there the day he was taken, Ralph. According to your account the Indians were demented to see him caught."

"But by now," Ralph insisted, "they may have written him off. As if he is somehow tainted."

"Whom should we ask? Who would know whether Arabanoo would consider the thing benign or not?"

The question was meant to stump Ralph, for Davy was tired, did not want an argument, and still had to write up his journal for this extraordinary day.

"There is a lag who knows him well."

"Bradbury I suppose. Bradbury is a happy fool!"

"Not Bradbury. The she-lag Dabby Bryant."

"You want us to get that Cornish woman in to judge the pouch for us? Has the play affected your mind?"

"Everything affects my mind, David," said Ralph, tired himself. "There is no need to talk to me as if I were a corporal."

Davy emitted a groan towards the glittering sky. "So she's done the savage a favour, eh?"

The question shook Ralph. Davy understood that Dabby Bryant performed ministrations. This must mean she had done something for Davy too, something for which he now used the ungracious word favour. He wondered what demon Dabby Bryant had spotted on the shoulder of this man. Ralph had never thought of Davy as prey to any particular fear.

"The native will certainly die," said Davy, "unless we present him with this pouch. He will probably die in any case. How could we explain to H.E. the grounds on which we would introduce such a woman as a receptacle of special knowledge on the matter?"

They rounded the harbour's Middle Cape. There was a small fire on the rock called Pinchgut, the Capri of H.E.'s empire, where some wretch waited for the *Sirius* or the *Supply* to take him to Norfolk Island forever. From abeam this isle, the lights of the women's camp could be seen and an expectation of hearths and she-lags rose pungently—so it seemed to Ralph—in the boat he and Davy shared.

They moored at H.E.'s landing and sent the Marines marching back over the stream to their side of things. Would Private Hunt go and speak with Nancy Turner the Perjurer tonight?

Davy and Ralph marched alone to H.E.'s place. Their disagreement over Dabby Bryant did not encourage any homecoming conversation. As they reached the gate in front of the viceregal house, they saw Robbie Ross and Jemmy Campbell emerging, gusted along by accustomed pique. Both Davy and Ralph paused to let them pass. "And here they are," Robbie said gratingly. "Military men in their prime, sent forth to fetch back some wee magic for a savage. Work of moment, that, wouldn't you say, Jemmy?"

Robbie's spleen restored Davy. "And I wish the divinest of just slumbers to you, Major!" he called after Robbie.

When they knocked at the door, it was Johnny White the surgeon who answered. He led them through to the parlour, where H.E. slept under his naval cape on a sofa in the corner. A decanter of brandy stood on the table, and a half-filled glass which was clearly Johnny White's. Johnny motioned them to sit down around the table. He asked them how their journey had been, but he wore a frown. There was great petulance in the air. Perhaps Robbie and Jemmy had left it behind.

"What foxes me about these men like H.E., these scholars . . . " said Johnny, taking a gulp of brandy before finishing the sentence, "is that they would not tolerate the use of charms by Brazilian or English peasants, but they send out expeditions to find them for sick Indians."

"You have been speaking to Robbie," said Ralph, laughing quietly, aiming to put some good fraternal feeling into the house.

"I thought you might return with another savage," said Johnny. "H.E. was hoping so."

"They mistrust us too much after the capture of the one we have," said Ralph. "I have to say I do not find their wariness unfair."

"Well," said Johnny, "you aren't to fret yourselves. For the native's fever has abated. That's the one reason you find H.E. asleep."

Arabanoo's fever had broken during the afternoon—Ralph and Davy surmised it was around the time they had met Ca-bahn, though they did not necessarily ascribe any cross-country magical influence to the native priest. Davy passed the pouch to Johnny, who pulled a candle closer to inspect it. "Why this is human waste." Johnny laughed. "Though of great age."

"I said so to Ralph." Davy yawned.

Johnny's fingers probed the pouch—what Ralph thought of as a surgeon's recklessness of movement was there. "There is something else in here," he announced. He extracted a button. "Where did this come from?" he asked. It was the sort of button gentlemen of good families wore on their jackets. A coat of arms was embossed on it. "My God," said Johnny White, "I know whose button this is. I am related through my mother to the family whose crest is here."

He held it close to the candle and invited Ralph and Davy to examine it. "See the lettering. *Nigra sum sed formosa.* I am black but beautiful. Holy Christ knows what the real significance of the phrase is—it is from the Song of Solomon. But it is the crest of the Banks family." He began to laugh. "This button and this dung both belong to Sir Joseph Banks."

Davy laughed madly too, suppressing it all at once so that H.E. could sleep on. There was a strong image of the great naturalist on the shores of Botany Bay nineteen years past, when the first European ship to visit this coast had been in that shallow and overpraised haven called Botany Bay. Taken short, Sir Joseph rushes in among the paperbarks, wrenches his breeches open and squats. One of his heavily used buttons falls to the ground. When he is finished and has gone, perhaps cursing the missing button but unable to find it, the people *ab origine* move in and inspect these droppings and the button. They are perhaps gauged by synods of native priests and tested for potency, malign or benign. In the course of normal trade between one doctor-priest and another, they move across the harbour and finish up to the north with Ca-bahn.

"But are they a curse?" asked Ralph. "Or are they a cure?"

"It can no longer matter," said Johnny. "For the native is now sleeping well. He has beaten the disease."

"Then there is no need to show him the pouch," said Ralph. "It would seem to me that shit is a bad omen in any man's language."

"On the contrary." Davy yawned again. "I have, in the days before the outbreak of the smallpox among them, seen a native singing languorously over a heap of ordure left there by some woman he desires. They have a child's innocence about these matters."

"I think," Johnny White murmured, "we can leave to H.E. the decision about what to do with this curious little package. No one loves the native more than he does."

It was agreed they would all leave H.E. asleep, but Davy wrote a quick note and left it under the pouch.

May 16th, 1789

Your Excellency,

We have returned this evening from the country north of the harbour, having had communication with the car-rah-dy named Ca-bahn. We encountered among the lagoons a fine figure of a native who called himself Bennilung and who seemed unmarked by the smallpox. He conducted us to a small grove of palms some twelve miles north of our landing place where we encountered a substantial body of warriors, all armed and bent on intimating by unearthly sounds and by militant gestures that they did not wish their priest to return with us. Other than by opening fire on their ranks, an expedient which would have left many dead on both sides, we could not have borne Ca-bahn away. On learning that Arabanoo was ill, however, Ca-bahn delivered to us a pouch, which I hereby present to you. Surgeon White indicates that the dark substance is human waste and has recognised the button as belonging to Sir Joseph Banks, Bart.

We are pleased to hear from Surgeon White that the Indian has recovered from the fever associated with the disease, and we therefore leave to Your Excellency himself to decide whether the native should be shown the pouch.

Your obedient servant,
David Collins,
Captain, Marines

Post Script: I shall present a more detailed report, as will Lieutenant Clark, who has some forceful views on the manner in which the capture of Arabanoo has diminished the trust the Indians once showed us.

Signed D.C.

T H E Y crept out through the hallway and then through the front door. When they were past the sentry, Ralph asked the surgeon how poor Harry Brewer was now.

"Kind of you to enquire, Ralphy," said Johnny White. "Everyone's forgotten poor damn Harry. His old friend H.E. had visited him only once before the Indian's fever arose to claim all his attention. Harry's lungs are growing congestive with lack of proper motion. I have him turned over three times by day, and twice by night, but it is not enough. He is wasting too. We can pour only a little broth down his throat a few times a day, and though his power to swallow is there, he gags after a few mouthfuls. In short, Ralph, it is my view we shall lose our friend."

Ralph found that hard to believe. It seemed to him the convict society of New South Wales would grow quite unbalanced if Harry Brewer were lost. He feared he would grow unbalanced himself. "Until the play is presented, I am free in the mornings and evenings. You must call on me, John, to sit by Harry."

Johnny accepted the offer with a solemn nod. "It's a long way from the Strand for a flash boy like Harry. And his tart has backslid and gone over the stream for company."

"The company of men?" asked Ralph, suddenly enraged at Duckling.

"The company of her Dimber Damber, her abbess, Goose." Johnny himself had a good command of cant talk. It came from treating convicts, Ralph surmised.

They passed Dick Johnson's place, where Mary Brenham and her child lay asleep—cunning arrangement of which the surgeon and Davy were unaware. But Ralph's own solitary understanding of Brenham's location filled him all at once with a ridiculous joy.

CHAPTER 24

The Watching of the Ill

H E wrote a letter to Dick Johnson.

My dear Dick,

John White tells me that our friend Harry Brewer is in great danger and needs a constant watch. A number of occasions throughout a given day, his body has to be turned to prevent the blood from pooling and the lungs from congesting. I would like to make use of the services of convict Mary Brenham in watching and helping to turn poor Harry—at least in those periods when she is not required for domestic service in your household. I would be grateful if you could send her to the hospital at nine o'clock, where I shall give her her instructions.

He had not left his hut for the hospital when a servant of Dick Johnson's came panting up the hillside to his hut with a reply.

My dear Lieutenant Clark,

Of course I am happy to provide Brenham for such a merciful service. As your spiritual counsel, however, I must advise

you that you are concerning yourself overly much in the movements and affairs of this woman, since this is the second time
in three days that you have taken a direct interest in her. I urge
you to beware of low motives hidden behind high ones. In Jesus
Christ I remain

> Your obedient servant,
> Richard Johnson,
> Pastor.

D I C K ' S clumsy spiritual advice made Ralph kick the leg of his
small camp table and then cross the room and pound the corner
upright of the hut. That mean Eclectic talking to him as if he were
a boy of twelve. It was a prime instance of the way Dick worked to
put a distance between himself and those who were willing to be
his clients.

But the anger gave way to an awkward shame. Dick had so
precisely read his motives. Ralph considered for a time whether he
ought to arrive late at the hospital, let Mary Brenham sit there
waiting with her baby son for an hour or so. But that would mislead
only Mary herself. She would have sixty minutes to sit and perhaps
occupy her mind with the Jewish epiloguist Wisehammer. Whereas
Surgeons Considen and White would understand his game exactly,
since they both seemed so competent in dealing with women.

Harry Brewer used to mutter a great deal to himself, rehearsing
arguments, some of which he had had years before and which were
beyond repair, or chastising himself for historic or present follies.
Ralph found himself so discomforted by Dick Johnson's letter he
now took up this habit without thinking; halfway to the hospital
he stopped and patted his hand emphatically against a tall eucalyptus tree. "I will be very curt with Dick Johnson in the future!" he
announced aloud.

H E surprised himself by being at the hospital before she got there.
He was disgruntled, too, to find on duty not Johnny White and

Dennis Considen, for whom he had prepared himself, but the rakish young Scot Balmain, who had come in from Rosehill for a few days and who proceeded around the hospital with stiff limbs, as if a more fluent style would hurt his head too much. He barely listened when Ralph told him a convict woman was being brought in to keep watch over Harry.

Mary Brenham and her child, both pleasantly breathless as if Mary had made a game of the short journey, got to the hospital a little later. The Reverend Johnson had detained her, she pleaded, fanning her face with her hand. The hurry she had been in had brought out a few childlike freckles under the fine skin of her broad forehead, and Ralph was reminded, despite her rich, full-lipped features, of how young she was. He led her into the room occupied by Harry. Harry's rankness did not seem to appall her. She had probably encountered worse on the convict decks of the *Lady Penrhyn*. She settled the child in a corner with a wooden jigsaw puzzle which Ralph recognised as belonging to the Johnsons. Then she crossed the room to Ralph for her instructions. He led her to Harry's pitiable cotside.

Harry lay under three blankets and on a sheet of sealskin. His breathing was very noisy. He was a man drowning terribly in his own flesh.

"Mr. Brewer must be turned twice every morning while you are here," said Ralph. He did not know where he got the number from, he knew simply that it was more than the surgeons and the orderlies would do.

He took back the blankets and there was Harry in nothing but a stained shirt. His legs were thin and blue, and his stubby little prick hung loose. For its sake Harry had embezzled and joined a criminal mob, a canting crew. Now it looked so negligible and, worse, as if the stroke had sundered him from it.

Mary Brenham began to behave with great capability and briskness. She suggested they lift Harry to another cot while she scrubbed down the sealskin. Shifting Harry was a task Ralph and Mary managed more easily than Ralph would have believed. She bundled Harry's small, failing body in the three blankets, so that only his head appeared, and Ralph carried him by the shoulders as she took the legs. Looking at Harry from behind, Ralph would have thought him a child.

Then Mary took the fouled sealskin outside to wash. Ralph was left alone with her son and with mute Harry. "Come there, Harry," said Ralph forlornly. "Time to stir. Your girl is living with Goose."

Ralph saw the child looking at him and smiled. "I am just talking with Mr. Brewer," he told the child, who returned to his game.

Mary came back with a bowl of water and a cloth. She raised the cloth to Harry's mouth. Harry's cracked lips worked at the cloth. "See," said Brenham. "He has the same thirst as a man in a good state of health."

She had laid the sealskin in the sun, and when it was dry she brought it in again and spread it briskly on Harry's empty cot. She and Ralph then moved the child body of Harry back across the room to where it belonged, and Ralph fetched a stool and a chair so that they could sit beside Harry. He insisted Mary take the chair, since she would be there longer. Before sitting she gave her child a scrag of dried beef to chew on.

"I am perhaps Harry's truest friend," said Ralph to his own surprise as he settled himself on the stool. "He is well liked. I think . . ."

"There is no need for you to sit, sir," said Mary Brenham. "I am here."

"I will stay for a while," Ralph insisted.

Within seconds they were talking of the play and then of the players.

"I heard that Turner the Perjurer," Ralph ventured, "is spending time with Private Hunt."

"Private Hunt?"

Private Joseph Hunt, he explained. The man whose evidence had hanged Nancy Turner's lover.

In the corner Small Willy Brenham was talking to a piece of jigsaw, an amenable child who was disappointed with the lump of wood he held rather than determined to cause it harm. His mother blinked. "I have seen them together once," she admitted.

"I think it is curious, that is all," said Ralph.

Mary Brenham rose and put the wet cloth again against Harry's lips. The lips worked away. They were what was most live of Harry now—Harry that man of complicated ambition and mysterious desire. Only the lips spoke for him in sucking against the rag.

"What if the poor man gets thirsty in the night?" asked Mary.

"There is a night orderly who gives him broth. And his hut mate Duckling should be here to ply the rag."

Mary Brenham blinked again.

"Do you know Goose?" he asked.

"She and Duckling are mother and daughter," said Mary Brenham. "Well, not mother and daughter in the ordinary way. But mother and daughter just the same. I can't answer for Nancy Turner or Duckling, Lieutenant Clark. They are dear friends in the play, but a puzzle to me in the flesh."

He saw his mistake. She thought he was plumbing her for intelligence on the two women. He changed the subject and began to talk to her about reading, since the source of her obvious writing and speaking capacities now interested him. He told her that from the start he had noticed how well she had taken to the reading of Silvia and how competent her transcriptions of the play had been. He asked her about her education, the years before she was convicted at Justice Hall in the Old Bailey . . . how long ago?

"It will be five years this eighth of December, Mr. Clark," she told him, staring at him directly. He had noticed this in the lags—they stated the dates of their convictions with great candour, for fear that to state them either shyly or sullenly would bring them undone with something like bitterness, would force them to a railing against destinies and governments.

Soon she was talking freely of her infancy.

Her grandfather had been a groom in the house of Sir Desmond White at Feltham in Middlesex. Her father had been the groom's clever son, a companion therefore to Sir Desmond's small son, the Honourable Horatio White who became in the end, so Mary Brenham told Ralph, a justice of the King's Bench. Grandfather Brenham—as his lag granddaughter called him in speaking to Ralph—was much trusted by the household. That enlightened

Whig Sir Desmond had no doubts about asking the chief groom's son into the household for lessons in the classics and geometry. The tuition was provided by a former scholar of Peterhouse, Cambridge, a man who was also an ordained minister of the Established Church. "My father," Mary told Ralph, "was said to be the equal of the Honourable Horatio in Greek and Latin, and better than him in mathematics and geometry. But when the boys were nine, the Honourable Horatio White was sent to Harrow and there were no further lessons for my father. There he was, you see, Mr. Clark, high and dry with some education—portable wares, you might say. But he couldn't take them anywhere. So at last Sir Desmond was aware of the cruelty of teaching the boy only so much, and arranged for him to go to one of the Dissenting academies—Sir Desmond did not believe in God. So the fact that my father would get a different doctrine at Sunbury Academy than the Honourable Horatio was receiving at Harrow made no difference in Desmond's mind. It made a difference in my father's—he used to like to talk of divine matters. When I was small, he taught me such words as Socinianism. I've remembered the name, though I cannot quite remember what its point is now."

Ralph laughed at her irony. This family history she had embarked on was, he was ecstatic to notice, proving her elegant, intelligent, a dazzling companion.

"When my father married my mother," she continued, "they set up a small academy of their own in Feltham, for the sons of small traders and farmers. It was awesomely hard though to get people to pay for the education of their sons, especially when those same people were often the butchers and grocers to whom my mother and father owed money. My father was already suffering from consumption. It killed him before he was twenty-nine years old. After we had settled all our debts in Feltham, my mother and I moved up to London. I was ten years old. I think my mother came to London not because of any dream she might have of that great city, but because she could see no future ahead of us in Feltham other than charity. Sir Desmond was dead, and his son mainly in London, and so there was no one to protect us from being labelled on parish books with that terrible name. The Poor."

Mary Brenham's mother began to attend Quaker meetings in Stepney, perhaps because the Quakers were well known for their charity. And so she found work on the fringes of benevolence, as a cook and housekeeper for the Society for the Ruptured Poor, a Quaker house of charity which took in and nursed those whose frames had been broken in mills and factories and who could therefore no longer work.

"She found me my position at the Kennedys' and I repaid her miserably," said Mary Brenham flatly, glancing at her child. "The consequence of my early years is that I do not fit the same tongue or have the same mind as those who have been felons from babyhood. I am not better than them, I am probably worse for having known better and still become a thief."

"No," Ralph hurried to say. "You mustn't flay yourself. Society does not demand that. It has taken your time and put you in a distant place. That is the extent of what you have to give."

"In any case, better or worse, the ones like Nancy Turner and Duckling I do not understand and therefore cannot—since they choose it so—be their friends."

The mention of Duckling again reminded Ralph that he was exploiting poor mute Harry as a species of table, a useful item of furniture, over which he received Mary Brenham's sweet confessions.

His sudden discomfort must have shown in his face, since she shook herself. "I have spoken at a terrible length, Mr. Clark."

"No, no," said Ralph. Her short history seemed almost infinite to him, full of questions, more ramified than that of the Roman Empire. "And does your mother still work in that Quaker house?" he asked.

"At the time my ship left the Thames, yes. My trial confirmed her position there, making her doubly unfortunate and so doubly worthy with the Brethren. I could say my crime confirmed her imprisonment with the Quakers, just as it assured my transportation."

Ralph laughed. "You do not like the Quakers?"

"Away from them, my mother might have found a new husband."

"And might have starved on the other hand," said Ralph.

"I do not think I could be a Quaker," said Mary. "It seemed to me they were very severe on ordinary joy."

Ralph wondered whether her concept of ordinary joy included John Wisehammer. He spent so long trying to imagine the framing of this question in a way which would not give himself away to her that he must have seemed to have become distracted. She employed this apparent drifting mental state of his as a signal that he certainly had heard enough of her life history, for now she changed direction and took exactly the course he wanted her to.

"Sir," she said, "there is John Wisehammer's epilogue, which I have helped him to write."

She had his attention instantly. "Yes?" he asked.

"May I say, Lieutenant Clark, that you have never wanted to see it, and therefore he thinks he is under a shadow with you."

"So much nonsense," said Ralph, knowing that a more competent lover, a Captain Plume, would have said, "He *is* under a shadow. He has taken a claim to a woman I desire."

"I had forgotten the epilogue," lied Ralph.

"If you could ask to see it, sir," said Mary Brenham, "it would —if I can speak freely—be the end of a terrible tyranny for me. For he writes it and writes it again, he edits out lines, he alters meters and rhymes, and he asks me continuously if I think it is ready for you to lay your eyes on."

"He is concerned to such a degree?" asked Ralph.

"All the players are becoming sick of urging him forward, telling him to show it. And I above all, since the main burden lies on me as John Wisehammer's friend and helper." She sighed and it was no false sigh. "If he gained your approval, then you would become an object of friendly devotion, and the weight would be lifted from me."

In the seconds after she had said this, it was apparent she was about to ask his pardon for being so frank. But Ralph had enough trouble suppressing his joy. Wisehammer was something of a nuisance to her! It took some seconds for him to understand that though he knew she was now free of claim, lag or otherwise, he lacked the stomach, what he would have called the ordinary gall, to recruit her as his lover. Perhaps he feared the world would be unbalanced, and Betsey Alicia sent into even more prodigious gales of extravagance. It was above all that he—who had once kept a journal—lacked the tongue for the task.

And it was while Ralph was suffering in that acrid way from his inability to speak to Mary Brenham, it was while he was cursing the Destinies which permitted Davy to speak to Ann Yates, George Johnston to speak to Esther Abrahams, but put a stone on Ralph Clark's tongue, that Johnny White appeared in that room at the hospital and stood in the door shaking his head.

H I s air of philosophic disapproval, however, had nothing to do with the sight of Ralph and Mary Brenham. He asked if he could see Ralph. Ralph joined him and stood in the main ward, where some of the sorrier cases of scurvy, flux, and starvation lay, for the most part older lags or those who had been cheated out of their rations through dice and card games and the superior cunning of their fellows.

"Without a word to me," said Johnny White, "H.E. showed the pouch to the native. The sight of the thing caused a violent fit in Arabanoo and the fever asserted itself yet again. The native is dead, Ralph. Now all that lies ahead are the excessive funerary rights. H.E. is determined to bury him in the grounds of the viceregal house. He is concerned at his lack of knowledge of the native burial ritual, and I would not be surprised if he sent out another armed party to gather information on this point."

"I do hope not," said Ralph. "The last expedition returned unharmed only through Davy's good sense—I must say that, despite any differences we might have had."

Johnny White drew his hand over his forehead and looked forlornly at his wardful of sad cases. "Damn me, I do not resent H.E., his interest in these unfallen and natural creatures. I have something of the same myself. But to bury one in viceregal ground, with Robbie Ross and Jemmy Campbell, those vile letter writers, looking on . . . It makes one see that H.E. is capable of grand folly. I do hope he is never captivated by one of the she-lags. For she will end as queen; she will sit at the head of table. Although again, if rumour is true . . . but we won't speak of that."

For the rumours were back, that H.E. was a sodomite—his passion for Arabanoo was seen by the more base-minded as mere pederasty, the assault of a high culture on a low.

"There is no change in Harry?" asked the surgeon.

"I have brought in a convict to watch him," said Ralph, attempting to control through his will the surges of blood inside his head.

"When Harry goes," asked Johnny White, "do you think he will merit burial in H.E.'s garden?"

O N the day before Arabanoo's funeral, Harry awoke. The left half of his face would not move, but he was able to speak. And he woke speaking, consumed with the same concerns he had had before his stroke. "Where is she?" he asked.

Only Mary Brenham was with him when he stirred. She sent a convict orderly at once to find Ralph.

Ralph had just heard he had been nominated as officer of the honour guard for the burial of the native. Since no Indian or *ab origine* performer of rites could be found without a major military expedition, H.E. had decided to fall back on the more accustomed resources of the British armed forces and the Established Church.

The funeral would further interrupt Ralph's preparation of the play. The space in his military career which the playmaking had nonetheless created enabled him to rush to the hospital immediately to visit the resurgent Harry. What he saw was a man who could speak only with one half of his face.

"Where is the Duckling?" asked the new Harry.

"She is staying with friends."

"On the east or west side of the stream?" Harry had never been sharper, despite the distortion of his face.

"We will send for her," promised Ralph. By motions of the head he signalled that Mary Brenham should see to this—the fetching of Duckling from whatever ancient tie now detained her.

Mary understood exactly and gathered up her small son, who

made a minor protest at being separated from his jigsaw, and set off
to summon Duckling. Tears brimmed out of both Harry's eyes. The
stroke had not frozen them in their well behind the gnarled face.
"They claim her back with such ease," Harry murmured. One side
of this mouth exactly articulated; the other was a mere slit. Yet he
forced both into service to speak of Duckling, that unprofitably
loved lag. Ralph had hoped that if Harry did return to a conscious
state, he might emerge without the memory of Duckling, having
lost her somewhere in the swamps of his coma. For it occurred to
Ralph and to most people that there was not a great deal in the girl
for besieged memory to cling to.

Next Harry said, "Is the Captain still alive?" He retained that
memory too, of shipping with H.E. before H.E. was a viceroy. But
Ralph told him the Captain was in excellent health and had been
to see him, that news of Harry's awakening would be a cause of
great joy to the viceroy. "Christ," said Harry, suddenly, licking his
palsied lips, "I am hungry." But as Ralph got up to go to the cook
orderly at the far end of the hospital and commandeer a bowl of
floury stew, Harry began to weep again.

"He will always be there, just out of sight," he told Ralph.
Ralph knew he meant Private Baker, that leering phantom. "And
they will always fetch Duckling right easy."

Almost at once he fell asleep again, as if exhausted. Surgeon
Considen came in and said, "We will first feed him and then see
how well he walks." Duckling arrived with Brenham and the child.
Duckling did not show any interest in inspecting the sleeping features of her master and sometime lover but sat silently on a bench
by the wall. Ralph approached her.

"Will you be kind to him?" he asked.

She looked up at the rafters. "Yes, Mr. Clark," she said.

"If you were not determined to be kind to him, it would be
better if you were sent to Norfolk Island, where you would have
greater liberty to choose your friends."

Now she lowered her gaze and engaged his eye. "I like the
friends I got here, Mr. Clark. I like you. I like them players. I like
that Brenham best of them."

He wondered if she was mocking him by naming Brenham like

that. Irony and warmth both seemed alien to her, and it was hard to find out which one this was. He told her she was to sit with Harry throughout the afternoon, that she was not to attend the rehearsals of the play, but that when Harry spoke she was to reassure him and try dissuading him of the existence of Private Baker's ghost.

I N the midst of funeral preparations for Arabanoo the following day, news of Harry's revival had reached H.E. He came over to the hospital for a short visit, during most of which Harry was tongue-tied or given to tears. It happened, too, that during the afternoon's playmaking, Surgeon Considen helped him trundle around the room and concluded that in a little time he might be able to take up again the duties of Provost Marshal. One thing, however, Considen told Ralph when Ralph reached the hospital that evening, Harry must be moderate answering the calls of Venus and must drink no more than a cup of brandy a day. "His history as a good bottleman," said Considen cheerily, "is at an end."

It was agreed too among Considen, Johnny White, and Ralph that Duckling should be permitted to sleep on a pallet on the floor of the same room Harry occupied. And indeed Duckling was there in the early evening when Ralph arrived and found a Harry still tremulous and tearful. It was Ralph's impression again that Duckling, by the questions her presence aroused, was poor company for the sick man. Yet Harry could not have been content with her absent from the room, because then he would have been plagued by questions of where she was.

Harry did ask Duckling to leave for a small time—he wanted to speak privately to Lieutenant Clark. She rose up obediently, almost gratefully. She could join the convicts in front of the fire in the main ward.

When she was gone, Harry began to tell the story once again of the night Goose had simply sent for the girl because Private Handy Baker had wanted her and had made an arrangement with Goose. And because too, since babyhood, since Soho and the parish of St. Giles, since the days when Goose ran an apothecary in Greek Street, in the shadow of the great Rookery of St. Giles—that island of criminal tenements looming near the Tottenham Court Road—since those days, Duckling had always obeyed Goose.

Ralph settled in to hear the great and engrossing history from Harry yet again. He believed he could half listen, for all he expected to hear rehearsed again was the mystery of Duckling's daughterliness to Goose.

F I R S T Ralph heard again how Harry had—one evening in the settlement's first days—discovered Duckling's absence from her tent across the stream. In those days, soon after the women were landed, Duckling occupied her own little bell of canvas close to Captain Jemmy Campbell's marquee, for whom she worked for a time as a servant. Harry had set the patrols of the convict night watch and then gone to Duckling's tent to see sitting in front of it Dot Handilands, the most ancient of the she-lags, rumoured to be eighty years of age. For then, before huts and locks, felons with little else to do were often employed for a small portion of food or liquor to keep watch over people's possessions.

She admitted, only after threats, that Duckling had gone to see Goose.

Harry crossed the stream in the last blue of the evening and walked up through the women's camp, which was then all tents or insubstantial tumuli of boughs, looking for an innocent glimpse of Duckling among the cooking fires.

Even in those days the apothecary she-lag, Goose, had achieved a superior dwelling. Her mere tent had been extended with a length of canvas to become a spacious marquee. It had therefore both an anteroom and a sanctum.

Calling Duckling's name, he went inside this elegant tent. There, on a pallet, the big Marine, Private Handy Baker, dressed only in a shirt, was plunging and rearing between Duckling's knees.

Harry launched himself, strangling away, onto Baker's shoulders, but was soon thrown, with all the diverted violence of Private Baker's desire, onto the clay floor. Baker landed on top of him now

and, with hands which held the odour of Duckling, began strangling *him*. A shadow passed over Harry's mind. For the first of the
two times he would manage it, Baker took Harry's senses away.

Waking later, Harry found himself seated on a square of canvas, a tumbler of spirits in front of him. As his brain reached
painfully for the memory of the latitude and the year—the common
bread of time and place without which Harry was not Harry—the
knowledge returned to him and he hurried to the corner of Goose's
tent to be sick.

Looking up he recognised Goose standing calmly by the flap,
some firelight from outside richly burnishing her red hair. He knew
now that he was still inside her tent. It was a further segment of it
than the one in which he had observed Baker and Duckling. Perhaps there was no end to the canvas Goose had already acquired.

She was the same ample, red-haired woman he had seen in
Newgate on the occasion he visited Duckling there. He had rarely
bothered to face her since the night of Duckling's commutation of
sentence. When he discovered that Duckling and Goose were both
in the same detachment of Newgate prisoners marched down to
Portsmouth and placed with over a hundred other female convicts
aboard the *Lady Penrhyn,* he had devoted himself to having Duckling transferred to the smaller female convict hold of *Charlotte.*
This expedient, he now bitterly understood, had been quite fruitless.

Goose sat on a folding camp stool and grinned at him. She
had mad, nut brown eyes. "You should never set yourself to stop
Handy Baker once he's in his stride. Handy Baker is a runaway
coach and four. Handy can take on three coolers a day."

Cooler was flash talk for *girl.*

She surmised aloud that Harry, in spite of the bruising he'd
had, wasn't planning any vengeance based on the letter of the law.
"All the camps might laugh at you then, Mr. Brewer," she told
him. Besides, everyone came over here to the women's camp to see
Mother Goose, she said, slapping her stomach. To ask Goose for
favours.

•

S H E had even told Harry—and Harry always told Ralph in retelling the tale—that Ralph had once been there. But Ralph was strangely unabashed, since Harry had confessed so much greater follies of his own. Goose said that the girl had been amused when tipsy Ralph had tried to show them all his little picture of his wife. But, Goose told Harry (and Harry passed on to Ralph), that when it came to the assizes of the flesh, Lieutenant Clark went at it as strong as anyone.

This Handy Baker, Goose had informed Harry as he sipped his brandy, was a good cove and had a position of favour with some of the officers. Harry, argued Goose now, had seen Baker flogged on the back and arse in Rio for trading in Tom Barrett's counterfeit Portuguese quarters. He would see Baker suffer again if he just waited for it. For Handy Baker had always gone to the trouble of arranging punishment for himself.

The longer Harry sat before her, trying to piece his head together, the greater and more terrible was the sense she made. Harry was not to think that Handy Baker and Duckling were somehow set, said Goose. Handy was settled in with the Huffnell woman. But he'd asked for Duckling to be sent over in return for some favour he'd done Goose. Baker knew Duckling was clean and in good health, said Goose, as if that explained entirely Baker's preference for her.

Harry's head had still been tolling from the blows and strangling Baker had given it, but he was capable of a slow, balanced, waiting fury. For one thing he picked up the brandy she had poured him and emptied it onto the clay floor. Then he had warned her not to send for Duckling again. To which Goose replied that Duckling had to come if her old mother and abbess sent for her—Harry knew that. These young things always answered the calls of their madame.

She was closer to Duckling, she argued, than mother, than law, than any favours Harry might give the girl. "I am the Flash Queen, Harry. He who tries to put the wind up my skirts finds vipers beneath. You give her little gifts of mugfuls of flour, and sips of rum. Good for you, Harry. It might keep a wife in a cottage. It won't keep the Duckling over there when her Queen calls."

Goose further elaborated the state of her nation to him. She would let him buy Duckling, but he did not have the wealth. And though he was Provost Marshal, he would find it hard to have her, Goose, sent before "the Beak," Davy Collins, and sentenced in any way. If she were put on a list for Norfolk Island, someone else would take her off it. "Because everyone talks to me, Harry."

Then she produced her brandy bottle again, refilled his glass, and advised him not to waste it this time.

Though he needed it to ice his brain a little, he struggled upright and walked away into the corner. He could not remember later what threats he uttered then—not only the noose but an array of inconceivable punishments. Yet as he left she clapped him on the shoulder. A maternal indulgence from a woman two dozen years younger than him.

When Harry got to the stream (as Ralph heard in all these retellings), Duckling was waiting for him, sitting propped on the handrail. Once she saw him she did not maintain this posture. She came upright and said nothing. There was such an expectation of blows in her manner that Harry could not remember how it was he'd ever wanted to punish her.

"A strong bastard, that Baker," he said to her then, to let her know she was safe. He hoped she showed to Baker the same whorish competence and coolness she showed him, the writhings which had no juice in them and were intended merely to move the customer along.

She assured Harry that he was her regular swell. She went so far as to touch his face. She murmured that no one could afford making enemies of the Marines.

There was one he intended to make an absolute enemy of.

Soon afterwards (again as Harry told it to Ralph), Harry and H.E. had one of their awkward conversations. It was over a glass of port on the Good Friday before that first Easter.

"This woman you know," H.E. had said quietly. "Do you think you would ever marry her? Or is she in the nature of a temporary solace?"

The question had struck Harry oddly, so that he wondered was it a test. Since H.E. saw the convicts as future yeomanry or, in

Duckling's case, future yeo-womanry, was he suggesting that gentlemen should be happy to marry them? Or was he doing what friends do everywhere, taking a hand in the grotesque passion of an elderly comrade for an unlikely young girl.

"If she were pardoned, I would marry her," Harry had said to his surprise. It was a thought he had never consciously held before. And H.E. remarked—as if he thought a girl ought to have a dowry —that when she had served her time, she would be given a land grant. That was to be the standard arrangement.

It was at this point that Harry chose to damn Goose with H.E. "There is a procurer working in the women's camp," Harry suddenly confessed. "A woman called Goose. A woman of many false names. She procures girls, even from this side of the stream, for Marines and for convicts with a bung, as they say, a purse. In terms of the women's camp she lives in grand style. She calls herself a queen."

H.E. closed his eyes for a time. "I shall have my adjutant look into it," he said.

H.E.'s adjutant was George Johnston, the affable young officer and paramour of Esther Abrahams.

About the time Harry mentioned the name of Goose, H.E. went off on an excursion across the harbour, traversing for the first time the country where Ralph and Davy would later meet Ca-bahn. In the meantime a lag named Joseph Levy died, a genial young cockney Jew. Harry and Lieutenant Johnston attended that funeral, and Dick Johnson was accommodating enough to allow the Jewish convicts, Esther Abrahams shawled among them, to sing Kaddish over Joseph Levy's grave. The seven-shilling kettle Joseph Levy had once lifted had brought him to the earth's further burial.

Dick Johnson supervised the ceremony, as if he suspected something infamous would take place, but at the end he remarked to Harry that it was a remarkable thing that Jews sang Kaddish in Aramaic and not in Hebrew, and he began to speculate on the historic reasons for that.

It was after this funeral that Lieutenant George Johnston took Harry aside. "Harry, His Excellency told me to look into this matter of Goose. What would you like to see done? A prosecution, is it? Because there is nothing to prosecute her with!"

It struck Harry that George was a little overheated on the matter, as if a friend of his had been attacked. At last though, he grew more jovial and put a hand on Harry's shoulder. "Harry, that woman keeps order for us in the women's camp. If not for her, it would be all Stygian chaos, believe me."

"She keeps order?" asked Harry, unbelieving.

Lieutenant Johnston had licked his lips and begun to tick off the fingers of his left hand. "In the first and best place of all, she keeps all those girls in the camp. Do you think you do it, with your night patrols? Do you think great space does not call to them? Remember that they are beings used from childhood to impulsive action. They have seen alleys and escaped up them without thinking of the wisdom of it. They have stolen whatever presents itself in the same spirit. Here we have an immense space, but most of the women choose not to flee into it. That, in the first place, is one of the services she does for us. In the second place, she works some order upon the disorderly desires of Marines and convicts alike."

"You mean," said Harry, "she manages the women's camp like a pushing shop."

"It *is* a pushing shop in any case, Harry," George Johnston said, and groaned. "It would be a bloody slaughterhouse without her."

"And it is not bloody now?" Harry pursued, remembering the damage Baker had done to his head and throat.

"Harry, old fellow," said George, "you must consider that girl might love one of those scoundrels perhaps better than she loves you."

"She doesn't love any of them," said Harry, deciding not to be angry. "She doesn't love me. It is too much to ask of someone who has been a whore from babyhood."

This disarmed George. He shook his head. "Anyway, Harry," he said, "there are always people like Goose. I think I find them more essential to society than parsons, probably more important to the tone of things than the military and officers of the law. And believe me on one point, Harry. They can't be expunged."

Harry had felt shamed. He had risked greatly in raising Goose's name with H.E., risked that friendship which went back to the *Europe* and the *Ariadne,* to the time of the war with the Americans. But all that had come of it was this picture of lag society as sketched by George Johnston.

When Johnston withdrew, he was muttering still about the lack of matter for prosecution.

CHAPTER 25

Withholding Prussian Blue

As the resurgent Harry Brewer now continued to tell Ralph, it was on the day after the six Marines were detained for trial that the young son of one of the Marine sergeants had come jogging over the stream with a summons from the woman Goose herself. After some delay, meant to signify his independence of her, Harry obeyed.

Crossing to the women's camp, he found Goose sitting in a straight-backed chair in front of her tent; her camp stool had been placed beside her and was waiting for Harry. She told him to sit on it but he refused, leaning instead against the tent pole and looking down over the disorder of the women's camp, which the day before George Johnston had chosen to call order.

"You didn't have to do me the honour, Harry, of dropping my name in your His Excellency's ear."

"Given a chance," said Harry, "I'll drop more than a name."

Goose clapped her dimpled hands. "Spirit, Harry! Love is very good for a man's spirit!"

She had then come out and asked him about His Excellency, what His Excellency's fancy was. If it was boys, she could find him boys. If he was a plug-tail . . . she said with half a smile, using the contemptuous cant word for sodomite.

"He's nobody's lover," said Harry. "It would be more merciful for him if he were. He is a true solitary, and so you can never rule him."

"But he never has a woman?" said Goose. She spoke speculatively, as if there were a gap she might one day fill. Harry began to laugh at the idea.

Suddenly, "You can keep Duckling," Goose told him.

Harry could not speak for a time. Then he ranted at Goose. "I can keep her, can I? I can *keep* her? I have Your Grace's *approval?*"

"I'll say to Handy Baker, ask for someone else, Jim."

"Thank you, my sweet abbess," Harry continued satirically, calling on his knowledge of Soho for invective. "May you piss pure cream." He was answering her in kind—with the cant alternative for catching the gonorrhoea. "What do I need to do to repay such generosity?"

"You could speak well of me to this His Excellency," said Goose without any smile.

Harry could see she was not joking.

"Speak well of me, I say. No words like abbess or bawd or Madam Ran or such."

"I cannot speak good of you, Goose!" Harry protested.

"Then don't speak bad." She stared levelly at him. "If you speak bad of me, I'll take your little Duck."

The pattern of society was now clear to Harry. George Johnston must have felt he kept Esther Abrahams at home and in his arms only by grace of Goose. That Mother Goose, if she chose to, could provoke unimagined havoc. And, watching her, Harry too had a sense above all of her power to reclaim Duckling. Part of his pride in being Provost Marshal, servant of order, bled away now. He felt foolish. He had often enough said to Ralph that the same arrangements which prevailed in St. Giles and other criminal covens must have been transported in the convict holds of the *Lady Penrhyn*, the *Charlotte*, the *Friendship*, and the others. From his mad youth, he believed, he had learned to be certain of this. Yet he had not really believed it, in the chambers of his blood, and now Goose was proving it to him. And in the chambers of his blood too he rejoiced that Duckling was now secured to him.

What was left of his pride as Provost Marshal, however, required him to make a hard contract.

"All right," he had murmured. "When others say you're evil, I'll call you mischievous. When others say you're vile, I'll say you're merely self-interested. If that's all you want, I'm your man. I shall never mention you unless someone else does, and if they do, and speak too highly, I shall moderate what they say down to a medium level, and if they speak of you poorly I shall improve your reputation in a small way. That is all."

She laughed at that and put out her creamy hand, which no tropic nor convict deck nor intemperate downpour had marred or made less immaculate. "Good for you, Harry Brewer." She squeezed his nose with her ivory fingers. Harry had the impression she was growing affectionate, and for the first time in his life chose not to take an erotic chance. When she saw that he intended to keep his reserve, she began talking business again. "And, Harry Brewer, above all you must guarantee this! If ever friends of mine come into your hands, you must promise to treat them swiftly, that's our contract too. Swift treatment without any rope tricks to string them out."

"I know no such tricks," he told her. "Neither does Ketch Freeman." Both Ketch and Harry were tyrannised in their sleep by the idea that some silly ineptitude of the knot could cause a terrible grievous drop.

"There are further mercies than mere hangman's mercy," Goose argued, patting her cheek and running a forefinger around her lips.

R A L P H had heard the story thus far at least four times in the past year, and as the stricken Harry came to the point where his bargain with Goose was sealed, Ralph began to congratulate himself that the tale was just about ended and that now Harry could rest, Duckling could be called in again, and he, Ralph, could go home. He felt petulant, therefore, when Harry continued the history, hinting at further and later arrangements with Goose. Harry's weakness was that he could narrate nothing in its short form.

Besides, there was a rankling concept which had arisen in Ralph, which he wanted to take away with him and look at in private. It was this: if he wanted Mary Brenham, did he have to bargain with Goose himself? Would he be bound to visit Goose the way a hopeful lover visits a woman's mother?

Yet now Harry's recital took a direction Ralph had not heard of before. After mentioning further mercies, Goose took something from the pocket of her jacket and kept it hidden in the palm of her hand. She took his hand by the wrist and dumped in his palm a little flute of glass with a blue fluid in it. Now that Handy Baker had been condemned she wanted him to enjoy a small mercy. Close to the execution, Harry would pass the phial to Baker, who would hold it in his mouth before the drop. When the ladder went from beneath him, his teeth would break the glass and he would feel—in Goose's words—"no more anguish."

Harry asked about the other Marines who were to drop. About Askey and Dukes, Luke Haines, and the others.

Goose told him they were not her concern to the same degree. Besides, it was likely they would be pardoned on the gallows. But there would be no pardon for Handy Baker, since he had been the chief actor in killing the Marine Bullmore.

"You have supplies of this?" Harry had asked her, impressed once again at the range of her governance. A regime which could place such a kindly substance on the tongue of a condemned creature could call itself merciful.

"I have some," said Goose.

Somehow she had transported it, a cache of maternal kindness, in the hold of the *Lady Penrhyn*.

"One for yourself?" asked Harry.

"Aye. And one for you, Harry Brewer, if you need it. It is an ancient trick. Without it the world would be too savage. When the surgeons see the bloodied lips of Handy Baker, they'll think he's bit his tongue."

Harry would have liked greatly to be able to put a name to the poison or opiate Goose had given him. Therefore he went to see Johnny White that night, asking for a small glass phial suitable for storing an abnormal and robust ant which he had captured.

"It had never occurred to me," Johnny White had said, "that you were a naturalist, Harry."

"Only when nature is poised to bite me," Harry told him.

Johnny White suspected Harry's story. "Your compassion is well known," said the surgeon.

"I was not aware of that," said Harry. "I thought everyone considered me a peevish old bastard."

It was not uncommon for surgeons examining the body of the hanged, said Johnny White, to find broken glass in the mouth of the corpse. Merciful people—perhaps an officer, perhaps a minister of religion—attempted to limit the victim's agony by handing him a phial filled with some swift poison or another.

"Hydrocyanic acid," said Johnny, "was distilled a mere ten years ago from Prussian Blue by some German chemist and is now commonly used by the higher classes of criminals, especially in Holland, where they hang like us, or in Spain, where they garotte. I would never make any fuss if I discovered splinters of glass between the teeth of a hanged felon. But I warn you as a friend, Harry, that the sharp, fast poisons must be handled with some care."

By now Harry was emboldened by the sight of Johnny White going for one of his medical cupboards and withdrawing a flute of glass stoppered at both ends.

"This ant of mine," he improvised, "reaches a length of at least two inches."

"I'm sure the Royal Society would be very interested in it, Harry."

Harry took the phial, and in crossing the stream uncorked one end of it, knelt, filled it with water, and sealed it again.

"I felt like a god and a criminal at the one time," Harry confessed to Ralph.

T H E next morning Harry went with Ketch Freeman to the civil prison, which had begun as canvas and was now brick, and put the nooses round the heads of the six condemned soldiers, and the tail of the rope in their chained hands. While this was proceeding,

Harry handed Handy Baker the phial of clear water tinctured with draughtsman's ink. This mixture had been made late at night, after Duckling was asleep, the phial of acid lying before him in candle-light to serve as an exemplar of how much ink should be added. Handy took the thing from Harry, as of right, and placed it in his jaw. The drop would break it in his teeth and give him release, or so he believed. He winked at Harry. "Winking back," Harry would tell Ralph, "I understood at last what a treacherous and vengeful son of hell I was."

The six men made their way then to the exemplary scaffold constructed by John Arscott, Ralph's Sergeant Kite.

"I was serene," the palsied Harry told Ralph. "I had withheld all mercy from Handy Baker and was saving it, you see, for some future and more deserving victim."

At the drop he always turned his head away, but this time he waited until he had seen awareness and alarm in Handy Baker's eyes. Handy's Dimber Damber, Handy's pontiff, the Goose, had failed him at the worst minutes of his life.

"It was not to be wondered," said Harry, using his new face, which only half worked as a face should, "that Handy Baker would subject me to visitations, should haunt me when I arose at dawn. But now you see, I am delivered of Baker. He has taken his measure of my flesh. I shall be, Ralph, a laughable hobbler. I am left with a mouth which cannot frame a kiss. Think of it. But at least Baker is gone. And now there is Duckling and Harry. Harry and Duckling."

Harry closed his eyes in contentment, and—watching him—Ralph felt homeless and willing to give up a fair proportion of his own powers just to find the equability, the freedom from ghosts that maimed Harry now apparently enjoyed.

PART FIVE

CHAPTER 26

Tattoo

OF all the most exquisite reaches of Farquhar's play, the one which gave Ralph most delight as the date of the performance neared and his desire for Mary Brenham grew absurdly and without rest, was when Brenham/Silvia and Rose/Mrs. Bryant appear at the beginning of Act 5. On the night of the performance and during the last rehearsals, Mary Brenham would be wearing a white gentleman's suit and Rose would be dishevelled and wear a mob cap, her hair escaping from beneath it. Neither woman was as yet fully acquainted with her costume—the seamstress Frances Hart was still working at Silvia's suit.

This segment of the play was oddly delicious, particularly because of what both women had suffered, though Ralph assured himself he did not relish directly the recent travails of either of them. But since her recovery from her bruises there was a new liveliness in Mary Brenham—she did her Silvia with gusto. And in Dabby a sort of smarting grief was apparent since the native had died, since she had seen him buried with his secret and glistening rope intact within him and heard Dick Johnson's play-hating God, instead of that celestial Mother and Son, invoked on Arabanoo's behalf.

Act 5 commences in an anteroom adjoining Silvia's bedchamber. Silvia enters wearing a man's nightcap. The nightcap was available—Frances Hart had run it up—and Mary Brenham looked very handsome and boyish in it.

Silvia had accepted the lusty Rose's invitation to share her bed as a means of avoiding sharing one fraternally with Plume, and since Silvia has had to stay buttoned up all night to maintain her disguise, Rose is not at the start of Act 5 very pleased with her night's rest. Her responses are in the characteristic Farquhar style.

Rose: How am I? Just as I was last night. Neither better nor worse for you.

Silvia: What's the matter? Did you not like your bedfellow?

Rose: I don't know whether I had a bedfellow or not.

Silvia ends up standing trial before her own father, Justice Balance, for ravishing Rose. Mary Brenham played the rakehell soldier beautifully in front of Ketch Freeman's Balance. It made Ralph wonder whether—if Brenham desired him at all—the suggestion of an alliance might not in the end come from her.

When Balance asks her what brought her to Shropshire, Silvia through Mary Brenham replies with male authority that she always knew country gentlemen wanted wit, and that town gentlemen needed money and therefore the two were made for each other.

And so, for a sweet joke, she aggrieves even her liberal father.

In Act 5 too, in what Ralph saw as the sublime way of plays, everything begins to coalesce. Worthy arrives at Melinda's place and indicates he is about to travel Europe for a year. As you would predict, Melinda/Nancy Turner at last begins to show an aggrieved humanity. "A year! Oh, Mr. Worthy, what you owe to me is not to be paid under a seven years' servitude." Worthy knows he has her, kisses her hand ardently (at least as Sideway played it), and replies, "And if I don't use you as a gentlewoman should be, may this be my poison."

And so as Ralph's version of *The Recruiting Officer* neared its end, as all characters grew not only redeemable but worthy of congratulation, the players and the playmaker Ralph himself were left with the sense that life *could* be easily amended, that love was an easy ploy, and that everyone really intended the best.

Ralph considered that in the real world it might also be the case except that there was always too much hidden, and too much to take into account. It was only within the circumference of a play, and particularly of a comedy, that all characters could be so deftly delivered from their meanness. Only in a play could Melinda, the Nancy Turner who sat by campfires with Joe Hunt, become so ennobled as to say, "I am going to Mr. Balance's country house to see my cousin Silvia. I have done her an injury, and can't be easy till I have asked her pardon."

As Ralph would soon have it proved again, though art perpetually improved itself, society went its reckless and complicated way.

S o o n after Harry's awakening, Ralph took John Wisehammer aside to ask him for his epilogue. His reason was not only that Mary Brenham had asked him to, to deliver her of the burden of Wisehammer's anxiety. It was also that Wisehammer's rendering of Captain Brazen was now less certain than it had been two weeks before. These days, in the midst of the scene where Brazen fires his pistol, or that other stage of sweet nonsense where Justice Balance tells Brazen he is laconic, and Brazen says, "Had not you an uncle Laconic that was Governor of the Leeward Islands?"—in the midst of such comic fervours, Ralph would find Wisehammer stealing glances at him. The reason was apparent to Ralph now. Because he had coveted Mary Brenham and believed her to be Wisehammer's girl, he had wilfully suppressed any laughter which Wisehammer's performance would normally and justly have evoked. He had praised Plume and Kite, the overseer Kable and the carpenter Arscott, and had choked back any praise of Wisehammer. And Wisehammer had probably thought it a matter of the ancient hatred of the Semite which he had seen surface frequently enough among the Marines, privates and officers both. Whatever cause Wisehammer had allotted to Ralph's coolness, Ralph now had no doubt it had unbalanced Wisehammer's playing.

So, after the day's reading, Ralph took Wisehammer aside and enquired pleasantly if his epilogue was finished.

"You ask me is it finished, Mr. Clark?" asked Wisehammer, blinking with delight.

"Yes, I do."

"The epilogue is finished, sir, and I believe it is suitable for our little play."

"For our large play," Ralph insisted.

"Indeed, Mr. Clark, for our large play. But I must tell you, Mr. Clark, that if in any particular it offends you, sir, I can mend it, I can make it to fit. For I am but a tailor of words."

Ralph could see, from Wisehammer's slightly overblown speech, that Captain Brazen had returned.

Ralph explained that he was going out to his turnip island, which he had greatly neglected since the work of the play had begun. Wisehammer could meet him at the dock about dusk and hand the document to him. "You must be aware I can give no promise, Wisehammer, that it can be used, since there are so many sensitivities abroad in this city."

Wisehammer nodded assent again and again. He was willing to have his work rejected. It was clearly having it ignored which had sapped his acting.

As Private Ellis rowed Ralph out to his island, the sun of early winter shone as sweetly as that of a Devon summer above the dun cliffs where the late Arabanoo had captured his shrewish tribal wife. Ralph felt himself ready, too, for a new world spouse. His mind idled over the prospect not only of accustoming Mary Brenham to the idea, but of so accustoming H.E. and all other British inhabitants, bond or free, that he and Mary Brenham could, without attracting any malice, float out here at will to the garden isle, Small Willy lolling amidships. By the mouth of the cave on the blind side of the island, they could sit before a fire and grill bream from the harbour. As pregnant as the harbour seemed this evening with such fish, so did the coming months seem pregnant with such opportunities.

Ralph found the old convict gardener Amstead undisturbed by the long lack of a visit from his master. Ralph felt, in fact, that had the strange lag enterprise been totally given up, had H.E. decided to cram all the people aboard the *Sirius* and abandon the city, the gardener would have continued on the island, wondering perhaps a little at the non-appearance of his rations of flour and beef, but making very good meals of mixed pots of vegetables. He had baskets of turnips, potatoes, and one of carrots for Ralph to take back to the town. "There be some grub got at them potatoes," he told Ralph. "It weren't here when first I come, when first I take up the task of gardener. So damn grub must be able to swim, the ruffian!"

In a boat full of the island's plenty and rowed inexpertly by Private Ellis, Ralph returned to the settlement.

It was dusk. From half a mile out, Ralph could see Wisehammer pacing the dock, glancing out across the harbour and then back inshore as if there were a whole crowd to whom Ralph's arrival needed to be announced. As Ralph's boat drew in, Wisehammer was waiting, avid as a hunting dog, on the bottom step of the quay. It was apparent now why Mary Brenham might find him wearing.

He thrust some papers into Ralph's hand even though it was now too dark for Ralph to be able to read them. "I shall look at these with great interest," he promised the Jew.

Later, by his fire, Ralph took out the pages and inspected the poesy of Wisehammer.

> To make this play we travelled by the mile,
> More distance than those gentlemen of Style
> You find around the Royal in the Lane.
> We beg you to ignore the felon's stain,
> And look upon our art without disdain.
> As we with humour bold before you file,
> We humbly hope we may excite a smile.

Ralph remembered how Mary Brenham had ranged around the tent, ticking off the rhymes on the fingers of her left hand. Mile, style, file, smile. A lesser Sappho making line endings for a clever poetaster.

> Upon the one hand we commend the Navy.
> Phillip and Hunter—may this be their gravy!
> Upon the second, we applaud Marines
> And hope their brave and robust spirit means
> They will enjoy the tenor of this play,
> This sunshine of our brief theatric day.
> May these our antics represent in sum

The first time you went marching to the drum
Inveigled by some handsome, martial Plume,
To give to King and country all your bloom.
And on the third hand, since we have three here,
We hope our play the felons will endear.
The lags of Dyot's Isle and Cornwall both
Will with our Silvia reclaim their troth,
And see in arch Melinda and in Worthy
Exemplars at the same time wise and earthy.
May each lag now his cull-ess quick bespeak
Avoiding all attentions of the Beak,
And Thus the holy state of marriage blazon,
As do our Silvia and Plume, Lucy and Brazen.
May every lag-ess now have wit to force
Upon her lag the matrimonial course,
And blessed will this felon shore then be
If your lag-ess says yes, as mine to me.
And so we hope our play begins with wit,
But ends with happiness derived from it.
And may our King be happy to display
This joyous penal place so far away,
And boast of happy culls and blooming molls,
Beyond the stars where great Orion lolls.
We hope the action has been fast and clear
And so invite your universal cheer.

It was as clever as any officer could have done, but Ralph calculated whether outright applause for Wisehammer's epilogue would excite the man so much he would now turn again to courting Mary Brenham. Then there might be congratulatory fondlings and so on, which Ralph found very painful to envisage.

A N hour before curfew, still tormented by this mean question, he was pacing back and forth from the fireplace to the bed, sitting briefly sometimes either on the cot or at the chair by his writing desk and repeating in a distracted way snatches of the play which he had now learned by heart, muttering them to himself as if they had a magical or a religious importance, when someone knocked jauntily on his door. At first he presumed it was Harry with a bottle of brandy, but then remembered all jauntiness had been struck out of Harry. The shrunken Provost Marshal had earlier in the day been carried in a chair by four convicts back to his home across the stream. Duckling had been there, dutifully at the door, but with a nomadic look in her eyes. She did not give any clue as to whether she would have preferred Harry to die and so release her to a sort of freedom over in the women's camp, or was happy that he had lived to ensure her a certain status on this side of the stream.

Ralph, on first hearing the knock and thinking it Harry Brewer, had felt guilty. He had cherished Harry as a friend, as a teller of whimsical and grotesque stories of criminal London, and above all as a confessor of such crimes—lechery, embezzlement— that one felt able to confess *anything* in his company. Yet Ralph understood now that when Harry Brewer had been struck down and rendered mute, he, Harry's friend, had without knowing it taken his death as read.

And so Lieutenant Ralph Clark, playmaker, manager of convict players, had broken an undertaking he had made earlier to the vertical, perambulating, joking Provost Marshal—that Duckling would be given no lines that were too gamy.

In Scene 5 of Act 5 a need had emerged for someone to say the lines of two common women who appear, one after another, in front of Justice Balance. These lines reek of carnal jokes. Rather than search for another player among the women who could be tutored in these lines, Ralph had—during the first days of Harry's stupor—had Duckling read them. The comedic wariness with which Duckling performed this section of the play newly opened to her convinced Ralph she was precisely the right choice. So that— in a sense—he had had a minor and underhand interest in Harry's never reawakening.

The first woman Duckling played in Scene 5, Act 5, was the wife of a young man Sergeant Kite had impressed into the Grenadiers—or as it would be in this city of convicts—Marines. Balance asks her is she married, to which she replies, "We agreed that I should call him husband to avoid passing for a whore, and that he should call me wife, to shun going for a soldier."

That "to avoid passing for a whore" worried Ralph guiltily. He feared Harry might come for an explanation, introducing another argument on top of the Wisehammer-Brenham dilemma he himself was already occupied with.

He opened the door and it was Dabby Bryant, looking witchy under a shawl, her sleeping girl child in her arms. She seemed a little blank-faced, as if she were still absorbing the mystery by which one who could travel among the stars and converse with the Emu-Mother and Daramalung her Son could also be quenched by something as average as smallpox.

Ralph told her to come in from the cold. He had never before had a she-lag inside his hut after sunset, but even if he were not contemplating having one there after each future sunset, Dabby Bryant, with her higher powers and mercies, would have been exempt from such narrow rules. Ralph gave up his own chair to her and sat her by the fire. If she had not delivered him of his relentless nightmares, he would never have been able to negotiate the distance between the dream Betsey Alicia and the one who had built up a debt with Broderick Hartwell's estate: the gulf between the two would have consumed him whole. The beneficent and dazed Cornish Gypsy who now sat at his hearth had saved him from that and so deserved the best chair.

He asked her would she like some tea, but she said no. The child called Charlotte slept as tranquilly as Mary Brenham's child. What mysteries of contentment you might take in with your mother's milk if you were Dabby Bryant's infant!

Ralph made some remark about the tragedy of Arabanoo. Dabby blinked at the fire. "Did you know," she asked, as if it referred to the native, as if it was a talent she and the native had shared, "that a person ought to be able to tell the time from the Southern Cross?"

"I don't have the skill myself," said Ralph.

"My father taught me," she said. "To some souls, the sky takes exactly after the high street of a village. You can look and see where the crossroads fall."

Her star talk, he was sure, referred to the trance she had suffered in the native's arms. She sat for half a minute—Ralph thought she had gone to sleep. He wanted to ask her was she plagued by Arabanoo still—did he come and take her on exhausting expeditions in her sleep.

"I don't rest well now," she said suddenly, her eyes still closed.

"I'm sorry to hear it. Is it the native? Or the play . . . ?"

She waved her hand dismissively at the idea of the play. "It's Mary Brenham," she said. She opened her eyes. "And it's you too, Lieutenant Clark, boy."

That "boy" struck Ralph strangely, but he had no doubt she was entitled to such a familiar appellation.

"I disturb your sleep?" he wonderingly asked. Yet he knew himself how it was possible to have the unhappiness of other people, as well as your own terrors, infest your peace.

"You and that Mary Brenham should settle to each other. But you don't, darling, because such is your nature. And she don't because of the tattoo on her arse."

"Tattoo?" That pagan novelty which adorned the bodies of sailors. The idea that Mary Brenham carried one was not only beyond belief but also extended and challenged his image of her. "She carries a tattoo on her body?"

"She carries on her arse a tattoo which says *Andrew Hilton I love thee to the grave*. She dreads you'll see it. It is the shame of her life. On account of it she tells the surgeons after the big black man bruised her that he did not try ravishing, even though he did. She feared Surgeon Considen seeing her arse and that *Andrew Hilton.*"

"And who is Andrew Hilton?" asked Ralph, trembling, he was sure, visibly.

"Why, her fence, wasn't he? She comes to London, a green girl of thirteen years. She's working as a maid, but running an errand she meets this lovely boy, who is foul, mind you, as an adder behind the sparkle of his face. He gives her gin and shows her his love, and when they are in one of those bad max fevers he puts it to her that she have that message carved in her sweet little flank. *Andrew Hilton I love thee to the grave*. And so she does love him to the grave, very near. For his sake she fumbles through all the wardrobes of her master and her mistress, handing him through the window all that good linen Mrs. Kennedy, that gentlewoman, wore on her untattooed arse, all those good tablecloths. So much good linen it came near to earning a wryneck day for our girl, if the Middlesex jury hadn't discounted the value of all that truck and lumber, because of her sweet face and her thirteen years. And because they knew there must be someone like Andrew Hilton behind it, some fly boy with dark eyes and a treacle tongue and a prick like a dagger! That poor Brenham kept herself buttoned up in Newgate and on the ship for fear people would see that tattoo. But her sailor boy saw it, of course. And the she-lags on the *Lady Penrhyn* see it when she gives birth to that little boy of his, *AndrewHiltonIlovetheetothegrave* heaves about then as the poor thing drops her kid. She would like to scar or burn it off, but how can she do it herself? And she can't trust them that offer to do it. She knows they would be likely to poison her blood, and then her small boy would be orphaned. And what a place for an orphan this is, darling."

The baby called Charlotte suddenly woke, struggled in its mother's arms, clawed itself higher, its feet finding purchase against Dabby Bryant's stomach, and stared at Ralph with an enormous infant limpidity.

Having inspected him for a time, the baby settled again and slept.

"So this awful thing, this tattooed arse of hers, you know it now, boy. You should do something with it. Unless you are the sort of mean mind who finds a tattoo too low for his touch, you ought to take her for your lag wife so I can have some peace from her."

"It means that Caesar ravished her?" he asked.

"So that's what it is, darling? In such a place as this you want a girl who's suffered no mishandling? A black man, bodied like a brick stack, comes into your house and says he might kill your child. Do you do battle with him, chuck? Not if you had your training on the *Lady Penrhyn* or the *Charlotte*. She is a good little duck. What else do you need to be told?"

"But the black man forced himself on her?" Ralph persisted.

"If that sours the girl for you," sniffed Bryant, "more than tattoos on her haunch, you should tell her, boy, so she can go and live with John Wisehammer."

"It isn't any such thing," Ralph said, getting heated over Dabby Bryant's constant suspicion that he might be a narrow and unmerciful lover. "It means nothing. The tattoo and Black Caesar. I would like to see her safe from attack and from shame as well."

Both the women I best know, or hope to best know, he realised, are in debt and subject to hard dealings. Betsey Alicia had never experienced the hard erotic business of transport or penal city, but in a way the closely managed estate of Broderick Hartwell would be a similarly merciless regime. And only Mary Brenham was available to receive the kindnesses he now felt himself brimful of. Betsey Alicia had to depend on the generous friendship of his friend Kempster. And Kempster was a man of such honour he would seek nothing from her, not even a kiss or a fondle.

"Ah," he said aloud, despite himself, "my two tormented girls!"

This scarcely conscious cry of his satisfied Dabby Bryant and she stopped harrying and accusing him of being affronted by tattoos.

"Will you speak to her?" Dabby asked all at once.

"I don't know that I can," Ralph confessed.

He sweated with his incapacity to approach Mary Brenham. To know that she was subject to similar torment did not help him at all. And so, almost coolly, almost with deliberation, he set aside this obvious new world duty of speaking to Mary in favour of fury against the Madagascan Black Caesar. The Fragrant One would not save him.

"We must catch that fellow!" Ralph said, on an impulse. "You could tell her that tattoos mean nothing to me. The idea of a convict misusing her means much, at least in the sense that I want the bastard found."

"Would Captain Plume call on a Cornish witch to take a message for him? To a poor she-lag with a tattoo on her arse?"

"I am not Captain Plume," said Ralph, understanding himself all at once. "I am Mr. Worthy. A frightened lover, who takes all signs in the worst way."

"You might do what other gentlemen do, and use your power, darling!"

"That is not my nature. It would be better if it were."

"You might give me rest, God damn you!" said Dabby Bryant, rising.

"Lifetimes aren't long enough, Dabby," he pleaded, "for me to make my tortured approaches."

"I seem to remember a time your approach was quick enough," Dabby cried. She had stood suddenly, heedless of the sleeping child in her arms, and shouting in the same reckless spirit. "Don't think I cannot curse you as easy as I cured you that time, boy. Others of my stripe have surely put a curse on me, don't you worry!"

"Don't you curse me, Dabby. Give me a little time."

"Holy Jesus!" said Dabby and, crossing the dirt floor, disappeared from the house. Ralph wondered desperately where he should go now—Mary Brenham was still at Reverend Dick Johnson's. Could he propose an arrangement to her under that roof? He decided instead to hold fast to his rage against Black Caesar. He searched for his greatcoat, found it, pulled it around his shoulders, and went out to see Provost Marshal Brewer, however marred by paralysis that official might be.

DUCKLING answered the door, opening it only wide enough to admit him if he inhaled. Harry, his stockinged feet sitting on one of the hot stones of the hearth, his upper body wrapped in a naval cape, looked expectant and amused at his arrival. He told Duckling to fetch Ralph some port. Surgeon Johnny White, he said, had cut him down to a tumbler of port and half a measure of brandy a day. "Just enough to get some warmth to the ancient extremities," said Harry, "but not enough to explode what's left of the brain."

He had already had his daily quantity, so Ralph would have to forgive him if he did not join in with the taking of refreshment.

When Duckling had brought the liquor in a cup, she fetched her clay pipe again and sat on a stool. Her air was that of a child waiting to be let from school. Again Ralph found himself speculating that if she could be sent to Norfolk and replaced in Harry's house by one of the more reliable she-lags, Harry could begin a better ordered life. He had got rid of the ghost beyond his door, and now all he needed for perfect balance of his mind was to be rid of the ghost on his hearth. But any list she was placed on, Harry had the influence to alter; as once, working in a broom cupboard at the Admiralty. Those were the days when he had hoped that by dropping the raw earth of her criminality through such an enormous sieve of latitudes and longitudes, her soul would be cleansed.

"Have you heard from H.E.?" Ralph asked Harry, not wanting to introduce his own exciting proposal at the very start of the conversation.

"I was visited. He is not well, the Captain. It is the death of this savage. On one side I could say to him, why grieve so long for the boy? He had an innocence, a frankness, indeed. But there are boys in England I could find who have an innocence and a frankness worthy of the affection of an older man. And don't misunderstand what I say, Ralph, as the rest of the officers' mess does. Sometimes I wish for his own sake he was *that* thing, or that he showed a preference among the convict women. There is something inhuman in the poor Captain."

It appeared to Ralph that Harry might no longer consider himself H.E.'s intimate, might have heard in fact that H.E. had spent more time at Arabanoo's bedside than at Harry's. In any case, Harry now smiled at Duckling, who puffed equably on her pipe.

"It was the first time I've seen the Captain and thought, Poor old boy! Another man might look at me and say that I was a poor source of law with half a working face and a hobble of one leg. But he told me he hoped I could continue in my duty, and since it is the only duty I could exercise here or anywhere else in the universe, I looked him in his eye and told him I was fit for it."

Ralph was pleased the talk had come round neatly to the point at which he wanted it. Did Harry know that Black Caesar the Madagascan was still at large? "He lives in the fringes of the forests," said Ralph, "and raids the town at night. He stole firearms from Private Meadows, he bruised and misused the convict Mary Brenham, and he stole flour from the brick kilns party. I know how he can be caught, at least I would hope so."

Harry blew air through his stricken lips and sat forward. "I would love to find that great bastard!"

"Never will conditions be better for that, Harry, than on Thursday when my play unwinds itself. Everyone will have his eyes fixed on it—I can't tell you how amusing the women will be—Dabby Bryant and Mary Brenham and Nancy Turner the Perjurer. And Kable and Arscott. Even Sideway and Wisehammer. They've transformed the normal arts of criminal dissembling into the better dissembling of the actor on stage."

Harry Brewer slapped his own knee—a sudden, youthful, unstricken movement.

"The Madagascan," Ralph continued, "is cunning in ways in which we are simple-minded, but simple-minded in ways in which we are cunning. If you were to create an improperly guarded store of food on the edge of the settlement, say at the brick kilns, if you would talk the Commissary into letting you have some beef and flour on a trust basis, then the black man would come into town to steal it. For everyone remarks he has no rationality in the matter of food. We think of the Madagascan as somehow having the same dimensions as the forest which hides him—as being as difficult to gauge and capture as that. But his appetites reduce the extent of the space he can occupy. That is, he is bound always to be close to the town."

"But now he has a gun," Harry said. "He can wander wherever he likes, living off kangaroo and iguana. There is no reason either why the savages wouldn't take him in as a brother."

Ralph shook his head. Even this degree of argument seemed to him mysteriously to advance his surreptitious approaches to Mary Brenham. Caesar first, then Brenham to follow! "If he were living well from kangaroo and iguana, and if the savages took him as a brother, he would not have needed to raid the convict woman."

"Are you suggesting that not only did he break into her house, but that he also raped her?"

Ralph, for no good reason, burned with shame. "The convict woman is very reticent on that matter," he said. He was very reticent himself.

Harry struck the ham of his leg again, with a force which took Ralph by surprise. The young rake who had embezzled Cuxbridge and Breton's accounts could not have slapped flesh with more impact. Duckling stared at him sharply but—Ralph thought—without understanding.

"This," said Harry, "is how I re-enter the live business of being a Provost Marshal. By capturing the Fragrant One."

Ralph again felt a sudden envy for Harry, who had rediscovered his profession, rid himself of phantoms and possessed—more or less—his love. "Black Caesar isn't the Fragrant One," Ralph corrected. "He calls his god the Fragrant One."

"Capture a man," shouted Harry, under the brunt of an excitement which might well be bad for his health but was certainly good for his spirit, "and you capture his gods."

CHAPTER 27

Celebrating the Part

BUT even the planning of the capture of Black Caesar had failed to ease Ralph's bewilderment over Mary Brenham. In the cold night air he felt warm with apprehension as he made his way toward the bridge of barrels over the stream. An inexactly played fiddle and the high laughter of two or three women sounded across the cove, yet you still had the feeling any noise made was barely resounding in an enormous silence. Over on that more populated and less sober side the nights of liquor, whoring, and thievery ended earlier than in the sweet humid nights of summer.

Nearing the Reverend Dick Johnson's place, he saw a man in a white suit pacing among the widely spaced trees which skirted Dick's garden. It was, Ralph felt sure, the little Irish dentist and surgeon, Dennis Considen, though why he should be wandering like this—like a man rehearsing an argument with himself—Ralph could not guess. The likelihood was that he had had dinner with Robbie Ross or Jemmy Campbell and that the experience had left him half drunk and angry, and that he was saying in the privacy of the native cedars what he believed a man of courage would have said at the table of whichever turbulent officer had had him to dine.

"Dennis," called Ralph. Considen paused in his exaggerated pacing and stared at Ralph. Then, as if Ralph's being there added further to his shame, he began to flee along the picketed edge of the Reverend Johnson's garden. Ralph was non-plussed but also alarmed for the little dentist. Considen's strange jerky running reminded Ralph of an earlier tragedy, of the exaggerated gait of Lieutenant Maxwell, who had gone mad in the Indian Ocean. In the settlement's first days he would run, bare-arsed and with that same broken lope, toward glittering stretches of harbour, intent on ecstatically drowning himself. Ralph did not want to see the little Irishman drown himself, so he began to pursue Considen, sure he was the only one in all the night who could save the Irishman from some Maxwell-like excess.

It was when one began to run that it became clear how the poor quality of the naval and penal diet throughout the lag city's existence—a diet only sometimes spiked with the liveliness and fibre of turnips or cabbages or kangaroo or fish—had sapped one's strength. Considen ran bent now, and not quite like a terrier, but one could not doubt he took energy from his frenzy, whatever it was.

He broke away now from the corner of Reverend Johnson's garden, making for the confused ground of boulders and sinewy acacias in the direction of the fishing camp. He fell once, over a ledge of sandstone, and Ralph heard him give a strange and pitiable bleat. He got up swiftly, but the fall seemed to have destroyed his certainty of direction. At last he knelt at the base of a boulder, as if now that speed could not be invoked he intended to call on powers and principalities.

Ralph reached him, but for some time had too little breath left to circle him, consider his face by starlight, and quiz him about his desperation. At last he staggered in a half circle to Considen's front and looked down at him. The surgeon was still kneeling.

It was not Considen in his white suit. It was Mary Brenham in her white suit, the one run up by the convict seamstress Hart out of calico, yet as perfectly cut as any suit anyone in the place owned. Mary began to weep. But Ralph, in his breathlessness, was exalted. All those movements and gestures which had seemed madness when he had associated them with Considen now had a sweet reason to them once you attributed them to her. To a Mary Brenham so consumed by the play that she asks Frances Hart if she might take her costume home with her, and then, after the Johnsons and their native child and Small Willy are soundly asleep, dresses in her calico coat, vest, and breeches and, defying the convict curfew, goes out to recite her lines among the trees and to take on the theatrical postures suitable to a Silvia in men's clothing.

Now arose what he knew to be the supreme moment of temptation in his life. He could take an air of authority with her, and this would defeat her yet still give him at least her body and her willing performance. With authority and the harsh question, he could take from her without turning over any mysterious gifts of his own, without becoming a fool as she had become a fool in her white calico suit in the night. This first possible procedure appealed indecently to him. His blood itched. He suffered a sharp and panic-stricken awareness that this was the way damnation was decided and Heaven and Hell apportioned. Yet he was still beset with the question of whether to tyrannise her when he heard his voice asking with humanity or even tenderness, "So you were rehearsing your part?"

"I know my part," said the girl.

"You were *celebrating* your part, perhaps? You were celebrating Silvia."

"I am always caught out," she said. "It seems to be a condition of my life that I cannot do anything secret without being found out."

Ralph reached out and touched the line of her jaw. The sweat dampened his hand. "Andrew Hilton I love thee to the grave," he said.

As he raised her she was looking away, as if the night itself were not adequate cover for her. He kissed her through the medium of those tears. They had their source, he fancied, in the night she had ransacked the Kennedys' wardrobes, passing the clothes of better people down to Andrew Hilton in the street. One crime, one capture, one sailor, one child, one Silvia. There was in her eighteen-year-old face and gestures the certainty that her vanity in Silvia too would turn to tears. He felt desperate to correct this assumption of hers. He kissed her throat. He encountered beneath the calico suit of white clothes the remarkable firmness and design of a young woman's body. Climate was canceled. He tore at the fabric so painstakingly sewn together by Frances Hart. Vest sundered, coat dropped, breeches tore apart at the buttons. And Mary Brenham tore similarly at his vest and breeches, which though adequately tailored by Lambton Brothers of Plymouth fell apart with the same ease as the works of the lag costumier. All at once Clark and Brenham were joined, blue as ice beneath that moon merely rumoured to be the same as the one which gave its light to Britain. His blue hand found the holy delta as she cried, "Oh soft, soft!" So the wonderful hard and liquid entering of his Silvia/Brenham commenced. How she appreciated his shoulders, how she tore him to her! What exquisite gasps compounded of Farquhar and unhappy criminality, of what Ralph thought of as lost years and unchosen motherhood, went into her cry as he entered. When he turned her over it was because he wished to demonstrate to her, at the peak of his joy, that her tattooed arse meant nothing. Raging as he gave himself, he saw the calligraphy of her thirteen-year-old folly shining like some runic inscription.

"Silvia," he screamed, delighted under that penal moon. "Oh, now." He laughed, recovering his breath. "Oh, now can our friend Rose forget us." He had used Dabby Bryant's play name, he would later suppose, since the mistaking of Mary Brenham for Considen, his pursuit of Brenham under the supposition that she was a young and dapper surgeon gone lunatic, and his astonished coupling with incarnate Silvia seemed to him as neat as anything Farquhar could devise, seemed to be a gift and a contrivance from poor Farquhar's comic genius.

What was most gracious about this gift was that Mary understood it too—the play and Ralph and Mary were of one mind.

"I altered my outside," said Silvia/Brenham, quoting Farquhar with a directness and a humour Ralph had before merely *suspected* she possessed, "because I was the same within, and only laid by the woman to make sure of my man. That's my history!"

Then, with the tears of the chase and the shame still in her eyes, she began to laugh as—aware of the necessities of time—she began to button herself back into her white calico suit for a return to Dick Johnson's house.

"I will have you built a hut in my garden," Ralph promised her. "You shall be by name my housekeeper and by night my beloved."

She nodded. She knew that was the way love was managed on that particular penal moon.

CHAPTER 28

Lag Matrimony

LAG matrimony was accomplished thus: between the scenes in which John Arscott played scandalous Sergeant Kite, he was detailed to the work of building a small wattle and daub hut close to Ralph's. Curtis Brand, who had fewer lines to speak, cut the lathes and wattles for the wall panels and dug holes in which to sink the corner posts. Ralph had not denounced him to Harry Brewer for taking joy in Duckling, and in Curtis's code of action this entitled Ralph to a certain quantity of grateful labour.

The roof was of that shaggy bark which could be cut in whole pieces from certain species of trees and which had, *ab origine*, kept the rain off the heads of the Indians.

Ralph did not explain the purpose of the hut to either Arscott or Brand beyond saying that it was for a servant. During the reading of those scenes in which Arscott and Curtis did not appear, sounds of adze or axe or hammer could be heard from the direction of Ralph's place, and a knowing flicker would, however, enter Mary Brenham's eyes. She and Small Willy, she understood, would be domiciled more in Ralph's house than in that outbuilding the two handy players were erecting. The hut would have its uses as a storeroom, an alternative kitchen, and a concession to the fiction that Mary was a mere servant.

In his nuptial frame of mind, he looked kindly at Nancy

Turner the Perjurer, who by now knew her lines intimately enough to let her true spirit and sharpness emerge as she strode, queenly and dismissive as Melinda. She had loved Private Dukes and spawned a false oath to save him—affronting solider deities for the sake of honeyed, treacherous Eros. In one sense, good for her!

Towards dusk Ralph went down over the stream to speak with Lieutenant Johnston, who possessed the power to direct convicts here and there, to this side of the stream and to that. George could well have been amused—he had been the first to declare a love for a she-lag. He had been mocked behind his back, though he was built so huskily and came of such obdurate Scottish farming lineage that very few made jokes to his face. He did not smile when Ralph told him that he required the convict Mary Brenham as his house-keeper, and Ralph was grateful. He at whom everyone had grinned had not descended to grinning now. In that there was something to admire.

George looked through his registers in the small office at the front of H.E.'s place. "This is Mary Brenham, who is presently with the Reverend Johnson?"

"That's the one," said Ralph. He thought it would be to betray her if he said that because she had worked in Dick's house she was known to be trustworthy. George Johnston knew, as did Ralph, that that was a narrow recommendation.

"Can it be done?" Ralph pleaded.

"Yes, Ralph, it can be done," said George. How sweet was the compassion of a fallible man like George. Their mutual weakness made them brothers.

"George, I am a bad cook, but if ever I should shoot anything worthwhile, then I hope you and your Esther will join me at my table."

It was only now that George showed some marginal amuse-ment. "Ralph," he said, "I would be honoured."

I have joined a club, Ralph concluded.

I N those last days before the play and the accomplishment of the marriage, the carpenter Arscott seemed to be driven to a fury of energy by the force of the mutual expectations of Mary Brenham and Lieutenant Clark. He rushed from the quickly done hut in Ralph's garden to the wildly accented scenes in which he represented Sergeant Kite, and then on to the work party which under his direction was making a rude stage in the new barracks building on which the play would be enacted. Here the thief of powder and perfumes John Nicholls painted flats and a backcloth on which you saw great oaks and parklands and country houses sublimer than H.E.'s place, and prepared himself for confecting and decorating the faces of the players on the night of the performance. One of the convict women made artificial flowers of coloured canvas to deck the stage, and both she and the powder thief too seemed to work with what Ralph thought of as a celebratory enthusiasm.

On the edge of the brick kilns, a similar hut to the one Arscott was building as matrimonial cover for Ralph was being constructed so that a small but tempting quantity of stores could be stacked there. On Ralph's one visit, he saw Harry Brewer limping about with crooked vigour. The calmer Ralph at the core understood that this access of vehemence and punch he saw in the world may have been an illusion. Harry, indeed, on a closer look, seemed not to be consumed by the sort of congratulatory sweetness Ralph was seeing in most people now, in his lag players, in George Johnston, in Nicholls and Arscott. Harry was plagued—as always—by questions to do with Duckling.

"My toxin is gone," Harry confided to Ralph. "The Prussian Blue I used to toy with. Duckling didn't give it to you or the Reverend Dick?"

On the morning of Harry's fit and collapse, Ralph and Dick had forgotten the little phial. They should have taken it and emptied it, but it seemed a small matter beside Baker's ravening ghost and Harry's stroke. Now Ralph suggested that Duckling, in her concern for him, might have poured the stuff in the roots of a tree.

"She denies it," murmured Harry. "If she returns it to Goose, that Pope of the Whores will know I failed to honour my contract with her!"

Ralph assured him Duckling would not do that. She was negligent perhaps but not treacherous. In his roseate state, he believed in the comfort he was offering Harry. Lucy/Duckling in the play could deceive Brazen by taking on the identity of her mistress, Melinda. But Duckling/Lucy of the penal city would not so abruptly betray Harry Brewer.

"You see," said Harry, "she may have thought—after I suffered that apoplexy—that I was good as dead, and so returned it to Goose. You can't tell with those people! You can't tell!"

The term *those people*, especially as it came from Harry, shocked Ralph for a moment. He had grown accustomed in the last days to seeing this earth and this population as one thing.

"I am not built any more," said Harry, "for a battle with Mother Goose. That big slattern is a galleon of Dimber Dambers, and I don't have the weight for it any more."

R E T U R N I N G to the clearing, the marquee, the new house-keeping residence, and, a little beyond it, the new barracks where the play would be performed, Ralph saw—waiting by the door of his own hut—the Reverend Dick Johnson and his wife, Mary. He considered hiding in a clump of cabbage-tree palms—indeed he took temporary refuge there and observed the Johnsons taking sightings up and down the length of the cove, on the lookout for him.

They must be faced, Ralph knew, and it might as well be sooner than otherwise. So he emerged from the cabbage trees and walked with what he thought of as an absorbed nonchalance towards his home, his canvas marquee, and his legal fiction of a housekeeper's hut. He was—he realised—more afraid of Mary than of Dick. The tightly built, bustling little olive-skinned woman believed in the Johnson dogma, which was that everyone misused her husband. She was prepared to say so militantly, without any of the pallid wistfulness which characterised Dick himself. She did not bruise as easily as Dick. Ralph decided to act at least as angry as she would, knowing that if he showed any penitence or doubt Mrs. Mary Johnson would flay him with it.

He was not prepared for the Johnsons' sage regret.

"Oh, Ralph," said Dick, staring at him with wounded eyes. "How you took advantage of me!"

"It seems to us," said Mary Johnson, "that you used our household to provide a refuge for your concubine until you had prepared your own household for her. We had a right to expect something less arch, Lieutenant Clark!"

"We spoke to the adjutant to dissuade him from assigning Mary Brenham to you," Dick told Ralph. "But we all know where he stands. He is delighted to compound his own guilt."

"So we intend to appeal to His Excellency," said Mary Johnson.

Ralph flushed despite himself at the idea of H.E., whom he thought of as a grey and preternatural presence, receiving frontally from Mary Johnson the news that Lieutenant Clark intended to cohabit with Brenham.

"That won't do any good either, my dear," said Dick Johnson, almost tranquil in his despair. "He is a viceroy who would rather build a theatre than a church." He turned his eyes to Ralph. "We are absolutely alone now," he remarked almost amiably. "Mary and I alone are united in something like righteousness and in regard for Christian doctrine. We cannot point to you any further as a paragon."

"I was always only a poor paragon, Dick," said Ralph.

"When the play takes place," said Dick in that same strange companionable tone, "Mary and I will be the only ones at home, a loaded pistol on the table between us in the event Black Caesar raids us." He put his hand across his eyes.

"Come, Dick," said Mary. "Fortitude, my love!"

Ralph had been prepared not to yield to clerical fury and denunciation. But Dick's wistfulness routed him. He found himself putting up a moral defence.

"It is better that she live with me than with a convict. Even the married convicts prostitute their wives."

He had no evidence that Henry Kable, who played Plume, prostituted his—Henry was a jealous spouse. Yet he argued on, hoping the example of Kable would not come to Dick's mind. "On the first Sunday after the women were landed," he said, "you married many lags of whom it could not be said with any certainty whether they had previously been single or married to persons left behind in that other country, the one they will never see again.

You did so on the instructions of H.E., who believed that it was better for them to marry here for the sake of this society than to maintain the mere letter of ruined marriages in another place—marriages which could never be resumed. The Dutch geographers, Dick, used to say that there *had* to be a great southern continent to act as a balance to the land masses of Europe and Asia. Likewise it has always been H.E.'s suspicion—and I must say it is my suspicion as well now—that people here have needed southern marriages, new world associations, to balance the marriages and associations they might have had in the old. We have travelled too far in space —perhaps we have come further than human creatures should— and the influence and the glow of English marriages and loyalties cannot reach us here. I wish it were not so, but too much space lies between. I shall honour my English marriage, Dick, and I shall not call upon you to sanctify this loosely termed marriage I undertake here. Yet it is a marriage, and it will have honour, even if you denounce it. My punishment will come when I must leave Mary Brenham.

"I ask you," Ralph continued, "why does H.E. not object to these arrangements? It is not, as you must realise, because he wishes to attack the morals of Christians. It is rather because he knows that these 'marriages,' these arrangements, are a leavening in this society. It is because he has an active understanding of the way whoring begets felonies. He is not satanic, nor is he bent absolutely on disappointing you, Dick. It is that he understands what is possible with human flesh, and what is not."

Dick had been becoming increasingly enraged throughout this speech. "Get thee behind me!" he now screamed. "There are always high-sounding arguments for sin, and Satan is a lawyer. But the Decalogue does not cease or become transmuted at the Equator. It is because such people as His Excellency and you believe the Commandments are altered here that this slub, this scrag end of civilisation stinks so high in the nostrils of Creation! Sin heartily if you must, but make no apologias, Ralph! There is no defence to save you from the lick of hell!"

"And remember," said Mary Johnson, "we who have been your friends are witnesses to you and your illicit association with Mary Brenham."

This idea frightened him. Did Mary Johnson feel bound to write to Betsey Alicia when the relief ships came?

"You would not tell my wife?" he begged. "You would not for the sake of the Decalogue ruin my English marriage and torment poor Betsey? I ask you to have ordinary human sense and compassion!"

"When I say witness," said Mary gently, "I mean that we will observe your sin, and the knowledge that you are observed will bring you shame and a final repentance. I am not a writer of poisonous missives, Lieutenant Clark. You must depend on someone else to write such a letter."

"Depend? Do you think I wish Betsey Alicia to be tormented? But no one will write it, since this sort of arrangement—a convict marriage let us say—is taken as normal here and below remarking."

"Oh, the truth, the truth!" Dick groaned. "Now that you have made such an arrangement, this city is entirely devoted to concubinage. This is the way the world goes, Ralph. First I come to you and counsel you against a play. The play finds fornication funny, fidelity a joke, and a woman a fickle organ of pleasure. But it is merely an entertainment, you say. Yet now I approach you under circumstances which have made the conditions of that play incarnate in this cove, on this shore, in your very household, Ralph. Adultery *is* a laughing matter for you now, fidelity *is* a joke, and woman *is* an organ of pleasure! The play—as I warned—has become your very life."

If Dick had not been himself an almost theatrical parson in his horror for the play, Ralph would not have been so pleased to feel anger coming to him like a friend. He embraced it gratefully. "Blame the Admiralty perhaps! They let you bring *your* wife, but refused me permission for mine. I have the letter from H.E. which says that for me to bring Betsey Alicia was contrary to Admiralty rules." He grabbed at the sentence which was forming, as it were, behind his back, a sentence to bludgeon the Johnsons with and brutally end the conversation. "Can you be sure, Mrs. Johnson, that if the Admiralty had not provided you with this long passage, after two years of fidelity Dick himself might not have been ready to find an honest companion?"

Dick covered his face from the possibility and Mary Johnson

became brick-red with rage. Yet her answer was unexpected. "Do not use," she said, "the possible crimes of one man to pay for the certain ones which you are about to commit!"

Ralph would have hoped for something a little less coherent from her. Nonetheless, thankfully, she took Dick's elbow and suggested they should leave. Ralph, she said, could not be diverted, and the struggle would be a long one. As he watched them go, two loyal friends supporting each other in what they considered a grief peculiar to themselves, Ralph began to feel a blinding shame, a grief at his betrayal of Betsey Alicia. Her mishandling of money and of debts suddenly seemed an enormous claim on him. It was one thing to imagine a spouse bravely managing while an officer was away and living with a lagwife. The idea of her bravely *mismanaging* was somehow more pitiable and more of a reproach.

He went to his hut and covered the butterfly collection he had made for Betsey with a cloth. Then he staggered off to the barracks, where the players were at work. Their lines, he was sure, would restore him. Perhaps the play was—as the Johnsons argued—his life incarnate.

T H A T same shame recurred at dusk when old Dot Handilands came trotting up to the clearing, the marquee, the now extensive Clark household, looking for Ralph. She had in her hand a bottle which she presented to Ralph. "Good max, the best gin," she kept saying, assuring him of its high quality. She said it was from Goose, who had heard of his good fortune and wished him well.

The old she-lag staggered away, the ancient perjurer, at eighty years of age an errand woman.

"Dot!" Ralph called on impulse.

Dot Handilands stopped and turned, fixing a strange stooped gaze on him. Ralph uncorked the bottle and let the gin flow out on the ground. "Tell Goose I do not look for her presents." For the first time since Dick Johnson had confronted him, he felt justified and restored.

CHAPTER 29

San Augustin

JUNE 1789

By the time the chief dish was served at H.E.'s great noonday dinner for the birthday of the distant King, Ralph was glimmering away at table with a wonderful tipsiness. He had had a celebratory brandy with his breakfast, which had been served for the first time in his history by Mary Brenham. She worked with the same mean rations as Ellis, but there is a difference between food that is willingly instead of sullenly handled. Mary had suggested the brandy to mark the day. She left it unclear whether she found her new world marriage, the play, or the monarch's birthday the cause for serving spirits. Breakfast brandy had put Ralph in a state where he could consider the night's performance of *The Recruiting Officer* with composure. For the sake of composure he had drunk well before H.E.'s dinner and was now drinking well at table, becoming more convinced with every mouthful of what a consummate group of men these officers were, glowing with affection for Watkin and Davy, and even finding the sullenness of Robbie Ross and Jemmy Campbell engaging in its consistency.

"Is the play up to viewing, Mr. Garrick?" one or other of the gentlemen would periodically ask Ralph, and he was ecstatic for this merely whimsical comparison of himself to the great actor-manager. "Mr. Garrick, the port if you please!" and "Mr. Garrick, will you pass along the salt?" became staples of the humor of H.E.'s table and filled everyone with increasing hilarity. The talk turned also, in such a military gathering, to old battles. There were four or five there at table who had seen Bunker Hill and could trade impressions. "If it were not for Bunker Hill," said Jemmy Campbell, morosely, though he had survived the musketry of the Minutemen, "we would not be in this ghastly place. Our lags would still go where they were intended by nature and geography—the Americas."

From his place at table, Harry Brewer began to rumble. "Warriors, are they? Those who faced the Americans. I was one such *warrior*. But do they deserve the name? We are not warriors. The Captain, when he served with the Portuguese, was a warrior!"

Enough of the younger, less embittered officers at the table heard Harry. They were not yet of an age or a narrowness where the mention of another man's glory was an affront to them. Davy and Johnny White the surgeon began to press H.E.—the Captain, as Harry still cherished calling him—to recount his adventures on the Brazil station.

And H.E. himself was in one of his rare companionable moods, less aloof than usual, capable of memorialising and storytelling. Sometimes he made a poor president of a dinner table, but today he was an excellent one. There was some slamming of plates and the bases of glasses against the table, a tattoo of sound created by the younger members of the company to encourage him to speak. And so, his dish of pork half-eaten, H.E. began. "You have to understand that I was Captain of a mere frigate for the Portuguese. Its title—oh, you have no idea how grandly the Portuguese entitle their ships—*Nossa Senhora do Pilar e Sao Joao Baptista!*"

Everyone laughed, this day of Hanoverian kings, at the Papist excess of the name of H.E.'s Portuguese frigate.

"There were a number of English and Irish naval officers scattered throughout the fleet, of whom this humble narrator was but one. Oh, and it had been a dismal year! The Pope had long ago divided the New World between the Portuguese and the Spanish at the fifty-first meridian west. The Portuguese had—for what you could call reasons of geographic convenience—created a city far beyond that meridian, on the Plate River opposite Buenos Aires.

They called that city Colonia del Sacramento and they peopled it with—well, I will leave it to you to guess who they peopled it with, but they call them *degradados*."

"Lags!" called a number of those at the table.

Rations were so short, said H.E., that the Portuguese monks at the Benedictine monastery ate meat only on the highest feast days, and then it was pickled dog! "We have not got so far yet in our Colonia here, gentlemen," said H.E. "Now the governor of the place I felt great compassion for—he was a soldier, a man of perhaps the age I am now—his name was da Rocha and he understood, all through the blockade, that he would be blamed for the loss of the place. And so he *was* blamed and even sentenced to death, though they commuted that and sent him to—"

"New South Wales," yelled one of the young officers and Ralph doubled up with the humour of it.

"To Africa," said H.E., "where he was to perish of blackwater fever. You see in all this, gentlemen, the object lesson for the colonial viceroy. You are forgotten until you are remembered. You are remembered when the day of blame comes."

"Oh, do not move us to tears!" Robbie Ross murmured snidely to the wall behind his chair.

H.E. now stood with abnormal suddenness and vigour and raised his glass of port wine. "Gentlemen," he said, "may we all in the service of His Majesty be delivered from the spirit of fear, delay, and inertness. Let us have no doubt that for damage it is matched only by the spirit of rancour."

There was a cry from Jemmy Campbell. He rose. Suddenly he was trembling and he asked in a thin childlike voice. "But, Your Excellency, how can we know whether the King is alive or not? And isn't it dangerous to drink to a dead king?"

There was such alarm in Jemmy's question that no one laughed. H.E. said gently, "I am sure the day finds him well, Captain Campbell. All the reports are of his recovery."

Tears appeared on Jemmy's face. "Reports? The reports are *years* old? How can we know anything here, Captain? How?"

He half turned as if to leave the table and then fell against the wall and subsided. Some of the younger officers laughed now, at the idea of Jemmy drinking too much and getting soulful. He was carried to a bedroom and soon forgotten, though he left a certain wistfulness behind him at the table.

M A Y B E to dispel it, Harry Brewer—farther down the table— had taken off his shoe and was beating the heel of it against the wood. "Tell them about the *Augustin,* Captain!" he was roaring from his crippled mouth. Meanwhile a fine pudding had been served. It was full of dried Brazilian fruits and had plums from H.E.'s garden in it.

As Ralph listened in an ecstasy, his mind half fixed on Mary Brenham's delicious tattoo, H.E. launched into a comic account of an engagement off the Brazilian port of Destêrro. One of H.E.'s colleagues blocked the path of a great seventy-gun Spanish warship called the *San Augustin,* but H.E. himself, in his little converted merchantman, drew near from astern, calling to the captain of the *San Augustin* consolingly in Spanish. The poor fellow thought that H.E. was in the service of the Spaniards and was disabused only when H.E. drew abeam and unleashed a full broadside volley at him. H.E. described this comic approach, this matter of confused identities, Ralph thought, as sweetly as Farquhar could have. When he announced that the *San Augustin* was repaired and com- missioned in the Portuguese navy and renamed the *Santo Agostinho,* and that he himself was placed in its command, and that then— further—when the Spaniards and the Portuguese came to terms the ship was handed back to the Spaniards and renamed the *San Augustin,* the table seemed to be consumed with hilarity.

And what was remarkable was that H.E. spoke that dinner time as Ralph never expected to hear him speak, like a man who had visitations from angels, one angel saying attack and another counselling him that imitating a Spaniard could produce large re- sults. Ralph felt too like a man subject to nothing but friendly visitations. Standing for Mr. Garrick, he floated closer to the great bulk of his *San Augustin,* that breastwork of impersonations, mock- eries, passions, and grand mistakes Farquhar had constructed and named *The Recruiting Officer.*

CHAPTER 30

Performance

A T some point in the afternoon, when he left H.E.'s table and floated across the town to his own marquee, he found his players transmuted by Nicholls the perfumier. They were ghost white, but their cheekbones were rouged and their eyes so starkly marked it seemed to Ralph they looked at him with refined knowledge and saw that, yes, he was justifiably tipsy, and judged that yes, that was not inappropriate.

Nancy Turner the Perjurer seemed to him totally swallowed by Melinda, her face a terrible alien white, her white, powdered breasts, marked here and there with beauty spots, scarcely held by her bodice. Oh what poor Private Dukes lost when he lost Nancy! Duckling too was ghost-white and fussily dressed. Mary Brenham had been costumed less ornately in the honest gown in which she would appear in Act One, Scene Two—a garment which would later be replaced by the white suit in which Ralph had mistaken her for Considen.

John Wisehammer, the epiloguist, his face marked with black lines to give him age, stood by the theatrical Robert Sideway, who wore a fine grey suit borrowed from an indulgent Commissary Miller. Arscott the carpenter carried a sergeant's jacket rakishly, and Nicholls had much ruddied up his features to give him a look of town-and-country rascality. Ketch Freeman as Balance wore a mask of ageless judicial seriousness. Curtis Brand, who would play Costar Pearmain and the bumpkin Bullock, had had his face skilfully painted a blank and witless blue. Rose, behind whose stark white face and emphasised eyes it was difficult to recognise the Cornish witch Bryant, stared at Ralph most omnisciently of all, and a strange and uninterpretable smile appeared briefly there. Lastly, the convict overseer Kable, in an excellently cut captain's coat and a superbly pomaded wig, in boots too which carried a fine gloss, did some practice strutting across the floor of the marquee and murmured lines to himself.

None of them would now take those rags off, wash the artifice from their faces and eyes, or become their accustomed lag selves until the performance had been done, the play perfectly rendered. They were locked up for the rest of the day in their characters. This gratified Ralph the playmaker, who would have been tempted —if he had had the power—to keep them like this forever.

A number of private Marines of Ralph's company had been detailed to shift furniture on stage. Ralph spent some hours directing them. A small sofa borrowed from Johnny White was necessary for the scenes involving Melinda, since Melinda was to be languid, and a sofa was an aid to languor. A table with a large cloth had been obtained for the Sergeant Kite fortune-telling scenes, and a series of counting tables loaned by the Judge Advocate and the Commissary needed to be placed together in the centre of the stage to form the bench at which Justice Balance would preside.

Among the soldiers who had been assigned to this changing of scenes was the perfidious Private Hunt, the one who had turned evidence against his co-conspirators in the matter of the pillaged storehouse. He worked blithely, Ralph noticed. Just as no one on the excursion to find Ca-bahn had avoided Hunt, so now the other five Marine stage-handlers showed no reluctance to work with him. When he had hold of one end of a table, there was no scuffle among his five brothers to avoid picking up the other. He helped lump the heavy counting tables on and off stage, while the others groaned in unison with him and gave him ample friendly advice as the things were eased in and out the barracks door and up the steps to the platform. And as the players found their way among the furniture, enacting their lines for the last time short of performance, and Hunt and the others watched from the side of the stage, the recent King's Evidence gave and received equal quantities of digs in the ribs at all the higher points of comedy and double meaning.

Arscott had cut two holes in the backcloth to coincide with the windows of what would pass as Justice Balance's Shrewsbury house. Through these, standing secretly in a small interstice between backdrop and the barracks rear wall, Ralph could see his creatures come and go on the bright stage. Throughout that promising afternoon he continued to make short visits to the place, especially to see Mary Brenham do her Silvia in that suit of white calico. Observing the players from his own special hide carried with it the same air of choice subterfuge as H.E.'s story of capturing the *San Augustin*.

He did not leave the barracks until it was dusk and the last, fully costumed rehearsal of *The Recruiting Officer* had concluded nearly faultlessly. Turner the Perjurer had once or twice been distracted by the laughter of the Marine furniture movers, her speech had frozen and all she could do was to adopt a brave but—Ralph could see—desperate queenly stance and wait for rescue. Rescue was Mary Brenham, who was the play's universal memory.

Ralph had believed it was particularly the laughter of Private Hunt, whose evidence had hanged Private Dukes, that distracted Turner. He had toyed with the idea of ordering him away, but that would have left the other handlers of stage items short-handed. So he waited.

The barracks was now entirely prepared for the performance. Candles had been put on spikes along the walls. Three braziers placed down the middle of the barracks-theatre would keep the audience warm. Flares dipped in pitch would light the stage. As the light vanished, Ralph stood alone in the midst of the floor. Everything was unlit, yet the stage seemed to him—though in the dimness the backdrop was barely discernible—to be still radiant with the latent energy of that afternoon's costumed enactment. Echoes not of past but of coming laughter filled the space. He turned and left the barracks, going home to collect the sea cape he would need for warmth. For he would not be part of the animal humidity of the audience. He would move from his hidden niche to the wings of the stage to the barracks back door, and out across the clearing. Pacing among the eucalyptus trees, he hoped to savour the noises of amusement indoors.

By the entrance to the marquee stood Hunt and Turner the Perjurer still in the form of Melinda. In spite of rumours he had heard of Nancy Turner being friendly with Hunt, Ralph had a powerful sense that now she was being abused. She stood very still, quiet—as Ralph's mind proposed it to him—as a trapped animal, her bodice down, her eyes distant, while Hunt caressed her magnificently powdered, rouged, and beauty-spotted breasts. A little light came through the fabric from the marquee, where the other players ate their evening meal and chattered, tremulously certain of future applause. It was not enough light to tell whether Hunt was in a rampant and runaway state or not. Yet Ralph was somehow certain of it.

That a man whose word had hanged six other Marines should now be enjoying Nancy Turner in their place, should be demonstrating in his flesh certain infallible signs of life while they lay mute and blind and loveless in a pit, unexpectedly enraged Ralph. There was also some element of protecting Nancy Turner, or of Melinda, in the action he took now. He grabbed off the ground a hefty fallen bough from one of those ungainly and unearthly trees and brought it down on the back of Hunt's shoulders. Melinda danced backwards from Hunt, as if she were concerned that the impact of the blow might somehow derange her costume. Hunt staggered and gagged and fell to one knee. It was one blunt blow, Ralph thought, to go with the hundreds of sharp ones to which Hunt had been sentenced by military courts in the past. Melinda adjusted her bodice but too hastily, at a wild angle. Captain Plume appeared at the door of the tent and calmly considered the injury Ralph had done Hunt.

The blow had not expended all Ralph's fury. He hauled Hunt up by the shoulder. He called him a whoreson and an oaf and told him he was there merely to move the inhuman furniture and not to interfere with the human. Ralph was chastened then to see Mary Brenham, dressed in her female costume for the start of the play, appear at Plume's side and look at Ralph with her characteristic equability.

Ralph told the Marine to go and eat his dinner somewhere. Nor was he to malinger or play sick from the blow, and was to return on time to move the play's furniture.

Dazed but upright now, Hunt nodded without resentment. Ralph could have struck him again just the same—for souring the evening.

Achieving something like normal breath, Hunt hobbled away.

"Are you well?" Ralph Clark asked Turner the Perjurer, wanting her to know his rage had been paternal.

"I am, Mr. Clark," said Melinda.

"Well then," said Ralph, "look to your costume."

She turned back gratefully to re-enter the tent. Captain Plume, the convict overseer Kable, said, "I might have kicked his arse early on, except the military get all prideful at such action."

Ralph smiled. "You keep your Plume intact, Henry," he told the overseer. Henry gave a theatrical bow, excessive enough to have come from Sideway, and himself re-entered the tent. Mary Brenham was still there, in the doorway. He feared unreasonably what she might think of his show of rage.

She walked toward him and took up a confiding posture.

"I have to tell you, you shouldn't be concerned for Nancy Turner at the hands of Joe Hunt, Lieutenant Clark." She still called him Lieutenant Clark in all circumstances, and always would, Ralph supposed.

"I don't see why she should have to be worried with Joe Hunt. Or *by* Joe Hunt, if it comes to it. It seems improper that he should caress her when she went to so much trouble saving her lover— even to the limit of taking a false oath and lying in court."

Mary looked away and he felt desire move in him. She was wearing a dress dyed lavender—God knew where the costumier had got the dye from. On her head was a large black hat which had probably been borrowed from one of the Marine wives, and around her shoulders a canvas shawl which Hart had worked on with a thin black brush to make it appear that it was made of mantua lace. Rouged up by Nicholls, she looked like the essence of Englishness transported beyond all sensible bounds, a divine little scintilla in the most un-English darkness. As if she had now completed the sum she was doing in her head, she returned her gaze to him.

"I have found out, since we last talked about this, that Hunt is her lover. She would wed him if he would hear of it. Nancy Turner did not perjure herself."

"I was in the court when she did," he told Mary, trying to keep from his voice that crackle of irritation which, he feared, could turn his wedding into a master and servant business. He did not want that sort of union. For the servant must do what the master says and enforces an inexcusable tyranny at the table and in the bed. Whereas Ralph needed his household to be a willing commonwealth.

"Lieutenant Clark," said Mary, putting her hand confidingly on his elbow, "Turner merely spoke the truth, but confident she would be disbelieved. The others had some grievance against Dukes, as thieves always do."

He took an instant to find her reference to thieves quaint, ironic, endearing. If he had not been so interested to hear the rest of her proposition, he might have teased her about it—"as thieves always do" might have become one of those regular lovers' jokes. But there was no time at the moment for establishing anything like that, for the gauging of the balances of affection which must be completed before such small and recurrent teasings could be uttered.

"As for Turner," Mary Brenham went on, "she'd got sick of Dukes, and he had been sent to the outstation at Rosehill in any case. So she told the truth in court, knowing it would finish Dukes. For Dukes was, as Nancy said in court, *not* a member of that crew, the ones who worked the storehouses with forged keys."

"This is astounding," said Ralph. "You must tell the Judge Advocate."

"But," said Mary reasonably, "he can't bring Private Dukes back to life."

She was asking Ralph to believe in what Harry Brewer had always been fascinated by—the mystery of criminal purpose, the mystery which manifested itself as much among the Marines as among the lags. She was asking him to remember how philosophic Baker and the others had been as Joe Hunt killed them with his evidence, and to believe that at the same time they were calm and cool and cunning enough then to settle an old grievance with Dukes. Didn't they know, Ralph nearly asked her, that they had to share a grave with Dukes? That he would lie close as a lover to them?

Ralph remembered that Dukes had tried to escape the twisting by naming other Rosehill Marines and convicts, but his evidence had not passed examination in court, and the other condemned or doomed Marines had mocked him for his effort.

"It can't be said, I think," Brenham surmised, "that that is a crime. In telling the truth? Even to kill someone by telling the truth? It can't be considered a trying offence?"

"It isn't a trying offence," he agreed distractedly.

"Hunt and Nancy Turner keep it pretty quiet," she told him, shaking her head at their artifice. "But they will not be apart much longer. Your Melinda means to move into Joe Hunt's cabin very soon. So you must not distress yourself for Nancy, Lieutenant Clark, even though it is good to see Joe Hunt take a beating, for he is a bad cull and a hound!"

"Do all the lags know this?" asked Ralph, still teased by the old criminal conundrum.

"They have *always* known it," she said. "Even I, who find out things last of all, discovered it in time. I steer clear of the London mobs and crews you find in the women's camp. I was never in a canting crew, you know. But even I find out in the end."

"You found out before me."

"But you are not a lag," she said, and smiled so richly that he put his hand out to her face, but with a little grief. For now he indeed knew that there *were* two worlds and two truths—H.E.'s explanation and the Tawny Prince's. The play would be performed for a divided audience and for two minds.

"I poured out the gin which Goose sent as our wedding gift," he told her.

"I am not owned by Goose," she said.

"Goose thinks you are."

She took hold of the hand which still lay on her face.

"We must think of the play, Lieutenant Clark, rather than *that*. The play is the most wonderful thing that has occurred in all my life."

F R O M the punishment of Joe Hunt, the enlightenment of Ralph Clark by Brenham, to Wisehammer's well-modulated utterance of the first words of the prologue seemed barely a confused instant. In that pulse of time, Ralph had had a chance only to take one glimpse of the two worlds sitting below the stage. Momentarily, and as many a theatrical manager before him, he was awed by the power of a play to summon people. "Against the spikes," as Sideway said they called it in the London theatre, and as you might call it in this fabulous place eight moons distant from Drury Lane, sat the agent of sweet reason and Portuguese naval stratagem, H.E. His substantial and crooked legs shone in white twill in the middle of the front line.

Beside him lolled Johnny Hunter, the impassive Scot, captain of the *Sirius*, the officer who had at the age of eight years nearly died in the Norwegian shipwreck of his father's vessel and had been revived in a fishing village between the radiant breasts of two Norwegian sisters. Johnny seemed to be taking a light nap at H.E.'s right side. Ralph felt confident the first word of the play would rouse him.

Over H.E.'s left shoulder shone the brown scholarly face and pale tunic of the astronomer Dawes. The surgeons Johnny White and Considen sat by him on his left, priests of surgery and dosage, autopsy and dentistry. The young Scot Surgeon Balmain had been rowed all the way down from the outstation at Rosehill to watch tonight's celebration. He looked too red-faced and heavy-eyed with liquor to appreciate Sideway and Brenham, Kable and Turner. If he got rowdy, Considen would try to hush him, and Balmain would challenge the little Irishman to a duel, and the play might be interrupted.

On H.E.'s left sat those robust enquirers, Davy Collins the Judge Advocate, and Tench Watkin, his brown eyes, which stood out from his head not unpleasantly, alive for amusement. Robbie Ross and Jemmy Campbell sat at the end of the line and had separated themselves from what they saw as His pernicious Excellency with the entire officers' mess—Lieutenant Creswell and George Johnston, Poulden and Lieutenant Long, elderly Lieutenant Alt, Lieutenants Furzer, Shairp, Davey, and Faddy, an old enemy of Ralph's in hardly a better condition to watch a play than Surgeon Balmain. Ralph knew that, if he himself had not been manager, he would have been employed in the same manner by Jemmy and Robbie—to help give flesh to the rampart of younger officers they had raised between themselves and Harry Brewer's Captain.

Missing were Harry Brewer himself, who had sent apologies but was out with the Quarter Guard waiting for a visit from the fugitive Madagascan, John Caesar, and of course Dick Johnson, whose Eclectic Society principles dictated he could not attend the theatre, even if Ralph had never pursued the white-suited Mary Brenham and brought her into his household.

Behind the line of officials, behind the two commissaries Miller and Clark, sat the married Marines and their wives and children, and then less regular, less discernible groupings of Marines and *Sirius* sailors and lags male and female. Ralph had time for one look at them. Meg Long, having seen the play at its rude beginning, was agog now to see its consummation. Goose sat by the brazier in the middle of the hall, her elbow room guarded and guaranteed by a cordon of young convicts. One held a bottle of brandy on one knee, and a goblet on the other—the bitch had a cup-boy!

In another segment of the barracks Will Bryant's lean, sad, knowing face was raised with touching and childlike attention toward the stage where his wife, Dabby, would be Rose. His daughter was probably asleep on blankets on the floor. Kable's Susannah sat nursing one child and heavy with a second. All this complicated audience, then, Ralph took in at one glance through the window of Justice Balance's country house, during the flux of time between Mary Brenham's consoling touch and Farquhar's first words.

In the constricted space by the back door of the barracks, all his players had gathered and were waiting for him. He could not prevent a frank conjugal smile from passing between himself and Brenham. As he faced the people of his play, he was aware of the smell of powder and fabric and excited sweat. "The audience is ready for you," he said, his voice quaking. "Please do them and yourselves the honours you have done me as your manager and playmaster." Dabby Bryant stared fixedly, with that gaze which had seen the Emu-Mother, into the centre of the small flame on the taper she carried.

"Rose and Bullock," he murmured. "Light the torches on stage."

Ralph heard a delightful gasp from one of the women players, but did not know whether it was Mary or Duckling.

As Rose in her robust country costume and Curtis Brand as a hobbling oaf appeared on stage with the tapers in their hands, a miraculous cheer rose from the crowd's desperate voices and became one voice, raising in Ralph for the final time the mad hope that his play would unify this remote planet of lags.

T H E play was begun by Wisehammer, speaking Farquhar's pro-logue, saving his own verse for the end of the event. Dressed as a captain of Marines, he intoned the lines with what Ralph thought, looking from the flats, to be a sublime mixture of grand eloquence and gesture.

> In ancient times, when Helen's fatal charms
> Roused the contending universe to arms,
> The Grecian council happily deputes
> The sly Ulysses forth—to raise recruits.
> The artful captain found, without delay
> Where great Achilles, a deserter, lay.
>
> Ulysses caught the young aspiring boy,
> And listed him who wrought the fate of Troy.
> Thus by recruiting was bold Hector slain:
> Recruiting thus fair Helen did regain.
> If for one Helen such prodigious things

> Were acted, that they even enlisted kings;
> If for one Helen's artful, vicious charms,
> Half the transported world was found in arms . . .

(Of course, Wisehammer put great emphasis on the word *transported*, and even the lags seemed to understand that this was a joke not intended by Farquhar. Wisehammer was therefore rewarded with the night's first thunderous laugh.)

> . . . Half the transported world was found in arms . . .
> What for so many Helens may we dare,

(He rolled his eyes and gestured over the heads of the dignitaries toward the wedges of she-lags scatttered about the barracks.)

> Whose minds, as well as faces, are so fair?
> If by one Helen's eyes, old Greece could find
> Its Homer fired to write, even Homer blind;
> The Britons sure beyond compare may write,
> That view so many Helens every night.

And so with grotesque Brazen-like gestures, which promised that when he returned later in the play they would be given better laughs still, Ralph's recent rival for the love of Mary Brenham backed from the stage. The action proper commenced with a drummer rat-a-tatting Sergeant Kite and the minor players onto the stage.

T H E next time Ralph was able to return to his hide behind the window of Justice Balance's country house it was close to the end of the long Scene One, where Plume is pensive for once in declaring to Mr. Worthy his admiration for Silvia.

"I hate country towns. If your town has a dishonourable thought of Silvia it deserves to be burned to the ground. I love Silvia, I admire her frank, generous disposition. There's something in that girl more than woman. Her sex is but a foil to her—the ingratitude, dissimulation, envy, pride, avarice and vanity of her sister females do but set off their contraries in her. In short, were I once a general, I would marry her."

He could see Plume's ruddy, well-made features, powdered up to resemble those of an officer, and beyond them in the dimmer body of the barracks the pale features of H.E. apparently engrossed in this extolling of the heroine.

The scene ended. There was a miraculous throaty burr of anticipation. Ralph noticed, among the furniture-movers dressing Melinda's apartment for Scene Two, Joe Hunt carrying on chairs and walking straight. His back had been so patterned and assaulted by the authority of the monarch whose birthday was being cele-brated that a branch of a tree wielded by Ralph must have seemed a minor business.

In a stillness which grew to howls and cheers and whistles from the lags in the dim reaches of the barracks, Silvia and Melinda entered. It was Nancy Turner's snowy beauty-marked breasts which evoked the enthusiasm—Priapus was in that roar, just as he had had a part in Joe Hunt's earlier encounter with those powder-white mounds.

But to Ralph's admiration, Nancy did not cease to be Melinda, she did not turn frontally to the crowd or bob her knee to them or wave or smile. She remained icy and poker-hot Melinda, as Mary Brenham remained honest Silvia. And of course, that is why she is so perfect, this Turner, Ralph saw now. That was why her act in court excited me as a prospective playmaker. I thought she was a perjurer playing the part of truth-teller, but her ploy was deeper than that—she was a truth-teller playing a perjurer and never breaking from that character no matter how much Jemmy Camp-bell might scream for her neck.

Ralph, seeing all this from the flats of the stage and then going to his hiding space behind Justice Balance's country house, found the perfection of the scene almost beyond bearing.

Melinda speaks: "Our education, cousin, was the same, but our temperaments had nothing alike; you have the constitution of a horse."

Silvia speaks: "So far as to be troubled with neither spleen, colic, nor vapours. I need no salts for my stomach, no hartshorn for my head nor wash for my complexion; I can gallop all the morning upon the hunting horn and all the evening after a fiddle. In short I can do everything with my father, but drink and shoot flying; and I am sure I can do everything my mother could were I put to the trial."

How they paused for all the laughter yet played ignorant of it!

T H E laughter took on an edge at Melinda's famous speech about that which Silvia is tired of:" . . . an appendix to our sex," says Melinda, "that you can't so handsomely get rid of in petticoats as if you were in breeches." Ralph in his niche feared for a moment that the laughter might relate to the new state of Mary Brenham and himself. Yet it soon showed itself to be universal laughter, not directed at any single being. Ralph could see Davy Collins laughing frankly, supported by more dimly discerned hilarity farther back on the barracks floor. It did not sound malicious, though it had an archness to it, he was sure, a certain welcoming leer which he found difficult to confront. So, flushing absurdly, he left his place and went to the back stairs and gently out of the door into the night. There he began to laugh delightedly, like a tittering child, as barks of laughter and delight came to him from within. He did not return to the barracks until the tempest of foot stampings and clappings signalled Silvia and Melinda had accomplished the closing of Act One.

For the greater part of Act Two, he found himself outdoors as well. While Justice Balance becomes so alarmed at Plume's intentions towards Silvia that he sends her to the country; while Robert Sideway/Mr. Worthy simpers and languishes for the termagant Melinda and Kite deceives honest country boys with lies of campaigning, Ralph paced the night. He could hear most of what the players said. When he could not, he would approach the barracks back door once more, tentatively, like a man about to receive a wound almost too pleasurable to bear. He had a sense that his players had somehow become their own actors, independent of him like grown children—that he was no longer bound to them by either pleasure or duty, that they had entered into a pact with the audience which was rightly none of his business and that only the approval of the crowd could justify them and assure the maturity of their craft.

Kite was still arguing with the bumpkins Costar Pearmain and Thomas Appletree, and Kable/Plume had only just entered with his song, altered to meet the facts of convict transportation—

> Over the hills and o'er the main
> To Flanders, Portugal or New South Wales,
> The King commands, and we'll obey—
> Over the hills and far away,

—when Ralph saw a knot of Marines and convict constables approaching the front door of the barracks, one of them carrying a torch, many of them speaking at once and willing to intrude upon the play. His sea cloak whipping behind him, Ralph ran to prevent them. They were only some twenty paces from the door, seeming already to anticipate bringing a roguish disruption to the laughter within, when Ralph reached them. Harry Brewer, Ralph now saw, was with them, hobbling crookedly and talking to the constable, Bill Parr. These were the members of the night watch and of the Marine Quarter Guard who had been deprived of the pleasure of the play by the necessity of giving the settlement some security. Now they knew they had something worth interrupting a play with, something which would direct the love and the laughter of the audience towards them. For shackled in the middle of them was the great Madagascan Black Caesar, who seemed to be full of the same theatrical excitement as Harry and the handful of Marines and constables.

"Your concept, Ralph," called Harry, joyously, "and my execution. We *have* the great black bastard!"

"But you cannot interrupt the play," said Ralph. He was consumed with a fury at Harry and himself and at the recaptured convict. When he had proposed the plan he had imagined a capture in the small hours, after he and Mary had been ages asleep in Thespian triumph. He had not intended that the Madagascan should supplant the play. And yet he knew he could not delay the entry of the constables and their captive through three more acts of Farquhar's—as it now seemed to him—modest magic.

"Please," he said to Harry. "Keep the Madagascan out here until Act Two ends."

Ralph raised his ear to find the progress his players had made. Plume was just eliciting laughs by pretending to chastise Kite for taking advantage of honest fellows like Pearmain and Appletree. Would the laughs be there, would they be so uncritically granted, once Black Caesar was introduced?

"Two minutes," Ralph pleaded. "Could you delay your entry two minutes?"

"Of course, my dear friend," said Harry, his words as muffled as usual yet full of comradely intent. "Two minutes, boys," Harry called to the Quarter Guard.

"No fret," said one of the boys benignly.

It was only now, having saved something of the integrity of his play, that he remembered the Madagascan had bruised and distressed his woman as well.

"For what you did to Mary Brenham," he murmured, close to the Madagascan's ear, "you will be heavily punished."

"Oh, Your Honour," Black Caesar told him, with a torch-lit gaze of transparent innocence, "I have been an evil fellow and will sure perish unless the Fragrant One smile on me."

An ecstatic Harry Brewer clapped Ralph on the shoulder. "This is your invention, Ralph, and I will not take the praise that belongs to you. I would, however, desire the honour of presenting Caesar to the Captain."

Ralph could hear Captain Plume's raised voice exhorting Pearmain and Appletree to sing the refrain with him, and singing it they marched off stage to volleys of applause. All that would have to be moved on stage for the beginning of Act Three was a little wooden sundial, and the capture of the Madagascan would so delay the play there was ample time for that.

Harry now limped forward to lead the night watch in, their mouths agape with the celebration of their capture, and Caesar seemingly as joyous as any of them. Ralph followed behind. Art had been supplanted by a criminal sensation, or at least Art was about to be. As Caesar and his captors entered the barracks, Ralph, following on, noticed that Harry had put the twenty-eight-pound ankle irons on the prisoner, who nonetheless moved more or less like a dancer.

When the crowd saw him they gusted him forward with applause. The captors were sportingly applauded too. It was all a game, a hazard, a contract which had been skillfully concluded by both parties to it, by the Madagascan and the night watch. Harry led Black Caesar on a roundabout route, not up the centre by the braziers and past Goose, but around the outer aisles of the barracks, past the young wives of the private Marines and their sleepy children lying on blankets on the floorboards. Everyone had risen, except these children drugged by noise and the redolence of gin and brandy and tobacco which hung around the walls. Everyone rose as if the monarch they were celebrating were not George but Caesar. As Caesar and the night watch made the front row and the Madagascan was presented to a mildly smiling H.E., willing to tolerate such sportiveness because of the day, Ralph dodged onto the stage and through the flats to see his actors. He thought they all looked wan—it was not simply the powder of their faces. They knew Caesar had out-theatred them.

"Act Three will be a little delayed," he told them.

He saw Mary Brenham, now wearing her white suit of men's clothes and her wig, turn and flee down the steps and out the back door.

"Have courage," he said to the others. "It is all progressing beautifully. Everyone is dazed with happiness and admiration. Otherwise they could not so applaud this villain from Africa."

He knew it was a brave battlefield speech, delivered quickly, with half an eye to the back door Mary Brenham had left ajar. But it seemed to revive them. They turned to each other. There were modest caresses of congratulation—not the grand gothic ones they had expected an hour ago to be able to extend, but worthy of people ruggedly and competently taking on themselves the burden of three more acts.

Ralph took one more look at the front of the stage. There Black Caesar was doing a little kick-up with his fourteen pounds of iron on either ankle. Davy, who would bring down death or some other heavy sentence on the Madagascan, applauded and laughed as hard as anyone. Ralph felt for a moment bereft of bearings. When is roguery laughable, and when is it hangable? Davy Collins seemed to know all the answers to those questions which left Ralph baffled still.

Ralph said a brief goodbye to his actors and went to find Mary Brenham. For the second time in his life he pursued a girl dressed in a white calico suit of men's clothes across the night.

He found her among the trees of the marquee. She had her back to him, one arm raised to the trunk of the thing, the other bent across her face.

"Come back," said Ralph. "He is wearing the twenty-eight-pound chains and is as good as sentenced."

"I cannot say my lines with him sitting in front of me there," she told Ralph. She covered one side of her face with her hand. The side he could see looked suddenly like that of an unwise thirteen-year-old, the one who had erred for Andrew Hilton. "Knowing, too, that I'll need to go to court and show my arse."

"If you say rape, he will hang, my dear. And if you say merely bruises, he will still be put on a rock in the harbour, or sent to an outstation."

"But you will want me to say rape. They will try to get me to say rape, so that they can have him, so that Ketch Freeman can twist him. And if I say rape, I will be forced to show myself. And you know by now, Mr. Clark, that I cannot bear it."

She turned to him, and he could see her shuddering distress. He put his arms around her. "I have not a line of Silvia left in me," she said.

He knew she was beyond reason—that he could not fruitfully explain to her that so long after the assault she would not need to show any limb or organ. Her face alone could hang Black Caesar.

"You do not have to say rape, and I will protect you from saying it. But please find Silvia's lines again, my love. Please, since the play still has half its way to run and yours is the foremost part."

He had to go on repeating his assurances about the trial of Caesar, and he did it energetically and without faltering.

"I fear for my son," she confessed.

"Remember," said Ralph, "the Madagascan stole food and weapons. He made incessant raids. His attack on you was simply one element in the whole cloth of his crimes. If I told Davy there is no reason for you to show yourself, Davy will believe me."

And so, with some halts, he coaxed her back across the clearing and to the barracks again. As she neared the door, Silvia revived in her. She asked Ralph if he could send the perfumier Nicholls out to her to restore the whiteness of her face, which had been somewhat furrowed by tears.

"Remember," said Ralph, about to re-enter the barracks, "that if he is permitted to sit down in his chains and watch the play, he will not know you in your suit of white clothes."

"He did not know me when he savaged me in my hut," she said. "Just that I had a body to be bruised, and a son to protect."

"So hide behind your Silvia mask and mock him," said Ralph, kissing her cheek and feeling her breast behind the harshness of the cloth.

"Lieutenant Clark," she told him, "you are such an honest poor fellow."

"I shall send Dabby Bryant to fetch you when the play is to go ahead," murmured Ralph, weak with her praise.

Back inside, Ketch Freeman the hangman, dressed in a scarecrow suit and heavily lined to pass as Justice Balance, was waiting at the head of the stairs like a child waiting for a parent. Ralph decided to be jovial.

"So it seems you will have the turning off of Black Caesar, Ketch."

"I never done anyone so heavy nor so big," said Ketch.

"You still have your lines as Balance?" Ralph asked, passing him.

"Balance is easy," said Ketch Freeman. "Freeman is hard."

"Wait and see, Ketch. He may not be given death. In the meantime, you are a fine Balance."

Ketch Freeman laughed as if Ralph had made a play on words. Mary Brenham's praise, thought Ralph, had transformed him into a sage and a wit.

Ralph eased along behind the backdrop to look out the window of Justice Balance's country house. The scene was like a multitudinous wedding feast. Caesar was making his way down the aisle, past the braziers. The constables and the Marine guard still flanked him. By the middle of the three braziers, Mother Goose, pontiff of the Tawny Prince in this penal reach, rose and clapped her hands. Her cup-bearer came to her side, uncorked the new bottle of fresh brandy he had been carrying all night and poured it into the goblet. When he handed it to Goose, Goose raised it high, to the level of Black Caesar's face. She took a great draught—three mouthfuls. A little of the third mouthful bled down either side of her mouth. The lags were cheering, had never seen such public honour done. With a gesture of beneficence from her left hand, Goose passed the goblet to Caesar with her right. Caesar smiled massively and turned on his heels to show the entire crowd the half-drunk goblet. By the time he had completed the circuit, had toasted Goose and had raised it to his own lips, Goose's mouth had opened wide and she had taken a throttling hand to her throat. Caesar took the cup from his lips without having drunk even a sip. He stared. The crowd began to moderate, except at its edges, in the noise it had been making. Ralph saw Goose emit three grunts —three clouds of blue mist—before she crashed to the boards.

Surgeon Johnny White rushed down the centre aisle as if he had seen the first signs of collapse in Goose and was out to combat them. Dennis Considen ran behind him. Johnny knelt by Goose's substantial fallen bulk and raised her eyelids and lowered his ear to detect breath. Ralph saw Black Caesar raise the goblet and start another circuit, crying, "Oh look, my brothers! The Fragrant One has delivered Caesar one more time!"

But Johnny White rose and grabbed the glass and emptied its contents onto the floorboards. After a conversation with Considen, he reached out and closed Goose's startled eyes. At that point an enquiring roar rose from the audience. Johnny found four young lags to carry Goose out of the hall, and it seemed to Ralph from his point of observation that there was a sort of inadvertence in the way the crowd took note of this bearing forth of the centre of felonry. The barracks were still loud with question and surmise.

But of all those who could have followed Goose weeping, only Dot Handilands, the she-lag of more than eighty, staggered behind, cursing God.

Any tolerance the front row theatregoers—H.E., Johnny Hunter, Davy—had extended to Black Caesar was now cancelled. Davy instructed Harry Brewer, and Harry Brewer instructed Bill Parr and the Marine guard to remove the prisoner. There was no applause for him as he left in the wake of Goose's corpse.

"It is apoplexy," Ralph heard Davy report to H.E. "The play should now go on without any more of this."

Goose—as Ralph would later discover—was laid down just beyond the barracks doorway and covered with a blanket. There were no sentimental visits from her cup-boy or anyone else. It showed you that in the lag commonwealth, fealty was exactly cut off at the instant of the sovereign's fall. There were no ceremonious or heartfelt obsequies. Everyone but old Dot stayed indoors to see the balance of the play.

Even without knowing these details at the time, Ralph—behind the backdrop—understood at once that her ungrieved death and the expulsion of Black Caesar had created a space in which his play could flourish. He hurried toward the wings of the stage where his cast was still waiting.

"It will be time in perhaps two minutes," he told them. He was distracted by the strange hobbling noise of Harry's approach and his appearance among the actors. Harry grasped Duckling by the arm and bore her down the back steps and out the door. Ralph followed, precisely because he did not wish to lose any further players. Emerging into the night, he saw Nichols applying a final coat of powder to Mary Brenham's face, a face restored and eager and as grandly familiar to Ralph as if he had known it all his life. "Perhaps only two minutes," he shouted to Nichols and Silvia.

Over by the marquee Harry raged at Duckling, "Do you have the phial? Do you still have it?"

Ralph, only a few steps away, saw Duckling reach into the bodice of her dress and drag forth a small tube of glass.

"Give it me!" Harry demanded. He saw Ralph there and glowered at him crookedly from a palsied face. "Oh Jesus," he said. "Thank God it's friend Ralph!"

He threw the phial to the ground and tried, in his uneven and crippled way, to crush it. Ralph held a hand out, conveying that Harry shouldn't strain himself, and raised his own boot and brought it down many times on the glass tube until nothing was left but silvery powder.

"Ralph," said Harry, "we are dependent on you."

"Dependent?" asked Ralph, for he had not yet pieced it all together.

"You understand, Ralph," Harry barked, more vulpine for having only half a mouth. "You understand, goddamn you!"

"But I thought she was indifferent," he said, pointing to Duckling. "I always thought she was indifferent."

"That's how much you and I know of loyalty and of whatever in the Christ this is. Or of poison and murder, whatever they are! You understand, this is a wedding present to you. And some sort of present to me."

She had said once she liked Brenham. When caught in carnal enthusiasm with Curtis Brand she had made some slack-mouthed speech about the play. And had there been something about gratitude to him as playmaker? Had Farquhar's play really conquered the Tawny Prince?

"Jesus!" said Ralph. "She has killed her own Dimber Damber." It was like water running uphill. It was science disproved.

Duckling stared at him in her frank, slightly sullen way.

"She grew up among those substances," said Harry. "Sitting there, watching Goose make up potions in Greek Street." He was trying to explain why Duckling looked no different from her daily self. Half-dead Harry said, "If you mention it to anyone, I will deny it on oath and to the death."

"You underestimate my love for you," said Ralph. But he was not really offended.

He turned to Duckling the poisoner. There was no sign of her motives, which lay in another universe than his.

"I hope," he said, dizzy and exultant, "that you still remember your lines."

EPILOGUE

WHAT is to be said of Ralph's play that night? Its local success in the city of lags was never in question. Both Davy and Watkin wrote of it in their journals. "In the evening," wrote Davy, "some of the convicts were permitted to perform Farquhar's comedy of *The Recruiting Officer* in a hut fitted up for the occasion. They professed no higher aim than 'humbly to excite a smile,' and their efforts to please were not unattended with applause."

Watkin wrote that the play was honoured by the presence of H.E. and the garrison officers. "Some of the actors acquitted themselves with great spirit and received the praises of the audience: a prologue and an epilogue, written by one of the performers, were also spoken on the occasion." Thus Watkin credited Wisehammer not only with having composed his own epilogue but also with the introductory verses written by George Farquhar himself eighty years earlier.

Seen from the immensity of time, Ralph's play might appear a mere sputter of the European humour on the edge of a continent which, then, still did not have a name. This flicker of a theatrical intent would consume in the end the different and serious theatre of the tribes of the hinterland. In the applause at the end of the evening, in the applause whether from H.E. or from Will Bryant, Arabanoo—had he still lived—might have heard the threat.

In recounting the further destinies of our playmaker and our players in that third world of the past, one is aware of the dangers posed by melodrama. Antibiotics and plumbing have made melodrama laughable to the modern reader. It is only in our own third world, where in the one phase of time lovers are sundered, clans consumed, and infants perish without once saying "Mother," that melodrama causes tears still to flow. The Sichuanese, the Eritreans, or the Masai would understand better than us the destinies which befell some of our players and in particular our playmaker, Lieutenant Ralph Clark.

For yes, though they are fantastical creatures, they all lived.

Even in the records of those players who had a happier existence than Ralph's there is a flavour of dramatic excess. Henry Kable would serve his time, become a constable, begin farming, go partners with another former lag in a sealing enterprise, rear ten children by his wife, Susannah, found a brewery (like Ralph's play, the first of its species in the penal world), run a public house, and live to be eighty-four years of age.

Robert Sideway, seven years after Ralph's version of *The Recruiting Officer*, opened his own playhouse. The authorities twice closed it down for the reasons authorities generally do such things —a suspicion that the theatre has too much influence. He would farm on the river between Sydney and Rosehill, marry a convict woman sentenced at the same Old Bailey sessions which had sentenced him, and—twenty years after *The Recruiting Officer* confirmed him in his theatrical ambitions—die of natural causes.

If the later histories of some of the players seem tame, it is mainly for want of information on them. We know that Nancy Turner lived to be pardoned and to beget a numerous family from a watch thief called Stokes. Duckling was shipped to Norfolk Island in the year following the play. It was no punishment, but the result of H.E.'s decision to shift a number of lags there as famine bit harder in Sydney. Harry Brewer, who stayed on in Sydney as Provost Marshal and who would live to a good age there, did not resist her transfer. The events of the night of the play had (so Ralph supposed) shown Duckling to be an affectionate daughter of Harry's rather than a lover, and in letting her go Harry absolved her from the burden of being filial to him. She would disappear from the records then—Harry had no hand in that, though clerical ineptitude might have—and whether she married and begot, and where she is buried, are not known.

Curtis Brand served his time, began to farm—quite close to Sideway's farm—and married and died before the age of forty. We are given the intriguing detail that he left his farm to a blind boy.

John Hudson, the youngest of Ralph's actors, would go to Norfolk Island on the same ship as Duckling and disappear for the same sorts of causes. Ketch Freeman would at last be exempted from any further hangings, find a convict wife, have seven children by her, and live into his sixties. John Wisehammer, thwarted in his love of Mary Brenham, began farming and trading at the end of his sentence, married a Cockney she-lag, and grew to be a respected merchant in a Sydney whose population had been augmented by further shipments of lags.

It is with John Arscott's records that melodrama bites deep. He was sent to Norfolk Island with Ralph Clark, behaved bravely when the *Sirius* ran up on rocks there, and helped extinguish the fires which started in her galley. At last pardoned, he had married a friend of Dabby Bryant's and accumulated wealth through his carpentry skills. He was one of the minority of lags who were able to afford to return to Britain. On the way home, in Torres Strait between Australia and New Guinea, a party from the ship, including Arscott, landed on an island to look for water. They were beset by natives, who killed six of them. Not able to find their ship again because of a cyclone which overtook them, they were forced to sail by open boat all the way to Batavia, now known as Djakarta. When their ship *did* find them there, Arscott was told that his wife, Elizabeth, who had once helped Dabby Bryant attack a spinster in a Cornish laneway, had died aboard of what the surgeon on the ship described as "a spotted fever" induced by drinking and grief.

Dabby Bryant herself would have made wry mouths at the idea that she would generate monographs in future times and be a historical curiosity. Instructed in astral navigation by Arabanoo, she escaped from Sydney Harbour in H.E.'s government fishing boat on a March night in 1791, taking with her Will, her two children, and seven male lags. They sailed all the way to Kupang in the Dutch East Indies, were eventually gaoled in Batavia, where her younger child, Emanuel, died of fever, as did Will. Dabby, Charlotte, her daughter of five years of age, and four convicts were shipped to the Cape, then to a British vessel, the *Gorgon*, which was bringing the Marines, including Ralph Clark, home from Sydney. So Ralph laid eyes on his physician of dreams one more time. He and Watkin showed many kindnesses to Dabby and the child, but the small girl was exhausted from her adventures and died at sea off the African coast.

Dabby herself was returned to Newgate to await trial for attempted escape from transportation. Her story was read by the passionate and generous Scot, James Boswell, familiar of Dr. Samuel Johnson, and he began a drive to get her a pardon. Cynics said he and Dabby became lovers—and why not, since like the more obscure Ralph Clark he was a man burdened by terrible marital dreams. There is a good poem by one of Dr. Johnson's literary circle on the subject of the supposed affair between Dabby and that warm and fallible Scot. In fact, Boswell settled ten pounds a year on her, even though he was always plagued by financial problems himself.

Then one night he said an affecting farewell to her aboard a ship in the Thames and sent her back to her family in Fowey. A letter from her in Fowey, thanking him for receipt of a bank draft, is the last we hear of her. At Yale University, in the Boswell archives, is a small package of wild tea leaves which Dabby brought with her from Sydney on her escape and gave to her benefactor.

It cannot be doubted that she carried her peculiar mercies and enthusiasms on to other associations. Imagination could create a plausible later career for her, but it could not say that she was ever convicted of further crime.

To Mary Brenham and Ralph, however, attaches the full brunt of melodrama—except that we know Ralph by now, and so the news of his last years, no matter how excessively tragic, will not be considered grotesque or laughable. When H.E. decided to send the annoying Robbie Ross to Norfolk Island, Ralph being also posted there as part of the garrison, Ralph ensured that Mary was among the convicts transferred to that outstation. Brenham bore him a girl child in July 1791, and five months later, after Mary and the child returned to Sydney with Ralph, she was christened Alicia. He sailed from Sydney with most of the other Marines late in the year. He leaves no record of his feelings at saying goodbye to Mary Brenham.

Mary was moved to Rosehill convict station, up the river from Sydney, towards Christmas that year. There placid Small Willy died of a sudden childhood fever, but the girl child Alicia flourished. Brenham and Alicia then disappear from the public record.

Returned to England, Ralph was stationed at Chatham on the Medway, and sailed aboard the *Tartar* for the West Indies in 1793. At some stage he was with the Marines aboard a ship called the *Sceptre*, and his young son, Ralphie, who could not have been much more than eleven years of age, was with him as a midshipman. In June 1794, the *Sceptre* was part of the squadron which trapped the French revolutionary Admiral Besseton in Port-au-Prince and engaged him when he tried to break out. Young Ralphie witnessed the fight from the gun deck of the *Sceptre* and was very elated by it.

Ralph himself suffered dysentery caught during a military excursion ashore to St. Nicole Mole, a location which would appear in most of Ralph's letters of the time. The position was for a time under great threat from the French. "All the Marines of the ships," he writes to Betsey Alicia in a letter dated May 8th, 1794, "and half of the seamen have been landed here since we expected to be attacked every moment, but thank God we are relieved from our fears in that head. For three days ago, the *Irresistible* of seventy-four guns with one regiment and the *Bellequieux* with two transports containing two regiments from Ireland arrived here, and in the room of their (the French) attacking us, we are making preparations to attack them."

Though it was through this campaigning ashore that he suffered dysentery, thoughts of the bonus or bounty money he would receive when the French surrendered their ships enlivened him during his recovery aboard the *Sceptre*. He wrote to Betsey Alicia that even young Ralphie was likely to receive over forty pounds as his share of the captured French ships and cargoes. But he complained of the price of everything. "I have received my board and forage money, but my dearest love, my illness has prevented me sending you part of it as I promised—for the first fortnight after I was taken ill it cost me from two shillings to half a crown a day for washing, I dirtied so many shirts and sheets a day. What do you think I paid for a pair of shoes for our dear sweet boy a few days since? No less than seven shillings and ninepence." Perhaps the finances of the Clark family had not yet recovered from the death of Broderick Hartwell, Ralph's old agent.

Sometime in June, sent with his friend, a Captain Oldfield, along the coast north of Port-au-Prince to accept the surrender of a French outpost, Ralph was fatally wounded by a random shot from within the fortifications. His body, dead or dying, was carried back to St. Nicole Mole and taken aboard the *Sceptre,* where Ralphie was suffering the ravages and sharp muscular pains of yellow fever.

In the catalogue produced by Sotheby's in another age to advertise the sale of Ralph's erratic journal, it is stated that father and son died on the one day. Neither of them knew that Betsey Alicia herself had suffered a stillbirth and died in the Marine hospital at Chatham. So in a pulse of time the blood and all the complex of dreams and very ordinary fervours of the Playmaker were extinguished, except for his lagwife Brenham and the new world child Alicia. Of them fiction could make much, though history says nothing.

Author's Note

The author would like to acknowledge that in making this fiction he found rich material in such works as *The Journal and Letters of Lieutenant Ralph Clark*, edited by Paul G. Fidlon and R. J. Ryan; David Collins's *An Account of the English Colony in New South Wales*, edited by Brian H. Fletcher; and Dr. John Cobley's compilation *The Crimes of the First Fleet Convicts* and the same author's *Sydney Cove, 1788–1792*. Information on H.E.'s Brazilian experiences was found in *The Rebello Transcripts*, by Kenneth Gordon McIntyre.